HONOR AT DAYBREAK

Also by Elmer Kelton

The Day the Cowboys Quit
The Time It Never Rained
The Good Old Boys
The Wolf and the Buffalo
Stand Proud
Dark Thicket
The Man Who Rode Midnight
Bowie's Mine
Joe Pepper
Manhunters
Eyes of the Hawk
Massacre at Goliad
Long Way to Texas
Llano River
Hanging Judge
Horsehead Crossing
After the Bugles
Wagontongue

A Novel
of One Town's
Battle for Justice

DOUBLEDAY
New York London Toronto Sydney Auckland

Daybreak

ELMER KELTON

PUBLISHED BY DOUBLEDAY
a division of Bantam Doubleday Dell Publishing Group, Inc.
666 Fifth Avenue, New York, New York 10103

DOUBLEDAY and the portrayal of an anchor
with a dolphin are trademarks of Doubleday,
a division of Bantam Doubleday Dell Publishing Group, Inc.

Library of Congress Cataloging-in-Publication Data

Kelton, Elmer.
    Honor at daybreak/Elmer Kelton.—1st ed.
      p.   cm.
    I. Title.
   PS3563.A2932C36 1991
   813'.54—dc20 90-36335
               CIP

ISBN 0-385-24893-8

10 9 8 7 6 5 4 3 2 1

In a broad sense this book is dedicated to all those hardworking oilfield folk who have ever bent their backs over pick and shovel and drilling bit, for without them the industry would never have delivered a barrel of oil. In particular it is dedicated to Bill Allman, who loved the cabletool rig to the end of his life, and to my uncles Paul and Charles Holland, who began laboring in the fields soon after the time of this story.

Prologue

INDIANS IN TEXAS used oil for medicinal purposes centuries before a Spaniard named Luís de Moscoso, in 1543, took seepage from oil springs near Sabine Pass to calk his ships. In the latter half of the nineteenth century, oil in modest quantities was found and used in or near such diverse places as Brownwood and San Antonio, Waco and Corsicana. But historians would later say the real discovery came the morning of January 10, 1901, when the ground rumbled beneath a slight prominence known as Spindletop outside the little town of Beaumont, just inland from the Gulf of Mexico. A mighty surge of gas, oil, mud and rocks knocked the crown block from atop the driller's wooden derrick. For days, a column of black, sulphurous-smelling oil spewed a hundred feet and more into the air, and Texas would never again be the same.

From all over the country, a surge of fortune-seeking humanity converged on this oil boom, and then another and another, new discoveries following like black pearls on a string. Each discovery breathed new life into old towns or created new towns where none had been before. Names like Sour Lake, Burkburnett, Ranger and Cisco became synonymous with sudden wealth and excitement, heartbreak and violence.

It was, in its own way, a continuation of the frontier experience into the automobile age.

Out on the rangelands of far West Texas, professional geologists had declared the region barren, sure that no oil would be found beneath its grass-covered prairies, its greasewood flats and its sandhills. A driller was considered lucky to find even water, much less oil. But in August of 1921, Carl Cromwell spudded in a cabletool rig on a site beside the tracks of the Orient Railroad, thirteen miles west of an isolated little ranching town known as Big Lake. Some of the money for this wildcat venture had come from a group of Catholic women in New York, who sent rose petals to be sprinkled from the derrick top for good luck. Cromwell christened the well Santa Rita, after the patron saint of the impossible.

For twenty-one slow, monotonous months, Cromwell's bit patiently punched deep into the ground beneath the waist-high greasewood. He and his wife lived in an unpainted shack beside the derrick. She planted a garden and raised chickens while drilling crews, mainly out-of-work cowboys, came and went. Finally, the morning of May 28, 1923, oil gushed over the top of the eighty-four-foot structure, and the rush was on.

Boomtowns flashed into life one after another as drilling spread quickly across this huge region underlain by an ancient inland sea known as the Permian Basin. They included Best, McCamey, Crane, Pyote, Wink.

And, in due time, oil came to another, a sleepy old ranching town in the sands below the rough and broken ground that marked the southern edge of the Llano Estacado.

It was called Caprock. . . .

One

Fire in the Earth

1

The Oil Rig

THE HEREFORD COW jerked her head up from her grazing in startled response to an unaccustomed noise from the drilling platform on the lee side of a tall sand dune. She held still, stems of green spring grass protruding from her mouth, and watched the tall wooden derrick for sign of a threat to herself or to the red whiteface steer calf that ran to her side, spooked by the sound. Warily she observed the men moving about at the rig, a hundred yards away. None of them evidenced any interest in her or her calf, so after a moment she extended her tongue to pull the rest of the grass into her mouth and lowered her head to strip off another bite. Her calf, still nervous,

3

remained close, keeping her between him and the strange machinery that had given him fright.

The grass had always seemed a little sweeter to her on this side of the big pasture. She had favored it before the oil men had moved in and set up their cabletool rig. Their coming and going, the frequent passage of trucks and automobiles, the high-pitched clanging of casing pipe, the loud clatter, thumping and rumble of the drilling operation had kept her frightened away at first. The lure of the sweet grass had brought her back, cautiously in the beginning, then nearer and nearer the rig as appetite overcame apprehension. She hardly even looked at the derrick anymore unless an unexpected loud noise drew her attention, as now. The other cattle, mostly younger, remained more timid and kept their distance. That left the best grass to her and her calf.

On the rough-planked rig floor, thin, slump-shouldered Autie Whitmore eyed the cow with misgivings. She was grazing closer every day. If not watched, she or her calf might venture into the hopeless muck of the slushpit beside the derrick. He had never seen a twenty-dollar cow that did not become a hundred-dollar cow when something happened to her that the owner could collect for. Whitmore hunched over the drill hole, his gloved right hand gripping the heavy cable that rose and fell with each up-and-down movement of the massive walking beam overhead.

He was forty-seven years old but looked sixty under the weight of a life spent at hard labor, trying in vain to work his way out of the poverty that had plagued all of his days. The gods of luck, it seemed, had always conspired against him. From the poor worn-out cotton farm of his boyhood to the oilpatches of Texas and Oklahoma, every time he appeared about to get a leg up, something came along and knocked his feet out from under him.

The bit was nearly three thousand feet down in the hole. It should be approaching the oil, if there was to be any. By a piece of red rag tied to the cable, he could tell that the bit had penetrated less than a foot in the last hour. He grumbled, "Come on, Goddamn you, take a bite!" The bit had been to the forge so many times that it could not hold an edge, pounding against the fierce resistance of ancient rock far beneath the sandy surface of this Texas ranchland. He would not be surprised to learn that it was old enough to have drilled a water well for George Washington, or at least for Abe Lincoln.

Well, that was about par for the company; it wanted to make its millions without spending any of them. The drilling rig was old enough to vote. The company management bought obsolete equipment on the cheap, and they had given Autie Whitmore the poorest of the lot. That was commensurate with his ranking at the bottom of the list of drillers currently on their payroll. The company preferred to hire "weevils," beginners just come from farms, ranches and towns, most of them strangers to the oilfield. Young men like that would work for next to nothing just to have a job, while a family man had to demand enough to feed his wife and kids. The company made sure it hired bachelor boys, too, so that if anything happened to them the compensation payments would not amount to much. That was the only reason they let him use his son Benny for a tooldresser on this job. Benny had grown up in first one oilpatch and then another. He was twenty-two and middling good help, even if he *was* Autie Whitmore's boy.

Autie needed to pull the bit from the bottom of the hole so Benny could heat it on the forge and hammer a new cutting edge onto it. But that took time, and the slave-driving company pusher had a knack for driving up here just when the drilling shut down. He had been riding Whitmore hard about this well going slow. Thinking of the pusher, Whitmore frowned at the blown-out two-rut road that crooked its way through the sands toward the booming town of Caprock. He saw no vehicle, but he nursed a strong hunch that those slick-handed, lace-boot sons of bitches from the main office were fixing to show up and fire him. They had been making noises like they had it on their minds, even though he was working for two dollars a day less than any decent driller in the Caprock field. Well, what the hell, he had been fired off of better rigs than this.

He watched the boiler man walking in from the pasture, dragging dead mesquite limbs through the sand to stoke the fire and produce the steam that kept the engine running. *Man* was not the right word; *boy* was more like it. He was a kid of nineteen or twenty, kin to one of the company bosses, who wanted him to learn the oil business from the ground up. Well sir, this was about as near to the ground as he could get. A boiler man had to

5

hold the steam on an even keel and not let the boiler explode. The steam pressure was dropping, for the man had been gone awhile. Whitmore grumbled to himself. Any decent outfit would have kept a supply of coal or wood on hand so the boiler operator wouldn't have to go scrounge it off the land. But this company was hell for squeezing its men and its machinery to get the most out of them while putting damned little into them.

One of these days, when I get a few dollars ahead, I'll walk into that office and tell them what Autie Whitmore thinks of them, from the stud duck down to the bookkeeper.

He was always intending to tell off somebody, but one way or another it seemed like he never got around to it.

This time, by God! This time!

He had been out of work for three months before he had gotten on as a driller for this wildcat well twelve miles out from the nearest proven pay. At least he had the day tour, which he pronounced *tower,* so he could be home nights. Not that home life amounted to much. He shared an old peaked-top tent in Caprock with his wife Flora, son Benny and daughter Tracy.

Flora and Tracy worked in a café, serving meals to a hungry horde of oilfield workers who sometimes stood in line for an hour to pay as much as half a dollar for a plate lunch that wouldn't cost more than thirty cents anywhere but in an oil boomtown. Usually the women didn't get off at night until ten or eleven o'clock. Flora would come dragging in with Tracy, too tired for a decent kiss, much less anything more. Even if she felt like doing more, the tent didn't allow a married couple any privacy. It was only about fifteen feet square. They suspended blankets on cotton rope at night to divide the tent into three separate sleeping areas, but even then it was almost like having four people in the same bed. Times, when the pressure got to working on him, Autie had no choice but to pay a visit to one of the ladies at Jolene's "rooming house." At least there they had walls.

Hell of a way for people to have to live, but many in Caprock lived no better, if as well. Some didn't even have a tent. Maybe one day he could do proper for his family, but that day looked a long way off. During the months he had been unable to get steady work, the family had lived on what Flora and Tracy brought home from the café, and sporadic pay he and Benny picked up at odd jobs like loading oilfield equipment, and even working as "pearl divers," washing dishes in the café.

Seems like the only kind of luck I ever have is bad.

It wasn't all just luck, he would admit to himself occasionally when nobody was looking. He had a reputation as a man who favored his whisky, good whisky when he could afford it and the rawest kind of Prohibition bootleg when fortune frowned upon him. Most outfits didn't like to take a risk with a driller who drank too much. His carelessness could cost them heavily if he dropped a string of tools or a joint of pipe down a hole. They knew about Autie Whitmore in every field from Ranger to the Santa Rita.

A rotten rig like this would drive anybody to drink, he told himself.

Benny Whitmore looked at the piece of rag tied on the rope to let the driller measure the descent of the bit. "Ain't moved down much, has it, Papa?"

The reply was testy. "Tell me somethin' I don't already know."

"Maybe we ought to run the bailer down there and clean up the hole. While you're bailin', I could be dressin' a new edge on the bit."

"You tryin' to tell me how to run this job?"

Benny always backed off under Autie's dark frown. He had been brought up to respect his father whether other people did or not. "Tryin' to be helpful, is all. We just don't seem to be makin' much hole."

"When they hire you for a driller's wage, you can drill. Till then, you're a roughneck, and you do what the driller tells you." Autie's eyes cast a stern challenge to the other young man in case he had advice to offer. He did not. Only Benny knew enough about the job to have any advice.

Autie knew Benny's suggestion was good, and he ought to take it. He didn't know why he sometimes rode the boy so cruelly. Maybe it was because he saw a latent ability in his son that he himself lacked. It wasn't fair. Autie had tried hard, worked as hard as anybody. But he had a feeling deep in his gut, a feeling that in three or four years Benny would climb farther up the ladder than Autie ever had. He knew he should be ashamed, feeling jealous of his own son. But damn it, he could have shown them if they had given him a chance. He wouldn't have turned to the bottle so much if his luck hadn't always been so bad.

All of a sudden, he began to feel the need for a drink. It was not a thing men were allowed to do at a rig, but what they didn't know in town wasn't going to hurt them. He said to Benny, "You take over the line for a few minutes while I go out and run off that cow."

"I can run her off, Papa."

"You been itchin' to do some drillin', so here's your chance. I need to get off of this floor for a little while anyhow."

Benny frowned. Autie suspected he knew his father's intentions. But he put up no argument. "Sure, Papa." He reached for the cable. Autie turned it loose, warning, "You mind now, we don't want a crooked hole."

"I know, Papa."

Autie stepped down from the floor into the sand. Sand, mud or rocky ground . . . seemed like just about every field he had ever worked in was on ground that made it difficult to get around. Some people said there had to be oil underneath because there sure as hell wasn't much of anything on top. But he couldn't tell that the Hereford cow had suffered any. She was fleshy enough that he could not see any of her ribs when she moved about, and her calf was mud-fat from the good milk flow she was affording him. This sand grass must have a lot of strength in it, Autie figured, even if it looked a little sparse in places.

He walked toward the pair, waving his hat. "Move on, old Sis," he shouted. "Git back away from the well." The calf ran, but the cow just stood and looked at him. He would have thrown a rock at her if he could have found one in the deep sand. He hurled his misshapen, oil-blackened old hat. She took notice of that flying apparition and trotted away after her calf. She did not go far, perhaps twenty yards. But that was enough to justify Autie's coming out here. He turned back toward his old black Model T, parked just far enough from the rig to be out of harm's way. A man in the oilfield needed a car to get him to work, because few companies furnished transportation. And if he happened to be "working for Street and Walker," which meant hunting for a job, he happened it to get him from one field to another. Few young weevils had a car, so the boiler operator paid Autie fifty cents a day for the ride. That helped buy gasoline and patch tires. Autie didn't charge Benny anything.

He walked around to the off side of the car so Benny couldn't see him. He reached beneath the seat and brought out a bottle, then sat on the running board and unscrewed the cap. He turned the bottle up for a long double swallow and sat there, enjoying the burn as the whisky made its way down. This wasn't the best stuff; it was some of Preacher Perry's bootleg squeezin's, aged in the truck. But it could warm a man's innards and make him forget his troubles for a little while. Put a couple of drinks of this under his belt, and a man became the best damned driller in West Texas. He relaxed a few minutes and took another pull at the bottle. He almost choked, for this one burned more than the first. But he felt a lot better. If that company pusher were to show up here now, Autie might just kick his ass plumb off of the lease.

A movement brought his gaze to the gap between two sand dunes, to a horseman riding through the low-growing bush-type mesquites and shinnery brush. The rancher, maybe, or one of his cowboys. Well, at least they hadn't seen him run their cow off, so they didn't have anything to complain to him about.

He heard something then, something that didn't sound right. It was a hissing sound from the well. For a moment, he froze, not knowing exactly what it was but feeling the same instinctive fear that always rose up in him when he heard a rattlesnake sound off. He pushed to his feet as realization struck him.

The bit had broken into a pocket of gas. The hiss turned quickly to a loud roar. Autie hurled the bottle aside and ran around the car, waving his hat, shouting.

"Get away! Get off of the floor!"

He saw Benny stagger in confusion, perhaps already feeling the effects of the gas.

"Benny!" he cried. "Run! For God's sake, run!"

The boiler operator had not waited. He was running as hard as the deep sand would let his legs move. But he did not get far. The ground shuddered to an explosion that blew the derrick apart. The crown block at the top seemed to waver for a second or two, then fell crashing into a huge ball of orange fire. The blaze billowed out and overtook the running kid. Even over the roar, Autie heard him scream. He saw him for just a moment, slumping to his knees, then he was lost in the roaring flames.

"Benny!" Autie cried again. He tried to approach the well, but the blistering heat stopped him. He retreated behind the Model T, but even there the heat was intense. He realized that the car's gasoline tank would probably explode. He began retreating through the sand, staggering, stumbling, scrambling for distance, and all the time crying for his son. He felt his back blistering, and his old work clothes began to smolder. He looked back, and in the fire and black smoke he thought he saw a huge death's head form for just a moment, then disappear.

The whisky. The Goddamned whisky. If I hadn't sneaked out to take a drink, I'd've been there and died with Benny.

That, he thought, might have been a good thing. How could he ever face up to Flora and tell her how he had escaped while their son had died? For a moment, he felt a strong impulse to turn back, to go back into those flames and die with the rest of the crew. But he could not face the terrible heat. He kept running, and when he could no longer run, he fell to his knees and crawled.

Trinidad Suarez had never trusted himself to ride all the way up to the drilling rig and actually visit with the crew, but he had enjoyed sitting on his horse and watching the activity from afar when his duties brought him to work in this pasture. He had been fascinated and at the same time strangely repelled by the sheer sense of immense power given off by the great bullwheel, the heavy walking beam, the rumbling steam engine, which he could hear but could not see within the sheetiron walls that protected it from the weather. As far back over his twenty-eight years as he could remember, Trinidad had been a cowboy or had been training himself to become one. He knew much of horses and cattle, saddles and ropes. He knew little about machinery. Only since he had been working on the ranch of Mr. Douglas Clive had he even learned to drive a car or truck, and that not particularly well.

He had dug many a posthole two to three feet deep with simple hand diggers. It strained his imagination to think of this mechanical monster pushing a hole down a thousand, two thousand, three thousand feet into the earth to find treasure mysteriously hidden there a million or even ten million years ago. That was too long a time for the human mind to grasp. It must have been before God, even.

Times, when he rode over here to steal a look, Trinidad wished he could be part of this exciting new life that had burst upon the quiet West Texas ranching country, that had exploded the sleepy little town of Caprock into a bustling chaos scattered over two square miles of what had been mostly cow pasture. But his life had always moved at a deliberate pace. He could not imagine himself rushing, pushing, shoving as he had seen so many of these people do. They hurried as if there would be no tomorrow, and all that was to be done had to be done today.

There was another point. Trinidad was Mexican, at least by blood. He had been born in Texas, as had his father and his grandfather, but whatever that might have meant in the eyes of the law, it meant little in the eyes of most other Texans. He was and always would be an outsider except within his own little group . . . an outsider, even a foreigner, despite the place of his birth. So far as he had seen in his limited observation of the Caprock oilfield, Mexicans had found little place, certainly not in the drilling crews. He had seen a few building pipelines, which was crushing, backbreaking work, and he had seen a couple on a muleskinning job, handling the large teams sometimes required to pull equipment through the deep, clutching sands where even the heavy trucks could not always go.

He had heard that the wages were high for those people who could get oilfield work. Roughnecks were paid like princes, often five and six and seven dollars a day, far more than the dollar a day he earned working for Mr. Douglas Clive. But Mr. Clive furnished groceries. He provided a house for Trinidad and Gabriela and the little one. True, it was not a large or elaborate house like Mr. Clive's own. It was a simple little box-and-strip. The wind drove sand into it around the doors and windows and up between the boards of the floor.

Good enough for Mexicans, he had heard Mr. Clive say when Mr. Clive did not know Trinidad was listening. Or perhaps he knew and did not care. Mr. Clive was not a likeable man. But his money was spendable. And Trinidad did not intend to work for him forever. Patience had been taught him from the time he was a child. What he did not like and could change, he changed.

11

What he could not change, he endured in faith that time and fate would make the change for him.

Riding through the low green scrub oak plants known as shinnery, Trinidad saw the Hereford cow and her calf. He had noticed lately that this particular cow—old enough for a considerable amount of bovine wisdom—had been grazing nearer to the derrick than the other cattle dared go. She was something of a loner anyway, impatient of others' company, quick to toss her horns if they crowded her or tried to push to the water trough ahead of her. He thought of something neighboring rancher Henry Stringfellow had told him. Mr. Henry was a kindly old gentleman who always found time to talk to Trinidad. The only talk Mr. Douglas Clive ever gave him was in the form of orders.

Mr. Henry had spoken of the pecking order among animals, including cattle. This cow never let anything peck at *her*. Gabriela would enjoy her spirit, for she had much of that fight herself. He remembered the first time he had ever been alone with her, and he had tried to take liberties. She had taught him a thing or two. Now that he had the sanction of the Church and the law to take liberties, he still left himself room to retreat with some grace in case she was not properly receptive. Happily, she usually was.

He stopped at a respectful distance to watch the drilling. He wondered at the function of the walking beam, a huge lever that worked up and down like the pumphandle that brought water into Gabriela's little kitchen sink. He found the rhythmic noise almost hypnotic. He noticed, after a bit, a man sitting on the running board of a black Model T, facing away from the rig. The man appeared to be taking a drink from a bottle. Drilling for oil must be thirsty work.

A sudden sharp hissing, whistling noise startled his bay horse, making it jerk its head up quickly. The horse would have turned and run had Trinidad not pulled up strongly on the reins. He saw the cow begin to run in fright, the calf close behind it. The man on the running board jumped to his feet. Trinidad thought he heard him shout, but he was not sure because the noise from the well was so piercing that it hurt his ears. He saw one man running away. Then came the explosion, a great ball of fire rolling up the derrick a moment before the whole thing blew apart and collapsed back into the roaring inferno. The running man was overtaken by a billowing flame. The man at the car turned and began running toward Trinidad, stumbling, falling, struggling in the sand.

The terrified horse came near throwing Trinidad in its attempt to break free and run. Even as Trinidad fought to stay in the saddle, he tried to see what was happening to the man who had been at the car. He saw the Model T burst into flame from the burning well's intense heat.

It was obvious that anyone on the drilling floor had died in the first seconds. Heat was rapidly overcoming the only survivor, for he sank down on his stomach in the sand, got up, moved a few feet and sank again.

Trinidad managed to get the horse quieted a little. He knew the man could not come out alive without help. Trinidad stepped to the ground, pulled off his shirt and tied it around the horse's head as a blindfold. He remounted and spurred hard, forcing the reluctant animal toward the fire. Trinidad's face burned. He knew the horse, even blindfolded, could feel and smell the huge fire and hear its roar.

The horse finally quit, refusing to go farther no matter how Trinidad spurred him and whipped him with the end of his rope. He dared not dismount, for the horse would almost surely break loose and run away. He shouted, "Come! Come to me!"

The man stirred. He struggled to his feet, took a few steps and fell again. Trinidad saw that his shirt was smoking. He shouted again, "My horse does not get closer! Come to me!" The man pushed to his feet and managed the last few faltering steps. The heat was almost unbearable. Trinidad leaned down and grasped the man's shoulder. "Take hold of the saddle." The man gripped the saddlehorn with one hand, the cantle with the other. Trinidad did not wait to get him all the way up. They had to get out of here. He held on to the man and put the horse into a run, away from the fire. The man's legs dragged in the shinnery and the low mesquite. But that was better than burning to death.

When they reached what Trinidad thought was a safe distance, he stopped the horse, let the man fall to the ground and swung down to roll him in the sand to smother the smoldering of the shirt. The man had been crying the whole time. Trinidad did not know if this came from pain or grief or fear. It did not matter; he was entitled to all three.

"Oh my God!" the man wept, looking toward the roaring fire. By this time, Trinidad was satisfied that nothing was left of men or rig except ash and melted, twisted, white-hot steel.

Trinidad tried to comfort the man. "You are all right. They will soon come. They will see the fire and the smoke from far away, and they will come."

"My son was in there. My son."

Trinidad made the sign of the cross. "He is in a better world."

2

The Dutchman's

SLIM McINTYRE had never seen so many fires in his twenty-three years. Through the streaked and dusty windshield of the rattling, chugging truck, through the open window on his side and across the driver to the other window, he could see fifteen or twenty separate orange flames licking the black night sky, so brilliant they overpowered the stars.

"Is the whole oilfield afire?" he asked, a little in awe.

The driver, a hand-rolled cigarette perched precariously on his lower lip, shook his head. "Nothin' that ain't supposed to be. Them's flares . . . torches. They burn off the gas because there's nothin' else to do with it. There's ten times more of it comes out of the oilwells than they've got a market for."

Slim marveled. There was a beauty of sorts in it, though the conservative side of him was appalled at the waste. "I'm glad I didn't doze off and just now wake up. I'd think I'd died and gone to hell."

"You'd've *thought* hell if you'd been here a while back and seen that wildcat well burnin' out yonder a ways. Taken two men with it, it did. Snuffed 'em out just like *that."* The driver snapped his fingers. "They was probably gone so quick they didn't hardly have time to scream." He dimmed his lights for what appeared to be a one-eyed car but turned out to be a motorcycle on the narrow, caliche-topped road. "Damned *sickles,"* he said. "Too dangerous for me. If I get myself into a wreck, I want to have a good solid truck around me to take the lick."

Slim looked back through the rear window. It was too dark now to see, but he remembered the truck was loaded with steel casing, heavy pipe manufactured to go down into a well. He had seen it when he had thumbed a ride out of Odessa at dusk. In event of a collision, that heavy load would come crashing through the cab and make pulp of anyone inside it. At least motorcycles didn't haul pipe. But gratitude for the ride made him keep his mouth shut. A lot of people had passed him by before this friendly young man, starved for talk, had stopped to pick him up. Silent Jim Kelly, he said they called him.

Kelly asked, "You sure you ain't lookin' for oilfield work? There's a right smart goin' on around Caprock these days for a strong-lookin' feller like you."

Slim shook his head. "I came to take a cowboy job. I wouldn't know nothin' about oilfield work."

"Hardly anybody does at first. Most of the people I know in the patch came off of a farm or a ranch someplace. Like me. You think I look like a farmer?"

"I can't say as I know what a farmer's supposed to look like. The ones I know come in all sizes and shapes."

Kelly was a wiry little man in his middle to late twenties, dressed in the same kind of blue work overalls Slim had seen on farmers and teamsters, cotton-gin workers and lumberyard hands all his life. He smelled of tobacco and sweat and something else pungent that Slim could not quite define. He supposed it was oil.

The driver said, "Most of these folks couldn't make a decent

16

livin' in the country and was lookin' to put meat and potatoes on their plate. I run off from my daddy's farm over in the East Texas piney woods. Place got to where it couldn't raise nothin' but chiggers, ticks and wild hogs. Got awful tired of eatin' pork, I did. You like pork?"

"I was always a little partial to bacon of a mornin'."

"You'd get damned tired of it if you was to have to eat wild hog three times a day. Even a mess of possum now and again got to where it tasted good. Drivin' a truck in the oilfield, I can afford me a steak once in a while. Ain't married, of course. If I was, I couldn't buy steak. But then maybe I wouldn't spend so much money at places like Jolene's."

"What's Jolene's?"

The driver chuckled. "You *did* just come off of the farm, didn't you? Never mind, you'll be huntin' for Jolene's when you've been out on that ranch awhile lookin' at nothin' but cows. Won't nobody have to explain it to you then."

Nobody had to explain it to him *now*. He hadn't lived his life in a convent. He had spent it with cowboys, who might act shy around womenfolk and outsiders but talked like muleskinners among their own. The world didn't hold many secrets from a kid who kept quiet and listened to cowboys. When they told a story, they left the hide and hair on.

The driver said, "I take it you've never been around an oiltown before."

"They haven't found any oil up where I come from. Just grass and a little two-bit farmin'. Folks up there take theirs from the *top* of the ground."

"And probably don't take much, or you wouldn't be down here huntin' for a job."

That hit a little close to home. The memory of loss was still painful. "I've *got* a job. It was promised to me. Do you know Douglas Clive?"

"Heard the name, is all. Seems like he's got him a cow ranch, ain't he?"

"He's the one. I'm surprised you don't know him, workin' around Caprock like you do."

"The folks that lived in Caprock before oil, they don't have much truck with us that works in the fields. They call us oilfield trash. They're glad enough to take the money that comes from what we do, but they don't want to rub up against any of us to get it. Like Jolene's place I was tellin' you about? I hear tell the buildin' belongs to a deacon in the church. She mails him the rent money so he don't have to go down there and admit to the world what he's gettin' rich from. Keeps his hands clean, but it comes damned close to makin' a pimp out of him to my way of thinkin'."

The road passed close enough to one of the oilfield flares that Slim could feel its heat through the open window. The flame came from the top of a huge upright pipe, standing forty or fifty feet tall. He caught a strong sulphur smell that he knew had to be crudeoil. "Stinks some, don't it?"

Kelly shook his head. "It stinks good. Smells to me like foldin' money."

Slim could hear the throbbing sound of a loud engine. Against the brilliance of the flare, he could see the silhouette of a tall wooden derrick. Men labored by lanternlight on its floor.

"They work all night?" he asked.

"Twenty-four hours a day, a lot of them. They got day *tower* and night *tower* on these rigs. You work twelve hours to a shift. What it is, you see, these people that own the leases, they're scared to death the man next door is fixin' to suck all the oil out from under their property before they can get it theirselves. So when a well is proven, everybody around it tries to get their own property drilled up and pumpin' as quick as they can. That's what makes an oil boom, everybody workin' hard and fast. When the production's all drilled up, the boom's over, like stickin' a pin in a balloon.

"You won't see no brick buildin's in Caprock except for the few that was already there when it was just a little cowtown. The rest of it's put up quick and cheap, because the boom could end by Saturday night week."

"Sounds kind of temporary. What do you do when it's over?"

"There's always another boom someplace. We just pick up and go. No ties and no tears."

"Sounds to me like cowpunchin' is safer. So long as those cows keeps shellin' out calves, you've got a steady job."

"And dull. What I like is the excitement. I wouldn't go back to my old daddy's farm for all the bootleg whisky you could load onto this truck." He pointed with his chin. "Well, yonder's

Caprock. If you ain't ever been to an oil boomtown, you better sit up and take notice."

Slim could see electric lights ahead. He became aware that they were passing a multitude of large tents. Lamplight flickered through the canvas so that he could see the shadows of people moving around inside.

"Ragtown," the driver said. "They ain't strung the powerlines all the way out here."

The vehicular traffic had become heavy. Most of the tents seemed to have cars or trucks parked beside or in front of them. He frowned. "Looks like folks that can afford to have a car could afford to live in somethin' better than a raggedy tent."

"They got to have a car to go to work in. And they can't throw up houses fast enough to get all the folks out of the tents, even if everybody wanted one. A tent's got its good side: you can roll it up and take it with you to the next boom. You can't carry a house over your shoulders, not even a sheetiron shack."

"Seems like a poor way to live."

"You live where the work is. And the work keeps movin'." Kelly slowed, gearing the truck down. "Any druthers as to where you want to stop at?"

Slim shrugged. "I reckon' it's too late to find my way out to Clive's ranch tonight. Drop me off at a café if you would, please. I ain't et since noon, and not much then."

"Right yonder is the Dutchman's. It's as good as any and better'n most. Just keep your hand on your pocketbook, cowboy. This town has drawed highbinders and highjackers that the devil himself wouldn't claim kin to. They'll steal anything from a straw hat to a truckload of oilfield equipment. They'll spot you for a mullet."

"Can't be any worse than Kansas City. I rode up there one time on a cattle train."

"Kansas City ain't seen nothin' like this. Chicago, maybe, but not Kansas City. You get to that ranch as soon as you can and stay out of trouble."

"Trouble won't come lookin' for me if I don't go lookin' for it."

"Well, I told you, anyway. Good luck, and don't forget your saddle."

Slim had his saddle, bridle and spurs in a towsack tied between the truck's right headlight and the bumper. His few extra clothes were rolled up inside two blankets. He shook the driver's hand. "Much obliged for the ride, Silent Jim. I'd like to buy your supper."

"Thanks, but they're probably already throwin' a conniption fit, hollerin' for this load of pipe. See you around, cowboy."

As soon as Slim retrieved the towsack and blanket roll from beneath the headlight, Kelly noisily pulled away. Slim watched a moment, feeling uneasy and alone. He regarded Kelly as a friend, if a casual one, and now he stood by himself in a strange, bustling, pulsing town in which he did not know a soul. The truck kicked up street dust, burning his eyes. The exhaust was strong in its wake, burning his nostrils. He heard the insistent *ooo-gah* of a car's horn and stepped back to let a Model T pass, carrying four laughing men who seemed to be in no pain. They reminded him of cowboys in town for a Saturday night, but this had no look of a cowtown.

Parking space seemed to be at a premium. Cars were parked not only up against the wooden sidewalks on both sides but in the center of the wide street as well. Some faced one direction, some the other, as if poised for a quick getaway. He saw a car back out, and another immediately pulled into the vacated place. A disappointed motorist who had been second in line honked his horn in frustration and passed on up the street. If this had been Saturday, Slim might have understood, but he was pretty sure it was only Thursday. He had lost track, hitchhiking down from the plains.

A stern voice said, "Stand out in that street very long and they'll make you a part of it. You better get up here on the sidewalk out of harm's way."

Turning, Slim saw a tall, athletic-looking man in cowboy-type khaki clothes and high-heeled boots. He felt for a moment that he had found a kindred spirit. But then he saw a badge on the shirt and a pistol on the man's hip. Slim always felt uneasy in the presence of lawmen, even though he hadn't done anything. He stepped quickly up onto the rough-sawed sidewalk, carrying his blanket roll and towsack. The saddle thumped solidly as he dropped it on the boards.

The lawman stepped up close enough that Slim could read the

word *Sheriff* on his badge. "What you got in there, burglar tools?"

"My saddle."

"What use you got for a saddle in the oilfield?"

"I come for a ranch job."

"I haven't heard of anybody hirin' on."

"Douglas Clive said he'd have a job for me."

The lawman frowned deeply. "You know Clive?"

"Met him a while back at a rodeo. He said he could use me."

"Douglas Clive says a lot of things. What's your name, cowboy?"

"Patrick McIntyre. Folks just call me Slim."

"I'm Dave Buckalew, Slim. Welcome to Caprock, such as it is. All I can do is wish you luck. You're apt to need it." The sheriff turned and walked up the street, his boots striking heavily on the boards.

Slim watched, a little perturbed. Was Buckalew implying something about Douglas Clive, or did he just regard Slim as an innocent about to be swallowed alive by Babylon? He didn't feel all that innocent. He had been to Kansas City.

Foot traffic on the sidewalk was almost as heavy as the automobile and truck traffic on the unpaved street. Slim kept to the edge of the walk and looked both ways, studying what he could see of the town in the glare of bare electric light bulbs strung from storefronts and in windows. Where he stood, most of the buildings were new and, as Kelly had said, built for haste and economy with little thought to endurance. They were mostly of raw lumber and sheetiron. Whatever had been here before oil must be farther down the street. He heard shouting and laughter and the distant sound of a drunken quarrel. In a moment, the quarrel turned into a fight, and men cheered the combatants on to maim one another. Boots thumped heavily on the wooden walk, and the sheriff brushed past Slim, hurrying to quell the disturbance. It was Slim's guess that a lawman could run himself into a frazzled remnant in a town like this.

Carrying the towsack and the roll, he moved in the opposite direction, looking for the Dutchman's. He passed a poolhall, where he heard the strike of a cue against billiard balls and the shuffle of dominoes on a wooden table. The scent of homebrewed beer struck him like a wet towel across the face. Prohibition was supposed to put a stop to such as that, at least in the open. He wondered if the sheriff had lost his sense of smell.

Music emanated from the building next to the poolhall. It was raucous, jazzy music. As he came to the plate-glass window, he could see couples dancing inside. A number of men stood in the front of the building, behind a sort of fence. Several women sat along one wall, and a few more in brightly printed cotton dresses loafed on the sidewalk out front, smoking ready-roll cigarettes. A couple had their hair bobbed off short as if they were trying to be men. But their skirts reached only to the knees, and their stockings were rolled down just below the hemlines. They had his full attention for a minute. He stared until one of them turned and met his eyes.

She rubbed her hand up her hip and stopped it under one breast. She said, "Want to dance, sport? The music's lively. Just a dime a dance."

He was tempted, but he knew what would happen. He would get caught up in the intoxication of those warm, soft women in his arms, and he wouldn't be able to call it quits. At a dime a dance, the night could melt away a goodly part of the hard-earned thirty-four dollars he had in his pocket. He hadn't had to go to Kansas City to learn that; he had learned it in Fort Worth.

"Another time," he said. He was relieved that the woman didn't press him any further, because his resistance might not have stood up to the challenge. Her perfume followed him, tempting him to turn back.

A drugstore stood next to the dancehall. Its marble counter and its ice-cream parlor chairs belied the cheapness of its sheet-iron exterior. This was probably not the first boomtown the shiny counter had graced. He saw two young couples at a small round marble-topped table, sipping ice-cream sodas. He remembered he was thirsty from the long ride, and the sodas looked good. But he was also hungry. His money would be better spent at the Dutchman's.

An empty lot separated the drugstore from the next building. The sidewalk ended momentarily. He boosted the two bundles up onto his shoulders and stepped down into the dirt. His boot struck an empty bottle, which he had not seen in the darkness. Kicking it away, he thought the town must look pretty junky in the daylight if folks threw empty bottles down where other people had to walk.

Just beyond the dark lot, he found the café. A small sign in the window said TEAGARDEN RESTAURANT. He had read about English teagardens in books. This in no way resembled his mental image. But he supposed it didn't hurt to try to pretty the place up with a nice name. Lord knew there wasn't much else pretty about it. It was strictly utilitarian, built of raw new lumber and plain as a pair of overalls. He paused a moment at the plate-glass window, wondering if he really wanted to go inside. The place was full of customers, many of them wearing clothes blackened by oil, their faces begrimed by the grease and dirt and rust and all the other unpleasantness that went with hard work in the oilfields. A big man stood at the cash register, burly as a barroom bouncer. Slim supposed that was the Dutchman. One young woman worked behind a long counter that had fifteen or twenty stools. Another worked out in the room, carrying plates in both hands high over her head as she maneuvered her way gingerly among the tables. Through a long opening behind the counter, he could see a third woman busy in the kitchen, her slightly graying hair done up in a bun at the back of her neck. She rubbed an arm across her eyes and forehead. She looked tired enough to drop.

He hated to add to her work, but he had to eat, and his abstinence wouldn't lighten her load enough to count. He started for the open door but found it blocked. A wizened, slightly stooped man of uncertain age stood there, staring in. Slim waited a moment, then said, "Go ahead, mister. You were here before me."

The man seemed startled. He backed off a step. "Pardon me, young feller. I wasn't goin' in. I was just lookin'."

By his appearance, Slim guessed he might be hungry. His worn old clothes and his gaunt face suggested that he might not have the price of a meal. Well, buying him something to eat wouldn't bust Slim's pocketbook. It would be better than spending his dimes in the dancehall. He tried to keep from sounding as if he were offering charity. "If you ain't et, I'd be tickled to have your company."

The man shook his head. "I don't eat much." Slim caught the smell of whisky on his breath. He might not eat much, but . . .

The man said, "That's my wife yonder, workin' in the kitchen. You go on in. You'll find that she's a right smart of a cook." His gaze went to the big towsack. "You ain't peddlin' bootleg, are you?"

"I've got a saddle in there."

"A saddle? Hell of a town to have a saddle in." The man turned and started up the street, his step unsteady.

Sheriff Buckalew came back, the fight broken up. He paused to watch the wizened man's retreat under the harsh light of the bare bulbs. He asked, "Autie hit you up for a drink?"

"He didn't ask for nothin'. I offered to buy his supper, but he didn't take me up on it," Slim said.

"If he ever does ask you for a drink, tell him no. He gets more'n enough." Buckalew looked into the café for a moment. Slim sensed that his gaze was directed toward the woman in the kitchen. The lawman's eyes softened with pity, which surprised Slim a little. *Not much like a couple of sheriffs I've known.*

Buckalew went on. Slim waited for a couple of oilfield hands to come out, then entered the crowded café. The interior was warm and stuffy despite the best efforts of three whirring ceiling fans. The noise of a dozen conversations assaulted his ears. The smell of oil was strong, for many of the workingmen had it soaked into their clothing, their shoes, probably even their skin. He looked for a place at the counter, but all the stools were occupied. His second choice was a table, but those too were busy. He stood holding the bag and the roll at arm's length, trying to gauge how long it might be before one of the men at the counter finished his meal and left.

A friendly voice said, "There's room at this table, partner, if you don't mind sharin' company with a stranger. Couple of the boys just now up and left." Slim turned to see a red-haired young man of near his own age, his sun-browned and freckled face lighted by a hospitable smile half a yard wide.

"If it wouldn't put you out none," Slim said gratefully.

"Glad to have somebody new to talk with. Everybody around here already knows my jokes." The young man turned to find the waitress. "Tracy, reckon you could clear off these empty plates? My friend's fixin' to sit down here."

Tracy looked as if she had her hands full already, carrying a plate in each one. "Hold your horses," she answered. "I'll get there when I can." She eyed the bag and roll. "You can put those over yonder against the wall, where nobody's apt to trip over them." It sounded like an order.

Slim did as she said, then took a chair that allowed him to watch his property. He remembered the truck driver's admonition about keeping his hand on his pocketbook. The waitress cleared the plates left by the two departed workers and swiped at the red-and-white checkered oilcloth with a damp rag.

The young man extended his hand across the table. "My name's Hap Holloway. I think they started callin' me Hap because I've got such a happy disposition."

The waitress said ironically, "Or maybe it was because you're so hapless."

Holloway grinned. "Tracy, what you need is a man to give *you* a happier disposition."

She sniffed. "I need a man like I need a broken leg. A broken leg will at least heal up. A man never gets better."

"How can you know till you try one? I'm available if you're shoppin' around."

"I know how available you are." She turned to Slim. "What can I bring you?"

Hap put in, "You ought to try a steak like the one I've got. Only costs ninety cents."

It had taken Slim three months to save thirty-four dollars out of cowboy wages, after meeting his responsibilities. "What's cheaper?"

"Special plate is fifty cents. Coffee included."

"I believe I'll just have the special. Make the coffee black." He watched the girl as she turned away. It was hard to guess her age, for the working day had run well into the night, and she was tired, like the woman in the kitchen. She probably looked older now than she really was. She was not what he would call a pretty girl. If anything, she was a little on the plain side, but that was probably at least partly because of the hard work. Give her some rest, some decent clothes, maybe even a little lipstick, and she might look a right smart better. Not that it made any particular difference to him, one way or the other.

Holloway gave part of his attention back to the steak, but Slim noted that he continued to watch the girl's movements. Slim ventured, "I've seen prettier ones. And friendlier."

"They don't have to be pretty. They just have to be alive. As for friendly, a man just has to keep workin' on that. Good things don't always come easy. New in town, ain't you?"

"Just now came in. Name's Slim McIntyre."

"You're roughneckin' on a rig, I suppose?"

"I'm a cowboy by trade. Came here for a ranch job."

"What you got in that big sack, a Shetland pony?"

"Just my saddle, mainly. And what goes with it."

"You probably wouldn't think so to look at me, with these oilfield duds and all, but I used to punch cattle myself. That's all my daddy ever done, all his life, and I was pretty damned good at it if I do say so myself."

"How come you quit?"

"Watched my daddy gettin' old and stove-up for damned little money. Decided if I had to work, there was better-payin' places than some dusty old ranch."

The waitress came back with Slim's coffee. She said, "Too bad you haven't found one of them. You could use a steady job."

"Now, Tracy, I get all the work I want to do."

"Which isn't much." She gave Slim a cautioning glance. "You better watch him, cowboy. He smiles pretty, but first thing you know, he'll be in your pocket."

Slim had to doubt that. Hap seemed like a lot of the cowboys he had known and worked with most of his life, not much concerned about the rainy days ahead but fun to be around in camp or in town, the kind of good old boys who would work hard all month just to whoop and holler for a night or two in town. His father had always said there wasn't a nickel's worth of harm in them so long as a man just enjoyed their company, accepted them for what they were and didn't try to follow them down the road. There were times when they could stop being fun.

Slim saw no harm in Hap.

The girl brought Slim's plate. The main part was meatloaf, to his notion a blasphemous way to treat good beef, but he was hungry enough to pretend it was steak. The red beans had a chuckwagon taste, and the French fries and biscuits made up for any shortcomings of the meatloaf. She filled his cup a second time. "You lit into that like you were starved, cowboy. They must not feed very good where you come from."

"They did fine. I just been on the road awhile."

Hap ordered a piece of apple pie and finished it. "Tracy, you better bring the cowboy a piece of that pie too."

She looked at him, asking the question with her gray eyes. He wanted to ask how much the pie cost but was ashamed. "No, I reckon I'll have enough when I've finished all this."

Hap smiled. "Well, there's nothin' I'd rather do than sit here and watch a hungry man enjoy himself, but I got places to go and people to see. Tracy, how's about my check?"

She took a pad from the pocket of her lace-edged apron, the only thing Slim had seen in this place that looked the least bit fancy. She flipped through it and tore off a page.

"An even dollar, hunh?" Hap dug into his pocket and brought up two coins. He stared at them as if in surprise. "Well, by damn, Tracy, looks like that's all I've got. Sixty cents. Looks like you'll have to put the rest of it on the cuff till I get paid."

If she had been blunt before, she became caustic now. She pointed to a sign up over the counter: IN GOD WE TRUST, ALL OTHERS PAY CASH! "You know Mr. Schwartz runs a cash business here. If you didn't have the money for that steak, you ought to've ordered a special plate like your friend here."

Hap's broad smile was confident, his teeth white as piano keys. "Don't know much we can do about it now. I don't think you want that steak back."

The burly gentleman came out from behind the cash register and pushed his way among the crowded tables like a bull looking for a fight. "Any trouble here, Tracy?" He put his hands on his hips. They looked like a pair of cured hams. Slim had a mental picture of those hands making fists and beating Hap's face into something like the meatloaf on his plate.

Slim became aware that most people had stopped eating and were watching to see the Dutchman take forty cents' worth of satisfaction out of Hap Holloway's hide. He said quickly, "No trouble. I'll stand for the rest of it." He brought out his wallet. His thirty-four dollars was mostly in one-dollar bills. They looked like a lot more than they were. He peeled off one. "Take it out of this."

Hap said, "Better take fifty cents. I wouldn't want Tracy to go without her tip."

Tracy gave him an angry look, then said critically to Slim,

"You ought to learn to take care of yourself, cowboy, and let these freeloaders take their lumps."

"Fifty cents ain't much if it keeps somebody out of trouble."

"It's just about what you saved by takin' the special instead of the steak. You'd've been better off eatin' the steak and lettin' this fast-talkin' cheapskate get what's comin' to him."

The big proprietor was more interested in making a profit than in making a point. "Take the man's money, Tracy."

She took the dollar bill and told Slim, "You'd better put the rest of that roll back in your pocket before somethin' happens to it." She turned away stiffly, carrying the money to the cash register.

Hap said to Slim, "I tripped this mornin' and fell flat on my face. Turned out I had stumped my toe on an old horseshoe. I taken that for a sign that this was goin' to be a lucky day for me." He stood up and shoved out his freckled hand. "Much obliged, partner. I owe you one."

"You owe me fifty cents, is all. If we don't run into one another again, put it into the collection plate at church."

"Church?" Hap seemed surprised at the idea. "Why, sure, I reckon I might be goin' to church one of these days." He gripped Slim's hand so hard that it hurt. "Good luck to you, cowboy. Next time one of them old bad broncs throws you off on your head and you're just makin' thirty a month, remember what I told you about a better way of earnin' a livin'."

Hap saluted Tracy as she came back from the register. Slim watched him walk out into the night, then turned his attention to Tracy.

"Your special is fifty cents. I went ahead and rung it up. That killed most of your dollar." She put his dime change in front of his plate. "No tip expected or wanted. You put that back in your pocket."

He had a feeling she was angry at him. "Hap seemed like an agreeable feller. I just didn't want to see him beat up or nothin'."

"It's a good sign for a man to be soft-hearted. But it's somethin' else to be soft-headed. You'll do well to learn the difference, cowboy."

A commotion drew their attention to the doorway. The sheriff stood there, supporting the sagging man named Autie. He gave Tracy an urgent beckoning nod.

Autie was protesting, "Ain't nothin' wrong with me. I'm all right, I tell you."

Slim caught a look of anxiety in Tracy's face. The sheriff said, "Somebody needs to take your papa home. He staggered out into the street just now and come within an inch of gettin' himself run over."

Autie protested again that he didn't need any help. A roustabout who had finished eating stood up and looked sympathetically at the sagging driller. "He's a friend of mine, Sheriff. I'll see that he gets home." He left some change on his table, took the man's arm and led him outside.

The sheriff said, "I'm sorry, Tracy. I hope your mama didn't see that."

Tracy sadly shook her head. "She'd've come rushin' out here if she had."

"I don't know what you-all are ever goin' to do with Autie."

The girl shrugged. "He's my papa. We'll just keep lovin' him, is all. Lovin' and hopin'."

The sheriff gave the crowd a quick appraisal, his gaze touching a moment on Slim. He nodded in recognition, then turned back out into the street.

Slim felt embarrassed for the girl. When her gaze fell upon him, he looked quickly down at his coffee. He finished it and stood up. He left her the dime and another like it in spite of what she had said. He retrieved his bag and blanket roll. Outside, he hoisted them up on his shoulders and started down the sidewalk. He had a hunch a hotel room would be hard to find in this town, even if he wanted to spend the money for one. He had slept on the ground a big part of the time the last few years, cowboying for one ranch and another. He would find himself a quiet place and roll out his blankets. In the morning, he would see about getting out to Douglas Clive's ranch.

As he came to the end of the sidewalk where the vacant lot was, a man stepped up to him out of the darkness. "Buddy, you got a match?"

"I don't smoke," Slim replied, "but I think I've got some matches rolled up in my blankets." He set his burdens on the ground. He heard a sudden movement behind him, then something struck him across the back of his head. He sprawled forward on the ground, his head feeling as if it were about to explode. A shower of stars fell before his eyes. He felt a hand searching through his pockets but was powerless to do anything.

He heard a man's voice shout, "Hey, what're you doin' there?" It sounded like Hap's. He heard the quick shuffle of feet as his assailants ran off into the darkness.

A hand gently touched his shoulder. "They hurt you, mister?" Then Hap said, "By damn, it's the cowboy. Take it gentle, Slim. Don't rush anything. Just get up real slow and let's see if there's anything broke."

Slim said grittily, "Feels like *everything's* broke." With Hap's help, he managed shakily to put his feet under him. His hat was lying on the ground. He bent to try to pick it up and nearly fell. The pain made him forget about the hat. He reached up and gingerly touched his hand to the back of his head. He felt something wet and warm and sticky.

"I must be bleedin' like a stuck hog."

"You need help, partner. Let's get you back into the café."

"My saddle. Don't leave my saddle."

Hap looked around, then shook his head. "There ain't no saddle here. They must've took it with them. Taken your blanket roll too, the way it looks."

Slim felt for his wallet, knowing it would probably be gone. It was. He groaned. "What the hell kind of a place have I come to?"

3

A Bad Beginning

HAP HELPED SLIM UP onto the sidewalk, supporting him so he would not slump to his knees. "Damned poor introduction to our little Sodom in the Sandhills. Let's get you back into the Dutchman's and see how bad they treated you."

Slim felt all eyes turn toward him. The café's rackety conversation turned to a solemn quiet. The waitress Tracy raised a hand to her mouth in shock but quickly moved toward him. "Hap Holloway, what did you do?"

Hap seemed aggrieved. "Nothin'. How come you always think the worst of me?"

"Because I've seen that side of you too many times." She

pointed to a door. "Take him into the kitchen. We don't want the blood turnin' the customers' stomachs."

Hap complained, "A man may be dyin', and you're worried about losin' customers."

"He's not dyin'," she retorted, "but he could've been, flashin' that roll of bills around for everybody to see."

"It wasn't but thirty-four dollars," Slim said defensively.

"For forty they'd've killed you."

The graying woman turned wide-eyed from the grill. "What in the world . . ." Her surprise turned to sympathy.

Hap said, "Somebody rolled him, Mrs. Whitmore. He's taken a lick on the back of his head. We need to wash the blood off so we can see how bad it is."

Hap guided Slim to a cane-bottomed chair and sat him down, then turned toward the sink. He picked up a wet dishrag, but Tracy stopped him. "You want to give him blood poisoning?" Her tongue was sharp. "We'll use a clean tea towel." She turned on the faucet and wet half of the towel, then began to wash the back of Slim's head. He flinched at the pain. "Got a gash there," she said tightly. "It's still bleedin'."

Mrs. Whitmore brought a handful of flour. "This'll help get that stopped," she said tightly. She applied it to the wound and stood back, staring anxiously into Slim's face. He thought he saw tears start in her eyes, which struck him odd, for he was a stranger to these people. Or perhaps the tears were his own; he was seeing things through a red haze.

Slim could not tell if the flour helped or not. His head throbbed as if someone were beating on it. But shortly Tracy said, "I believe the blood has stopped." She went back to work with the towel, cleaning around the edges of the gash, her fingers careful. He flinched anyway.

She demanded, "Who did it?"

Slim started to shake his head, but it hurt too much. "I wouldn't know; I'm new in town. Besides, I only saw one face, and that was in the dark."

She sounded suspicious. "Where was Hap when this was goin' on?"

"It wasn't him. He came to help me."

"Probably lookin' for another free meal." She finished the cleaning. "That's startin' to swell up. You're goin' to have a knot

32

the size of a cantaloupe. But it's not bleedin' anymore." She went to a small cabinet and fetched a bottle. When she poured its contents over the gash, he felt as if she had dumped a pan of hot coals on his head. He gritted his teeth and gripped both legs so tightly that they hurt. He heard a hissing sound and knew he had made it himself. But he managed to choke back a few cowboy terms the women would not appreciate.

She said, "Sorry, but that was necessary."

"That's what they say to the horse with a broken leg when they shoot him."

"I'll tear up a couple of these tea towels and make a bandage, such as it is, just to keep the gash clean." As she was finishing up, the big Dutchman stood in the door, watching. "If you're through with him, Tracy, we've got more customers out there than Mabel can handle by herself."

"I've done all I can do for him." She stepped back and surveyed her bandaging job. "Not pretty, but then I never went to nursin' school. That'll have to hold you, cowboy. Wouldn't hurt to let a doctor see you."

"I've got nothin' to pay a doctor with. They took it all."

The Dutchman said, "Hap, he done you a favor while ago. Now you do him one and take him to the sheriff."

Hap shifted uncomfortably. "Sheriff ain't goin' to catch them robbers."

"He won't if he don't know about this. Use the back door. One of the ladies got so sick to her stomach that she went outside and lost the supper she'd just et."

Slim feared he was about to lose his own, thinking about losing that money, his saddle, everything except the clothes he was wearing. The Dutchman reached out with those huge ham hands and helped Slim to his feet. Slim swayed and caught himself by extending a hand to the wall. When he had been on his feet a minute, the swaying eased.

He glanced at Mrs. Whitmore. She had never stopped staring at him the whole time. He said, "Thank you, ma'am, for your concern. I'll be all right."

She still had tears in her eyes. She said to Tracy, "Don't he look a little like Benny?"

The girl answered quickly, "He doesn't look a bit like Benny, Mama. You've got to quit lookin' for Benny in everybody you see." She turned back to Slim. "Next time don't you be flauntin' your wealth in front of a crowd."

"There won't be any wealth, not anymore." At the door, he turned. "Thanks for takin' care of me."

"I'd do it for a dog. And maybe even for Hap Holloway."

Outside, Slim found he could walk on his own, once Hap helped him down the single wooden step to the ground. He said, "That girl has got your name written real big on her list. What'd you ever do to her?"

"Nothin', by damn!" Hap sounded hurt, but after a moment he admitted, "Well, a while back I reached up under her skirt, tryin' to find out what she had above her stockin's. My eye was black for a week."

Slim marveled. He would never have had the nerve to try a thing like that. Truth was, he probably would not even have thought of it. "Didn't you know she'd hit you?"

"You never know for sure till you try. You'd be surprised how many women'll let you."

In the cowtowns Slim had known, such a liberty could get a man killed by the woman's friends or relations, or at least beaten so grievously that his mother wouldn't know him. Maybe things were different in the oilpatch.

Hap bent over in the darkness and picked something up from the ground. "I believe this is your hat." He was at about the place where Slim had fallen. "Good thing you had it on when they hit you, or that gash'd be worse. I'll carry it. You probably couldn't get it on your head right now anyway."

The sidewalks were still busy, the street carrying a constant stream of cars and trucks. Slim didn't know what the hour was, exactly, but back where he had come from it would be considered time for honest folks to be getting ready for bed.

They walked past the drugstore, then the dancehall, where the music still played loudly and couples were fast-stepping to its quick beat. Hap paused a moment to look wistfully inside. "All them good-lookin' women, and me without a dime to my name."

Slim couldn't help him now, not even if he felt like it. He didn't have a dime either. "How far to the sheriff?"

"A ways yet, to the old town. All this stuff here was built after the oil come in."

It was two blocks, but it felt like two miles. Slim's head ached, and his feet seemed to weigh a hundred pounds apiece. They came finally to older buildings, some of brick, some of lumber, but all more solidly built than the rest he had seen.

Hap said, "Yonder's the courthouse and jail."

Like most other county-seat cowtowns Slim had seen, this one originally had centered around a small two-story brick court-house, which had the central block all to itself, shared only with a small jail built of the same bricks. He saw several men sitting or lying on the ground around a large old chinaberry tree. Not until he was closer did he realize they were all handcuffed to a heavy chain, its links half the size of his fist. He glanced at Hap in surprise.

Hap said, "That's the auxiliary jail. I've spent a night or two on that chain myself. Come on, sheriff's office is in the court-house."

The door stood open at the top of half a dozen concrete steps. Slim labored a little, making the climb. Hap helped him. The hall was dark except for light spilling through one open door. A sign nailed to the doorframe said simply SHERIFF.

Hap walked ahead and peered in. "We're in luck. He's here."

Buckalew was seated at a desk, his broad-brimmed hat still on his head. He looked up from some papers he had been leafing through. "Well, cowboy, didn't figure to see you again so quick." He saw the rude bandage. "What happened to you?"

Slim was glad to slump into a hard wooden chair and let Hap do most of the talking. Buckalew walked up to Slim and in-spected the bandage more closely. "Tracy's a good girl, but she's got a long ways to go before she makes a nurse. You say they got everything you had?"

"Even my saddle," Slim lamented. "Now, I can see them takin' my money—what there was of it—but what use could they have for my saddle?"

"Probably take it to Odessa or Midland and hock it. I'll phone the sheriffs over there and have them keep an eye on the hock-shops. Can you give me a description of it?"

Slim told him all there was, which didn't amount to much. It had been a plain working saddle, nothing very fancy to make it look different from a thousand others. It had the maker's name stamped behind the cantle, and a number, but he didn't remem-ber what the number was.

35

"Not much for us to go on," the sheriff told him flatly, "but we'll do what we can." He cut his gaze to Hap, and it was not friendly. "You said you saw them. Who were they?"

Hap turned up the palms of his hands. "It was dark, Sheriff. I can't even tell you if they was white, black or polky dot."

The sheriff appeared not quite to believe him. "Seems like you know just about every lowlife that hangs around this town."

"I wouldn't've known my own brother in that dark."

"If you had a brother, I wouldn't be surprised to learn that he was out there." Buckalew turned his gaze back to Slim. "Since the boom started, we've got everything from pickpockets and sneakthieves like them that hit you to highjackers that'll pistol-whip a driver and steal a whole truckload of drillin' tools."

Hap said, "You'll have to admit, Sheriff, that most of these oilfield folks is good people. They don't cause no trouble and don't want none."

"I know, but it's that other bunch I've got to contend with. There's enough of them that I don't sleep good like I used to. Speakin' of sleepin'," he said to Slim, "where're you spendin' the night?"

Slim shook his head and wished he hadn't, for it hurt all the more. "Hadn't given it much thought. I was just goin' to find me a place to spread my blankets. Now I don't even have any blankets."

Hap said, "I can take him with me. Ain't but three of us sharin' a tent. I'll give him my cot and sleep on the floor."

Buckalew grunted. "I don't like the looks of your head, cowboy. With all due respects to Tracy, I think I'd like a doctor to take a look at it in the mornin'. Why don't you stay here?"

"In your office?"

"Next door. Come on, I'll make a place for you."

Hap said, "I've already seen what's next door. I don't care to be seein' it again without I'm forced to." He thrust his hand toward Slim. "Good luck to you, partner. Maybe I'll be runnin' into you."

Slim couldn't have helped liking Hap's grin, even if he tried. "I'm obliged to you."

The sheriff turned out the office light and led the way down the dark hall, shutting the door behind him when he was outside on the broad first step. "Watch you don't fall, now."

Slim made his way carefully down to the ground. The sheriff jerked his head toward the jail. "This way."

Slim missed a step. "You puttin' me in jail?"

"No." The sheriff seemed surprised. "Well, not in the way you're thinkin'. I'll clear out a cell so you'll have a cot to sleep on. I won't shut the door on you."

They passed the men locked to the chain. "Hey, Sheriff, have a heart," one of them pleaded.

"Buckalew, this ground don't get no softer," another said.

Buckalew ignored them. He entered the jail's front room. A man sat at a desk there. Behind him were several small cells. The man stood up as Buckalew entered. The badge on his shirt was smaller than Buckalew's. "Catch you another one, Dave? There's still room on the chain." The deputy seemed to take pleasure in his work.

Buckalew said, "Slim, this is my deputy, Waddy Fuller. Waddy, this boy got a rude introduction to our town tonight. You still have Ox in that back cell?"

"Right where you left him."

"Roust him out and put him on the chain. There's no use an old rowdy like him havin' a good cot at county expense when this boy needs a place to lay his head."

"Ox is liable to raise hell."

"That's what got him in here."

The deputy was a beanpole, six feet tall like the sheriff but without Buckalew's athletic build. He wouldn't weigh a hundred and twenty with his clothes on and soaking wet. He had light blue eyes with a washed-out, transparent appearance, as if there might not be anybody at home behind them.

The man named Ox was built like a blacksmith, his face burned brown except where it was bruised to a deep blue or cut to an angry red. That he had been in a hell of a fight was obvious. His clothes were torn and blood stained and smelled of beer. He staggered, almost dragging down Deputy Fuller, who kept a grip on his arm. Fuller was no match for the man's great weight.

"Where you takin' me?" Ox demanded. "It ain't mornin' already, is it?"

"Not yet," Fuller said. "You're just changin' beds, is all." His eyes were asking Buckalew for help.

The sheriff cautioned, "Waddy, don't you put him anywhere close to Choctaw. They'll just fight again."

Slim watched the pair lurch out the door toward the chain that was firmly hitched around the big chinaberry. "You use that chain much, Sheriff?"

"Most every night. This old jail's not half big enough, and the county commissioners don't see fit to build another one. They're afraid the oil play'll die out and they'll be hung with the debt."

"What if it rains?"

"Those boys won't melt, and the water has never risen high enough here to drown anybody. Come on, let's see about puttin' you to bed."

The cell was tiny, just long enough for a steel cot and about half as wide. The only furnishings besides the cot were a wooden washstand with pitcher and bowl and a white enameled slop jar with a lid to help contain the odor. Slim sniffed. The lid wasn't doing its job very well.

The sheriff said, "Ol' Ox is a real stinker. If I was you, I'd want to empty that before I bunked down." He pointed toward the toilet. He did not volunteer to do the job himself. Slim decided the use of the cot was worth a few minutes of unpleasant duty.

He said, "The longer I think about it, the madder I get. I worked long and hard to save that money. If they wanted money they ought to go and work for it like I did."

"Welcome to Caprock," Buckalew said.

The jail was stuffy and warm, smelling faintly of sweat and tobacco, of human waste. Though the cell door stood open, the iron bars around Slim gave him claustrophobia. His head ached, and he had a hard time finding a way to lie without the pillow aggravating the burning wound. This was going to be a long, sleepless night. He lay thinking about the loss of the saddle and his other belongings, as well as the thirty-three dollars he had had left after paying for supper. He alternated between anger and despair. Sometime during the night, he finally drifted off to sleep.

He awakened to find sunshine streaming through the cell's barred window and reflecting brassily off of the ceiling. It hurt his eyes at first, so he had a hard time keeping them open. Presently he heard boots striking the floor.

Dave Buckalew stood in the open door. "I've brought Doc Tolliver to take a look at that wound. Afterwards, you can have some breakfast if you're of a mind to."

Slim felt of the back of his head. The bandage had shifted during the night. Most of it hung loosely down against his neck. A little of it was firmly stuck in the dried blood, however. As the girl Tracy had predicted, a sizeable knot had arisen.

Doc Tolliver was a paunchy little gray-haired man in his sixties, wearing an old-fashioned white suit that made him look like Slim's vision of a Kentucky colonel. He carried a little black bag, from which he extracted a bottle and began using its contents to soak the bandage loose from Slim's head. Whatever it was, it smelled terrible and burned worse. But the bandage came away. The old gentleman clucked sympathetically. "They sure put you a pumpkin on there, lad. But it's some distance from the heart. I think you'll live."

"I was kind of hopin' so." Slim squinted against the burning of the medication. The doctor put a new, much smaller bandage in place.

Slim said, "Doctor, I'll pay you when I can."

"No charge. Didn't take me five minutes. If you were to break a leg, of course, or die of some loathsome disease, I'd have to seek some kind of payment." He stood up and took a long glance at his handiwork, then put the leavings back into his black bag. "That'll hold you, I think. Now I've got to go see about a mare that's about to foal."

Slim watched the doctor depart. "Mare?"

Buckalew said, "He's pullin' your leg. But when he first came here, before the oil boom, there were days when there wouldn't be a single human patient show up. He'd take care of folks' animals, just for somethin' to do. Now people keep shootin' each other and fallin' off of oil derricks and turnin' their cars over. He's got so much business he's had to build him a clinic."

If the doctor applied that burning stuff to a mare, he would probably get kicked clear across a fence, Slim thought. "I don't suppose you've found the ginks that did this to me?"

"No, but I think I've found some of your stuff." Buckalew pitched two folded blankets and some clothing on the cot. "See if that's yours."

It was.

"This was left a little ways from where they hit you. I expect they went through it to see what they could use, then threw it away."

"But my saddle . . ."

"No sign of it. They probably figure on hockin' or sellin' it someplace. Come on over to my office. A little breakfast'll make you feel a lot better."

Slim counted fewer men on the chain than he had seen last night. Buckalew explained, "We let some of them go after daylight, if they're not chronics. A night on the chain does more good sometimes than a month of Sunday sermons."

Slim noticed that the man named Ox was still there, sitting quietly on the ground, his legs crossed. He held a tin plate of bacon and scrambled eggs in his huge, bruised hands. He asked, "How long, Sheriff?"

"How long do you think it'll take you to decide that fightin' and breakin' up furniture ain't the way for a grown man to behave around this town?"

"It wasn't me started it. It was Choctaw."

Farther down the chain, another man almost as large as Ox raised his head and glowered silently at his adversary with eyes so brown they were nearly black. This man had a dark face, a little like Ox's, but in his case the darkness came from more than exposure to the sun. Slim suspected from his name that he was at least part Indian. His eyes said that whatever their disagreement had been, a night on the chain had not put it to rest.

Buckalew said, "You ought to know better than to provoke a man you can't whip."

"I can whip that damned Indian any day of the week."

"Not as long as you're on this chain. Eat your breakfast."

Slim followed Buckalew up the courthouse steps and into the sheriff's office. On a table sat a plate of bacon and eggs, several biscuits and a blackened steaming, coffeepot. Slim said dubiously, "I can't pay you, Sheriff."

"It's on the county. We've got a contract with the Dutchman's to feed the prisoners. A couple of the ones we let off of the chain didn't feel up to eatin' anything, and it's a shame to see good food go to waste after the taxpayers have footed the bill."

Slim was hungrier than he had thought. Breakfast made him feel as if there might yet be hope of survival. "I'm obliged to you for everything, Sheriff. Now I guess I'd better be startin' for Douglas Clive's ranch, if you'll point me the way."

"Afoot? It's a right far piece. Are you sure you've got a job waitin' for you there?"

"He told me. I met him at a little hometown rodeo a while back. He was bettin' on me, and I won the calf ropin' and the bronc ridin'. He said he could use a good hand if I ever came down this way."

Buckalew poured himself a cup of coffee from the pot. "Did he split any of his winnin's with you?"

"No. Was he supposed to?"

"A lot of people do. I wouldn't figure Clive to do it, though. Well, you won't have to walk out there. I saw his Mexican in town while ago, loadin' up some feed. I asked him to come by and pick you up—if you're really wantin' to go."

"Why wouldn't I want to?"

Buckalew stood at the window a minute, looking out. "Yonder he comes now. All I can do is wish you luck, Slim. And this . . ." He extracted a ten-dollar bill from his wallet.

Slim protested, "I can't take your money."

"It's not a gift, it's a loan. I'll expect to get it back when you're able. Us cowboys have got to stick together."

Slim warmed. "Maybe this isn't such a bad town after all."

"It used to be a good town. When all this oil foolishness finally plays out, maybe it'll be a good one again."

The sheriff followed him out to the curb, where a dark-skinned young man stood beside a black Model T truck that had some chicken and horse feed stacked on its wooden bed. Buckalew said, "Slim, this is Trinidad Suarez. Trinidad, Slim McIntyre."

"Mucho gusto," Suarez said.

Slim didn't know any Spanish, but he supposed that meant *howdy,* or something of the sort. He shook the Mexican's hand. "Pleased to meet you." He wondered if the man spoke English. If not, he didn't know how they were going to communicate.

Suarez said, "You are ready to go? No saddle?"

All Slim had was the recovered blankets, rolled and tied. "No saddle."

Suarez turned toward the truck door. *"Adiós, Cherife."*

"Adiós," the sheriff said. "Don't you bounce this boy too much

41

on that rough road. He's had a hard knock." He stepped to the front of the truck, indicating that he would crank it for Suarez.

Keeping his blanket roll—he didn't want the feed dust getting into it—Slim climbed into the old truck. The sheriff cranked, and Suarez got the engine started. He pulled out into the street, joining the already-heavy morning traffic of automobiles and trucks, all raising dust. Immediately around the courthouse and jail, the older part of Caprock still retained much of its original cowtown look. But after a couple of blocks, the difference was even more apparent by daylight than it had been last night. Raw lumber and sheetiron construction were the rule. A grocery store had a black tarpaper exterior. Some of the buildings had the look of having been hauled in from elsewhere and set down on heavy wooden blocks. Here and there, even before they reached the section the truck driver yesterday had pointed out as Ragtown, he saw a number of large tents, mostly twelve or fifteen feet square, some boarded up partway as a measure of weatherproofing.

"Sure ain't much for pretty, is it?" he said.

"People must live. Who is to say what is pretty?" Suarez philosophized.

Arriving in the night, Slim had been unable to see much of the oilfield except in the light of the gas flares. By daylight, the flares were much less obvious. Now he could see the tall wooden derricks standing like a man-made forest in the midst of a gently rolling sandy countryside. Each had a massive walking beam that pumped up and down with a steady rhythm. Through the open window, he could hear the steam engines, each with its own cadence, some disciplined and regular, others with an uneven popping sound. He could see crews of men busy at every derrick. Large storage tanks of wood or steel stood at intervals, receiving the black flow from the wells. He found himself marveling at the level of energy being expended here. He tried to calculate mentally what each of these wells must be pumping, and his lost thirty-three dollars looked small. Except that all this belonged to someone else, and the thirty-three dollars had been his own.

"Leaves a man short of breath, don't it?"

Suarez glanced out his side window. "It makes me afraid sometimes, so many people, so many machines, so much noise.

42

And so much smell. I look at these wells and I think, what if this one blows up, or that one?"

"You ever see one blow up?"

Suarez shuddered. "Yes. On Mr. Douglas Clive's ranch. I was there when this one was all of a sudden a big fire. I saw those men killed. And I saw . . ." He hesitated a moment. "I saw the face of the devil himself in the smoke and the flame. He was laughing. I think they drill these holes so deep, they find where hell is and the fire comes up."

His eyes reflected the horror, as he made a sign of the cross.

Slim's curiosity was aroused, but he saw the pain the dark memories had aroused. "I reckon ranch work is plenty good enough."

"It is all I know, all I want to know."

Suarez went silent for a while. They passed the last of the derricks. The truck stopped at a red-painted wooden gate with a small sign bolted to it: CLIVE RANCH. Slim got out and opened it, swinging the gate shut when the truck had gone through. Climbing back in, he saw that Suarez looked solemn. The Mexican broke his silence after a mile or so.

"Mr. Clive, he will hire you?"

"He said he had a place for me."

"I wonder if he fires me, then?"

That thought had not occurred to Slim. He felt suddenly guilty. "Why should he?"

"You are not a Mexican. Maybeso he would like you better."

Slim found himself in a quandary. He had never been around Mexican people. He had spent his life on the plains, farther north, where not many had migrated as yet. He was aware that prejudice existed against Mexicans, but he had not observed it himself. He had not considered that Clive might be hiring him simply so he could get rid of a Mexican.

He said, "I only met Clive once. What kind of a man is he?"

Suarez pondered before he attempted an answer. "He is not a man to like very much. His pay is not very good. But a little pay is better than no pay at all, and a boss one does not like is better than no job. I have a wife, and a little one."

Slim made up his mind. "If I find out he's fixin' to fire you so he can hire me, I won't take the job."

The Mexican said, "I think you are a pretty good man, Mr. Slim."

"No Mister to it. Just Slim."

Suarez stretched out his hand. "Slim." Slim shook with him.

4

The Clive Ranch

THE WIND HAD PICKED UP by the time the truck reached the Clive ranch headquarters. It whipped sand from the shallow borrow ditch at the edges of the bladed road. Slim could feel its grit in his teeth. He kept working at it with his tongue but could not get rid of it all.

Chinaberry trees seemed to grow well in this sand; he could see a dozen or more of them about the headquarters, clustered around a large surface tank of water, shading a large old ranchhouse and a small box-and-strip house that sat at some distance away, nearer the barns. He surmised that was where Trinidad lived. A thin, dark young women worked out in front, sweeping the yard clean.

"My wife, Gabriela," Trinidad said. "And there is our baby, Manuela." Slim saw a small girl toddling along behind her mother.

Slim's attention went to the larger house. "Mr. Clive's?"

Suarez nodded. "I do not know if he is at home now. Miss Lauralou can tell you where to find him."

"Lauralou? His wife?"

"His daughter. Mrs. Clive, she died. There are those who say the loneliness, it killed her. Me, I do not know. My Gabriela seems content here."

Trinidad stopped the truck at a feed shed. Slim started to help him unload the feed sacks, but Trinidad waved him away. "This is not good for you with your hurt. Anyhow, you do not work here yet. When you work here, you can help."

Slim took his blanket roll under his arm and walked up to the house. It was of an old bungalow style, its roof pitched upward from four sides almost to a point instead of the conventional comb astraddle its longest dimension. From its look, he judged that it had been built about the turn of the century by some predecessor of Douglas Clive. A screened veranda extended all the way around. A windmill in the backyard clanked and groaned as the west wind turned its wheel and pumped water into a seeping wooden storage tank standing on a tower ten feet tall. Chickens scratched for bugs at the edge of a little patch of Bermuda grass that struggled for existence against the constant challenge of the moving, cutting sand. The place spoke of modest comfort but not of luxury.

He knocked on the screen door at the front of the house. A voice responded from somewhere within. Presently a young woman stepped out onto the veranda. He stared, his mouth open. She was beautiful. Moreover, she was a blonde, and he had not seen many of those, not real ones, anyway. He wondered if that color was by nature or by choice. She wore a schoolgirl's blue dress that in maturity she had outgrown a little. Two of its top buttons were undone. Cooler that way, Slim surmised. For her, anyway.

She considered him a moment with clear and unblinking blue eyes. "Yes?"

He stood on the second step from the top, his eyes about even with her bosom. "I've come to see Mr. Clive."

46

"He's out in the east pasture. Who are you?"

"Name's Slim McIntyre. He told me a while back that he had a job for me."

She seemed surprised. "First I'd heard of it. He's got Trinidad. Doesn't seem like he'd need anybody else." She studied him as if she could see beyond his eyes into his mind and know what he was thinking. He hoped that was not so, for she would have reason to slap his face. He glanced at her left hand and saw no ring, then wondered why he had looked.

She opened the screen door. "You're welcome to come in and wait. I'm Lauralou, his daughter."

He wanted to say something sophisticated, but all that came was, "Much obliged."

Slim went onto the veranda, out of the morning sun. It was cooler here, a little breeze finding its way through the screen. The girl turned away for a moment, and when she turned back he saw that she had closed one of the buttons. It made the dress look even tighter and left him more uncomfortable, for it meant she was aware of his staring. Still, she smiled as if she didn't mind. He wondered what she was thinking. Probably puzzling about the bandage on his head.

He volunteered, "I got robbed in town. They clubbed me with something."

"You been workin' in the oilfield? Papa doesn't have much use for oilfield folks."

"No, I've cowboyed all my life."

"Papa would like to have some good oilwells, but he hates what's happened to Caprock. I don't. It used to be such a sleepy old place. Now there's life and excitement and somethin' new every day. I love every bit of it."

Slim was at a loss to know how to respond. He had already tasted enough of Caprock's excitement to last him until Christmas of '29, if not longer. "Yes, ma'am."

She said, "It's already got warm this mornin'. Would you like somethin' cool to drink?" Her gaze went to the door that led into a dark hall.

He felt uneasy about following a young woman into a strange house when nobody else was at home. Such a thing led to talk. An honorable man didn't compromise a woman that way. "No, ma'am, not really."

47

"Well, I would. Come along."

He left the blanket roll lying on the veranda's boot-scarred pine floor and with some trepidation followed her down the hall to the kitchen. He saw no electric lights, just kerosene lamps. Electricity had not yet made it this far out into the country. The kitchen was large but plain, a big Majestic wood-burning range standing out far enough from one wall that its heat would not set the partition ablaze. Beneath the range lay a metal sheet that guarded the floor's linoleum from falling coals or embers. Lauralou chipped ice from storage in the top of a wooden icebox and, with long, thin fingers, put it into a glass. She filled the glass from a water pitcher on the wood-topped cabinet. "Sure you wouldn't like something?"

He felt his face warming. Being close to pretty women did that to him. "If there's coffee in that pot on the stove, I believe I could stand some."

She handed him a china cup, stepping so close that he could feel the warmth from her body. She did not retreat. "Men and their coffee. I don't think I'll ever understand how you can drink that strong stuff. I guess I'm just too delicate."

He might have thought of other descriptions, but not *delicate.* He poured coffee into the cup and held it in both hands, wondering if she could see their trembling. He backed away from her a little. Perhaps she had no idea the effect she had on him. Or perhaps she did, and was enjoying it.

He thought, *What a dandy place this would be to work.* But then he considered the delicious misery of seeing a woman like this every day and knowing that he dare not reach. Life could sure get frustrating.

He finished the coffee much sooner than he wanted to. It was only lukewarm, but he barely tasted it. "Maybe I'd better go wait for your father outside."

"It's warm out there."

Kind of warm in here too, he thought. He set the coffee cup on the cabinet. "Sure much obliged. But I *had* best be goin'."

As he started for the hallway he heard the screen door slam and heavy boots thump on the floor. A blocky man in his mid-forties appeared suddenly in the kitchen doorway. He had the ruddy face and red-veined eyes that bespoke a considerable acquaintance with whisky. His voice was angry. "Lauralou, who you got in here?"

Lauralou said quickly, "Just a cowboy, Papa, come for a job."

Douglas Clive's face was clouded with threat as he glanced at Slim, then back to his daughter. "I've told you a hundred times: I don't want you bringin' people into this house when I ain't here. Especially strangers."

Slim's throat was tight, but he managed to extend his arm, inviting a handshake. "Remember me, Mr. Clive? I'm Slim McIntyre."

The hand was ignored. "Who?"

"Slim McIntyre. We met at a little country rodeo up in Dickens County. Remember? I won the calf ropin', and the bronc ridin' too. You bet on me."

Clive's eyes narrowed as he studied Slim's face. "Can't say that I remember. What're you doin' here?"

"You offered me a job, Mr. Clive."

"I sure don't recall anything like that. I got no job here for you."

Slim swallowed, feeling new misgivings. "But you said you always had a place for a hand like me. Said all I had to do was come and see you."

"If I said that, I must've been drinkin'."

"Yes sir, a little."

"Don't you know better than to hold a man to what he says when he's drinkin'? Ain't fair to take advantage of a man when he's drinkin'."

"I wasn't takin' advantage. I didn't think you was drinkin' that much. And it wasn't me that talked about a job. It was you that asked *me.*"

"What happened to the job you had?"

"I was workin' for Ol' Man Wilson, over on the Double Mountain Fork. He went broke. Bank taken everything he had and sold the place out from under him. I remembered what you said, and here I am."

"You've come a long ways on a fool's errand, is all I can say. I got all the help I need here. I take care of this place by myself, just me and my Mexican." His eyes narrowed. "I don't especially like havin' a Mexican here, but they work cheaper'n a white man.

49

Maybe if you're willin' to work for what I'm payin' Trinidad, I'll fire him and take you on."

Indignation began to sting Slim. "No sir, I wouldn't have it that way. I wouldn't throw another man out of a job so I could get it."

"He's just a Mexican. Who'd care?"

"*I'd* care. I was raised different, Mr. Clive."

"You'd better go back to where you was raised, then. I've got no place on this ranch for a damn fool." Clive squinted, noticing the bandage on Slim's head for the first time. "What's that? You been fightin'?"

"No sir. I got slugged and robbed in town last night."

Clive did not believe him. "Probably got it fightin'. Another thing I don't need on this place is a man who don't know how to stay out of a fight." He pointed toward the door. "I think we've finished any business we had together. You can leave now."

Slim tried to force down the anger that nearly choked him. He managed, "Thanks for the coffee, miss. It was nice." He turned and started down the hall, then stopped. "At the least, Mr. Clive, could I get somebody to take me back to town?"

"I don't remember invitin' you to come here. The day is long, and you've got two good legs."

Lauralou protested, "Papa, I could take him . . ."

Clive turned harshly on his daughter. "You mind your own business. And the next time I find you in the house with a strange man . . ."

Slim picked up his blanket roll and left the house as quickly as he could, letting the screen door slam. He could hear angry voices behind him, Clive declaring, "Ain't you got any judgment at all, girl? Anything with pants on, you go runnin' after it like a heifer in heat."

Lauralou stormed back, "And look who's talkin'. My mama wasn't hardly cold in her grave before you started bringin' women out here from Jolene's place."

"What would you know about Jolene's?"

"I know a lot. All I have to do is watch you!"

Slim tasted the cold ashes of disappointment. What in the hell was he going to do now?

The young Mexican woman and the little girl were watching him. He swung the blanket roll over his shoulder and started for the front gate, his face hot with anger. He set out on the road he and Trinidad had traveled in the truck. The wind whipped sand up from the bladed surface and into his eyes. The spring sun was warm. It would be downright blistering after a while, and it was six or seven miles into town, maybe more.

As a cowboy, he had never spent a lot of time walking. High-heeled boots were made for stirrups, not for the road. The heat of the sand soon penetrated the leather, and his feet felt as if they were on fire. Fire! That made him think of an appropriate place for Mr. Douglas Clive to go, the sooner the better. The longer he thought of Clive, the hotter and angrier he got. He tried to think instead of the blue-eyed Lauralou. That did not cool his indignation, for he had gotten an inkling that her father's brutishness extended to her too.

He had to stop several times and rest, sitting on the edge of the road, dangling his legs down the slope of the borrow ditch. His hat perched precariously, not quite fitting over the bandage. Sweat ran down from the leather band inside and burned his eyes.

After a time, he heard the soft thud of a horse's hoofs in the sand. Turning, he saw Trinidad Suarez, mounted on a pretty little sorrel pony. Trinidad reined up and asked, "You ride double?"

"Beats hell out of walkin'." As Trinidad freed his left foot from the stirrup, Slim eagerly put his own foot in and swung up behind him.

"Won't Mr. Clive be mad at you?"

"What Mr. Douglas Clive does not know, he will not be mad about. I will take you to the gate. After that, pretty soon you can get a ride with somebody from the oilfield."

"Thanks." Slim felt a little sheepish now. "I think you were tryin' to tell me what to expect from him without bein' straight-out about it."

"Mr. Clive is not a man to like."

"Truer words was never spoken. Treats his daughter kind of hard too, don't you think?"

Trinidad did not answer.

The pony had a rough trot, and he pounded Slim's tailbone considerably. But his tailbone had been pounded many times before. That was better than blisters on his feet.

They had ridden a couple of miles when Slim heard the *ooo-gah* of an auto horn from behind them. For a moment, he feared Clive had caught up with them, and Trinidad would be in trouble. He watched an old black Model T come up the road and stop. A thin-shouldered man of late middle age stepped out from behind the wheel, leaving the motor running. His hair was gray, almost matching the color of his friendly eyes. He took a dark brown pipe from his mouth.

"Howdy do, Trinidad," he said jovially. "The Clive outfit runnin' out of horses that you got to double up?"

Trinidad said, "*¿Como está?*, Mr. Henry."

Slim sensed strong regard in Trinidad's tone, a feeling reflected in the older fellow's gray eyes. The man wore a dusty, shapeless black hat that looked as if it had been run over by a dozen oilfield trucks. He had a threadbare blue work shirt, khaki trousers held in place by blue-and-white suspenders, lace-up black shoes, scuffed and dry and old.

Slim said, "Trinidad was givin' me a lift to the front gate."

"My ol' jitney might be more comfortable than that pony's backbone. Git down, and I'll take you with me."

Slim slid to the ground and introduced himself. The man said, "I'm Henry Stringfellow. Most folks call me Uncle Henry. I'm headed for Caprock, if that's the way you're goin'."

"Sure is."

Trinidad and Stringfellow visited a few minutes about the calf crop and the rain and the grass. Slim surmised from the conversation that Stringfellow was a rancher. Trinidad remounted the sorrel, bade the two men *Adiós* and started back toward the ranch headquarters.

"Git in, son," Stringfellow said, "and I'll have you in Caprock in a jiffy. Don't know why you'd want to go there, though. You look like a cowboy, not an oilfield hand."

Slim explained why he had come to Caprock, what had happened to him last night and what had happened to him at Clive's. He said nothing about Lauralou. He didn't see that she was pertinent to the account.

Stringfellow puffed his pipe and nodded sympathetically. "Everybody knows Douglas Clive is a horse's ass. Dave Buckalew could've warned you."

"I guess he tried, in his own way. So did Trinidad."

"Clive inherited the money he bought that ranch with. Now he's hopin' to get rich from oil, only they ain't found any on his place yet. A cheapjack oil company had a wildcat workin' on it a while back, but it went up in flames."

"Trinidad told me about that."

"Clive had better strike oil pretty soon. What with his drinkin' and gamblin', and the fact that he ain't much of a rancher anyhow, he stands a fair chance of losin' everything he's got."

Slim couldn't say he would weep over such a spectacle, except that Lauralou Clive wouldn't seem to deserve the predicament it would put her in.

Stringfellow said, "Sorry your hopes about that job went a-glimmerin'. Wisht I could help you."

"You're a rancher. Do you need an extra hand?"

Stringfellow laughed. "Some say I'm a rancher, and some say I'm not. I got me a little sheep outfit over yonderway, adjoinin' Clive's far side." He pointed his thumb. "You ever herd sheep?"

Slim said with a touch of cowboy pride, "Two things I've never done: I've never picked cotton, and I've never herded sheep."

"Everybody ought to herd sheep once in his life. Teaches him humility and gets him a little closer to God. Wisht I had a place for you, but I got a hand named Miguel, brother to Trinidad's wife. Good with sheep, these Mexicans are. It's their patience, I reckon. Sheep'll either teach you patience or drive you to the asylum."

Slim wondered if he was desperate enough to herd sheep. He doubted it. What if the boys back home ever found out? "Looks like sandy country for sheep. Doesn't the sand get into the wool?"

"Wool sells by the pound. A little sand makes it weigh more."

"You got some oil on your place?"

"A wildcatter named Underwood has drilled two holes on it. Dusters, both of them. He's fixin' to try another, but I'm afraid he's about to lose his butt. Looks like the oil formation has missed my little ol' outfit."

"Too bad," Slim said, meaning it.

"It'd be nice to have some oil come in. That'd make me a smart rancher instead of a dumb old sheepman." Stringfellow laughed, but Slim sensed that his humor was dry, like his would-be wells.

Stringfellow changed the subject. "What you fixin' to do now? I doubt there's a ranch job to be had in forty–fifty miles."

"Go find me some cow country, I reckon. But I've got to earn a little money first, somehow. All I've got is ten dollars, and that belongs to the sheriff."

"You can probably find work in the oilfield." Stringfellow pointed his thumb at the tall derricks they were passing.

"I wouldn't know the first thing about it."

"Nobody does at first. Everybody's got to learn. You're a husky-lookin' young feller. There's roughneckin' and pipelinin' and tankin' crews. Muleskinnin' and truck drivin' too. You'd be surprised what you can do when you're up against the taw line and have to."

"I'm up against the taw line, all right."

They drove through Ragtown. Slim looked dejectedly through the dust at the rows of faded tents and crude shacks, at trash on the ground and vagrant pieces of dirty paper drifting on the wind. He thought of the ranches he had lived and worked on over the years. The pay might not have been much, but the living was a damned sight better than this.

Stringfellow said, "You just got to make up your mind to tough it out and do the best you can. You'll make it, cowboy."

"I'd sooner take a whippin' with the double of a wet rope."

ranch out in the sandhills, too small to earn him a living but large enough to tie him here.

Ofttimes he wished he could simply be a cowboy again, with no responsibilities except the specific tasks assigned to him. As a working cowboy, he had not been called upon to make stressful daily decisions, and he had always known what he was doing. He had spent no sleepness nights floundering in self-doubt. He sometimes wished he had stuck to his original *no* when some of his friends suggested running him for sheriff after his return from the trenches in France. At first, being sheriff had been a lot easier than ranch labor. As a cowboy, he had ridden horseback from can't-see to can't again, working for outfits that paid twenty-five or thirty a month and gave him more need for a lantern than for a bedroll. There hadn't been much strain to the sheriff's job in those times. He rounded up an occasional drunk cowboy or sheepherder and mediated an occasional quarrel between neighbors over a fence or the proper reading of a cattle brand on a disputed animal. It hadn't been much of a challenge. The ornriest part had been the paperwork, for his boots had not been made to rest beneath a desk. Caprock had been a quiet little community where everybody knew everybody else's kids, horses and dogs by name. Nobody had anticipated oil discovery and the sudden surge of restless, questing humanity that would turn this place into a clamorous Babel.

Damn it to hell, why couldn't they leave well enough alone?

Times, he was sorely tempted to pitch his badge onto the desk and inform the county that it should call a special election. He wouldn't have to listen to old Judge Potter holler anymore about the costs of running the county and complaining about every gallon of gasoline used by the sheriff's car, the cost of meals for county prisoners. But who would wind up with the job if he abandoned it? Waddy Fuller? Waddy had been so incompetent as a cowboy that several ranchers had persuaded Dave to appoint him deputy and get him on the county payroll where he wouldn't hurt anybody. It had been the next thing to charity; they didn't want to see Waddy and his mousey little wife go hungry. It also ended the guilt they felt for passing him over when Waddy asked for a ranch job. He wasn't much better as a deputy than he had been a-horseback, but at first it hadn't mattered. Dave had assigned him to take care of the jail, a simple task that did not require much competence. Times now, the challenge threatened to overwhelm Waddy. Dave wished the court would authorize a second deputy, but it shepherded the county purse with a vigilance approaching miserliness. When this boom ended, Judge Potter reminded Dave at every opportunity, they would be glad for every dollar they had managed not to spend.

A transient hunger pang reminded him it was time to go for supper. Maybe the crowd had thinned at the Dutchman's so he wouldn't have to stand around waiting for an empty table or a stool at the counter. Times, he wished he had a house like most people, and a kitchen where he could fix for himself, instead of a small corner room on the second floor of the Stockmen's Hotel. Better still . . .

He heard music from somewhere, a harmonica. The melody drifted through the open window in fleeting fragments, for the wind kept carrying it away. It could have been any song he wanted it to be. It reminded him of accordion music at another time, another place, of a girl with whom he had danced. He closed his eyes, remembering. He sat down at the desk and opened a drawer. Carefully he took out an old photograph and studied it. Even when he closed his eyes he could still see it. For most of ten years, he had memorized its every detail. An old regret cut him like a knife, and he placed the picture back where it had come from with a care that bordered on reverence. The melody still came to him from somewhere outside. He stood up, went to the window and closed it, shutting out the music.

Walking down the hall and down the steps, he paused for a look at the chain. Most of last night's guests had been released, making room for more if tonight's activity so dictated. It was Waddy's task to take the prisoners off the chain one at a time and escort them to the jail toilet so they could relieve the pressures of nature without outraging the community's sensibilities on the courthouse square. Waddy was walking back out with the big man named Ox. They were a contrast in size, Waddy a string-bean, Ox looking like the animal he was nicknamed for. His size was his living, for he worked as a bouncer at Jolene's.

Dave watched Waddy secure Ox to the chain with a set of handcuffs. "Everything all right?"

Waddy declared confidently, "They know better than to mess around with me."

Ox could have made breakfast of Waddy in three bites. So could the dark Choctaw, secured farther down on the chain. Dave dreaded the day when Waddy might have a truly dangerous prisoner to handle without help. That kind—and fortunately they had been few—Dave had managed to control without putting the deputy into harm's way. He wondered sometimes if Waddy had any conception of the possibilities. Waddy enjoyed the feeling of authority the badge gave him—he had never had any authority before—and the respect he saw or imagined in the eyes of people on the street. But Dave would hate someday to have Waddy on his conscience.

Ox demanded, "Hey, Sheriff, don't you think I been on this damned chain long enough? I need to get back to work."

His work at Jolene's house was to keep the customers from getting out of line, making sure none of them beat up a girl and, most of all, making sure they paid in full. Few there were who risked running afoul of Ox.

Dave said, "Repent ye first, and all things shall be opened." He doubted that was an exact biblical quotation, but Ox wouldn't know the difference. To Waddy, he said, "I'm goin' over to the café and get me some supper."

Waddy frowned. "When you ever goin' to get married, Dave, and have a woman to fix for you? I don't eat *my* meals in no damned café."

Dave supposed Waddy ate well, but it never showed on him. Waddy Fuller threw as lean a shadow as any man Dave had ever known. "There aren't many women around like yours, Waddy, who'll put up with the kind of hours we work."

Waddy beamed. "That's so. They don't grow on trees, not like Annabelle."

Annabelle had been an impressionable young schoolgirl, dazzled by the badge on Waddy's shirt. He had plucked her before she had come to full blossom. The original citizens of Caprock still looked out for her welfare the best they could. The new ones, the ones who had come with the oil, didn't even know her. Dave remembered once when a half-drunk pipeliner had accosted her on the street, mistaking her for one of the girls from Jolene's. Annabelle was so sheltered that she hadn't quite understood what he was talking about. She didn't understand why Dave firmly led him away; the man was just trying to be friendly, she said.

If she had been any brighter she never would have hooked up with Waddy, and he would be getting *his* meals in a café.

Dave watched the evening traffic moving both directions on the unpaved street and wished for some rain to settle the dust. But too much rain would just turn the streets into a loblolly of mud. Didn't seem like there was any way to win. He paused in front of the dancehall. The music was playing. A few couples were out on the floor dancing, but the place hadn't come to full life yet. Give it a couple more hours and Shemp Oliver, the proprietor, would be raking in dimes by the sackful. Dave watched the movements of the women on the dancefloor, re-membering another woman, another place, remembering how she had glowed in his arms. There had been a deep and almost childlike devotion in the way she had clung to him; there had been nothing crude or vulgar and certainly nothing approaching the desperation he saw in some of the women here. He knew that many of these worked in the dancehall because no other jobs existed for them. This was—they hoped—just a temporary pause in their long-term plans for a regular life . . . marriage, home and kids. Many were honest girls who danced out of hun-ger and despair. They had come from farms or out of destitute families in distant towns and cities. Others saw this as an alterna-tive to warming the beds at Jolene's or some other house of its kind. He would see some of these dancehall girls in church Sunday, if he went. Others would be sharing quarters with hungover oilfield workers who offered what they considered a fair price for their services overnight.

Either way, Shemp Oliver gave them a few pennies out of each dime and considered himself their philanthropic protector.

Dave paused again at the vacant lot where somebody had slugged the young cowboy last night. He would talk to the Dutchman about putting a light on the side of his café. There had been altogether too much of that kind of thuggery around here. Damn these people who thought they were too good to work but weren't too good to take from those who did.

The café was crowded; he had known it would be. A lot of the oilfield workers were bachelors, and many others were married men whose constant moving made it difficult for their families to follow them. Dave wondered which would give way first, their backs from the hard labor in the fields or their stomachs from grabbing whatever they could get in greasy oilfield cafés and hamburger joints. At least the Teagarden had Mrs. Whitmore in the kitchen. Considering the pressure she was under, cooking so fast for so many, she turned out a reasonably decent meal most of the time. That the hard work made her look fifteen years older than she was couldn't be helped. Dave thought it a pity that her daughter Tracy appeared to have set her feet on the same path of drudgery and privation.

He saw the cowboy, Slim McIntyre, sitting at a small table alone, picking uninterestedly at the lowest-priced special plate chalked up on the Dutchman's blackboard menu. The solemn way the cowboy stared at his food told Dave more than he needed to know about the outcome of McIntyre's visit with Douglas Clive. He asked, "Mind if I join you?"

Glumly McIntyre responded, "I'd be tickled."

Dave sat down. Tracy Whitmore came along in a moment, bringing a glass of water and her order pad. "Evenin', Sheriff. What gastronomic delight can I bring you?"

"What's the least apt to kill me before mornin'?"

Tracy never took offense at Dave's jokes even though her mother did the cooking. A lot of other people joked too; it made life at least half-tolerable. "The chicken-fried steak isn't too bad. It's only been in the warmin' oven for about an hour."

The biggest trouble with the Teagarden's menu was that it didn't vary much. In about three days, he would taste everything it offered and meet himself coming back around. "That'll do."

He turned his attention to the cowboy. "I hope nobody got killed out at Clive's today."

He saw a flicker of concern in McIntyre's eyes. "There wasn't any trouble. Why, did he call you or somethin'?"

"No, he never calls. Clive and me, we never did see eye to eye."

"I can understand why."

"Sorry it didn't work out. I should've told you, I guess, but I thought maybe for once he had really meant what he said."

"He meant what he said *today*. He told me to git and not come back."

"I don't know any reason you'd ever want to go back."

"I did need the job, real bad. *Any* job."

"You won't starve. You've still got what I lent you. Worst come to worst, I can lend you some more."

"Thanks, Sheriff, but it's not as simple as just bein' able to eat. I've been payin' off my old daddy's debts. I was doin' pretty fair at it till my last job folded up under me."

"Is your father sick or crippled or somethin'?"

"He's dead. He died worse than broke; he still owed on a bunch of money-losin' old cows. I sold them after he was gone, but they didn't near pay what was owed. I been doin' it ever since, out of my wages."

Tracy had brought Dave's chicken-fried steak, but she stood with it in her hand, caught up in what Slim was saying. Dave saw something in her eyes, admiration perhaps.

He said, "Look, Slim, your daddy's debt died with him, outside of what estate he might've had. You've got no legal obligation to keep payin' on it."

"Not legal maybe, but moral. He was an honest man. He wouldn't want anybody the loser on his account."

"Looks to me like *you're* losin'."

"Not when you figure what he gave me. He was a good man. I can't feel like he's restin' easy till everything is paid."

Dave saw no way of arguing with that. "You got anyplace to sleep tonight?"

"I'll spread my blankets on the ground unless I run into Hap Holloway and take him up on that offer to share his tent. I don't reckon you've seen him?"

Dave's tone had an edge of disapproval. "No, but I haven't been lookin' for him."

Slim's eyebrows went up a little. "I already gathered that you don't have much use for Hap. What's the matter with him?"

"He's a shade wild, but at his age he's got no patent on that. What bothers me most is his choice of friends. He hangs out with some old boys that're knockin' on the doors of the penitentiary, tryin' to get in. That kind generally makes it sooner or later. Feller gets caught up in a crowd like that, he's apt to hear those big steel doors clang shut on him too."

"I haven't met any of his friends, only Hap."

Dave glanced up at Tracy, who was still listening. "I can't help feelin' like you may have met a couple of them last night."

Slim's mouth dropped open in disbelief. "I can't believe Hap had anything to do with that."

"Maybe not, but I'll bet he knows who did, even if he swore he couldn't recognize them in the dark."

Tracy finally set the chicken-fried steak in front of Dave. She had held it long enough for it to get half-cold. She told Slim, "If you're through with your plate, I'll take it to the kitchen."

He nodded, and she picked it up. In a minute, she was back with a slice of pie. Slim looked at her in surprise. "I didn't order that."

"Just eat it. You'll feel better after you've put down a little sweetenin'."

"I'm trying to save my money."

"This is on the house. Nurse's orders. Eat it." She turned away, leaving him no chance for further argument.

Dave smiled at the astonished expression on Slim's face. "I been eatin' here ever since the Dutchman opened this place, and I don't think they've ever brought me pie on the house."

"I like to pay my own way."

"A good rule to live by. But it don't hurt a man to let people do somethin' nice for him now and then. If it makes them feel better, why rob them of that pleasure?"

"If you put it that way . . ." Slim dug into the pie. "Maybe it'll help make up for what's been a calf-slobbers kind of a day."

Dave took his time with the steak, enjoying watching Slim get outside of the pie. He said, "You don't have to sleep on the ground tonight."

"If you're offerin' me the use of a jail cell again, thanks, but I'd rather sleep in the open. It smells better. Besides, I'm already beholden more than I want to be." He finished the pie and sat in thoughtful silence for a minute. "One thing you *could* do for me, Sheriff. You could spread the word that I'm lookin' for a job. Any kind of a job. I don't know beans about the oilfield, but I've got willin' hands and a strong back."

"I'll see what I can do."

Slim stood up and shook his hand. He left fifteen cents tip on the table for Tracy, then went to the Dutchman at the cash register to pay his fifty cents for the supper.

It was going to be hard for a young man to save a lot of money if he left fifteen cents tip every time he ate, Dave thought. He watched through the window. Dusk had turned to full dark. Slim did not go onto the dark lot. He started across the street, braving the traffic to stay where the light was better. Tracy came up with coffee as Slim reached the wooden walk on the other side. Dave pointed that way with his chin. "You'll be pleased to know that the cowboy learns fast."

"Why should it mean anything to me?"

"That piece of pie. I haven't seen you do that for anybody else."

"I'd feed a stray pup that was lost and couldn't find its way home. He's got that look about him, like a lost pup."

"He may not find his way home, but I have a notion he'll find a way to fit in wherever he's at."

"He looks like a fish out of water around here."

"There's a lot of us like that. Caprock used to be home to me. Now sometimes I feel like I've been dropped into a foreign country."

"I suppose it feels that way when you have all this happen to you so fast. To me, it feels natural. Our family's been livin' in or around the oil boomtowns ever since I was six or seven. If I were to find myself in Caprock the way it used to be, I'd probably feel lost myself." Her eyes went sad. "Speakin' of feelin' lost—we . . . Mama and me . . . we're grateful for your patience with Papa. He just hasn't been able to keep his feet under him since . . . what happened to Benny."

Dave thought he saw a tear in her eye, but she had too much pride to let it get away from her. She blinked quickly.

"It'll pass, Tracy. All things pass with time."

"Not all things. Some things just stay there until people die." She turned away, going back to her work.

Dave finished his chicken-fried steak and a third cup of coffee, then got up from the table. He dug a dime from his pocket for a tip, started to walk away, then came back and added a nickel.

He stopped on the courthouse square to take another look at the chain. Only four men were on it. Maybe he would be lucky tonight and not have to add any more. He didn't enjoy putting the overflow out here like this, but the only other choice was to turn them loose. In his book, an offense unpunished was likely to be repeated. He had never put anybody on that chain for singing too loudly in church.

He had locked his office door. As he entered the hall he saw a khaki-clad man in tall lace-up boots sitting on the steps that led up to the courtroom on the second floor. "Evening, Sheriff. I've been waiting to see you." The man stood up, taking a pipe from his mouth. He was well into his forties, his hair showing some gray, his face betraying lines and creases from hard work out-doors. His eyes showed the stress that came from trying hard and failing big, and worrying about the probability of doing it again.

"Howdy, Mr. Underwood. How can I help you?"

He had no more than a hand-shaking acquaintance with Victor Underwood, who had come here shortly after the first oil discovery. Underwood was an independent wildcatter, a crap-shooter who took the long odds while the major oil companies accepted the safer bets. Underwood had had a lot of luck here, and most of it bad from what Dave had heard.

"You have my man Choctaw out yonder on the chain. I'm about ready to spud in a new well on the Stringfellow place. I need Choctaw. What is his bail?"

"To tell you the truth, Mr. Underwood, I never did actually file any charges. Him and Ox in a fight was like two bull ele-phants runnin' amuck. I thought they both needed some time as guests of the county to reconsider the blessin's of peace."

"Choctaw is a peaceable man out on the job. He's like a big gentle bear."

"He was like a bear lookin' for red meat when him and Ox tangled together. But if you'll take responsibility for him and keep him out of town awhile, I'll turn him a-loose."

"I would be in your debt, sir."

Underwood had a polished way of speaking. Dave had heard somewhere that he had once been a college professor, but that seemed unlikely. Why would a college professor be wildcatting out here in this crazy man-made jungle, fighting temperamental drilling rigs and bad weather and cantankerous crews, knowing his chance of striking it rich was about like a snowball's chance in hell? A college professor belonged in a nice, quiet ivy-covered hall with a big, cool library and a chair soft enough to swallow him whole.

Dave said, "I hear you've already come in dry on two holes out at Uncle Henry's. What makes you think you've got any better chance drillin' there again?"

"If you're a wildcatter, you drill where no one else has drilled, and where you have a lease. Unfortunately, the only lease I have is on Henry Stringfellow's. In my present financial state, that is likely to be the only lease I *will* have. I will make it there or I will become a wage slave for some major company again. That, sir, is the last thing I ever want to do."

"I don't pretend to understand you oil people, but I'll have to admit that you've got guts."

"Your forebears who first brought cattle into this country faced obstacles just as formidable in their own way, Sheriff. This is a challenging land. They faced the challenge with a horse and saddle and rope. I face it with an old cabletool rig. We are not all that different."

"Maybe not. But I still like the horse best. Come on, I'll turn Choctaw loose." Dave paused at the courthouse door. "Just out of curiosity, how'd you happen to latch onto that Indian?"

"I was drilling in Oklahoma. A lot of Indians came to work on the oilfield gangs there. A few of them, like Choctaw, have followed the booms into Texas. Choctaw is a good, stable hand. We get along."

"Well, you enjoy him for a while. I've had about enough of his company for the time bein'."

Choctaw sat placidly on the ground, one wrist handcuffed to the heavy chain. He looked up expectantly at Underwood and the sheriff, but he did not condescend to beg for his freedom.

Dave said, "Let me see your wrist, Choctaw." He unlocked the handcuffs. The big man pushed shakily to his feet. He had had no exercise on the chain. He had spent a night and all of the day sitting or lying on the ground. He rubbed his wrist, left raw by the bite of the steel. Dave said sternly, "I don't want to see you back in this town for a while. When you do come back, I want you to damned sure behave yourself."

Choctaw said nothing. His dark eyes met Dave's for a moment, but they betrayed none of what might be on his mind.

Underwood said, "I want to know what you fought about."

Choctaw looked at Dave, who wondered whether the Indian

intended to give an answer, and if he did, if he would tell the truth.

Choctaw said, "He called me a damned Indian."

Underwood said firmly, "You are an Indian."

"But I ain't no *damned* Indian. You ready to go, Mr. Underwood? I'm mighty tired of this place."

Dave had heard from eye-witnesses how the fight had started. The *damned Indian* comment had come up rightly enough, but it had not been what the fight was about. Underwood had a fine-looking young wife about half his own age. Ox had made some remark about not seeing any young men from Underwood's drilling crew in Jolene's house. He speculated that they didn't need Jolene's; they were probably helping the old man do his homework. Big as Choctaw was, Ox probably had a good thirty or forty pounds on him. But Choctaw had been winning when Dave broke up the fight.

Ox complained from his position farther along on the chain, "If you're lettin' that Indian go, how about me?"

Dave replied, "I haven't heard anybody say they needed you." Underwood thanked Dave and guided the Indian toward his truck, parked on the uncurbed edge of the courthouse yard. For a moment, Dave was distracted by the lights of a car pulling in to park, and he lost Underwood and Choctaw in the glare.

Ox said, "It ain't fair, Sheriff, you turnin' that Indian a-loose and keepin' me here. It was him started the fight."

"I heard about that. It was his fist that struck the first blow, but it was your big mouth that caused the ruckus."

"I didn't say nothin' that I ain't heard others say."

"You said it to the wrong man. Far as that's concerned, you didn't need to say it atall. In the first place, it's probably a lie. And even if it isn't, it's nobody's business."

"You goin' to do the fair thing and turn me a-loose? This chain don't do much for a man's pride."

"If you had any pride you wouldn't be a bouncer in a whorehouse."

"The pay's good, and I get to audition the new girls. Beats hell out of sheriffin'."

Dave reached into his pocket for the keys. "I can't argue with that. Raise up your hand." He unlocked the handcuffs. "I told

Choctaw I wanted him to stay out of town for a while. And I want you to stick a rag in your mouth. Now git!"

The sheriff watched the big man lumber off across the yard, aimed in the general direction of Jolene's place at the near edge of Ragtown. It was in his mind that so long as he was cleaning house he had just as well go the whole distance. He freed the other two prisoners from the chain and bade them get out of sight before he changed his mind. Watching their retreat, he was unaware that two other men had walked up behind him until one of them spoke his name.

"Sheriff Buckalew?"

Dave turned quickly, half expecting trouble. The two were strangers to him, but he recognized the type. Both were well dressed in neat khaki clothes and cowboy-style hats. He knew they were lawmen even before he saw the pistols strapped to their hips and town lights reflected from silver badges on their shirts. More than that, he knew they were Texas Rangers. Officially, they had no uniform. Unofficially, they tended to look much alike. It was something in their bearing.

"I'm Dave Buckalew."

One of the men extended his hand. "I'm Harvey Grissom. This is Tol Carmichael. We're Rangers, and we're here lookin' for a couple of men."

"I'd've been glad to give you the pair I just turned loose. You-all've come a little late in the day."

"On purpose, Sheriff. We came after dark so they wouldn't be so apt to notice our car. We don't want to flush the birds before we're ready to shoot."

The remark was made in an offhanded manner, almost jokingly, but Dave sensed that the man was deadly serious.

"When you say *shoot*, do you mean that?"

"Depends on them. I'd say there's a mighty good chance."

Dave felt a knot forming in his stomach. It *had* been a calf-slobbers kind of a day. "Come on up to my office. We'll talk."

6

The Rangers

THIS WAS NOT THE FIRST TIME since the oil boom had begun that Rangers had visited Caprock. They always made Dave a little nervous. He could not help taking their presence as a reflection against his law enforcement performance. He realized it was not intended that way, but the feeling persisted. He unlocked his office, flipped the light on and dragged a hard-backed chair up close to his desk for Grissom. "Have a seat." Carmichael, the junior of the two, got his own chair.

"Who you lookin' for? Somebody I'd know?"

In the light, Dave could see that Grissom was a man of roughly his own age, midthirties to perhaps forty, moderately tall, looking strong enough to wrestle a two-year-old steer to the ground.

His companion was younger, possibly thirty but no more than that. Both men had the somber faces that marked their calling.

"I doubt you'd know them. We've got a picture of only one, but Tol here knows the other man by sight. All he needs is a good look at him." Grissom handed the picture across the desk. "That's Roscoe Poole. Damned fools paroled him out of the penitentiary about ten days ago. Good behavior, they said. Right away he teamed up with one of his old partners, named Blinky Trask. They both did strong-arm work for Big Boy Daugherty for a little while, till Big Boy got wind that they were pullin' jobs on their own and booted them out. Two days ago, they held up a fillin' station over close to Cisco, probably for eatin' money. Just out of pure meaness, Roscoe shot a black feller that was changin' tires in the station. Said he always hated niggers."

"What makes you think they've come down to Caprock?"

"Just a hunch. Roscoe always favored oil towns on the boom. More money floatin' around. Last seen, they was comin' southwest. Caprock seems like as good a bet as anyplace. What he generally does, he lays up two or three days casin' a town, seein' where the money is at, then he pulls a couple or three quick holdups and lights a shuck for other parts."

"There's five, maybe six thousand people in and around Caprock right now, scattered all over Ragtown and the oilfields. How do you propose settin' out to find these two?"

"Roscoe has a real weak spot for the women. After bein' in prison, he's got a lot of catchin' up to do. He generally, first thing, finds the best whorehouse in town. I know Jolene from other times, other towns. I expect her place would be the best, wouldn't it?"

Dave frowned, wondering if Grissom was hinting that Dave had sampled them all. "That's what people say. There's a couple others, and some girls that just work on their own."

"Roscoe never liked complications. He'll just go to the best one."

The younger Ranger had his eyes half-closed. He said, "Prostitution is illegal. And we noticed some beer joints when we came in. That's against the federal prohibition law. Don't you enforce the laws, Buckalew?"

Dave felt a spark of resentment. "There's just me and one deputy. We've got more than we can do just tryin' to keep the peace without us worryin' about unenforceable laws somebody has passed a thousand miles from here." His voice went a little sterner than he intended. "If the feds think so damned much of their prohibition law, they can come and enforce it themselves."

Carmichael made a sly smile. "Besides, you wouldn't want to cut your own throat, would you? What's your percentage of the take?"

Heat rose quickly to Dave's face. He raised up from his chair and leaned across the desk. "If you're tryin' to say that I've got a shakedown goin' . . ."

The older Ranger lifted his hands. "He had no business sayin' such a thing, Buckalew. I apologize for him. He hasn't been in the service long enough to learn his manners."

Dave's anger lingered. He suspected the two were playing with him, testing his honesty. It was an old ruse, one antagonist, one apologist who appeared to take up the victim's defense to trick him into giving information. "He needs a Spanish bit in his mouth. That'd curb his tongue." A Spanish bit was a cruel instrument sometimes used on a fractious horse to bring him under control.

"That's not part of the standard issue," Grissom said, flashing Carmichael a look that said to be quiet. "But it is worth consideration. Now, though, back to Roscoe Poole. How well do you get along with Jolene and her women?"

"Mostly I leave them alone and they leave me alone. They've got their own bouncer to take care of trouble, so I haven't had to go in there much."

"You'd be amazed how much help those women can be if you stay on their good side, Buckalew. They don't want any trouble, most of them, and they'll go out of their way to help you in return for you leavin' them alone. We've caught a lot of bad criminals on tips from one sportin' house or another."

Dave gave Tol Carmichael a hard look. "Seems to me like you-all don't enforce all the laws either. Otherwise you'd close the houses."

Grissom said, "We know our limitations. Close one today and it reopens tomorrow, somewhere out of our sight. Better to recognize reality and use it for our own purposes."

Dave could not argue with that view, for in many ways it was his own. He had known from the beginning that he could not prevent bootlegging and prostitution and many of the other ills that accompanied a sudden boom. Their proportions were overwhelming for a country peace officer. At best, he could perhaps regulate them a little and keep down the violence that was so often a part of the scene. Better to have it in plain sight where he could watch it than to have it hidden where he could not even find it.

He said, "You want me to go with you to Jolene's?"

"We think it would be better that way, involvin' the local peace officers. How about your deputy?"

Dave dismissed that idea quickly. In an emergency, Waddy Fuller was likely to be more handicap than help. He might even mess around and get shot. "Three of us is enough."

Grissom stood up, his face grim. "You ever killed a man, Buckalew?"

He didn't think France counted. "It's never come to that."

"It might this time, if we find Roscoe Poole."

The look in Grissom's eyes gave Dave a chill. He thought for just a moment about telling them to go by themselves. But that would be taken as cowardice. The pistol on his hip seemed to weigh a hundred pounds as he moved to the door. "You want to drive, or walk?"

Grissom said, "We'll walk. That star on our car door gets too much attention. We'll just walk and act natural. Maybe nobody'll notice us."

Dave doubted that. Three lawmen with badges and pistols, attract no attention? A rooster could more easily overlook the sunrise. But Grissom knew what he was doing. They walked on a back street where the light was poor and traffic thin. They came upon Jolene's house from the off side. Like many of the newer buildings in town, it was of simple frame construction, two stories tall, nothing on the outside yielding any clue to the nature of the commerce conducted within. It could easily have been a hotel. In fact, Dave remembered that it had been built with that purpose in mind, but the economic potential of its current business quickly outweighed other considerations. Its owner rented it to Jolene for what Dave had heard was enough money to pay for it in six months. She had already been in it for most of two years.

71

At the front door, the younger Ranger asked sardonically, "You want me to knock?"

Grissom flashed him a look of rebuke and pushed the door open. Dave followed the Rangers inside. They had the immediate attention of everyone within sight. The front parlor was equipped with soft chairs and a couple of long couches on which some of the girls sat with prospective customers, mostly men in oilfield working clothes. One girl was holding hands with the bruised Ox. The girls wore dresses or kimonos; none was showing more than a modest suggestion of skin. Jolene claimed to run a respectable house.

The arrival of three armed lawmen brought all conversation—and all negotiations—to an abrupt halt.

Ox demanded worriedly, "You ain't come for me again, have you, Sheriff? I ain't had time to do nothin'."

"No, Ox. I've got no interest in you right now."

Jolene was a woman of perhaps forty, showing the lines of her years and her profession but still worthy of being called good-looking, Dave thought. She probably weighed twenty pounds more than in her prime, but the extra weight was not unattractive. Her dress was conservative. Had Dave met her as a stranger on the street, he would have assumed she was an oilfielder's wife and not given her a second thought.

She eyed the lawmen with misgivings, especially Grissom. "Well, Harvey, it's been a while. Is this a raid?"

"No, Jolene. The sheriff and us, we've got some business. How about your office?"

It was the first room on the right in the long hallway, just off the parlor, where she could keep an ear turned to whatever was going on.

The Rangers entered first. Dave looked back at the women and the customers in the parlor. Three of the men quickly exited through the front door. Business was about to take a dive here tonight.

Jolene slumped into a chair behind a small desk on which a considerable pile of greenbacks was stacked. She evidently had been counting them. "Business, you say?" She looked at Dave in disappointment. "Well, I knew it was too good to last. This is the first town I've ever operated in where I didn't have to cut some of the local laws in for a piece of the take. How much do you want?"

Grissom glanced at Dave, approval in his eyes. "Nothin' like that, Jolene. We need your help. We're lookin' for a killer." He brought out the picture of Roscoe Poole. "Have you seen him?"

Dave knew by the sudden flicker in her eyes that she had. She gave the picture a long study, then looked up, her eyes a little frightened. "He was in here this afternoon, him and another man. They each took a girl upstairs. You say he's a killer?"

"As cold-blooded as you'll ever want to meet."

"I don't want to ever meet him again. Fact is, he got mean with one of my girls. I heard her scream, and I went up there with a baseball bat." She turned her gaze accusingly to Dave. "You had Ox on the chain, Buckalew. Any other time, he'd've been here to put a stop to such as that. This time I had to do it myself."

Dave refused to feel guilty about locking Ox on the chain. "Did he do anything to you?"

"He didn't have the chance. I hit him where it'd do the most good and got him the hell out of this house." Her face showed anxiety. "You think he's liable to come back?"

Grissom said, "Not if we find him first. You have any idea where he went?"

"No. He sat out front a little while, waitin' for his partner. They drove off in a Ford roadster."

"What color car?"

"Black. Like most of them."

"That's not much help. Could we talk to the girl he was with?"

"She's in her room. He bruised her up some, and I thought she'd ought to rest tonight. I'll bring her." Jolene left the office for a couple of minutes. Dave heard her footsteps on the stairway.

Grissom used the time to give Dave an apology of sorts. "I'm sorry for the test Tol and me put you through a while ago. Like she said, in most of these boomtowns the local laws get all mixed up in the traffic. We just took it for granted . . ."

Dave did not back away from his resentment. "The county pays my salary. I eat good. That's all I need."

Jolene returned with a pretty young woman Dave thought was probably in her late twenties. She had a nice, trim figure, but what caught his attention most were her large hazel eyes. They looked at him in wonder, and for a moment they took his breath. They reminded him of eyes that had haunted him for years.

Jolene said, "Lydia, these men want to ask you some questions. This is Sheriff Buckalew, and Ranger Grissom, and . . ." she stumbled over Carmichael's name. Carmichael touched fingers to the brim of his hat and told her. It struck Dave odd that the young Ranger felt compelled to show such deference to a prostitute. Perhaps he too had been surprised by her eyes.

The young woman had a bruise across one cheekbone, and a slight swelling on her chin. Grissom showed her the picture. "Is this the man who did that to you?"

She glanced at the picture and shuddered. Her whispered yes was unnecessary.

"We want very badly to find him. Sometimes a man will tell a woman things, more than he intends to, when he's . . . under the influence of her charms. I want you to think hard. Did he say anything that might indicate where he would be goin' when he left here?"

She pondered a moment, those hazel eyes moving from one man to another. They seemed to linger longest with Dave, and he felt warm under their scrutiny. "No. He was strictly business. He didn't talk much except to tell me what he wanted. Some of what he wanted, I didn't want to do. So he started to hit me. That's when Jolene came up."

Grissom was disappointed. Dave wondered what he had expected. It seemed unlikely that a man on the dodge would spill all his plans to a woman he had casually bought and paid for.

Grissom pressed, "You sure there wasn't anything else?"

The woman thought a minute. "About the only other thing he said was when we first came upstairs." Those hazel eyes looked ashamed under the men's staring. "He said he liked the way I felt. He'd bet I was a good dancer. Said he loved to dance. Even offered to pay for my time if I'd go with him to the dancehall tonight. I told him Jolene wouldn't approve."

Grissom looked triumphant. "Miss, you may have paid him back for those bruises." He turned to Dave. "Well, Sheriff?"

Dave said, "Shemp Oliver's place. It's down the street."

He felt the woman Lydia's eyes follow him to the office door. Jolene trailed the three lawmen through the parlor and out onto the porch. She looked balefully at the couches, empty except for Ox and the women. "You sure played hell with business."

"The night is young. You'll make it up," Grissom said.

She turned to Dave. "I'll take it kindly if you don't ever let on that we told you anything. If he gets away, he's liable to come back to get even with us. Or send somebody to do it for him."

"We'll hope he doesn't get away."

Grissom assured her, "If we spot him, he won't. Don't you be worryin' your head."

Jolene stood on the porch and watched them as they walked back down toward the dark street by which they had approached.

Grissom said, "I suppose the dancehall has a back door?"

"Sure. There's toilets out behind it."

"You'll go through the front door, Sheriff. Anybody who's uneasy with the law will be lookin' at you. Tol and me, we'll slip in through the back door. If Poole and Blinky Trask are in there, we'll catch them between us."

"I wouldn't want any innocent people gettin' hurt."

"How many innocent people do you suppose you've got in this town?"

Dave thought Grissom had been in too many oil booms; he had become jaundiced. He found himself saying, "They're good folks, most of them." It was not an admission he made lightly, given his resentment over the chaos of the boom.

They came upon the dancehall from the back. They watched for a minute or two in the darkness. Two men came out of the hall's rear door and went into the sheetiron toilet, a four-holer as best Dave could remember. Grissom glanced at his partner. "You don't suppose?"

Carmichael shrugged. "One way to find out." The two drew their pistols, threw the toilet door open and shouted, "Texas Rangers! Up with your hands!"

Dave saw the flicker of a match, then heard Grissom say in disappointment, "Go back to what you was doin'."

Dave waited for the Rangers to come out again. "Wrong men?"

Grissom nodded. Carmichael said, "One of them won't be dancin' anymore tonight. Not unless he goes home and changes his britches."

Dave felt sympathy. "I hoped the innocent wouldn't suffer."

Grissom said, "They weren't innocent. They both smelled like a bathtub full of home brew. You go on around yonder and enter from the front. If I was you, I'd have my pistol in my hand. We'll watch back here till everybody is lookin' at you, then we'll come in."

Dave reluctantly drew the pistol from its holster. Not many times during his career as a sheriff had he had to do so.

"Don't forget, he's a cold one," Grissom said gravely. "Don't hesitate or give him a chance. If he shows any resistance, kill him!"

Dave's blood chilled. He had known from the time he had first put on the badge that he might one day be forced to shoot somebody. But it had been only a vague possibility, something far out in the nebulous future. Now that the time was here, a sour taste twisted his mouth. He made his way along the side of the long sheetiron building and up onto the wooden sidewalk that fronted it. He paused to look through the windows, wondering if he might be lucky enough to spot Poole. He hoped he would not, that Poole was not here, that he had already left town to become somebody else's problem. He saw several faces he knew, including Hap Holloway's. Hap was out on the floor, grinning as if he had good sense, dancing his wages away with a cute little black-headed girl whose skirt did not come down quite to the knees. Dave thought about the cowboy Slim McIntyre, wondering if he had found Hap, if he might be in here too. If so, he was fixing to receive an object lesson about keeping bad company.

Dave's mission was to get everybody's attention, to distract them from the Rangers. He stepped through the front door, holding the pistol high in his right hand, about even with his head. He rough-counted some twenty couples out on the pine floor, dancing to jazz from a hand-cranked console phonograph. Shemp Oliver sat at the gate that led from the waiting area out onto the floor, taking up the dimes. He saw Dave and the pistol and came quickly to his feet, dropping a cigarette that had dangled from his lip. The dancers stopped moving, first one couple and then all the others, though the music went on because no one thought to shut off the phonograph.

Desperately Dave searched among the men's faces. He saw

one man leave a girl and start to trot toward the back door, almost running headlong into Grissom and Carmichael. Both Rangers held pistols. Grissom shouted in a voice that boomed over the noise of the phonograph: "Texas Rangers! Everybody against the wall!"

The man who had run for the door stopped in his tracks and raised his hands. For a moment, Dave was distracted, wondering if that could be Poole. The man's back was turned. Then the tail of his eye caught a movement out on the floor. A man pressed a short-nosed revolver against the back of a woman's blond head. As the man turned, Dave knew the face was the one he had seen in the picture. He saw terror in the woman's wide eyes.

"You Rangers," the man said, "you back away. I'm leavin' and I'm takin' this young lady with me. One wrong move from any of you and I'll blow her brains out. Come on, Blinky."

The man who had run for the back door lowered his hands. His face was drained pale from fright, but he said, "I'm with you, Roscoe."

Dave stood gripping his pistol, unsure what to do. If he fired, the woman might die.

He saw Ranger Harvey Grissom calmly drop to one knee, both hands firmly clasped on his pistol. Flame and smoke leaped from the weapon. The explosion racketed and reechoed through the room. The woman screamed and dropped to the floor. Roscoe Poole's blood was splattered all over her. Poole sprawled, his body twitching. The revolver lay beside him, unfired.

The phonograph played on, the jazzy music a bizarre contrast to the bloody scene on the dance floor.

Dave recovered from the momentary surprise and rushed to the screaming woman, fearing she had been shot. But she was simply in shock from fear, shaking uncontrollably.

Blinky Trask was on his knees, his hands trembling above his head. "For God's sake, Rangers, don't shoot me." Tol Carmichael quickly handcuffed him.

Some of the women recovered enough from their own astonishment to go to the fallen one's aid. Dave knelt beside Roscoe Poole. Whatever life remained was rapidly ebbing. Poole's eyes were open, but the back of his head was blown away.

Dave's surprise changed to anger. He pushed to his feet as the older Ranger came up, the smoking pistol in his hand. "God-

77

damn you, Grissom, you could've killed somebody. Or caused Poole to kill this woman."

"I did kill somebody," Grissom said flatly and without remorse, "the one we came for. He'll never murder anybody else. As for the woman, what's one whore more or less? There's a-plenty more."

Dave could hardly bring himself to look at the body now. He felt as if he might have to go outside and lose his supper. He could see no emotion in Grissom's face except relief. Sharply he demanded, "Don't it bother you at all?"

"Not one Goddamned bit. This way nobody'll ever parole him again. I've seen too many of them walk out through the prison gate. I've never seen one crawl out of the grave."

A curious crowd gathered around what was left of Roscoe Poole. Dave saw a woman reach into Poole's pocket and remove the wallet. He started to protest but decided not to. What the hell? Poole didn't need it anymore. He didn't need anything except a box to be buried in.

Grissom looked around for Shemp Oliver. "You the proprietor? If you'll call the undertaker, you can get started cleanin' up this mess."

Dave marveled at the man's coolness. As for himself, he was still shaking. Grissom said, "It's a damned shame somebody didn't do this a long time ago. I just wish it was Big Boy Daugherty himself lyin' there."

Dave remembered he was still holding his pistol. He slipped it back into the holster. "You mentioned this Big Boy once before. I've heard the name, but I can't tie anything to it."

"Just hope you never have to. He's got a way of movin' into boomtowns like this one and takin' over. He keeps a handful of thugs around him for enforcement. We get one of them occasionally, but we never can pin anything on Big Boy. If he shows up here, you'll be in for a lot more trouble than you and one deputy can handle. You'll be sendin' for us."

Dave listened to the weeping of the woman who had momentarily been taken hostage. *It'll be a cold day in July before I do that,* he thought.

Carmichael brought Blinky Trask up, securely cuffed, eyes rolling in the aftermath of terror. Grissom said, "Too bad Blinky didn't keep runnin' for the door. We wouldn't have to worry about takin' care of a prisoner."

Carmichael made a cold smile. "It's awful dark outside. He might decide to try runnin' for it."

Blinky began to cry, realizing how near he had been to sudden death, how near he might still be. "It was all Roscoe. It was Roscoe done the robbery at the fillin' station. And the killin'. I didn't want him to."

Dave knew the Rangers were baiting Blinky into telling everything. They would have him singing like a canary.

Grissom said to Dave, "We'll need the borrow of your jail to put Blinky away for the night. And I'd like to use your office. We've got to phone in a report."

Dave handed him the keys. "Help yourself. I'll go down to Jolene's and let her know she can stop worryin'." As much as anything, he wanted to get out of the choking atmosphere of the dancehall and into the clean night air. The biting smell of powdersmoke still burned his nose.

He realized the music had stopped. The phonograph was emitting the repetitive scratching sound that came at the end of the record when nobody shut it off.

Hap Holloway stood at the door, his freckled face a little strained from what he had seen. "By damn! Some night, wasn't it, Sheriff?"

Dave turned on him with a flash of anger. "I want you to take a good look at the man on the floor and at the one in handcuffs. Especially the one in handcuffs. Like as not he'll go to the chair as an accessory to murder. That's what happens when you don't pay attention to the company you keep."

He couldn't tell that what he said had reached Hap at all. Hap said only, "Some night. I'll bet the dancin' is over."

Dave's only consolation was that Slim McIntyre hadn't been there. It was no place for an honest cowboy.

He found Jolene sitting on one of the couches in the parlor. The hazel-eyed Lydia sat beside her. Ox slumped in a chair, watching over them protectively. Both women looked up, half in fright, as Dave pushed through the front door.

Jolene said, "We heard a shot."

"I came to tell you that it's over. Grissom shot Roscoe Poole."

"He's dead?"

"He'll never be deader. You won't have to worry about him anymore."

The younger woman lowered her head and began to sob. Jolene motioned for one of the other girls to come and get her. Dave watched them disappear up the stairs. Ox went to the stairway, his gaze following the women.

Jolene said, "She was scared half to death. She'll be all right now." She gave Dave a close study. "Are *you* all right? You look kind of peaked."

"I didn't know it showed. I saw men die in France, good men. I ought not to let it bother me so much, watchin' a bad one die."

"I've been in this business for twenty years, Sheriff. I've been in some tough towns, and I've seen them die, men and women both. You never get to where you can look at it without bein' a little sick."

"I just wish this boom would get over with. Then everybody would move on and leave this town quiet like it used to be."

"I can't join you in that wish, but I understand your feelin'. You've got a heart, Sheriff, too much heart for a job like yours in a town like this. What did you used to do before you were a sheriff?"

"I was a cowboy, is all. It was hard work, mean work sometimes. But it never gave me a night like this one."

"You need somebody you can go home and talk to. But you're a bachelor, aren't you?"

"Yep. When I go to my room, there's nobody but me."

"You'll always be welcome to come over here. I've got several girls who would be glad to help make you feel better. No charge." She smiled thinly. "As a matter of fact, I haven't got anything special to do right now."

Dave felt his face commence to burn. He backed toward the door. "Thanks, but I don't believe some of the folks would see that as proper. *I* wouldn't see it as proper."

"*Proper* doesn't mean much in a town like this."

"It still does to some of us. Good night, Jolene."

"Good night, Sheriff. Come over any time."

7

Underwood and Co.

VICTOR UNDERWOOD'S TRUCK seemed to be missing on one cylinder as he negotiated the narrow, two-rut road across Henry Stringfellow's ranch with the questionable help of the two dim headlights. He hoped the trouble was something he or somebody on the crew could fix, so he would save himself a garage bill. He didn't need that right now on top of his other worries.

He barely missed a whiteface Hereford cow that had bedded down for the night in one of the wheel ruts. He brought the old truck to a shuddering halt while the cow slowly stood up, hind end first, blinded and confused by the lights. Choctaw banged the palm of his huge hand against the outside of the door and hollered until the cow reluctantly gave up the road, allowing the truck to pass. He heard her bawl for a calf, somewhere out of sight in the darkness.

Choctaw said, "I thought Old Man Stringfellow was a sheepman." It was the first time he had spoken since they had left Caprock.

"Most sheepmen keep a few cows for respectability. I don't know what it takes to make an oilman respectable."

Choctaw was not usually a big talker. He said emphatically, "They can take us as we are or leave us the hell alone."

Underwood had never known whether Choctaw was fullblood or not. It never had mattered a nickel's worth one way or the other. The big man knew his way around a drilling rig, and he could lift weight that would have put Underwood in traction. The main thing that mattered on a drilling crew was whether a man carried his own load or not. If he did, few in the working force cared much who his daddy was or where he had come from. It could make a difference to the coffeepot polishers in town, of course, one reason the oilpatch people tended to stick with their own kind. A special kinship and tolerence existed among those who worked the oilfields, much like the kinship Underwood had noted among cowboys and others of the ranching persuasion, who tended to set themselves apart from the mundane rest of humanity.

He had not questioned Choctaw any further about the fight, once they had left Sheriff Buckalew's infamous chain. He had heard enough in town to know there had been more to it than simply the big man's being called a damned Indian. Choctaw would about as soon cut out his tongue as tell Underwood the straight of it, that the fight had started over a disparaging remark passed about Elise. That the big man worshipped Elise Underwood, there was no doubt; it showed in his black eyes every time she was within his sight. Had it been someone else, Underwood might have resented it, but he could not resent Choctaw. The big man's love was protective. Not in a thousand years would the Indian do or say anything to hurt her. Underwood could not have found a better bodyguard for his wife when he had to be away from her.

He felt a gratitude that he could not afford to express, because it would imply what Choctaw's simple explanation had denied. He felt guilt, too, that it had been Choctaw who had come to his wife's defense. *It should have been me.* But that was a futile thought. He had not been there. It was just as well, for the massive Ox would have destroyed him. Underwood's strength had always been in his mind and in his working hands, not in his clenched fists. Times, he even felt out of place among these hardier men who did the mean and heavy jobs in the field, the roughnecks who wrestled the drilling bits, the slippery, treacherous pipe, the huge wrenches that seemed to weigh half as much as a man. They worked hard, played hard and, occasionally, fought hard. They spent their sweat-won earnings freely, most of them, living as if the good times would never end. Underwood could not enjoy that luxury. His energies had to remain focused on business, for he was an entrepreneur, if not a particularly lucky one, looking always for that one big chance, perhaps that last chance.

He was in his middle forties now, hair thinner than it used to be, and a lot grayer. Some mornings he hated to get out of bed, for arthritis had begun to nag at him. Facing these signs that he was past the halfway mark of his life, he was driven by an increasing urgency that never gave him rest. He had to make it soon or it would be too late. By oilpatch standards, where youth was prized for its strength and energy, he was rapidly getting on.

The rig was dark, for the hole over which it stood had been dry. Huge wooden runners had been bolted securely to the legs. The rig was to be skidded across the hardland pasture tomorrow, to a new location staked for the next attempt. Underwood always dreaded a skidding operation, for there was ever the chance of toppling the tall wooden derrick. But skidding was cheaper than tearing it down and rebuilding it. He had to save a dollar wherever he could.

He felt a quick pleasure when he saw the lantern hanging outside the little frame house, its yellow light showing him the way home. He could see a dimmer light through the cotton curtains in the windows. Elise was still up, waiting for him. He glanced at Choctaw, who was looking at the lantern too. But for Choctaw there would be only the canvas tent he shared with the rest of the working crew on the other side of the rig, away from the rude little house that belonged to the driller and his wife. House! A shack, really, just a bedroom and a combination kitchen and dining area. Not enough room in there to cuss a cat, the roughnecks would say. Underwood had offered to find Elise better lodgings in town, but she had elected to live out on the location with him.

He knew that was one of the factors prompting speculation in Caprock that she might be dallying with younger members of the crew while he was busy elsewhere. That and the difference in their ages made many people whisper about their pairing.

Stopping the truck and slamming its door, Underwood heard a mule's loud protest as another one challenged it for room or for feed. Good! The teamsters who were to move the rig and machinery tomorrow had gotten here and set up camp. He said to Choctaw, "You'll probably find the boys over with the mule-skinners, attempting to lose last week's pay."

Choctaw made no comment. He walked around the slushpit where the cuttings and mud from the drilling operation had been dumped, then headed straight for the sleeping tent. He was a few years older than most others in the crew. Gambling had been burned out of his system. Underwood wished the drinking had too. But at least Choctaw never drank while a job was under way. He saved it for those times when he wasn't needed, then would go on a glorious drunk that might endure for three or four days. A lot of the oilfielders did it, especially the bachelors not tied to family responsibilities. For the hard work and the hazards of the job, Underwood had always felt they were entitled. Times, he envied them that freedom. But he wouldn't trade, for he had Elise.

A set of runners had already been bolted to the sides of the little house, for it would be skidded to the new location tomor-row, after the derrick. This would be its second move since a couple of derrick-building carpenters from town had hurriedly nailed it together. Underwood could only hope that it would not strike against some immovable obstacle and collapse. It had no conveniences, no running water, no indoor toilet, no electricity. Elise cooked on a small woodstove, washed the clothes outdoors with a tub and rubboard, and by night read romances in the light of a kerosene lamp.

He had spent a little money on cheap wallpaper with pictures of roses to brighten the inside, but the outside was unfinished, covered with black tarpaper to resist the wind and the rain. The ill-fitting windows and the single door were little barrier against sand that the wind carried in from disturbed ground around the rig. Times, wind whistling beneath the house would push through the cracks between the planks in the flooring and ruffle the throw-rugs Elise had spread.

It was a real comedown for a man who once had taught geology at Colorado's school of mines, who once had superintended a U.S. mining operation in South America. For himself, it would not have mattered. Comfort was a relative thing. But it galled him that this was the best he could offer the young wife who had pledged herself to him for better or worse. He had given her none of the better and a lot of the worse. He had promised her the moon but had given her a tarpaper shack and a slushpit for a yard.

He lifted a cardboard box of groceries from the bed of the truck and carried it through the screen door. Elise stood at the little stove, poking at some dry mesquite wood to bring more heat out of it. "I heard your truck comin'," she said cheerily, "so I put the coffeepot on. You had any supper?"

"No, I was too busy. But I'm not hungry."

"It won't take but a jiffy to fix you somethin'," she said, smiling as if the chore brought her joy. She rattled the round stove-lid back into place and hung the poker on its hook. She came to him, her chin upraised, her pretty little mouth asking for a kiss. He dropped his hat on the floor and took her in his arms, warming quickly, feeling a hunger that nothing she could fix on that stove would satisfy. She stepped back for breath, and he indulged himself a moment staring at her, wondering as he often did how he could be so lucky as to have her. Lucky in love, unlucky in oil. She didn't weigh a hundred pounds; he could have carried her under one arm. Her father had once said she wasn't much bigger than a watchfob. She had light brown hair bobbed in a Colleen Moore-Louise Brooks style, easily kept under these primitive living conditions. Her brown eyes were dark as coffee beans and twice as shiny. She had a cute button nose and an elfin figure that he thought should be shown off in a cheerleader's uniform instead of a plain yellow cotton dress.

People who did not know them often assumed them to be father and daughter. That always seemed to tickle Elise, but it rankled Underwood more than a little. He sensed what people were saying behind their backs, that he had robbed a cradle, that she had married him for the money she expected him to make someday. He knew the dirty little riddle that had passed around the oilpatch: how many times does forty go into twenty? One of the few times he had indulged himself in violence was shortly after their wedding, when he heard a roustabout ask that question and snicker. Underwood had broken a knuckle, but the roustabout had to have help to get up from the ground.

"If you're bound to cook something, just fix me a little bacon and a couple of eggs. They'll rest easy on my stomach," he said. With all the worry and strain that had gone into drilling two dry holes and burning up most of his financial resources, his stomach had been troubling him considerably.

She said, "That sweet old Mr. Stringfellow came by this afternoon and left us a leg of mutton."

Old. That hurt, because Underwood was only about ten years younger than Stringfellow, or maybe fifteen. "Tomorrow," he said. "Bacon and eggs will do nicely tonight."

Elise accepted with a frown. "I hope your stomach's not hurtin' again."

"It's all right."

"Did you get Choctaw?"

"He went to the sleeping tent."

"He's such a quiet and gentle man. I can't imagine him gettin' into a fight."

"Even a gentle man can be provoked."

"How? What could anyone say that could make him forget himself?"

He hoped no one ever told her. "They can call him an Indian . . . a *damned* Indian."

"Oh." Elise gave him a quizzical look that said she had not thought of Choctaw in that light, at least not in a long time. Choctaw had been around so long she probably never considered him in terms of his blood. She saw him only as a friend. Elise had led a sheltered existence, first with her father and now with her husband. She had never been exposed to some of life's uglier aspects. He hoped he could keep her that way.

She went to the box of groceries he had brought in. "Peaches!" She held up a can. Her brown eyes sparkled. "I didn't ask you to bring peaches."

"I know you love them. I couldn't afford diamonds."

She reached deeper into the box.

"Careful," he said. "There's another surprise in there, standing up against one side."

She made a little squeal of delight. "Records!"

"They had a new Ruby Vallee I thought you might like. And I found another song you've been humming lately."

Each of the two black records was in a paper sleeve of its own, a large round hole in its center allowing the title to be read while the paper protected the grooves from scratches.

" 'Ramona,' " she said with joy.

While the bacon fried, she opened a small black portable phonograph on top of the painted dresser, wound the spring and placed one of the new records on the turntable. She sang with the music.

He had bought a copy of the Sunday *Denver Post* at the drug-store; it was always available before the weekend. He tried to read it while Elise scrambled the eggs, but he abandoned the effort. He could not concentrate on the newspaper for watching her move, for listening to her voice as she sang. She put the bacon and eggs on a plate and poured a fresh cup of coffee for him. "Here. I'll have you some toast in a jiffy." She laid a slice of buttered bread flat in the skillet that had just held the eggs.

Finished, she turned off the phonograph and sat down to face him across the little table while he ate his supper. "I shouldn't think Choctaw would care what outsiders think about him. He knows how *we* feel."

He decided a change of subject was in order. "I saw Knox Anderson in town this afternoon. He just brought in another good producer with that rotary rig of his."

"Good for him. But you'll get one too. Just you wait."

Knox Anderson had courted Elise and lost. Underwood had thought often of that, speculating that Elise would have been better off to have married Anderson instead of himself. Anderson was ten years younger and by most standards already a wealthy man. If Elise were Mrs. Knox Anderson she would have a good house in Caprock, or perhaps even Midland; she would not be living in a makeshift shack on a field location twelve miles from town.

She surprised him by saying, "Sometimes I feel sorry for Knox."

"Why?"

"With all his money, all his luck, he's still livin' by himself. He doesn't even seem to be tryin' to find a wife."

Probably waiting for Old Man Underwood to drop dead so he can have another chance with Elise, Underwood thought. He said, "He probably can't find a woman who suits him. I'm sure he judges all of them against you."

"That's a sweet thing to say, Victor, but he travels in fast circles. He needs a woman who can keep up with him. And he's well educated. I never even got to finish high school, the way Daddy always moved us around."

Underwood was well educated. "That has never been any obstacle to me," he pointed out.

"Besides, I'm too plain and simple for a man like Knox. Just look at me."

"I am. I never saw a prettier woman. And I'll bet Knox never did, either."

She reached across the table and placed her small hand over his much larger one. "You're a sweet liar, Victor."

Any lies he had ever told her had been of omission, like not telling her the real reason for Choctaw's fight. He could not look into those trusting eyes and tell her anything that was patently untrue.

She said, "Let's forget about Knox Anderson. He's a grown man. Let him take care of himself."

"He manages to do that very well." Sometimes he wished he could hate Knox Anderson, but he had no real cause. Anderson was an agreeable chap. He had worked hard for whatever good things life had given him. His only faults from Underwood's viewpoint were his relative youth and his incredibly good luck. It was too much strain to hate a man like that. He would have to admit that Anderson would have been a good catch for Elise. He would *still* be.

That was an unsettling thought. "I think I'll fill my pipe and go outside for a bit. I want to take a look at the rig." The smoke would be a little heavy for Elise in this tiny house.

"Go ahead. I'll wash the dishes." She stood up first, leaning down to place her hand across his cheek and kiss him gently. "Don't stay too long."

He paused just outside the door to light his pipe in the benevolent glow of the lantern. He heard her start the phonograph again and sing along with the record.

"Ramona, I hear the mission bells above . . ."

His mind drifted back unbidden to another woman, some twenty years ago. He had felt this way about Mary, too, but he had been much younger then, starting a career as an assistant professor at the school of mines. After their marriage, Mary suffered a miscarriage that almost killed her and put a lasting blight upon her health. Later, when he was offered the mining job in South America, she willingly went with him. But the change in climate and the harsh living conditions were too much. Too late, he had brought her back to the States, only to see her wither and die. He had buried her in Boulder, a town she had loved, a town far, far north of the Texas oilfields.

He had never expected to love a woman ever again, not the way he had loved Mary. But the years passed more quickly than he realized in the oil booms of Texas and Oklahoma. Elise had been the daughter of a driller, Huck Portwood. Underwood had watched her grow from a girl into a young woman. He had been enchanted by her youth, her prettiness, her delight in simple things he would have passed over without notice. Around her, he had begun to feel young again. When Huck got careless on the job and broke his neck in a fall, Underwood had been there to comfort Elise, to see that she wanted for nothing. Unlike many independent oil operators, Underwood had carried insurance for his workers as a matter of conscience, so she had not been left destitute. But he had felt an obligation just the same. That feeling of obligation had turned, with time, into something much stronger.

He could not shake the image of Elise with Knox Anderson. Often—much too often—he had wondered why she had chosen Victor Underwood instead. He wondered if she had mistaken gratitude for love. If she had, the time might come when some younger man would show her the difference.

He walked out to the rig and stared up at the skeletal derrick, stark against a moonlit sky. It was eighty-four feet tall from the ground to crown block. It was known in oilfield parlance as a double, because two twenty-foot joints of pipe could be stood up within it, screwed together, and still leave headroom for a man to work high up in the derrick. He stepped up onto the heavy plank flooring and lighted the rag wick of a yellow-dog lamp. In its wavering light, he inspected the wooden runners that had been bolted against the legs.

Most drilling companies worked day and night, using two crews. When he was drilling, he usually took the day shift, or *"tower,"* and had another driller for the night tower. Many like Knox Anderson had modern rotary rigs that bored holes far more rapidly than this old standard cabletool outfit of his. But rotaries were much more expensive. *Poor folks have poor ways,* he had heard some of the roustabouts say.

If he didn't make a well soon, he would be among the poor folks, no question about that.

He heard Choctaw's voice before the man moved into the lamp's errant light. "Anything wrong, Mr. Underwood?"

Always, it had been *Mister.* He often wished it could be simply *Victor,* or better still, just *Vic.* But the men paid him a deference that he found confining even as it massaged his ego. "No, nothing wrong. I just wanted to take a last look. Otherwise I might not sleep tonight for worrying about it."

The truth was that the derrick itself was not one of his major worries. His main concern was what would happen when they drilled on the new site a quarter mile or so to the north.

Choctaw said, "We'll strike it this time, Mr. Underwood. I got a feelin'."

"I wish I had it."

"Indians get feelin's about things. I know you're goin' to make it."

Underwood argued, more for his own benefit than for Choctaw's, "The information has looked right all along. From what I can see from the surface, I am sure we're right on top of the anticline. Yet we've come in dry, twice."

"Oil ain't always where it's supposed to be."

Underwood nodded sourly. The science of geology could show only where oil *might* be. He had heard many old-time drillers disparage the school-trained geologists like himself. They still preferred to work on hunches, by the seats of their pants, perhaps helped along a little by what they called "creekology," looking for hopeful surface signs in old creekbeds and washouts.

He remembered a time when, fresh out of college and eager to show off his geology training, he had applied for a job with an old wildcatter. The wildcatter had turned him down: "You'd cost me too much. I'd rather take the same money and buy me a whore and a dog. The whore would give me pleasure, and the dog would give me friendship. I can find the oil for myself."

He could not argue that these old wildcatters' rates of success were any poorer than his own. Some of the biggest strikes ever known had come from creekology and somebody's strong hunch.

"Dr. Drill," he said.

"Who?"

"Some of the oldtimers say the only one who can tell you if oil is down there is old Dr. Drill."

Choctaw said, "In the long run, I guess, the only way to know is to make hole. But I'll string along with you, Mr. Underwood."

"I do appreciate that." Underwood snuffed out the lamp. "Good night."

"Good night, Mr. Underwood. It'll be a good day tomorrow."

Underwood walked back to the shack, slapping his pipe against his knuckles to knock out the warm ash. He blew out the lantern that hung in front of the door.

He found Elise in bed, the sheet and light blanket pulled up to her narrow waist. Her pink gown did not entirely cover her small, perfect breasts. He could only stand and stare.

"Is somethin' the matter, Victor?"

"Nothing. Just looking at you."

"You see me every day."

"I never get tired of looking."

He undressed, hanging his clothes on a hook on the wall because there was no closet. He turned back to her and said, "You have no idea how beautiful you are. Knox Anderson is an unlucky man."

"Forget Knox Anderson. Blow out the lamp and come to bed."

He did. As he crawled beneath the thin covers, she slipped the gown over her head and reached out for him. He forgot about Knox Anderson, about the rig, about tomorrow. She moved her body beneath his and sought his mouth with her own. He even forgot, for a time, about his age.

TWO

The Weevil

8

Mr. Birdsong

SLIM McINTYRE paused dejectedly before the wide sliding door at the front of a corrugated sheetiron building and looked up at a sign: PERMIAN OILFIELD EQUIPMENT. He had trudged the length of Caprock this morning, stopping at almost every place of business, inquiring if anyone needed a hand. The replies had ranged from "You should've been here yesterday" to "Hell no, and don't bother me." His feet hurt, for the high heels of his boots were hard on his arches. He dreaded another in a long line of rejections. A puff of west wind whipped dust from the tire-gouged street and hurled most of it into his face. He watched an empty truck heading north and for a moment considered hitchhiking out of this place. Anywhere, just about,

95

would be an improvement. But his debt to Sheriff Buckalew prodded his conscience.

Caprock might mean a boom to others, but it had been a bust for him. The sheriff's ten dollars had dwindled to six despite Slim's best efforts to be frugal. He hadn't even eaten supper last night, settling for a nickel candy bar. He had considered spending a quarter for the picture show—it was a Tom Mix Western—but he felt it would be foolish to skimp on food and lavish borrowed money on entertainment. Breakfast was the cheapest meal, so he had made up for the evening's abstinence with a big plate of scrambled eggs, bacon and biscuits at the Teagarden. For the moment, at least, he was not hungry.

While he hesitated, a curious-looking small truck chugged to a stop in front of the building. On a closer examination, he saw that it was not really a truck but a Studebaker coupe with rumbleseat removed and a modified truckbed bolted in its place. On the bed was a large steel box of some kind and a cable reel toward the rear. On each side, he saw a pair of steel racks shaped like a U. He reasoned that they were for carrying pipe.

A small, wiry, sixtyish man wearing a cap, khaki jodphurs and tall lace-up boots alighted and moved toward the sheetiron building in short, quick steps. He gave Slim a brief glance and a breezy, "Good morning, young gentleman. Beautiful day."

Slim had not noticed much beauty in it except for the bright, warm sunshine, which could be expected almost every day in West Texas. Rain, now, *that* would have been unusual. "Mornin'," he responded, leaving off the *good.* At least the little man had spoken to him first. Not everybody had been so friendly.

He squared his shoulders and made himself walk through the door. The long, narrow building was a warehouse. A wide assortment of tools, pipes, pumps and miscellaneous mechanical equipment was stacked on racks that reached the ceiling. Through an open door and dirty windows in the back, he could see a pipeyard extending for some distance to the rear.

At a plain counter built of raw one-by-eight lumber, the little man was talking to a clerk who wore green eyeshades and had a pencil resting over his right ear. The clerk said, "Yes, Mr. Birdsong, those shells came in from Odessa yesterday. We got them stacked for you right yonder."

The clerk then glanced at Slim, and the busy look in his eyes gave Slim a sinking feeling that rejection would be swift. "Somethin' I can do for you, young fellow?"

Slim summoned his waning courage. "I was wonderin' if you need any help, or if you know of somebody who does?"

"We're full up here." The clerk gave Slim a moment's study. "You look like a weevil to me. Had any experience on a drillin' crew?"

Slim had already learned that a weevil was a beginner in the oilfield. He was encouraged by the show of interest. "No sir, but I'd sure be willin' to learn."

"Just come off of the farm, I suppose?"

"Yes sir. Ranch, anyway."

"Well, if you can, try to get on with a jarhead crew and not one of those swivel-necks till you learn your way around." He grinned to see that he had Slim confused. That had obviously been his intention, and he winked at the little man, sharing his joke. He explained, "Jarheads are the ones who work the old standard cabletool rigs. Swivel-necks are the rotary outfits. There's too much goin' on with a rotary outfit; a man can get killed if he doesn't know what he's doin'." The clerk turned away, walking toward the back of the building, chucking to himself over having stumped a tenderfoot.

Slim shrugged, disappointed. At least the man had offered friendly advice; he hadn't bitten Slim's head off.

He noticed that the little fellow named Birdsong was studying him intently. "You are looking for a job, young gentleman?"

"I sure am, sir. Anything at all."

"Tell me, then, are you a *smart* boy or a *working* boy? I've *had* some smart boys."

"I guess I'm not too smart, or I wouldn't find myself in this fix. As for workin', I've never had an easy job in my life."

"But you *are* a weevil? That is to say, you've never worked in the oilfield before?"

"No sir, I'll admit that I don't know beans about it."

"That can be an asset in some situations. We don't have to unteach you anything. I prefer to take the raw clay and mold it to fit my own pattern."

"Does that mean you're hirin'?"

"It does, if you are ready to go right now."

"I am, sir, I sure am." Slim felt like hollering with joy, but he bottled up that emotion.

Birdsong's eyebrows knitted. "Aren't you even going to ask me what the job pays?"

Slim had not thought about that. A job at any pay beat what he had been doing. "I expect it'll be all right, whatever it is."

Birdsong still frowned a little. "I should have asked if you are a family man. Married? Any kids?"

"No sir, never been married. There's just me."

"Very well then. The pay will be seven dollars a day. The days are usually only ten or twelve hours long, but on occasion they may stretch to twenty-five."

Seven dollars. Slim swallowed. He was used to thirty-five a month on the ranch. "That's mighty fine, sir." Even allowing for expenses, he ought to be able to repay Sheriff Buckalew in two or three days.

Birdsong thrust his hand forward. "Done." Slim shook with him. For a little man, Birdsong had a crunching grip. He smiled thinly. "You didn't ask me what sort of endeavor your employment will entail."

"I don't see where it makes any difference. For seven dollars a day, I ain't fixin' to be choosy."

"I believe in paying what a job is worth. Seven dollars is not too much for a good man. Seven cents is too much for one who does not choose to work."

The man had a rapid pattern of speech a bit strange to Slim's ears. Slim figured him for some kind of Yankee. Granddad had fought the Yankees, but that had been a long time ago. Slim had no grudge against them if their money was good.

The clerk was back in a few minutes, followed by a grimy, greasy young helper in blackened work clothes, pushing a cart on which were stacked a dozen or more tin cylinders several feet long, shining like silver. Birdsong motioned to Slim. "You can help him load those onto the truck."

The clerk followed the helper and Slim out the wide door and onto the wooden sidewalk. He studied Slim with a little surprise. "You hired out to Mr. Birdsong?"

"Sure did." Something in the man's eye gave Slim pause. "Anything wrong with that?"

The clerk shook his head. "No, his money is good. I was just rememberin' what I told you about not workin' on a rotary rig. Seems kind of wasted."

"I don't follow your meanin'."

"Well, be sure you follow Mr. Birdsong and do exactly what he tells you. Otherwise, your job isn't likely to last long."

Slim wondered if the clerk was trying to tell him Mr. Birdsong was a hard man to work for despite his benign appearance. Well, he had worked for hard bosses before. He had usually found that so long as he did his work he had nothing to worry about. He followed the young helper's example by stacking the tin tubes in the racks, which appeared to be made just to fit them. They were open on the top end, with a welded-on bail something like the one on a milk bucket, and came to a closed point at the bottom, with a set of small hooks. They did not look like any pipes he had ever seen. The helper tied down the tubes so they would not slip out of place. Slim could see Birdsong at the counter, paying the clerk from a roll of greenbacks. He wondered how Birdsong could get away with carrying a roll like that when somebody had slugged Slim for thirty-three dollars.

Birdsong came out onto the sidewalk and took a quick look at the truckbed. He tugged at the tie rope. Satisfied, he said, "Crank the truck, would you please?"

When the motor kicked over, Slim got into the vehicle, feeling pleased but a little nervous. It was the first time he had ever had a job that did not involve a horse. He told himself he had no reason to be concerned; Birdsong had expressed no reservations over his lack of experience. Slim had always been able to learn anything he put his mind to. If all the people he had been watching around Caprock could do it, so could he.

Birdsong pulled into a center parking space across from the Teagarden. "I'll run in and pick up a couple of sack lunches. You stay and keep the motor running."

It was an even better job than Slim had thought, if Birdsong was going to furnish meals at work.

Birdsong was gone only two or three minutes. The girl named Tracy Whitmore followed Birdsong out onto the sidewalk and shaded her eyes with her hand. As she recognized Slim, her mouth dropped open. He gave her a small, tentative wave.

"I got a job," he shouted, doubting that she could hear him over the noise of the passing traffic.

Birdsong dropped two brown paper bags onto the seat between them. "That's forty cents," he said. "You can pay me now or you can pay me out of your first day's work."

Slim smiled wryly, another assumption gone wrong. "I never liked to be beholden. I'll pay you now." He dug into his pocket. Birdsong accepted the coins, holding them in his palm while he counted them. *A careful man,* Slim thought. It was just as well. In his first oilfield job it was not a bad idea to be working with a careful man.

Driving out through Ragtown, Slim thought the place looked a little less depressing than before. The tents, the rough sheet-iron and wooden shacks with water barrels standing by the front doors, the piles of mesquite stovewood, the shirttail young'uns playing in the sandy little patches that passed for yards, the paper and other light debris drifting about on the breeze . . . it seemed more tolerable now that he had a job.

He saw a familiar figure at a washstand in front of a tent, drying his face on a towel. Hap Holloway glanced up as Birdsong's converted automobile passed, stirring dust in its wake. Slim felt a smile tug at the corners of his mouth as he looked at Hap's freckled face and saw surprise in Hap's widened eyes. Slim hollered, but Hap only stared.

At least now Slim knew where Hap lived. He made a mental note of the tent's location.

Birdsong asked, "Do you know that young fellow?"

"We met the night I got here. He was of some help to me."

"I am glad to hear that, because he was of little help to me. He is a likeable young man, but he has as much use for hard work as a cat has for a swimming suit. We parted company by mutual consent after one day."

"He does seem to favor a good time," Slim conceded. "But I'll deliver you a day's work for a day's pay."

"I would hope so. Did I hear it said that you come from a ranch?"

"Yes sir. Cowboyin' is all I've ever done."

Birdsong mused. "That must be a most unpleasant life. It seems to me that most of the labor I encounter in these Texas oilfields has come from ranches and farms. They seem to be attempting to escape that life in large numbers."

"It's a good life, but sometimes it's hard to stay. Ranchers and

100

farmers go broke a lot, and if you're workin' for them you find yourself out of a job. I take it you're not from Texas?"

"Pennsylvania. I worked the oilfields up there as a very young man. When Spindletop blew in, I came to Texas to seek my fortune. After more than twenty-five years I fear it continues to elude me. But oil is an addiction, like alcohol or narcotics. It is a smiling mistress who promises much and takes much from you but sometimes yields little in return except eternal hope."

It sure hadn't made him fat, Slim observed silently. The man probably didn't weigh a hundred and twenty, even in those tall laced boots, worn by many in the oilfield for protection against thorns and rattlesnakes. Birdsong's face was wrinkled like a prune, the skin stretched over high cheekbones and a pointed chin; turkey wattles hung on his skinny neck. But his eyes were bright and full of life, the eyes of a man still young in his heart and making a liar of the calendar.

Slim said, "I don't expect to stay in the oilfield very long. Soon's I can make me a little stake and pay off some obligations, I'll be goin' back to a cowboy job somewhere."

"I have heard many of them say that. They intend to go back to the farm or the ranch, but not many do. They get caught up in the momentum of the fields and the boomtowns, and they begin liking it. They spend their money as rapidly as they earn it, and they cannot leave even if they want to."

"That won't happen to me."

"Perhaps."

The road had been wet down with waste crudeoil to retard blowing, but it was rutted and bumpy. Slim watched with interest the many derricks they passed, most of them wooden, a few of steel. The oil smell was strong, but it seemed less objectionable now than before, when he had been out of work. He wanted to ask Birdsong if any of the wells were his, but he thought it judicious to refrain from unnecessary questions. He had learned early in his cowboy career simply to watch the boss and take his cues in silence. At length Birdsong braked to a near-stop where several colored ribbons had been tied to the outstretched branches of a low-growing mesquite. Just past the bush was a set of ruts worn in the sand by passage of heavy vehicles.

"Hold on," Birdsong said, and pulled out into a pair of the ruts.

101

The crude road wound its rough and windblown way through mesquite and knee-high shinoak that thrived in the sand. A wooden derrick towered over the mesquites. Similar derricks stood on both sides, a few hundred yards apart. Slim had heard talk in town about state-required spacing to avoid overpumping the underground pools. In earlier boom fields, wells were drilled so close together that in places a man could jump from one platform to another without touching the ground.

He saw many lengths of wet and shiny steel pipe standing inside the derrick, and a crew on the derrick floor was pulling more pipe up from the hole, using chains and the big bullwheel. He heard a loud clanging as a man standing on a platform high up in the derrick caught a stand of pipe and swung it back against the rest, releasing the chains.

Birdsong said, "They are not ready for us. That is just as well, because we are not ready for them either."

A man came down from the derrick floor and walked out to meet the Studebaker as Birdsong pulled to a stop. Slim took him to be in his early thirties, though his face was streaked with oil to a point that it was difficult to judge. The man shoved his hand forward. "Good morning, Mr. Birdsong. As you can see, we are still tripping pipe. We should be ready for you about lunchtime, or soon afterward."

He spoke in a gentle manner, and his pronunciation indicated that he had taken on more schooling than Slim had managed. Maybe even college. On his head was a hard tin hat, but instead of the coveralls or jeans which marked most of the roustabouts, he wore what had evidently been a good white shirt and a nice pair of trousers before he had ruined them with oil and slush from the well. A mud-spattered necktie drooped at half-mast. Slim would bet there weren't many neckties in the Caprock field.

"We will be here, Mr. Anderson." Birdsong turned to Slim. "This is Mr. Knox Anderson, Slim. We are going to work on his well this afternoon."

Anderson reached out a oil-blackened hand. Like Birdsong, he had a grip that could bend iron. "My pleasure, Slim. I was afraid Mr. Birdsong was going to have to do the job all by himself. He sometimes has trouble finding help."

Slim counted at least four men on the rig floor, pulling pipe.

That looked like a lot of help to him, but it was not his place to ask questions. "Pleased to meet you."

Birdsong asked, "How deep?"

Anderson said, "Two thousand nine hundred, lacking about ten feet. The casing quits at twenty-seven hundred. The best we have been able to pump from it has been about thirty barrels. Those wells on either side have been pumping two hundred or better. We assume there must be a blockage of some kind."

"How much do you want in the hole?"

"I want to be conservative. Let's try about a hundred quarts and see what happens."

"Very well. That's what I'll bring."

Slim listened but had no idea what they were talking about. It stood to reason that oilfielders had a language all their own, just as cowboys did, unintelligible to anyone from the outside world. It was a badge of brotherhood, shutting out those who did not belong within the circle.

Birdsong turned back toward the truck, so Slim took the cue to climb in on the passenger side. The grinding noise of the tripping operation and clanging of pipe as it found its place in the stack were far louder than any bawling cow herd he had ever driven. Birdsong took his place behind the steering wheel but paused to look at the rig. "I never found my fortune, but Mr. Anderson has certainly found his. He has brought in more good producers than any independent in this field."

"A lucky man, I guess."

"You could say that. But I have found that the harder a man works, the luckier he gets. Mr. Anderson has invested a great deal of fortitude, judgment and plain old-fashioned hard work as well. He is deserving of whatever success may come his way."

Slim had long observed that many men resented those more successful than themselves. He detected no such resentment in Birdsong. The little man said, "It is our job today to see if we can make him even richer."

Birdsong drove back out the same rough road by which they had come, the little truck bouncing hard once as it ran over a mesquite root uncovered by the shifting sand. Birdsong stopped, got out and studied the ruts. "I didn't see that. But I'll see it next time." He reached up and broke a springy mesquite branch with both hands, letting it sag. "That will mark the spot."

Slim wondered why it made any real difference. The bump had done the vehicle no damage.

Birdsong turned left on to the broader oiled road. The derricks thinned out as they neared the edge of the explored and developed area. Slim noticed two-rut roads leading off at intervals, much like the one they had used in reaching the Anderson well. Each was marked by ribbons of various colors attached either to mesquite trees or to tall wooden stakes. Now and again one was marked with small signs carrying such identifications as MAGNOLIA NO. *3* or ANDERSON NO. *7*.

"Magnolia is one of the majors," Birdsong explained, "like Gulf and Humble. Mr. Anderson is an independent. However, he sometimes contracts his drilling equipment to make hole for one of the majors when theirs are all tied up and he is not too busy with his own enterprises. He does not like his equipment and crews to stand idle a day more than necessary. Those rotaries of his can put a bit down three thousand feet in a week or two, depending upon the formations. Mr. Anderson is a go-getter."

Slim figured Birdsong was at least twenty, maybe twenty-five years the elder, yet he still said *Mr.* Anderson, with respect. Not just to the man's face, but even in speaking about him.

Birdsong slowed, then turned off onto a set of ruts not marked by either ribbon or sign. When Slim commented upon that lack, Birdsong said, "It is just as well that not everybody knows this road."

For a moment, Slim asked himself uneasily if he might have gotten involved with a bootlegger. He remembered the two men talking about a hundred quarts, or whatever the number had been. But a hundred quarts of whisky didn't fit in with the other bits of conversation he could recall. Birdsong's look, though eccentric, did not coincide with Slim's mental picture of a professional bootlegger as a mean-eyed, iron-fisted thug, the way such characters were usually depicted in the picture shows.

They reached a bend in the road, skirting around a green mesquite thicket, and came to a strange box-shaped building with walls of plate steel. Birdsong got out and began fingering a ring of keys, looking for the right one to open a huge padlock that hung from the door. He said, "Leave five of those shells on the truck and bring the rest in here for storage."

Slim surmised that "shells" meant the tin cylinders. They were light in weight, so he was able to tuck one under each arm. As he carried them through the open door, Birdsong said crisply, "Careful you don't bump anything with those. Lay them down gently, over there against the wall."

It was dark in the building, and there were no windows. Except for the open door, the only light came through a pair of metal ventilators on the roof. Slim could hear the whirring sound as they turned in the wind. Birdsong walked outside and opened a second door on the opposite side of the building, letting sunlight stream in. Slim unloaded the rest of the equipment as ordered. He found that Birdsong had moved several square containers out into the middle of the floor. Each had cork stoppers in its top.

"Now," the little man said, "if you please, I would like you to go out and open the steel box in the bed of the car. I'll bring these and set them in it."

Slim frowned. The containers looked heavy. Birdsong was of slight build. "Why don't you let me carry them for you?"

"In time, young gentleman, once I have learned what you can do. For now, this is a job I prefer to do for myself."

As Slim walked around behind the vehicle, it occurred to him that he had never seen the rear of it. When he did, he stopped in midstride. On the back was a sign with big red letters: DANGER EXPLOSIVES. He swallowed hard and looked toward the building. Birdsong was coming, carrying a square container.

Slim shouted, "What's this mean, *explosives?*"

Birdsong did not give him a straight answer. He said, "Please open the box. I do not want to stand and hold this."

Slim opened the top of the steel box. Inside he saw rubber padding dividing the space into many sections about the size of the container Birdsong carried. He realized that the container was to nest inside one of those sections, atop a well-padded bottom. Birdsong carefully set the container on the end of the bed, next to the cable reel, then climbed up and cautiously lifted it again, setting it down into one of the padded sections.

Slim's hands began to tremble as realization came. Several pieces of Birdsong's conversation with Anderson began to fit together, and he wished Birdsong *was* just a bootlegger. He suddenly felt cold as ice.

"You didn't say we'd be workin' with nitroglycerin."

Birdsong blinked, his eyes innocent. "Didn't I? Purely an oversight, young gentleman. I suppose I never thought it important. As soon as we've loaded the rest of the containers, we'll have our lunch."

Slim felt more like losing his breakfast than eating any lunch.

9

An Education

SLIM HAD SPENT many a hot summer afternoon branding calves or doctoring screwworm cases, but he doubted he had ever sweated more than now. The spring day was not actually all that hot. Yet every time he looked through the rear window at the heavily laden truckbed, he broke out in a fresh sweat. He frequently rubbed his sleeve across his forehead.

Birdsong glanced away from his driving. "You do not look well, Mr. McIntyre. Did the lunch not agree with you?" Slim thought the little man was suppressing a smile. That innocent look was probably a cover-up for a sadistic streak.

"The dinner was fine." He had left most of it uneaten at the steel-sided magazine building.

Birdsong said, "I find that most men become quite nervous in the presence of nitroglycerin. I did so, myself, once. But I am two years on the downhill side of sixty, and for nearly half of that life I have been a professional shooter. You can see that I am still more or less in a single piece. I have never had an accident with nitroglycerin."

It won't take but one, Slim thought darkly.

Birdsong slowed almost to a stop when he reached the ribbons that marked the crude road out to the Anderson well. He made the turn with care, then drove slowly, seeking out the smoothest parts he could find in the rutted path. That was only a reminder to Slim—as if he had needed one—that the cargo was highly volatile. Birdsong stopped when he reached the broken mesquite branch that marked the exposed root and the rough spot it caused.

He said, "A shovel is tied on your side. I think it might be wise if you covered that root and smoothed out the roadway."

"Yes sir."

Slim untied the shovel with care not to bump it against anything. He sweated afresh as he looked at the heavy metal box containing the liquid explosive. He left the door ajar, reluctant to slam it hard enough for the latch to catch. He had always hated pick and shovel work when it was necessary on one ranch or another, but he attacked this task with a stern sense of purpose. He filled the hole with sand, stopping often to stomp on it and pack it with his feet. When the root was well covered, he patted the sand with the shovel to smooth it. Birdsong started the Studebaker moving forward. Slim's impulse was to drop the shovel and run, but he stood his ground, watching the tires cut deep into the sand despite the packing he had done.

The right rear wheel raised up as it came upon the root, dropping three or four inches down the other side. Slim shut his eyes. He did not open them until he was aware that Birdsong had stopped. He heard the man say, "You did well. I do not believe we will have any trouble the rest of the way."

The wind seemed cold, driving through Slim's sweat-soaked shirt and onto his skin. With trembling hands, he tied the shovel where it belonged, then got back into the truck. Birdsong smiled. "If I had all the nitro today that I have carried over rough roads in my time, it would probably fill three tank cars on the Texas & Pacific Railroad."

Slim wondered how many towns three tank cars of nitro could blow to hell and gone.

As they approached the well, he could see that activity there had stopped. Stands of pipe were stacked in the derrick. He saw no men on the floor. The only person in sight was Knox Anderson, still wearing the oil-ruined clothes, even oilier now than before. The soiled tie still hung loosely from his neck, incongruous in this setting.

Slim asked Birdsong, "Where'd all the men go?"

"The regular crews leave when I come to shoot a well. This is a job they prefer to leave to a professional."

Mighty good judgment, Slim thought.

Anderson strode out to meet Birdsong and Slim. He glanced in the rear of the truck. "It is all ready for you, Mr. Birdsong. Do you need anything from me before I go?"

"Just time and patience, Mr. Anderson. Time and patience."

Anderson pointed his chin at a derrick to the south. "I'll be over on Number Seven if you should want me." He got into a Packard automobile and pulled out across the sandy pasture toward the other well. Slim could not help feeling that they had been deserted. But no such thought seemed to bother Mr. Birdsong. He whistled a tune as he walked up onto the rig floor. He stared for a moment down the dark, deep hole, then up into the tall tower.

"Very well, Mr. McIntyre. I will fetch the soup, and you may bring the first of those tin torpedoes."

Torpedoes. The very name sounded ominous.

Slim paused a minute to stare. This was the closest he had ever been to an oilwell. The immensity of the derrick, the huge bullwheel, the heavy walking beam, the sense of tremendous mechanical power . . . all these seemed momentarily overwhelming.

Birdsong broke the silence. "The torpedoes, Mr. McIntyre."

They were secured tightly with rope to prevent their banging against the heavy box. Birdsong had mentioned, very casually, that metal striking against metal was to be avoided lest it create a spark. A spark, he said, would be all it took to spoil the day's work. Slim untied the shells and carried them to the rig floor.

109

Birdsong brought one of the containers, then tied a manila derrick rope onto the bail at the top of the first tin shell. He lowered the tube into the well's steel casing until its top was about waist high. There he stopped, putting a funnel into place.

"Now," he said, "you may hold the shell steady while I pour the nitroglycerin in." He unstoppered the container and tilted it. A creamy liquid, almost bronze in color, began to flow into the funnel. Slim closed his eyes, half expecting an explosion as it fell all the way to the bottom of the tube.

"Never fear," Birdsong said. "It only blows up for the careless. Or the unlucky. How do you feel?"

"Not as lucky as I did when you offered me this job."

"Try not to breathe the fumes. Nitro can give you a terrible headache." Birdsong emptied the first container. The tube was hardly half-full. "Hold the torpedo steady while I go bring some more." He had that tiny smile again. "I do not think you would want it to bang against the casing."

That had been the most unnecessary statement Slim had heard all day. He thought he could hear his own heart pounding.

Birdsong repeated the operation, pouring from the second container. "You will notice that I am careful not to let any spill onto the outside of the torpedo. Any friction as the torpedo goes down into the hole could touch off the charge prematurely. We would not want to damage Mr. Anderson's equipment, would we?"

"What about *our* equipment?"

Birdsong let his smile come to full flower. "It has been my policy to keep the customer's interests always paramount."

Slim tried to hold his hands steady, but they wanted to shake. The soup moved with the consistency of thick cream. Sweat crept from beneath his hatband and trickled down into his eyes. He tried to blink away the stinging, not daring to move a hand from the tube to rub his eyes.

Birdsong said, "Step back, take a few deep breaths and think of something pleasant. You will feel better."

Slim tried to think of himself on horseback, pushing a herd of cattle to cool water. But there was no forgetting, even for a moment, the volatility of this material.

Birdsong said, "The first experience is the hardest. We'll just take our time. Remember, I am paying you by the day, not by the hour, so there is no need to rush."

Slim's hands gradually steadied. When the first torpedo was full, Birdsong lowered it farther into the casing and hooked the bottom of a second shell to the bail. He let the empty one down to the same level as the first had been, then resumed pouring slowly and carefully, filling it from the square containers. The old man's calm manner finally began to reassure Slim to a degree. The third torpedo was hooked to the second, the fourth to the third, and finally the fifth and last was filled most of the way to the top.

Into that one, Birdsong inserted a long, thin tube to which was attached something that resembled an alarm clock. "This is the time bomb. I am setting it to go off in two hours. When it explodes, the nitroglycerin goes as well."

He unrolled part of the steel cable from the reel on the back of the Studebaker's bed, ran it through a pulley overhead and hooked it into the top bail of the last torpedo. "Now, Mr. McIntyre, we shall slowly and gently lower this precious cargo to the bottom of the hole, below the casing. If all goes well, the blast will fracture the formation down there and allow the oil to move more freely. That, in turn, will add to Mr. Anderson's fortune. And to ours."

Birdsong slowly unreeled the steel line, allowing the five-torpedo charge to descend into the dark hole. The tin shells were smaller in diameter than the steel casing. "The trick now is to lower the torpedoes without letting them bump too hard against the pipe. Sometimes, especially on these rotary rigs, the hole becomes a little crooked, and the shells scrape against first one side and then the other. If they should wedge, we shall be in for a spot of bother."

To Slim, the taut steel line played out at a snail's pace. He had no watch, so he did not know how much of the two hours had been used up. He tried to judge by the sun, but the sweat kept burning his eyes so that he did not see well.

Birdsong studied Slim's face. "You look better at this stage than your friend Hap Holloway did. He was a sick shade of green."

"I feel green inside."

"Time and patience, as I told Mr. Anderson. One should

111

never lose his fear of nitroglycerin, for when he does he is likely to become careless. But one should not let that fear paralyze him, for he is just as likely to make a fatal mistake out of panic as out of indifference. One must respect the danger but not give in to it. I should think it must be something like riding a bad bronco."

Slim said, "I don't see any comparison."

He felt he had aged a year before the lowest torpedo finally came gently to rest at the bottom of the hole, more than half a mile down.

Birdsong let the line go a little slack, then began to reel it up from the well. The hook at the end had released from the top torpedo's bail. "Now comes the hard part."

"Hard?" Slim wondered what could be harder than what they had already done.

Birdsong said, "That shovel seemed to fit your hands rather nicely when you filled the hole in the road. As soon as the cable is up, I want you to shovel that pile of pea gravel into the casing."

"On top of the nitro?" The thought was disconcerting.

"Any explosion will follow the path of least resistance. We want its main force to go out to the sides of the hole, to break up the formation. We don't want it wasted, coming back up the open casing like a blast from a shotgun barrel. So we tamp a yard or so of pea gravel on top of the charge."

Slim was dismayed at how long it took to move a yard of gravel a shovelful at a time. He kept glancing toward the sun, trying to guess how long it had been since Birdsong had set that bomb. He could hear the gravel racketing off the inside of the casing as it plunged down, down into the well. Birdsong appeared as calm as an usher in church.

Not until the last of the gravel had gone down the hole did Birdsong take out his pocketwatch and check the time. He frowned. "I fear I may have cut this one a bit close. Let's move the truck out of the way. It would not be a bad idea for us to watch the proceedings from a little distance. One prepares for the contingencies, but one can never foresee every possibility."

If Birdsong wanted to move, *Slim* wanted to move. He took a deep breath, then cranked the truck. He walked briskly beside it as Birdsong drove. He made it a point to keep the vehicle between himself and the well.

He had been eying an embankment of sorts, obviously man-made. He decided to climb over and wait on its other side. From its top it looked a little like a surface tank that a rancher might build with scrapers and mules to hold water for cattle. Its bottom was flat and dry-looking.

Birdsong shouted with concern, "Do not go down there, Mr. McIntyre. You may have a great deal of difficulty coming back out. That is an old slushpit."

Slim said with surprise, "It looks dry to me."

Birdsong joined him at the top of the embankment. "Looks can be deceptive. There may be several feet of old oil in the bottom. The top has congealed, and sand had drifted over the surface to hide it. I once saw a cowboy drown his horse in just such a pit."

The sand looked solid enough to Slim. "How'd he do that?"

"He caught a coyote killing a calf and set out in chase, hoping to rope it. The coyote fled across a pit like this. Its weight was not enough to break the surface. But the horse went down like a stone. Once its nostrils were plugged by that thick old oil, it suffocated. We almost lost the cowboy as well. I think you had best wait on this side with me."

The wait was short. Slim felt the ground tremble beneath his feet. Dust billowed from the hole, gravel striking the legs and braces of the derrick like a hundred charges of buckshot. A little of it rained harmlessly down around Slim and Birdsong.

"There you have it, Mr. McIntyre. A hundred quarts of nitro, and not a hair on your head so much as singed. There is no great mystery to it."

"There's one."

"Oh? What could that be?"

"Why I didn't take and run off the minute I first saw what we were fixin' to fool with."

"You would not be the first. You would be surprised how difficult it is sometimes for me to find help."

Slim kept watching the well, expecting any minute to see oil surge up out of the hole and spout over the derrick's top. Nothing of that sort happened. He asked about it.

Birdsong said, "Some of these wells will flow by heads. Oil will bubble up out of the hole, subside and flow again. Others never do. Mr. Anderson will have to pump this one, more than likely, to see if we have accomplished any benefit for him."

"And if we haven't?"

"We will come back and use two hundred quarts, or three hundred, whatever it takes. I have exploded as many as a thousand quarts in one shot to bring a well in."

A thousand quarts. Slim calculated in his head. They had used five torpedoes to put down a hundred quarts. Each torpedo had weighed on the order of sixty pounds. Fifty torpedoes at sixty pounds each . . . that would probably be enough to blow the whole town of Caprock as far as Odessa, or maybe Midland.

Knox Anderson drove back across the pasture in his Packard, his floor crew following behind him in a truck. They had probably been able to hear and perhaps feel the underground explosion all the way to that other well. Anderson stood with hands on his hips and surveyed the scene without emotion. Dirt and gravel were scattered all over the drilling floor and the machinery. To Slim, it looked like a mess. But Anderson was unperturbed. Slim figured he was used to it.

Anderson said to Birdsong, "Well, I am glad to see that you are both still in one piece."

Birdsong smiled. "You doubted it?"

"I always doubt it. I would not have your job for all the gold in Fort Knox." He glanced at Slim. "How much is he paying you, cowboy?"

"Seven dollars."

"Well earned. Well earned." Anderson turned back to survey his well. "We'll get started bailing out the rubble. I hope we can test it by tomorrow or the next day."

Birdsong said, "And I hope we have made a producer for you. If not, we'll come back and feed it some more." He jerked his head. "Come along, Mr. McIntyre. It will shortly be suppertime."

Slim doubted Birdsong meant to feed him, but he was glad enough to get back on the rough, sandy road and put the well behind him. Birdsong held silent until they turned out onto the wider graded and oiled road that led toward town.

"You did nicely today, for a beginner. I have seen several men wet themselves. I even had one faint once. He was about as much help as a dead cat. You held up better than I expected."

Slim said, "Thank you." He had never considered that he had any option, once he was into it.

"I would like to have you continue to work for me, but I will not hold you to your commitment or think ill of you if you decide today has been enough."

Seven dollars was not going to get Slim out of the sheriff's debt and feed him for very long. He nearly strangled on the words, but he made himself say, "I'll keep workin' for you."

They drove through Ragtown as the sun was going down. Slim saw women dipping water from barrels in front of their tents or standing in canvas doorways to watch children play in the sandy yards. Men walked along the street, shoulders hunched in fatigue from the long day, clothes oil soaked and torn. As each reached his own home he waved at the others and turned in. Slim watched a father take a child's hand and walk with him the final steps to the family's clapboard shack, tousling the boy's hair and laughing. Somehow Ragtown looked better to him now. He no longer dwelled upon the tents and the shacks and the debris and the squalor. This time he saw the people.

He noted the tent where he had seen Hap, but he saw no one there now. Hap was probably still at work, he thought. Or perhaps already out on the town.

Birdsong asked, "Where do you want me to let you out?"

"In front of the Teagarden, I guess. It's about time to eat supper."

Birdsong found no parking places on the busy street, so he double-parked and ignored the honking of a horn behind him. He dug the roll of bills from his pocket and counted off seven. "A day's pay for a day's work." He paused. "You did well enough that I believe you deserve a bonus." He reached back into his pocket and produced a dime. "Have yourself a slice of apple pie tonight. On me. Pick you up here at six-thirty in the morning?"

Slim fingered the dime as if it were a dollar. "Six-thirty it is."

Carrying his rolled blankets, he walked between two parked automobiles to get out of the traffic, which had bunched behind Birdsong's truck. He stepped up onto the wooden sidewalk and paused to hold out his right hand to see if it still shook. It had become remarkably still. It occurred to him that the people walking along the street paid no attention to the modified Studebaker with the words DANGER EXPLOSIVES emblazoned on its rear. He supposed oiltown people were used to living with hazards.

He gave a moment's study to the empty lot beside the Teagarden, the place where he had been struck and robbed on his first night here. He had thirteen dollars in his packet now, counting the six left from the sheriff's money. Be damned if he intended to let anybody take that without a fight, especially seeing how hard seven of those dollars had been earned. He glanced around half belligerently, as if someone might be stalking him even now. The most threatening thing he saw was two young women standing before the dancehall a little farther down the street, enticing men to dance away their day's wages.

On another night, he might be tempted, but he was tired and wrung out, not so much from hard work as from the tension. He probably couldn't have danced twenty cents worth.

The evening crowd was heavy in the restaurant; it always was. Slim saw that he would have to wait awhile for a place at the counter or a table.

Down the street, past the poolhall, was a narrow hole-in-the-wall hamburger joint with a sign proclaiming ELITE CAFÉ. People pronounced it *Eee*-light. There a man fried hamburger meat and toasted buns on a flat, black grill right in the front window. They smelled good and tasted good, and they cost just a dime. But Slim had not put away much of his sack lunch at noon, and he was hungry now. He did not think a hamburger would carry him until breakfast.

So he waited, watching the gray-haired Mrs. Whitmore hustle in the kitchen, watching her daughter Tracy and another waitress tend to the crowd. Dutch Schwartz stood at the cash register, taking the money and letting his formidable size warn any wayward customers about the hazards of walking out without paying. A cardboard sign behind him reinforced the message: WALKERS BEWARE! SURVIVORS WILL BE PROSECUTED!

Somebody shouted, "Hey, Slim!" The voice came from out on the sidewalk. It was a familiar one. Hap Holloway came to the doorway, a couple of tough-looking young roustabouts just behind him. Slim felt cold toward the pair on first sight. Both had the close-set eyes that had always raised a warning flag with him;

116

most people he had ever seen who looked like that had been trouble of one kind or another. He guessed that the pair might be brothers; they resembled one another a lot, one no handsomer than the other.

Hap moved into the restaurant, but the other two remained outside. Slim noted that the Dutchman gave them a hard stare. They had probably ignored his sign at some time in the past.

"Howdy, Hap," Slim said. "Want to eat supper with me?"

Hap shook his head. "We've done et. Me and the Haskell brothers are fixin' to go down the street and dance awhile. Might even go to Jolene's afterwards. How about you comin' with us?"

The prospect held no fascination for Slim tonight. Besides, he would be a long time forgetting what he had gone through to earn that seven dollars. "I'm too tired. I'm goin' to eat supper and then go roll out my blankets someplace."

"You can roll them on the floor in our tent. You seen me there this mornin', so you know where we live. Ain't no need you sleepin' out in the open."

By Slim's standards, Hap's tent was almost the same as the outdoors. About the only advantage it offered was a shelter from the rain, if it ever rained. "Thanks, but I'll do fine."

Hap frowned, "You may not do very long. I like to've swallowed my teeth when I seen you this mornin' with Old Man Birdsong. By damn, I didn't know you was so hard up for a job that you'd take one with that crazy old man and his soup wagon."

"I took the job before I knew what it was."

"I'll bet you lit a shuck soon's you found out."

"No, I stayed with him. We shot a well this afternoon, and I'm still alive. Shook some, but alive. And his money's got a nice green color to it. He even paid me a bonus." There was no reason to tell Hap it had been only a dime.

"You ain't goin' out with him again, are you?"

"Tomorrow mornin', six-thirty."

"You're crazy, Slim. If I was you, I'd hide out."

"I gave him my word."

"I gave him mine too, but just to get rid of him. Come the next mornin', I laid low till he gave up and left. Won't nobody think the worse of you for doin' the same thing."

"I would. I promised him."

"You always keep a promise?"

"Always."

Hap shrugged. "Well, it's your funeral. Only, there won't be no funeral because there won't be enough left of you to bury. If you change your mind about tonight, you know where to find us."

"I'll think on it."

A girl's voice said, "You'd better think on it a long time before you go with that bunch. They'll get you in trouble." Tracy Whitmore stood there, a glass of water in her hand, a washcloth over her arm. "I've got you a table now, if you're not in a strain to go follow after Hap." Her tone could be taken as accusatory. Slim didn't see where he had done anything to be accused for.

"I've got no such intention."

"Glad to hear it." She led him to a small table against the wall. She wiped the red-and-white checkered oilcloth and set the glass of water down. "You ready to order?"

"The special plate."

"You don't even know what it is."

"I'll take my chances."

"Sounded to me like you took the same kind of a chance, acceptin' a job from Mr. Birdsong without knowin' what he wanted to hire you for."

"He hired me for seven dollars. That was all I had to know."

"Greed'll be the ruination of the world," she declared, then went to the kitchen. When she returned with a napkin and utensils she said, "Mr. Birdsong is a decent old man. He won't kill you if he can help it. But you could make a mistake and kill yourself."

"I don't figure it for a lifetime occupation. But I gave him my word. I'll stick with him till I get a little money ahead or till he says he doesn't want me anymore." He frowned. "What difference would it make to you one way or the other?"

He suddenly wished he had not asked, for he remembered hearing what had happened to her brother.

If that thought came to her, she covered it well. "You've been a steady customer. This place needs all the customers it can get."

Some men vacated the next table and left a copy of the Fort Worth *Star-Telegram* behind. Slim picked it up and read from it while he waited for his supper. He turned back to the farm and ranch page and looked at some Frank Reeves photographs of Hereford cattle on the Swenson ranches. He felt homesick.

A girl's voice said, "Hello there." It was not Tracy's. He looked up in surprise at Douglas Clive's daughter Lauralou, of the blond hair and large blue eyes. He stood up quickly, dropping the newspaper and almost knocking over his chair.

"Why, hello," he blurted. "What're you doin' here?" He realized it was a stupid question, but nothing more intelligent came to mind.

She said, "I'm sorry my father was so curt to you the other day. I hope you've found yourself a suitable job."

"Well, a job, anyway." He stared at her, trying to think of something meaningful to say. He realized he had not so much as offered her a seat. He pulled out a chair. "Won't you sit down? I was just fixin' to have some supper. I'd be tickled to buy yours too."

She smiled and accepted the chair. He tried to slide it up under the table but could not move it with her weight in it. Awkwardly he turned loose of the chair and let her adjust it to suit herself. He stepped on the newspaper and in trying to pick it up let it fall apart on the floor. His face went hot. She had every right to laugh at his awkwardness, he thought, but she did not.

"Your name is Slim, isn't it?"

"It's Patrick, but Slim's what everybody calls me. You can use whichever name you like best."

"Slim is fine. There used to be a cowboy at the ranch named Slim. He was nice. Daddy fired him, though." He thought he saw a flicker of regret in her eyes before the smile covered it up.

Slim looked around, trying to spot Tracy and catch her eye. He saw that he already had it. Lauralou had it, at least. But Tracy took her time getting to the table, waiting first on a couple of men who had come in after Lauralou. She finally made her way across the room. "Hello, Lauralou." Her voice was matter-of-fact, not exactly unfriendly but hardly warm with welcome. "Slummin' again tonight?"

Lauralou said, "And how are you, Tracy? Still addin' up all those big tips?"

Tracy had her order pad in her hand. "What'll you have, Lauralou?"

"Whatever Slim's havin'. He looks like a man of good judgment."

"That could be a matter of opinion." Tracy glanced at Slim. "Will all of this be on one check?"

Slim felt a little irritation. What kind of man would let a woman pay for her own meal at his table? "You bet."

When Tracy left for the kitchen, Lauralou looked over the crowded room. "It's always excitin'."

"What?"

"All these people. So much goin' on all the time. You don't have any idea what a dead town this used to be. The same old faces, nobody doin' anything. I thought I'd go crazy from boredom. Then the oil came, and this . . ." She waved her hand. "You can feel a pulse in this town now, like the pulse in your arm. I love it."

Slim had spent his life around small towns. He had never found any quarrel with them, for at their slowest they were still a nice diversion after long weeks at the ranch. "It's sure different, I'd have to say that."

"What kind of work did you find, Slim?"

"I just found it today. I'm workin' with a Mr. Birdsong. He's a shooter. Nitro."

Her blue eyes went wide as half dollars, then sparkled with delight. "Gracious, that must be excitin'. I wish sometimes I were a man, so I could do somethin' like that. Wouldn't Papa throw a fit?"

Slim didn't figure she would have enjoyed shoveling pea gravel down the well, but there was no point in compromising her mood.

Tracy brought the plate specials and coffee for Slim, iced tea for the girl. "Anything else?" she asked Lauralou.

"If I think of anything I'll let you know." Lauralou's smile was sweet, but her eyes lost a bit of their brightness.

Slim felt a little uneasy after she mentioned her father. "Your daddy didn't seem to think much of me. He might not like it if he saw the two of us eatin' supper together."

"Papa's busy with interests of his own. I just came in to see the picture show. We never had a picture show in this town until the oil people came. I go now every time I can." Her eyes warmed again. "Would you take me to the show, Slim?"

120

He had not been to many movies in his life, for he had lived far out in the country. The ones he had seen, he had enjoyed tremendously, especially the Westerns.

"They had a Western on yesterday," he said. "I'll bet it's good."

"It's a romance tonight. Do you like romances, Slim?"

"They're all right, I guess." He thought he would enjoy any kind of picture show if he sat with Lauralou.

For a fleeting moment, he figured up what her supper was going to cost him, and the picture show. But the moment passed and he gave it no more thought, for he had thirteen dollars in his pocket. He spent Mr. Birdsong's dime on pie, and added one of his own for Lauralou.

When they finished and Tracy brought the check, Slim said, "We're goin' to the picture show. Would it be all right for me to leave my blanket roll here till afterwards?"

Tracy gave Lauralou a moment's study. "It's no skin off my nose. Are you sure you won't be wantin' it?"

Walking down the street with Lauralou, Slim wondered what in the hell Tracy had meant by that.

10

The Hijack

SHERIFF DAVE BUCKALEW hated nights when he did not get enough sleep. The next day often brought him an upset stomach and a sluggishness that set him to considering a different line of work. The insistent honking of a car horn brought him awake, momentarily disoriented. He was not in his hotel room. He lay on a cot in his office, where he had flopped down with his clothes on at two o'clock in the morning after a Saturday night that seemed more than usually overrun with drunken roustabouts, knuckle-bruising fights and general mayhem.

The sour taste in his mouth reminded him that he had taken a long drink of confiscated whisky, kept in a desk drawer to calm his nerves in such contingencies. When the oil rush had begun, he had tried to hold himself above the wilder element whose unrestrained behavior overwhelmed the conservative standards of the old and settled ranching community. Now he found himself reluctantly slipping into partial acceptance of the new ways. He was drinking more and more often, not enough to get in his way but more than he had ever expected.

Maybe I can't lick them, but I'm damned if I want to join them, he thought, half angry at himself.

He squinted toward the big railroad clock on the wall. He barely noticed its tick-tocking in the daytime, but now the dogged movement of its pendulum sounded like a blacksmith's hammer against an anvil. Seven o'clock. He would like to have slept another hour or two, but once awake he knew that was a futile wish. It was already shamefully late by cowboy standards. He swung his feet down and felt around on the bare wooden floor, searching for his boots.

He walked to the window and looked down on the big chinaberry tree and the men who had spent the night, or a goodly part of it, attached to the heavy chain. Occasionally he could muster some sympathy for them, but not this morning. Because of them, he felt a headache coming on, and an acid stomach. He counted to be sure he still had as many prisoners as when he had finally managed to tromp up the courthouse steps in the wee hours and hit the cot. He shaved in a tin washbasin, cold water from the tap bringing him fully awake but making the razor scrape painfully against his skin. He would have to go to the Dutchman's in a little while and order up breakfast for all the county's overnight guests.

The Teagarden, where Autie Whitmore's wife and daughter worked. That reminded him about Autie. He had not had the heart to put Autie on the chain last night, though it was inevitable that he sooner or later must if the man didn't find it in himself to quit staggering around the streets. To Dave's knowledge, Autie had not drawn a sober breath since the wildcat well blowout had killed his son. The town had given Autie its sympathy, but sympathy had a way of evaporating when a man played on it too long.

He walked down the stairs, out past the men on the chain and over to the jail. He had let Waddy Fuller go home last night because they had no felony prisoners to worry about. At least Waddy should have gotten a decent night's sleep. All of Saturday afternoon, they had searched for a stolen black Chevy coupe. If they had been able to find it and the thief, Waddy would have had to spend the night in the jail as a precautionary measure. But Dave figured the coupe was probably halfway out of the state by now, and a disgruntled company toolpusher was having to look for a new way out to his rigs.

Dave found one prisoner sitting on the edge of his iron cot, rubbing a hand carefully over a face badly bruised and cut in a fight over a two-bit pool game. He never got over being amazed by how little it took to make some people go to fist city. If the man had been a first-timer, Dave would have opened the cell now and let him out, but this was at least the third time since Christmas the same man had been in a scrap. This time he had hurt a rig builder badly enough to require a doctor's attention, so Dave intended to let him stay awhile and contemplate the blessings of peace from behind the cold steel bars.

Autie Whitmore was still asleep, snoring on a cot in a nearby cell. Dave had not closed the door on him last night, for he did not consider the driller a prisoner; he was a guest of compassion, as the cowboy Slim McIntyre had been the night he was assaulted and robbed. The jail frequently had guests of that nature these days. The town's hotel would have grounds for complaint about government competition with free enterprise were their own rooms not usually full anyway.

The poolhall battler called out, "Hey, Sheriff, how about some coffee?"

"When I'm good and ready," Dave replied irritably. "Be quiet. This man's still asleep."

"If I'd done what he done, I'd have to drink myself to sleep too. Swillin' on the job, gettin' his crew killed . . . He ought to go to the pen."

State authorities experienced in such matters had conducted an investigation of the blowout. Dave had heard the accusation that Autie had been drinking at the rig, but nobody had proven it. The investigators said the blowout would have occurred in any case, for the drill bit had punched into a pocket of gas, which somehow had ignited. Nothing Autie could have done, drunk or sober, would have altered the situation. Fate might have been merciful, however, if he had died with the others and had not been left carrying an intolerable self-imposed burden of guilt that could be relieved only by the oblivion of a drunken stupor.

Dave considered taking the black car the county furnished him but decided the fresh morning air might clear his head if he walked to the restaurant. Old Judge Potter would probably like it better too, his saving gasoline for the county. Dave paused to admire the color of spring flowers growing at the base of the courthouse wall. The old part of town still had time and inclination for some decoration, a spot of fleeting beauty when and as allowed by the dry West Texas climate. The new part, the boom-town section, had little such inclination because of its transient, temporary nature. To him, it remained a blight, an eyesore, symbolic of the wild rush to grab whatever payoff the oil might afford and then abandon the wreckage as the scramble for money shifted elsewhere.

He noticed a new crack in the plate-glass window at Shemp Oliver's dancehall, the result of some altercation, more than likely. Nobody had called him about it; a lot of these oilfield people preferred to take care of their own problems rather than bring in the law. That suited him fine. Times, he wished the troublemakers would all kill each other off. Then maybe he could get a full night's sleep.

Sunday or not, the Teagarden had been open since five-thirty to accommodate those men going to work early, fixing their breakfasts, preparing sack lunches to be carried to the job. But it would close about nine so Mrs. Whitmore and her daughter could go to church, and it would not reopen until about one. Dutch Schwartz had grumbled, but the Whitmore women were too valuable for him to lose, and he would lose Mrs. Whitmore if he pushed her to give up church. If she left, Tracy would go too. Dave had noticed one thing about oilfield wives: most were hellbent for church, even those whose husbands were just hell-bent.

At the front door, he could smell the coffee, the bacon. Tracy Whitmore saw him and pointed to a table. By the time he got there, she already had set down a steaming cup of coffee that had been meant for another customer.

"Breakfast, Sheriff?"

He had not seen her gray eyes laugh much since the tragedy.

125

"Not now, but I'm obliged for the coffee. When you-all can get to it, I've got fourteen men to be fed over at the jail."

"Fourteen? Kind of a bad Saturday night, wasn't it?"

"Bad enough. One of them's your daddy."

She flinched, glancing toward the kitchen where her mother worked. "I was afraid of that when he didn't come home."

"He's not *in* jail, exactly, he's just in the jail. There's a difference. I never locked the door on him."

"A fine point of law, I suppose."

"Whoever brings the breakfast up can take him home. He was still asleep when I left." Dave frowned, watching Mrs. Whitmore moving about in the kitchen. His first thought was that she ought not to have to work such long hours. But on consideration, he decided staying busy probably helped keep her mind off her loss. "Maybe if you-all got your daddy away from this place . . . away from the memories . . ."

Tracy shook her head. "He brought a lot with him when we came here. This would go with him anywhere we went. The best thing would be another job to keep him occupied, but people are afraid to hire him now. It doesn't matter what the state investigators said."

Dave saw Slim McIntyre at a corner table, eating alone. The sheriff nodded, and Slim nodded back. Slim had paid Dave his ten dollars within a week after borrowing it. He asked Tracy, "Is the cowboy still workin' for Old Man Birdsong?"

She glanced in Slim's direction. He thought a little of the sadness faded momentarily from her eyes. "You wouldn't figure it, would you? I thought by now he'd've gone back to his cows or horses or somethin'."

"I saw some broncs in my day that were about as dangerous as a load of nitro. Maybe this isn't so different after all." Dave hesitated, knowing it was none of his business. "He ever ask you out?"

"No." She looked surprised at the bluntness of the question. "And if he did, I might not go."

"Why not? Seems to me like a decent young man. Havin' a friend like him to lean on might be good for you."

"He's taken Lauralou Clive out a few times." She spoke the name in the same tone as she might have used in saying *strych-*

nine. "Picture show and such as that. He doesn't seem to need me any worse than I need him."

Lauralou Clive. Dave could not say he was surprised. Lauralou had a certain sparkle and shine, like tinsel on a Christmas tree. To a young man who had grown up too far out in the country to have seen much tinsel, she probably made a girl like Tracy look plain.

He thought of a proverb a German friend had told him once: "Too soon old, too late smart." Looking at Slim across the room, he remembered errors of his own youth. "I still think he'd be good for you."

Tracy sloughed off the suggestion. "I'll take breakfast up to the jail soon's Mama gets it ready."

The county commissioner's court would be raising cain with him about the cost of feeding the prisoners. Then they would turn around and complain that he wasn't doing enough to control the hell-raising. Old Judge Potter, especially. He was strong for law and order, but he wanted it cheap.

Someone called from the doorway. "Sheriff?"

Dave saw a chunky, red-faced man standing there, beckoning him urgently with his fat chin. Preacher Perry was the most popular bootlegger in Caprock. Old P.P., many of them called him. Usually he did his best to stay clear of the law's sight. It struck Dave odd that the man was actually seeking him out. *Damned unlikely that he's bringing me any good news,* he thought darkly.

He took a big swallow of his coffee and left a dime on the table. "Thanks, Tracy."

Perry waited for him on the sidewalk. He was normally a happy-faced man, and he had a right to be; he probably had more money than anybody in the oilpatch except driller Knox Anderson. But his expression now was one of agitation.

"What is it, Preacher?" Dave asked, figuring somebody had probably made a raid on one of Perry's booze caches.

"Out to my car, Sheriff." Perry pointed and started walking. He had a short but quick step, and Dave took long strides to keep up with him. Perry owned the best automobile in town, a blue Packard newer even than Knox Anderson's. Dave had never tried to outrun it; he doubted that his county vehicle could catch it in a fair race. He saw a man slumped in the front seat.

Perry said, "Look what the Lord led me to this morning, wandering around out in the sandhills."

Dave bent to the open window on the passenger side. He recognized Knox Anderson, his hair matted by dried blood. The driller tried to look at him but seemed unable to focus.

Perry said, "Hop in, Sheriff. We'll run him over to Doc Tolliver. He says two thugs highjacked him yesterday afternoon and stole the payroll he was taking to the men on his rigs. They hauled him out into the sandhills, clubbed him over the head and left him there."

Dave could well believe the man had spent the night crawling around in a ranch pasture. His shirt was torn, his trousers crusted with sand. Bits of dried grass clung to his clothing. Anderson's customary necktie was gone.

Perry declared indignantly, "It's an outrage and an abomination in the sight of the Lord, the liberties some people take with the law."

Dryly Dave said, "I don't suppose you'd want to tell me what you were doin' out in the sandhills in the early light of a Sunday mornin'?"

Perry hesitated but a moment. "I was hunting for bear."

"There's never been a bear sighted in these parts."

"I didn't find one either."

It was common knowledge that Perry had a still at an old abandoned homesteader shack on the Clive ranch. Dave had never bothered him. Perry at least was an honest bootlegger, within the limitations of his trade, and he never had hurt anybody so far as Dave had ever heard. He was even considered a minor philanthropist, giving or lending money to people in need so long as it didn't cost him *too* much. There were worse bootleggers working the patch than Preacher Perry. If the federals wanted his operation busted up they would have to come and do it themselves.

Because of the demands of the oil boom, Doc Tolliver had built a long extension onto the old frame house he had made his office, a hallway leading to several rooms where he could keep patients too sick or too badly hurt to go home.

While Tolliver cleansed and dressed the wound, Anderson painfully recounted what had happened to him: "I withdrew the payroll money from the Odessa bank yesterday morning, as I do every Saturday. I had some telephone calls to make from the hotel, so I didn't get started out to the rigs until three or three-thirty. That would've been plenty of time to get all the men paid before the end of the *tower*. I noticed a car behind me when I left town, but I didn't think anything of it. There's always traffic on that road. But when I turned off toward the first rig, the car followed me."

"What kind of a car?"

"A black Chevy coupe."

"Probably the one we hunted for all yesterday afternoon," Dave said. "It was stolen."

Anderson went on, "There's a sandy strip in the road out there. I've gotten stuck in it two or three times, and I did again. When I looked up, that Chevy was sitting right behind me, and there was a man on each side of my car. One of them pointed a pistol at me. The other one had a knife."

"Anybody you had ever seen before?"

"I can't say. They wore handkerchiefs over their faces. All I know is that one was built like an athlete and one was little. They made me get out of my car. They took the satchel the money was in and told me to get into the Chevy with them. They blind-folded me and drove me into the sandhills. When they finally stopped and told me to get out, I was sure they were about to shoot me. But the little one hit me over the head instead. When I came to I was lying in the sand, and it was dark. If Preacher hadn't come along, I'd be out there yet."

Dave tried to keep his anger from showing. Partly it was anger against the men who had done injury to the driller, and partly it was against the oil boom that had brought this kind of criminal activity to spoil a quiet cowtown. He wondered if he was compe-tent to handle the situation. Criminal investigation of this cali-ber was beyond his experience.

"Who knew you'd be carryin' that money?"

"I don't guess it's any secret that I pay my men every Saturday afternoon. I always pay in greenbacks because most of them need the money right away. It isn't easy for them to cash a check."

"So anybody could've done it that knows your habits."

"I suppose. But it's never happened before, here or anywhere I've been."

Perry remained indignant, his face even redder than its normal hue. "Bad enough that they robbed him. But to slug him over the head and go off and leave him . . . Without God's mercy, he could've died. I hope you catch them, Sheriff, and punish them to the full extent of the law."

Dave suppressed a wry smile. For a man who lived by breaking the law, Perry had a fine sense of justice in regard to a different class of felony. But he supposed the man had a genuine regard for Knox Anderson. Most people around here did, if they knew him well enough not to envy him for his success.

He remembered what had happened to Slim McIntyre his first night in town. He had been slugged the same way, not that this was an unusual procedure in a violent robbery. Dave had long harbored a strong suspicion. The Haskell brothers, and their good buddy Hap Holloway . . . He thought it was about time those boys had another little visit from the law.

He pushed to his feet. "You goin' to be all right, Mr. Anderson?" He reflected on the fact that he called the man *Mister* even though they were about the same age. The power of wealth, he supposed.

Anderson nodded painfully. "I've got work to do. I'll heal on the job."

Preacher Perry said, "When Mr. Anderson feels like it, I'll take him out to find his car."

Dave shook his head. "Don't. Right now I've got a hunch. If it doesn't prove out, I'll want to check around that car for clues. Mr. Anderson, I'll need you to go with me when I do."

"Anything you say, Sheriff. I'll be over at the hotel when the doctor finishes with me."

It was not a long walk back to the courthouse, where Dave's own car was parked. Waddy Fuller met him at the bottom of the steps, his hands animated. "Guess what, Dave? You know that Chevy we hunted for yesterday? It turned up this mornin', parked over behind the schoolhouse. Somebody had hot-wired the ignition. I called the owner, and he come and got it."

"Did you check for fingerprints?"

Waddy blinked. "Never thought of that. Maybe we can go run him down."

"It's too late now," Dave said brittlely. "They'd already be smudged up." Seeing Waddy's chagrin, he added, "The thieves probably wiped everything clean anyhow." He told about the robbery of Knox Anderson.

Waddy's eyes widened, then angered. "Stealin' cars, robbin' payrolls . . . What's this place comin' to?"

"Or goin' to. Hell, most likely. Come and go with me, Waddy. We're fixin' to call on some boys."

They drove out into Ragtown, past several blocks of shacks and tents, past a crudely constructed tabernacle church that would shortly be full of devout oilfield workers and their families. The contrast in people had struck him as strange almost from the day the boom had begun. On the one side were some of the roughest, hell-raisingest reprobates it had ever been his misfortune to meet. On the other were a formidable number of churchgoing folks who supported God, country and Prohibition with evangelical fervor. How they managed to mix at work in the fields he would never understand.

He knew which tent the Haskell brothers and Hap Holloway lived in. He had visited it many times, hoping to catch them at something that would give him a chance to put them out of Caprock's misery for a while. They were either more innocent than he could possibly believe, or they were too slick to be caught. But he would catch them. Sooner or later he would, and this just might be the day.

Waddy knew the tent too. His eyebrows went up. "You think the Haskell boys done it?"

"They're the first ones that popped into my mind."

Dave got out of the car and walked up to the front. The canvas tent was an old one, probably army surplus out of the war, stained by rain and dirt and rust but still more or less waterproof. The boys had not bothered to board up the bottom two or three feet, as many people in Ragtown had done. The water barrel beside the tent flap had a wooden cover, held down by a couple of cement blocks. Every now and again, a stray horse or cow meandered down these rough streets, testing the water barrels for a loose cover. At a dollar a barrel, such an invasion was more than a nuisance for hard-pressed families; it was a financial setback of some importance. Dave suspected that the Haskell brothers stole more water from their neighbors than they ever paid for.

131

He checked the washpan that stood on a wooden box beside the water barrel. It was dry, probably not used this morning.

"You Haskells," he called. "I want to talk to you."

He received no answer and called again. Hand on his pistol, he pulled the flap open and stuck his head in. Nobody was at home. It occurred to him that if the boys *had* taken Anderson's payroll, they might have left town for good. It would almost be worth the price, to him if not to Anderson.

He moved into the tent, telling Waddy, "You stay outside and keep your eyes open."

He saw nothing of particular interest. The tent was too small to hold a lot: three cots, a small woodstove with its chimney vented out the back, several stacked boxes that served in lieu of a dresser. He found only thin mattresses on the cots but no blankets, which struck him oddly. He turned all the mattresses over, vainly hoping to find money. He felt along the seams for signs that something might have been stuffed inside. He examined the clothes and miscellany in the boxes.

Waddy said from outside, "Maybe they went to church."

"Damned unlikely."

Shortly he heard a female voice. "The boys ain't here. They're out on a pipelinin' crew."

He exited through the flap and found an attractive girl of seventeen or eighteen talking to Waddy. Dave demanded, "You say they're gone? When did they leave?"

"Been gone three–four days. Hap promised he'd take me to the show on Saturday night, but he didn't."

A hefty woman came out of the next tent, looking ready to challenge the men until she recognized that they were officers. "What's the trouble, Sheriff? My daughter been up to somethin'?"

Dave tipped his hat. "No, ma'am, we were just askin' her about the Haskell brothers and Hap Holloway."

"*They*'re in trouble, then. It don't surprise me a particle."

"I can't say they're in trouble. I'd just like to talk to them."

"I hope you can catch them at somethin', Sheriff, and send them off somewhere a long ways from here. I been tellin' that Hap to leave Milly alone. But every time my back's turned . . ." She gave her daughter a hard stare.

"She says they're on a pipelinin' job. Do you know where?"

"North of town, out on the Magnolia lease from what I heard. Workin' for a pipeline boss named Phillips. I don't expect it'll last long. There's two things them boys can't stand. One is hard work. The other is the sound of unspent money jinglin' in their pockets. I hope you get them good."

The girl protested, "Mama, Hap's all right."

"All right my foot! If you don't stay away from him you'll come up one of these days with your belly all swelled, and he'll skin out of here like the devil runnin' from holy water."

Uncomfortable, Dave thanked the woman and her daughter and turned toward his car, Waddy following. The woman called after him, "You put him away for a long time, you hear?"

Waddy said quietly to Dave, "That Hap. Ain't he a pistol with the ladies?"

"I'd like to see him unloaded for a while."

Dave knew where the Magnolia lease was. He made some inquiries at a drilling rig and was directed to the pipeline job, leading eastward from a place where numerous wells had been brought into production and crudeoil was stored temporarily in big steel tanks. He saw a number of sizeable tents. Men, mules, wagons and trucks were scattered over several hundred yards of sandy mesquite-dotted ground. He drove as close as he figured was proper without getting in the way. He watched for a couple of minutes as men carried sections of large pipe with heavy steel tongs, working in four teams of three men each, two teams to each side of the pipe. A long string of completed pipeline lay atop wooden blocks behind them, beside a ditch. Farther back, men worked with mules and scrapers, dragging sand to bury pipe already tarred, wrapped and lowered into the ground. Far ahead of the pipe-laying gangs, other men worked with picks and shovels, digging more trench.

He remembered the pipeline boss, Phillips. They had drunk coffee together a couple of times. So far as Dave could tell, he belonged to the upright majority of oilfield workers. At least, Dave had never seen him raising hell on a Saturday night and had never put him on the chain. That he was working a crew on Sunday might raise some question, but the oilfield kept running seven days a week.

Phillips was a large man, muscular as Victor Underwood's Choctaw or Jolene's bouncer, Ox, but lacking the layers of fat

133

that Ox had added to the muscle. He hollered instructions at one of the gangs before walking out toward the car. Where joints of pipe were being screwed together to make the line, Dave could hear a peculiarly rhythmic ringing sound, made by a ballpeen hammer beating out a cadence on the steel for the tong men to follow so that they all worked in unison.

To an outsider, the oilfield might appear a study in chaos. But it had its own peculiar order, its own patterns of procedure understood by those who worked in it. Dave doubted that he would ever master it. He would always remain an outsider looking in. He was not sure he regretted that.

Phillips greeted the lawmen civilly but suspiciously. "Mornin', Sheriff. Somethin' I can do for you?"

"I was told you have three men workin' for you, the Haskell brothers and Hap Holloway. Are they here now?"

Phillips turned, squinting a moment, then pointing. "That's Holloway yonder on one of the tongs. The two Haskells are farther up, on the picks and shovels. I'd have to say they're employed here, but as to whether they work here or not, it depends on how close I watch them. Minute I look away, they're leanin' on somethin'.."

"Were they by any chance off the job yesterday afternoon?"

Phillips said, "They were here. I remember because I damn near fired one of the Haskells. He got reckless and hit one of the other ditch diggers with his pick. I let them fight for a little while to get it out of their systems."

Dave sagged a little.

Phillips frowned. "Did I say somethin' wrong?"

"Just made my job harder than I expected, is all. I suppose I ought to feel relieved when a suspect turns out to be innocent."

Phillips grunted, looking toward the ditch-digging crew. "I wouldn't go so far as to call them innocent, but they were here all day yesterday. And they'll stay here till I get this pipeline contract filled or I'll stove their heads in with an axhandle."

"Try to do it without witnesses, would you? I don't want to be hearin' about it." Dave turned toward the car. "Waddy, we crapped out on that one. Let's get back to town."

Later in the day, he took Knox Anderson out to the site of the robbery. Anderson's Packard was there, undamaged, still stuck in the sand. Dave looked around for anything that might serve as

134

a clue, but the sand told him nothing. Anderson's crews, coming off of the job, had found the Packard and stomped around all over the place. If the robbers had left any trace, the curious workers had obliterated it. He dug under the tires and threw clumps of beargrass beneath to give them traction. Anderson managed to get the car up onto firmer ground.

Dave admitted, "I can't promise I'll catch whoever did it, much less get your money back. But I'll do my best."

Anderson grimaced. "It's not the money that bothers me so much as this knot on my head. I'm going to see if I can find a big, mean bruiser with a pistol as large as a cannon to go with me when I carry the payroll. Do you know such a man?"

"You might borrow Choctaw from Victor Underwood. Or Ox from Jolene's place."

Anderson started to leave but paused. "Could I make a suggestion, Sheriff?"

"What's that?"

"The Rangers have a lot of experience handling situations like this. What do you think about calling them in?"

Dave felt a chill, remembering the shooting in the dancehall. "I'll handle it."

Walking into his upstairs office, he found Waddy Fuller sitting with his boots up on top of the desk as if it were his own. Waddy swung his feet down quickly, looking guilty as a boy caught smoking a cedar-bark cigarette. He said, "I don't reckon you found anything?"

Dave did not take offense so much at Waddy's sitting behind his desk as at the deputy's assumption that his investigation would prove fruitless. He had fretted all the way back to town over Anderson's suggestion. If he had to call in the Rangers, he had just as well admit incompetence and hand in his badge.

"I studied the lay of the land," he said. Like much of the land around here, it was more sandhills than anything else.

"Which reminds me," Waddy said, picking up a Western pulp magazine and vacating the desk, "you had a telephone call. Jolene says she'd like you to come over to her place at your first convenience." Waddy's eyebrows went up. "You ain't been doin' somethin' I ought not to know about, have you?"

Dave thought he saw a wishful look in Waddy's eyes. As attached as Waddy was to his wife Annabelle, he still exhibited a lively curiosity about what went on behind closed doors at Jolene's. Annabelle was probably not much for innovation.

"Waddy, I'm ashamed of you."

Waddy became apologetic. "I didn't mean nothin', Dave. Honest to God, I know you wouldn't . . . well, I didn't much think you would."

It was broad daylight, and Dave felt self-conscious about going in the front door of the long frame building, where anybody on the street could see him and trigger speculation. But he reasoned that if anyone saw him enter by the back door, the gossip would run even wilder. He grasped the doorknob and stood on the narrow porch for a moment in a spirit of defiance, as if daring the town to see. He was not without experience regarding places like Jolene's. He had gone to war, and such establishments had catered to the men in uniform everywhere. After his return from France, he had visited more than one in an attempt to put down old memories, old hungers.

Pushing the door open, he was immediately struck by the heavy odor of cheap perfume, perhaps overdone in an attempt to mask the faint smell of the oilfield that lay always over the town. Line of duty or not, he felt a little flustered when one of two kimono-clad young women arose from a couch in the parlor, smiling as automatically as if she had flipped a switch. She was new at the business, evidently, for she did not immediately recognize him as an officer.

"And what can we do for you today, sir?" she asked, her eyes suggesting she already knew. Then her gaze fell to the badge, and the smile went out like a light.

"Would you please tell Jolene I'm here?"

Her fearful look told him she assumed this was the prelude to a raid. "I just got into town today," she said quickly. "I've done nothing."

"Just go tell Jolene, would you please?"

Jolene had evidently heard his voice, for she stepped out of her small office and almost ran headlong into the girl.

"It's all right, Delia, he's not here to arrest anybody." She gave Dave a moment's contemplative study. He thought she was looking at him the way she might look at a studhorse if she were in the market for one. She beckoned him into the office. She closed the door behind him and motioned toward a soft chair. "I heard what happened to Knox . . . Mr. Anderson. It's a crime."

"Robbery always is. You called me over here. Do you know somethin' that I need to know?"

She lighted a cigarette. He noticed her hands shaking a little. "I can't say I know anything, but I've got some suspicions. Nothin' concrete, just two and two that add up to four. You've heard of Big Boy Daugherty?"

"Yes, but I never saw him."

"Well, you may be fixin' to. You see, a couple of weeks ago a new girl came in here lookin' for a place. Carried some good references from people I know, so I took her in. Calls herself Flower Sweet."

Dave smiled. "That's a made-up name if ever I heard one."

"Most of them are. Anyway, I gave her a place here. She's a cute little redheaded thing, but awful nervous. About a week ago, she was sittin' in the parlor when two men came in that I hadn't seen before. I could tell the minute she saw them that they knew one another, but she pretended like they were strangers. That's not unusual; it's good business sometimes for these girls to have a short memory, or to at least act like it. But there was somethin' about these two—and the look on Flower's face— that made me wonder. One of them took her upstairs. Tall, good-lookin' fellow who called himself Smith. The other man, kind of a slippery-lookin' little weasel, picked another girl. He was back downstairs in just a little bit. But Smith stayed with Flower for a long time.

"A couple of nights ago, Knox was in . . . Mr. Anderson."

Dave was surprised, though he knew he shouldn't be. "Mr. Anderson is one of your customers? Somehow I never thought of him that way."

"He's a man, like any other, and a bachelor. Why shouldn't he? Why shouldn't *you*? Anyway, he's a gentleman, always kind to the girls, generous with his tips. Always comes in the back way, very discreet. He was real taken with Flower the first time he saw her. He always did go for the petite little women, not the big busty ones. He's been to see her two or three times.

"You have to understand, none of this started addin' up for me until I heard about him bein' robbed and hit over the head. But I remembered that real soon after he left here that night,

Flower came down and used the telephone. Wasn't any of my business who she called, so long as it wasn't long distance that I'd have to pay for. But in a little while, this Smith came back, and he went upstairs with Flower again. Last night he was back for the third time. I thought to myself that she sure must have somethin' special."

"I don't see any connection between this and the robbery."

"Like I said, there may not be, but hear me out. You remember Lydia, the girl you met the night the Rangers came in?"

"The one with the eyes?" Dave had waked up in the night more than once, thinking of those eyes.

"She didn't see Smith the first two times he was here. But she happened to open a door and see him as he was leavin' the third time. Upset her some. She says his real name is O'Dell. They call him Irish."

"That doesn't mean anything to me."

"She says he's one of Big Boy Daugherty's main strong-arm men. Works under a thug by the name of Turk Radke. I've seen this Radke once or twice. You ever look a rattlesnake square in the face, Sheriff?"

"Yes, but I don't see . . ."

"It all came together for me when I heard what happened to Knox Anderson. I sent Flower off on a fool's errand and searched her room. I found a roll of bills up there that'd choke a Louisiana alligator. She told me she was near broke when she came here, and I believed her."

Dave was moving ahead of her now. "You think that money came from the holdup of Knox Anderson?"

"I'd bet a gallon of Preacher Perry's best whisky. I think she was sent here to spy out the town and look around for easy pickin's. Mr. Anderson probably told her somethin' he oughtn't to've. You'd be surprised what some men'll tell a woman when he's feelin' the glow. Then she tipped off O'Dell. When he came back here last night, he gave her a split of the take."

Dave's skin prickled. "You have any idea where O'Dell is at?"

"He's drivin' a red Ford coupe. I saw it parked by the Permian Hotel, that sheetiron *palace* over across the highway."

"I know the place. I'll get Waddy, and we'll go see if the gentleman's still there."

He started to rise, but Jolene motioned for him to wait.

"There may be more to this. The highjackin' of Mr. Anderson may be just the first chapter. I want you to talk to Lydia."

As she started toward the door, he said with genuine admiration, "You're a shrewd woman, Jolene. I'll have to start watchin' you a little closer."

She smiled thinly. "I've already told you, I wouldn't mind." She went out into the hallway.

While she was gone, he noticed a picture on her desk, its back toward him. He reached over and turned it. He saw there a little girl of six or seven, possessed of some of Jolene's features. The automobiles in the background told him it was too recent to be a childhood picture of Jolene herself. Funny, he never had thought of her as a mother, and he wondered where the child was. Probably boarded out somewhere far from here, with relatives perhaps, being raised in a proper manner. Hearing footsteps, he quickly turned the picture back the way it had been.

He stood up as the two women entered the room, thinking after doing so that he was being unnecessarily formal with such a pair. But it came from his upbringing, which demanded deference to all women without regard to their standing in society. He had fought against downgrading his ways to those of some in the boomer community, though he knew that in certain respects he had slipped.

The first thing he saw about the woman Lydia, as the other time, was her eyes, large, hazel in color. They fascinated him. "Glad to see you again, Lydia," he managed to say. The last time, her face had been bruised from a beating. It was clear now, and pretty, not hard like some of the women in places like this. But it was the eyes he looked at, not her other features. In their depths, he saw beauty, and tragedy.

She was ill at ease. "Hello, Sheriff." She seated herself on the edge of a chair as if to remain poised for quick flight.

He said, "I'm not here to cause you any trouble. I'm here as your friend. Jolene tells me you know this O'Dell."

She glanced uncertainly at Jolene, who nodded reassuringly at her. In a very quiet voice, she said, "Yes, I do."

He could see he would have to coax her. "It looks like I may have to meet him too. It would help me to know as much about him as I can."

She stared at him a moment before she answered, her voice

gaining confidence. "One thing you'd better know, Sheriff: he's not like most of those men you've put on your chain. He's not just some workin' stiff from the oilpatch who gets a little fight in him when he drinks too much. He's been one of Big Boy Daugherty's enforcement men for several years. He can smile real pretty at you, just before he knocks you down."

Jolene's eyes were somber. "I don't think he showed up here just by chance. I think Flower was sent here to look things over for Daugherty. She's asked me a lot more questions than most of the girls ever do—about the town, the people, the law. Rumor has it that the Rangers are sprinklin' salt on Daugherty's tailfeathers up in the Panhandle, so the old buzzard's lookin' for a new place to light."

He said, "And robbin' Knox Anderson gave O'Dell a chance to pick up a little money while he was at it?"

Jolene was silent a moment, judging him. "It also gives him a chance to see how strong the local law is before Daugherty and Radke move in."

Dave sensed challenge. He admitted, "I'm not sure how strong it is myself."

"You're a cowtown sheriff. Daugherty and his bunch, they're professionals. They'll run over you like a Mack truck over a jackrabbit. In your boots, I'd call for the Rangers."

That stung him. First Anderson, now Jolene. "You know what happened the last time they came into this town."

"They did their job in short order and showed they meant business. There was a murderer here who needed killin', and they killed him. Quick, neat and without any slick lawyer shenanigans. They'd take care of O'Dell the same way."

"But we don't know for sure that he's done anything here."

Jolene turned to Lydia. "I think you'd better tell him all of it, hon, so he'll know the caliber of men he's up against."

Lydia stared at the floor. "I can't. I can't talk about it to a man."

Jolene put a comforting arm around Lydia's shoulder. "Then I will. Lydia wasn't born into this business. Not many of us are. We kind of slide into it one way and another, generally because of some no-account man. Lydia was a farm girl like me, except I came from Louisiana and she came from East Texas. She hated the farm, same as I did, and she married the first fast-talkin' slicker who promised to take her away from it. She didn't know there's worse things than an old worn-out East Texas cotton farm." She gave Lydia a gentle shake. "You ready to tell the rest of it?"

Lydia looked up reluctantly, her hazel eyes glazed. "We followed the oil booms. It didn't take me long to find out that Jim didn't have much use for honest work. He was bad to gamble, and he generally lost. I knew about Big Boy Daugherty and his gang, but I had no idea Jim had fallen in with them until he was way over his head.

"That was when I met Irish . . . Michael O'Dell. Nice-lookin', good manners. He could talk an apple down from a tree. He wanted me, right from the first. He acted real sweet to me, sweeter than Jim ever was. Every time he came around, he was lookin' for excuses to touch me, and I'm ashamed to admit that sometimes I let him. He asked me to run away with him, said he was tired of workin' for Radke and Big Boy Daugherty. He kept tellin' me Jim was no good anyway, and I knew he was right.

"The gang got Jim so far into debt that he couldn't've paid them off in ten years. Radke said he'd tear up all the IOUs if Jim would help him highjack a money shipment. I begged Jim not to be any part of it, so at the last minute he turned and ran out. Almost got Radke killed. We tried to get away, but Radke caught us. You never saw a man so crazy mad. He took Jim behind a tank battery and shot him. Said he could get six men to declare they'd seen me do the killin'. Then he swore he'd make me work off Jim's debts two bits at a time. He dragged me to a house like this one, only ugly and mean, and ordered me to get to it. I told him I wasn't that kind of a woman. He called a bunch of the gang in to take turns at me till I wished I could die. Then he said, 'You're that kind of a woman now.'

"I begged Irish to help me get away, but he was scared of Radke and Daugherty. He took his turn with me like the others, and kept comin' back. Radke seemed like he was obsessed with makin' me pay for almost gettin' him killed. He told the madam that if she let me escape, he'd break both her arms." Lydia paused, wiping her eyes. "I finally managed to slip out of there one night, but I guess by then I was marked. Radke was right when he told me I was that kind of a woman. I don't know how to get away from it. God knows I've tried."

"What happened to the madam?"

"I don't know. It doesn't matter. She was a sow."

The pain in her voice roused Dave to anger. "I don't see how anybody could get away with such as that."

"It was Big Boy's town, and Radke's. They either bought off the law or ran it off. If Big Boy decides to move into Caprock, he'll first try to buy you. If that won't work, he'll try to scare you. If that doesn't work, he'll send Radke or Skinny or Irish to kill you."

Jolene said, "First thing you know he'll own a piece of just about everything in town that has money in it. He'll take over the bootleggin', the dancehalls, the girls. He won't let anybody operate unless he gets his share. Anybody who resists gets beat up to where he's glad to sell out for a dime on the dollar, just to leave town alive. That's why you'd better call for the Rangers and head him off before he ever gets here."

Dave said with some doubt, "I can't see any man bein' all that strong. If people would just stand up to him . . ."

"Most oilfield people are here today and gone next week. They know they won't have time to put down roots, so mostly they take care of what's theirs and mind their own business. You're well meanin', Buckalew, but you're just a cowtown sheriff who's stayed on till the water's up to your armpits. You're a babe in the woods against pros like Radke and Big Boy."

"I expect they put their britches on just like I do."

"Big Boy's are a lot bigger britches than yours, with pockets deep enough to pay off people you never thought could be bought. He'll turn this town into a cesspool."

Dave stood up. "I'll go see if I can find this O'Dell."

Lydia reached out as if to touch his arm. "Be careful." She realized what she had done and withdrew her hand, but her eyes reflected deep misgivings. "He'll talk like a saint, but he's closer to bein' a devil. Don't go by yourself."

The woman was genuinely concerned about him. That stirred him a bit. He told himself he had no real interest in her. But those eyes . . .

"I'll be careful." He glanced at Jolene. "And whatever I do, I'll do it without the Rangers."

Jolene's jaw was set grimly. "You'll change your mind sooner or later. I just hope it's soon enough."

Walking out of the office, he found himself face to face with a small, slim young woman whose long red hair reached halfway to her waist. She smiled automatically, like the girl in the parlor, but it was an uneasy smile as she saw his badge. He had a feeling that if he made any untoward move she would run like a cotton-tail rabbit. He suspected that this was Flower Sweet. He wondered if she might somehow be Radke's prisoner as Lydia said she once had been.

He saw Ox sitting in the parlor with one of the girls, reading the sports section of a San Angelo newspaper. The big man was uneasy at the sight of Dave. "I ain't done nothin'," he said quickly.

"Let's see that you keep it that way."

Dave walked out onto the porch. A feeling of dread built in his stomach. He looked in the direction of the Permian Hotel a couple of blocks away, wondering if he might see a red automobile all the way from here. He did not. He stepped down onto the ground and started toward his black car. Halfway there, he met the young cowboy, Slim McIntyre. From McIntyre's surprised expression, he surmised that the cowboy had seen him come out of Jolene's.

"Sheriff," McIntyre said by way of nervous greeting, as if sharing an unwanted secret.

Dave replied, "It's not what you think. I was there on law business."

"I wouldn't have thought no other way, Sheriff."

"You weren't fixin' to go in there yourself, were you?"

"No sir. I've never lost nothin' in that place."

"Glad to hear it. How's Old Man Birdsong to work for?"

"Fine. I'm off today. He doesn't work on Sunday."

"A religious man, is he?"

"I don't know if he's religious or just superstitious. He says he knew a shooter once who worked on Sundays. One Sunday he went out on a job, and all they ever found of him was his left boot. Says a man who does business on Sunday is askin' for retribution."

Dave thought about the business he had ahead of him. "He could be right."

He started to turn toward his car, but he held back. He liked this young man; he supposed it was because they had the same background. He noticed that Slim no longer wore his high-heeled boots. He had a pair of heavy brogan shoes like most oilfield hands wore; they were more practical for the work. He still had his cowboy hat, but it was badly stained by oil and grime. It would never be the same again.

"I'm a little surprised you're still workin' in the oilpatch. I figured you'd've gone back to punchin' cows," Dave said.

"Haven't heard of anybody hirin'. Anyway, Mr. Birdsong pays me seven dollars a day, and sometimes a little extra when everything goes real good. That's as much as I used to make in a week on horseback."

"Sounds fine. But how far does it stretch?"

Ruefully McIntyre said, "I can't seem to hang onto much of it. Time I pay for that little old bitty room I found at Mrs. England's roomin' house, and eat and buy a few things I need, there's not much left."

"That's the trap. The money draws people into it, and then they can't afford to get out. Looks like Ragtown has got you hooked, Slim."

"I'll get out, don't you worry. Soon as I get a little money together . . ."

Dave had heard that from others. Most were still here or in some other oilfield. There seemed to be something about oil dollars that made them evaporate faster than other money.

"Well, you just hang and rattle, cowboy. Maybe you'll make it."

He looked once more in the direction of the Permian Hotel, then climbed into his car.

11

The Permian Hotel

H E KNEW Waddy would have a dozen questions to ask about Jolene's, and he was not disappointed. Waddy spent a lot of time talking about such things, but Dave suspected that his deputy had never been in such a place. He was tempted to find some pretense to send him there on official business, just to watch his reaction. He suspected Waddy would be nervous as a cat in a dog pound and escape in a dead run at his first opportunity.

"Waddy," he said, "we're goin' to see a man." Waddy was wearing his pistol. He almost always did, though he had never been called upon to fire it at anyone. Dave doubted that he could hit a barn from the inside. He took a set of keys from a desk drawer and opened the rifle rack. He removed a shotgun and loaded it. "Maybe you'd better take this, just in case."

Waddy's eyes went wide as bucket lids. "We fixin' to shoot somebody?"

"I hope not. But if it came to that, I think you'd be better off with a shotgun."

Waddy's hands trembled as he took the weapon. He had talked often about what he would have done in the big war if he had been old enough to go. He had also wished aloud that he could have been there to help the Rangers the night they had shot the murderer Roscoe Poole in Shemp Oliver's dancehall. Talking was easy. "You really think we'll need to use our guns?"

"I don't want to, Waddy. But if it happens, that's what the county's been payin' us a big salary for."

Waddy was uncharacteristically silent as Dave drove to the Permian Hotel. Sure enough, a red Ford coupe was parked a couple of spaces down from the front door. He had hoped it would not be. He had hoped O'Dell had decided to leave town with his loot and become somebody else's problem. He got out and stepped clear of the car. Waddy slammed the door on the passenger side and stood with both hands clenching the shotgun. Dave had a feeling that it wouldn't take much to make the deputy wet himself. "You ready, Waddy?"

Waddy answered only with a slight tilt of his head.

The hotel was an unsightly frame structure that had already seen service in at least one other boomtown. It had been partially dismantled, moved here and put back together on cement blocks so that it stood a couple of feet off the ground. Its sides were covered by corrugated metal. Long pieces of partially rusted sheetiron had been nailed around its base as a protective apron. Wind had removed or bent back some of these, giving several town dogs easy access to the cool shade beneath the building. The appearance put Dave in mind of a mouth with several teeth missing. It was hardly one of Caprock's beauty spots, but it provided shelter to transients who could afford the rent. Its guests were mostly company people, geologists and lease hounds hunting for the one big deal they hoped would make them rich.

The two lawmen walked into the lobby. It was tiny, for lobby space returned no revenue. There was room only for a couple of

146

chairs, a wood-burning heater, cold now because it was spring, and the front desk behind which a clerk sat reading a true-detective magazine. The clerk lowered the magazine as he recognized the officers. His eyes widened at the sight of Waddy's shotgun. "You-all lookin' for somebody?" he asked with a tremor.

Dave said firmly, "I want to talk to the gent who goes with that red car outside. Name's O'Dell, I believe."

The clerk lost all interest in his magazine. "He's registered as Smith. His partner is Jones."

Dave said, "I've met a lot of their kinfolks. Which room?"

"Number Seven. Down the hall." The clerk stared apprehensively at the shotgun. "We got some day sleepers. I hope you ain't fixin' to do somethin' that'd wake them up."

"I hope not too." Dave beckoned Waddy with his chin.

He saw the clerk hurry out the front door as they started down the hall. One bare bulb gave all the light there was in the narrow passageway. The number seven was painted large in black on a white door, however, so it was easy enough to see. Dave drew his pistol and waved Waddy back, then tapped the barrel against the door.

A voice shouted from within, "Who's out there?"

"Sheriff Buckalew. I want to talk to you."

He half expected a blast through the door, but none came. The voice shouted, "We don't know any Buckalew. Go away."

"Open up, O'Dell. One way or the other, we're comin' in."

He heard the voice say, "Open it, Skinny." Footsteps sounded on the bare pine floor, and a key turned in the lock. The door opened a few inches. A thin, hostile face appeared behind it, and eyes that hated him on sight. One hand held a knife. The voice was as thin as the face. "Ain't you got no respect for the Sabbath?"

Dave pushed the door open, forcing the little man back. He kept a firm grip on the pistol while he swiftly surveyed the room. In a plain wooden chair in a corner sat a darkly handsome man Dave assumed to be O'Dell, one hand hidden beneath a coat spread across his lap. Dave was sure the hand held a pistol. He could almost smell it. Like the lobby, the room was not a foot larger than it had to be to hold the necessary—two narrow cots, two chairs, a washbasin, a hat rack and a painted dresser that

147

looked old enough to have come across the continent in a covered wagon.

Dave held out his free hand toward the thin man, who reminded him of a ferret. "I'll take that knife."

The man hesitated until the other one said, "Give him the shiv, Skinny." Skinny sullenly handed it over.

Dave focused his attention on the tall man. "You're Michael O'Dell?"

The man's dark eyes gazed at him with an air of injured innocence, not giving up an inch of ground. Dave knew instinctively that this was not just a penny-ante thug like the Haskell brothers or some of the other pickpockets and drunk-rollers he had encountered in this boom.

"My name is Smith. That's Mr. Jones."

"I've been told your name is O'Dell."

O'Dell shrugged, faking a smile that would melt butter. "My sweet old mother gave me a name, but you can call me by another if you want to. You have the advantage with all that artillery." He gave a glance to Waddy, whose face had paled perceptibly. Dave hoped nobody made any quick moves, for Waddy was likely to squeeze the trigger out of pure jumpiness.

Dave said, "I'd like you to take your hand out from under that coat."

O'Dell did not move. "It's cold. I forgot my gloves."

"We've come to search your room."

The little man was as nervous as Waddy. He moved closer to O'Dell. Calmly O'Dell said, "I suppose, you bein' a law-abidin' officer and all, that you've brought a search warrant with you?"

"We've never gone much for formalities in this town. Waddy, put your shotgun on the gentleman with the cold hands. If he wiggles a finger, shoot him."

"Okay, you can have the pistol. How could I know you were really a sheriff until I saw you?" O'Dell carefully slid the coat to the floor and offered a revolver to Dave, handle first. "We're just a couple of honest workin' men who stopped here for a few days of relaxation, a little whisky, a couple of girls. Surely you'd see no harm in that."

If Dave had not known better, he might have bought the man's guileless front. He could see how O'Dell's put-on boyish charm, his easy smile and good looks, might turn the head of a woman already vulnerable. He took the pistol.

"One formality we do observe in this town is a law against concealed weapons."

O'Dell said, "I didn't know who was at the door. A man can get robbed in a town like this."

"A man did, yesterday afternoon."

"And you think we might've done it, me and Mr. Jones? Just because we're strangers in town?" O'Dell shrugged. "Go ahead then and search."

O'Dell's confidence told Dave that if they had robbed Anderson—and all his instincts told him they had—they would not have the money in their room or in their car. They would have it safely stashed somewhere. He went through the motions nevertheless, searching the two men, rifling the dresser drawers, two Gladstone cases, ripping the covers off the cots and feeling over the striped mattresses. O'Dell never rose from his chair. His smile never faded, for this amounted to a victory of sorts. All Dave found, beyond clothing and a bottle of whisky, was another pistol in a shoulder holster, folded in one of the Gladstones. Its mere possession was no violation of Texas law so far as he knew.

"Satisfied?" the Irishman asked.

Dave would not admit defeat. "I could jail you both for that concealed weapon."

"If it makes you happy, I spit on the sidewalk this morning. You could jail us for that too. But what would you gain by it?"

"It would tell Big Boy Daugherty that this town has got no use for your kind or his."

"Daugherty? Who's Daugherty?" O'Dell looked at his partner. "Mr. Jones, do you know anybody named Daugherty?"

Skinny did not reply. He had never let his gaze drift from Waddy's shotgun, for good reason. Waddy's hands trembled, his finger poised on the trigger.

Frustration left Dave's stomach even more sour. He had made a weak showing. If anything, by his ineffectiveness he had issued an invitation for Big Boy Daugherty to come to Caprock.

He said, "I know you robbed a driller yesterday."

O'Dell had the satisfied manner of a gambler who had just pulled the winning card out of his sleeve. "You can't take us out and string us up like in the old days, Sheriff. You'd have to prove

149

your case in a court of law, and without evidence you'd stand no more chance than a bottle of whisky at an Irish wake. Where's your evidence?"

Dave had none, but he could not let these men get away without at least a token showing of his authority. "You-all have a permit to own these pistols?"

"There's no law says we need a permit."

"This is my county, and I say you need a permit."

"Who do we have to see to get one, then?"

"Me. And it'll be a snowy day in July . . ." He took both pistols. "You've got just a little while before checkout time. I'd advise you to save another day's rent and be gone by then."

"You can't just run us out of town, Sheriff. There's a thing called due process."

"Never heard of it. I'm givin' you ten minutes. Otherwise I'm jailin' the both of you. Come on, Waddy. I believe we're through here."

O'Dell stood up. He was as tall as Dave, and even broader of shoulder. "You're righter than you know. You're through, Sheriff."

Dave took his watch from his pocket and looked at it, hoping his frustration did not show. "Ten minutes."

Waddy did not turn his back on the two men, though Dave was sure he had confiscated the only weapons in their possession. The deputy sweated as if he had just dug a deep ditch. In the hallway, he said, "They're the ones done it, ain't they?"

"I'd bet a thousand dollars, if I had it."

"We could've just shot them. Wouldn't nobody care. We could've shot them and said they pulled guns on us."

"I thought about it, Waddy, tell you the truth I did. But you and me, we'd've known the way it really was. Would you want to live with that?"

"I could. They'll come back and rob somebody else."

Dave had no argument that would stand up against Waddy's logic. Maybe the Rangers would have done it, and few people in the oilfield would have criticized them. Very possibly the day would come that he would regret not having done it himself.

The hotel clerk was standing on the sidewalk. He appeared relieved at sight of the two lawmen leaving the building. He gave

Waddy's shotgun particular attention. "I didn't hear any shootin'."

Dave said, "I expect your two guests will be wantin' to check out pretty quick." He walked to O'Dell's car. It stood to reason the pair would not have the money in it, but he thought he would be remiss not to search it just the same. He turned the seats up and felt under them. The rumbleseat was not locked, so he checked it too. He found nothing but a couple more bottles of whisky. Just for the hell of it, he poured their contents on the ground and pitched the empty bottles back where he had found them.

"Prohibition," he told Waddy. "This stuff is contraband."

Waddy watched in surprise. The sheriff had never made any fuss about bootleg beer or whisky. Dave went then to his own car. Waddy asked, "What we goin' to do now, Dave?"

"Just sit here and wait for our friends." He seated himself behind the steering wheel. The sun had heated the idle vehicle, so he left the door open. Waddy sat sideways on the passenger seat, his booted feet on the ground, hands still clenching the shotgun. Dave said, "You better take the shell out before you blow a hole in the county's jitney."

"You think they'll go to wherever they've got the money stashed?"

"Not likely. Even if we hid where they couldn't see us, they'd know they're bein' watched. So we'll *let* them see us, and feel us ridin' on their tail all the way to the county line."

In a few minutes, O'Dell and the sharp-faced Skinny appeared, carrying the two Gladstone cases. O'Dell wore the coat now, and a short-billed cap. His searching eyes quickly spotted the officers sitting in the sheriff's car. O'Dell got in on the driver's side while the little man cranked their Ford. Waddy did not have to ask. He cranked the black car. When the red Ford backed out into the sandy street, Dave pulled right in behind it. The coupe made a lefthand turn onto the main street.

"Testin' us," Dave said, and followed closely.

Just past the courthouse, the red Ford turned to the right, and Dave did the same thing, pulling up so the space between the cars was only ten feet or so. O'Dell drove out into Ragtown before he made another righthand turn. In a little while, he turned left onto the unpaved road that led toward Odessa. Dave allowed none of the Odessa-bound traffic to pull between the two vehicles. He came near hitting the coupe's bumper, swinging in behind and claiming a position.

The road was rubboard-rough in places, blown-out sand in others. O'Dell challenged Dave by speeding up when the road was decently smooth, but the rough spots and the clutching sandpits would soon betray him. Once the Ford stuck in the sand. O'Dell was obviously not experienced at driving this kind of road. Dave stopped and watched, making no move to help. O'Dell rocked his red car back and forth a few times until the tires finally managed enough momentum and traction to pull out. When they reached the county line, Dave brought the harassment to a halt, pulling off to the side of the road. O'Dell slowed, as if waiting to see whether the lawmen would follow into the next county. When they did not, he stopped and backed up. He got out of the car.

Dave got out too, walking up even with the white wooden marker that signified the line between the two counties. O'Dell grinned.

"I'm disappointed in you, Sheriff. I thought you might come right on across."

"They've got their own sheriff over there where you're standin'. Soon's I get back to town I'll phone and tell him he's got company comin'. He'll probably meet you and see that you get across his county all right."

O'Dell gave him a long, half-amused study. "Looks like you're figurin' out in front of just about everybody. I heard in town that you used to be a cowboy. Ever get caught in a stampede?"

"Never did."

"They tell me that a man who don't get out of the way of a stampede is apt to get trampled into the ground. You might want to give it some thought."

Calmly Dave replied, "My old daddy was in a couple of stampedes. He said one way to slow them down was to shoot the lead cattle. You may want to give *that* some thought."

He stood watching until the red car was lost to sight over the hill. Waddy complained, "We let him get away."

"We couldn't do anything else. But he knows we're serious. Come on. I meant what I said about callin' the next sheriff. Time

O'Dell gets an official escort across several counties, he'll re-member Caprock."

"I still say we ought to've shot them both."

When he had finished telephoning, Dave returned to Jolene's to tell her what he had done. Lydia, in the office with her, declared with dark conviction, "Irish'll be back. They'll all come."

Jolene expressed the same regret as Waddy: "Damned pity he didn't give you an excuse to blow a hole through his brisket. He'll come back to haunt us."

"Not today, he won't." The sheriff to the north had promised not to let O'Dell stop for anything but gasoline, and to request the same treatment by the sheriff in the county beyond his. "Wherever he stashed the money, he didn't have a chance to pick it up."

Jolene said, "Then he'll sure as hell be back."

"Maybe. Or maybe he's got somebody here who can pick it up for him. That girl Flower, has she heard from anybody today?"

Jolene glanced quickly at Lydia, as if in sudden realization. "She got a phone call about the time he'd've been leavin' town. The voice was a man's. Could've been O'Dell."

"Did she leave the house?"

"No. She hasn't been out from under this roof today."

Dave pondered. "My guess is that she'll wait till dark, maybe even the wee hours of the mornin', then slip out to wherever O'Dell hid the money." He was compelled to look at Lydia, at those hazel eyes. "Have they still got any kind of a hold on you?"

"If you ever once belong to Turk Radke or Big Boy, they think you always do."

Dave frowned. "Everybody keeps talkin' about Big Boy. I can't quite feature a man like that."

Lydia shuddered. "Did you ever see a big fat tick, all bloated up on blood it had sucked out of some poor creature that couldn't help itself? That's Big Boy."

"If you want to leave town . . ."

Lydia looked at Jolene. "I've been better treated here than anywhere since I left the farm. Where could I go that there wouldn't be a chance of runnin' into Radke or Big Boy or Irish O'Dell? I'd as soon stay here."

153

"I'll do the best I can." Dave turned to Jolene. "I wish you'd keep an eye on Flower. If she leaves, try to see whichaway she's headed and call me at the office. Come dark, Waddy and me'll set up a watch outside. Maybe she'll lead us to Mr. Anderson's money." He started for the door.

Jolene said, "Buckalew, I don't imagine you think too much of us and the kind of business we run here. We're just tryin' to make our way in a world that ain't always kind. You help us, and we'll help you as much as we can."

"Biggest help you can give me right now is to keep an eye on Flower."

He found the office quiet, Waddy reading the Sunday comics in the Fort Worth paper. He said, "You go along home, Waddy. I'll pick you up about dark. Me and you, we're goin' to stake out Jolene's place tonight."

Waddy was immediately interested. "Sure enough?"

"From the outside," Dave added.

Waddy was a little disappointed. "Be kind of interestin' to see who goes in, won't it?"

"I'm more interested in seein' who comes out."

Waddy gone, Dave looked down at the empty chain. He and Waddy had turned most of the overnighters loose earlier. A pair of poolhall brawlers who merited a longer stay had been moved inside, behind bars. They were not of the class of felons who required constant vigilance, so he saw no need for anyone to stay on full-time duty in the jail. Nobody was likely to sneak in and turn them loose. Most of their acquaintances would probably prefer to see them remain where they were.

Dave sat at his desk, idly running through a small stack of mail he had already looked at once. His mind drifted back down the street to Jolene's, to Lydia. He had never asked her last name, and she probably would not have given him her real one anyway. When he closed his eyes, he could see hers. Gradually, because he had missed so much sleep last night, he dozed off in the chair. He slept a good while, for when he awakened the railroad clock showed it was past five-thirty. He walked to the window and saw the shadows lengthening, though full dark was still a couple of hours away. He tried to return to the mail, but it held no interest for him. He reached into the drawer of the desk and drew out the old picture he had studied so long and so often. Yes, it was the eyes, he thought. They looked much the same.

The telephone jarred him. Jolene's voice brought him back to reality: "I been watchin' her all afternoon, and she hasn't made a move."

Dave had a moment of doubt. They could be wrong about this whole thing. The evidence was all circumstantial. But, no. Jolene was a woman of experience and strong instinct. His own instinct told him she had called this one right. "Waddy and me, we'll be over at dark. You won't see us, but we'll be there."

"I'll see you," she said. "I'll be watchin' for you."

He hadn't eaten much all day because of his upset stomach, and hunger was beginning to nag him. He ate supper at the Teagarden, sharing a table with the old sheep rancher, Uncle Henry Stringfellow, whom he had known since long before oil. Uncle Henry's presence was a comfort, a tie to better times, or at least calmer times. Dave asked, "How's your oilwell?"

Stringfellow shook his head. "Looks like those woollies are goin' to have to support me the rest of my life. Victor Underwood is still drillin' like he expects to find him a gusher, but I haven't seen anything come out of that hole except rock and sand. Poor feller'll be herdin' sheep for me if he doesn't find somethin' soon. Can't say I'd mind havin' that little wife of his around the place, though. When she smiles, it's like all the lights had come on."

Dave knew Underwood's young wife by sight. He had heard the nasty little jokes and speculation about her marrying a man many years older than herself. From what he had heard, if she had done it in hopes of tying into a fortune she had made a poor choice. Underwood was widely regarded as a prime candidate for the poorhouse.

"I don't understand what drives those oil people," he said.

"Partly it's the same thing that drives us all, money. Ranchers, oilfield folks, no matter how good a livin' we make, we want a little more, and a little more after that."

"Ranchin' is more than a livin', though; it's a way of life."

"So's the oilfield, Dave. These people like Underwood, like Knox Anderson, they get it in their blood, and pretty soon it goes beyond money. You remember the excitement you used to feel when you got a new horse? You'd tell yourself this was goin'

155

to be the best one you ever had. They get the same feelin' every time they buy a new lease or spud in a new well. It's an intoxication, like. We've all got to have some kind of intoxication to keep us goin'. They just drink a different brand of whisky, is all."

"I wouldn't trade a good ranch for the whole damned oilfield . . . if I *had* a good ranch instead of that little old saddle-blanket outfit out yonder."

Stringfellow's eyes took on a twinkle. "I might trade my horse pasture for a couple of good wells." The old sheepman looked in surprise toward the restaurant's front door. "Speak of the devil."

Turning, Dave saw Underwood's young wife enter. Knox Anderson followed. Anderson's head was bandaged. Anderson nodded at Dave and Stringfellow. Both men got to their feet as the pair approached. Anderson asked, "Sheriff, have you ever met Elise Underwood?"

"Not actually met," Dave said, "though I've seen her in town." He added pointedly, "I know *Mr.* Underwood. I suppose he'll be comin' along pretty soon?"

Anderson said in haste, "Elise and I are old friends. When she heard what happened, she came to town to make certain I'm all right."

Elise Underwood nodded self-consciously. "Victor was anxious to know too."

Anderson shook hands with Henry Stringfellow, then said, "I couldn't send her back out there hungry. Come, Elise, I see a vacant table."

Dave watched them move toward a back corner.

Stringfellow said quietly, "Don't have such a suspicious mind, Dave. I know the young lady, and I know her husband."

"I wasn't thinkin' anything," Dave said defensively. But he was remembering what Jolene had said about Anderson's preference for small, petite women. He hadn't seen many more petite than Elise Underwood.

He drove by Waddy's house and picked him up at dark. Waddy asked eagerly, "You bring my shotgun?"

"I don't think we'll need it. I brought flashlights instead." He drove up to the corner of the block where he had a good view of the front door of Jolene's place. "Waddy, I'll stay here. I want

you to go find yourself a place where you can see the back door."
He described the prostitute known as Flower, though he added,
"I doubt you'll know her in the dark, so if any woman goes out
the back way, you come right quick and tell me. But don't let her
see you."

"You mean that's all we're watchin' for, is a woman?"

"That's all. Whatever else goes on is none of our concern."

Waddy took the bright view. "The back door is the most
interestin' one anyway. I'm anxious to see who goes in."

"None of it is any of our business except that woman." Waddy
was willing and able to start a lot of gossip. It would be hard to
make him keep his mouth shut when this was over.

Dave watched Waddy walk down to the corner, cross the street
and disappear behind the building. He wished the deputy had
enough imagination to have gone the long way and come back
around surreptitiously, but he decided it was his own fault for
not telling him. Chances were slim that Flower had seen him
anyway, or that if she had seen him she realized he was an officer.
The moon had not yet risen, so the night was black. He settled
back in the car seat for what was likely to be a long wait.

It was much longer than he expected. He glanced at his pocketwatch every quarter hour or so, tilting it so that dim light from
nearby windows would pick up the hands. He watched the passing traffic, the sporadic stream of business in and out of Jolene's.
He could not help wondering idly if she might be making more
money than just about anybody in the oilfield. Of course, she
had a lot of expenses . . . rent, lights, a number of women to
feed and to pay. Even allowing for this being a Sunday night, her
establishment was doing more than a creditable amount of
trade. After ten-thirty or eleven o'clock, it tapered off fairly
rapidly, however. Sunday pleasures had to give way to Monday-
morning realities.

His watch told him it had been an hour since the last man had
entered the house, at least by the front door. He had kept a
rough count, and most if not all had left by a little past midnight.
Even if Flower had done her share of the business, it was likely
she was through by now. She might be slipping out at any time.
But he waited, and watched, and waited some more. Most of the
building's lights had long since winked out, even the one in the
front lobby. He looked at his watch. Past one-thirty, going on
two.

He didn't need two sleepless nights in a row. But it looked as if this one was going to work out that way.

Two o'clock. He began seriously thinking about driving around to pick up Waddy and abandoning the vigil. Sleep weighed heavily on him. He had to fight to keep from giving in to it. He wished he had a cup of hot, black coffee.

He saw a movement on the dark front porch, and he sat up quickly. A form moved briskly toward him. He could tell that this was a woman by the way she moved, and that she was probably not the one he had been watching for. He could not make out the details of the face, but the voice was Jolene's.

"Sheriff, she went out the back door."

"Waddy's back there. I told him to come get me."

"I know where he's at, and he hasn't moved. I think he went to sleep on you."

"Oh hell," he exclaimed, jumping out of the car. "Do you know which direction she went?"

"I sent Lydia out to follow her."

He saw another woman trotting toward him in the dim light of the moon. She hurried up to the car, pointing eastward. "Sheriff, she's goin' up the alley, that way. She's not movin' very fast, stayin' in the shadows. You'll want to be careful not to scare her."

"East," he said. The Permian Hotel came quickly to mind. "You-all go punch up Waddy for me, please. Tell him to follow after me but to try to make less noise than a remuda of horses."

Jolene remarked, "With that kind of help, you sure need the Rangers." The two women disappeared in the shadows.

Flashlight in his hand but not turned on, Dave walked due eastward, then turned at the next corner and cut across to the alley. At first he saw nothing. Then he heard a dog bark. Against the faint light of someone's back-porch lantern, he glimpsed a movement, a slight figure moving along the alley a block ahead of him. One moment it was there, and the next it was gone. It had to be her. He followed, trying to make up some of the distance without moving into more than an easy trot, keeping to the shadows himself. She reached the unpaved highway and crossed in quick steps, looking back over her shoulder. He stopped and stood still, hoping she had not seen him.

He was certain now; she was heading for the Permian Hotel,

where O'Dell and his partner had stayed. He lost sight of her, however, in dark shadow where none of the faint moonlight penetrated. He held up at the edge of the highway, fearing she might see him and be frightened away. He waited a painful minute or two, then decided the risk of losing her was greater than the risk of scaring her off. He crossed over, walking as quietly as he could in his high-heeled boots.

He reached the corner of the hotel and stopped, looking. He saw her nowhere. He moved around to the front of the building. If she had been there she was gone. He retraced his steps. He could not see her on the off side either. Maybe on the other end. He started that way, then halted abruptly as a dog growled. The sound came from beneath the hotel. A second dog took it up. His first thought was that they heard his footsteps and were growling at him.

Then he saw a faint light, shining like a firefly through a hole in one of the metal sheets that made up the apron around the hotel's foundation. Just ahead of him, a sheet of it was bent back. He saw a beam of light reflected through the opening. Someone was crawling around under there with a flashlight, stirring up the dogs that used the space beneath the hotel as a sleeping area. He heard a dragging sound, then the light went out. He moved back flat against the wall. He saw a head emerge from the opening in the apron. The woman looked quickly in both directions, failed to see him, then crawled out on hands and knees. She stood up, holding something bulky.

Her back was turned to him as he stepped up close. "Young lady, I'll take that satchel."

She gasped in fright and dropped it.

He shined the flashlight beam in her face. "You're under arrest, Flower."

She sank to her knees and began to sob. About that time, Waddy came running up. Dave shined the light on him to be sure. Waddy exclaimed, "I wasn't asleep, Dave. I just didn't see her come out."

"There were two of them came out. You didn't see either one." Damn it all, he needed to find Waddy some other line of work. "Pick up that satchel she dropped."

Waddy complied. "You reckon this is Knox Anderson's payroll?"

Short of patience, Dave demanded, "Why? You thinkin' about runnin' off with it?"

"No, Dave, you know I wouldn't do such as that. I'd never . . ." He stopped, realizing Dave didn't mean it. "I'm sorry, Dave. I didn't mean to go to sleep. But it got awful quiet . . ."

Dave put his hands under Flower's thin arms and gently brought her to her feet. "Come on, young lady. We're not fixin' to hurt you, but we've got some talkin' to do."

Waddy asked, "We takin' her to jail?"

He hadn't guarded many women prisoners. Dave thought he could already sense the worry running through Waddy's mind. What would Annabelle say, him spending the night in the jail with a female prisoner?

"We're takin' her back to Jolene's first. She'll be needin' to gather up her things."

"Good idea." Finally, Waddy was going to see the inside of Jolene's place, and on official business.

Flower walked haltingly at first, trembling with fear. She said nothing all the way back to Jolene's. The light was on in Jolene's parlor. The madam evidently was expecting Dave's return. "Open the door for us, Waddy."

Waddy bustled ahead to obey. "I don't know what I'm goin' to tell Annabelle."

Dave suspected Annabelle was just as curious about Jolene's as Waddy.

Jolene and Lydia stood waiting in the parlor. Jolene's voice was angry. "Damn you, Flower, you tryin' to give my house a bad name?"

Lydia's voice was tinged with regret. "I'm sorry, Flower. I wish you hadn't gotten mixed up in a thing like this."

Dave motioned for Flower to sit on a couch. "Suppose you tell me about it."

Tears shining on her cheeks, Flower kept her head down. "I can't tell you anything."

Dave said, "Suppose then that I tell *you* what happened. You fingered Knox Anderson for O'Dell. When I didn't give him a chance to get the money before he left town, he phoned you to get it for him."

She looked little and alone, sitting there forlornly on the

couch. In a breaking voice, she said, "I can't tell you anything. They might kill me. That Skinny would, for sure."

Lydia sat down beside Flower and took her hands. "What kind of hold do they have on you?"

Flower shook her head but did not answer.

Jolene declared, "I don't see where that matters. She helped rob one of my good customers."

Lydia told Flower, "Turk and Big Boy had a hold on me once. I finally managed to get away from them. You can too. Sheriff Buckalew's a just man. If you tell him what he wants to know, he can keep them away from you."

Flower sobbed. "No. They'll kill me."

Dave said sternly, "The alternative is jail. Probably the pen. You're an accessory to armed robbery."

She did not look at him. "Better jail than to have them come after me. You just don't know them."

Lydia squeezed Flower's hands. "*I* know them. What're they holdin' over your head?"

"Murder. A girl where I used to work. I didn't kill her; Skinny did it with his knife. But Turk said they'd prove I did it if I wouldn't do what they told me."

Lydia looked up at Dave, those hazel eyes pleading. "Give her a chance, Sheriff."

Dave was tempted. He opened the satchel and spilled the money out onto a table, then counted it. "Somethin' like three hundred dollars short."

Jolene said, "I found about two hundred in her room. Like as not, damn them, they spent the rest."

The girl said, "The money in my room is Mr. Anderson's. Most of it, anyway. He treated me nice. Give it back to him."

Dave sat down beside her. She drew away from him, leaning to Lydia. He said, "It would help a lot if you'd talk. We could put them away on your testimony to where they never could hurt you again."

He could see that she was far more fearful of the gang than she would ever be of himself or jail. She did not look like a prostitute now, or an accomplice to robbery. She looked like a lost little girl.

"Where's your home?" he asked.

He could barely hear her voice. "Ohio."

161

"Did you ever tell any of them where you came from?"

"I never told anybody. And I never gave them my real name. I didn't want my folks to ever find out what I was doin'."

"How'd you like to go back home?"

"I just wish I could."

Dave looked at the other women. Jolene frowned. Lydia looked pleased. He said, "There's a bus that leaves here about seven-thirty in the mornin', goin' to Fort Worth. There you can connect to wherever you want to go. I think Mr. Anderson might be glad to see us use a little of his money for a bus ticket and expenses. Reward for you findin' his payroll."

She blinked away the tears. He saw first disbelief, then joy in her eyes. "You mean it?"

"I'll buy you the ticket and put you on the bus myself. All I want is your promise that you'll never come back, and that you'll find some better way to make your livin'."

Flower turned into Lydia's arms and cried a little. Dave glanced at Jolene, seeking support. Jolene looked dubious. "If you want to trust a little whore . . ."

Lydia said, "I don't think she'll let you down, Sheriff. But that Skinny's a man who likes to use his knife. I'd hate to think what he'd do to her if he thought she had taken the money and run off with it."

"That's what he *will* think," Dave said. "All the more reason for her to go back home and stay there where he can't ever find her."

Lydia smiled at him. "You're a good man, Mr. Buckalew."

"I just hope I'm not a stupid one." He studied Flower critically. "Where's her room?"

Jolene pointed toward the stairs. "Up yonder."

"I want to get the rest of the money that belongs to Mr. Anderson. I'm goin' to lock it up where nobody can get at it."

Waddy said hopefully, "You want me to come with you, Dave?"

Dave knew the deputy was boiling with curiosity. "Might be a good idea. You can keep an eye on Flower." He knew that was not necessary, but the trip upstairs would give Waddy something to talk about for a month. The three women went up with them to Flower's room. Flower retrieved the money from a cardboard suitcase that reeked of bad perfume. "About twenty of that was mine to start with," she said.

Dave said, "Take out what's yours." After she did, he put the rest in the satchel. He glanced at the window. "You've never jumped out of a second-story window, have you?"

"No."

"Well, don't. It's a mighty hard bump when you hit the ground. You'd be broken up a way too bad for a bus ride. But not for a jail cell." He walked back into the hallway, waited for Jolene and Lydia to come out, then asked Jolene, "You have a key to this door?"

Jolene produced a long key from her pocket. Dave used it, tested the doorknob and found it secure.

Jolene said, "I could roust Ox out and have him stand guard here all night."

Lydia shook her head. "You know how Ox would guard her. He'd be in bed with her whether she wanted him there or not." She turned to Dave. "I'll vouch for her, Sheriff. I'll have her at the station before bus time."

Dave glanced at Jolene. She said, "With that door locked, she can't go anywhere but out the window. And like you said, it's a long ways down."

He looked back at Lydia. "I'll be at the station ten minutes before the bus pulls in."

Lydia's eyes were warm with gratitude. "I do think she deserves another chance, Sheriff. I'm glad you're givin' it to her."

"I just hope she isn't givin' it to *me*."

Jolene still harbored reservations. "There isn't anything to keep her from gettin' off that bus anywhere she wants to."

He said, "Sometimes you just got to put faith in people." ·

"And keep a billy club hidden behind your back."

He sent Waddy home and locked Anderson's satchel in an empty jail cell. He thought that ought to be as safe a place as any; he had never heard of anybody breaking *into* jail. There wasn't enough night left to justify his going to his room in the hotel. He set an alarm clock he kept in his rolltop desk and bedded down on the cot in his office, not taking off anything except his boots.

It seemed he had barely placed his head on the pillow when the alarm sounded. He got up grumbling to himself about the perversity of a good little cowtown that had allowed itself to get caught up in the turmoil of an oil boom and spoiled as sweet a job as a man could ever ask for. He had gotten up a lot earlier than this in his cowboy days, but he had usually gone to bed soon after the chickens. It seemed to him that part of this town never did go to bed. Sometimes he wondered why he went to the expense of keeping a room. Too many nights, he didn't get to use it.

He started to shave but thought the hell with it. He didn't have to put on a show for anybody in this town. They could take him as he came or go around. He felt the need of some strong black coffee, but there wasn't time. He pulled on his boots, washed his face in cold water and walked down to the little stuccoed frame building that served as bus station. He was a few minutes earlier than he had to be, and he considered buying a cup of coffee in the station café. But he had been burned in that place before. Its coffee was worse than the skimmings from Preacher Perry's worst batch of bootleg. He would wait and have breakfast later at the Dutchman's.

He stood outside on the wooden walk rather than face the smell of burned toast and coffee spilled on a hot stovetop. He saw the two women walking hurriedly along, just as promised. Flower was the one he should be concerned with, but it was Lydia he watched. She was a fine-looking woman, he thought. It was a damned shame that circumstances had shoved her onto the wrong road and closed the gate. *That's the oil business for you. Ruins whatever it touches.*

Flower had all her belongings on her back and in the single cardboard suitcase. She set the suitcase on the sidewalk. "I'm here, Sheriff."

"Good. We'll go in and buy your ticket." He picked up her suitcase, then considered how strange it might look to anybody passing by, seeing him carry a suitcase for a prostitute who technically was under arrest. *Well, the hell with them. It's too early in the morning to worry about what anybody thinks.*

She was about to tell the name of the town where she wanted to go, but Dave stopped her. It occurred to him that if O'Dell or anybody came looking, they would probably check out the bus station. A few dollars would loosen the tongue of the station clerk. He said, "We'll buy you a ticket to Fort Worth. When you

164

get there, you buy what you need for the rest of the trip." In a place as busy as Fort Worth, no ticket seller was likely to remember Flower.

She said, "You trust me, Sheriff?"

"You think I shouldn't?"

"I gave you my word. I'll keep it."

The bus pulled in three minutes ahead of the posted time and discharged half a dozen passengers. Dave looked them over carefully, though he doubted it would do him any good. He could not meet all the buses, and even if he did, he could not judge most people by their outward appearance. Some of the roughest-looking roustabouts he had seen in the oilfield knew the Bible backward and forward, while some people who looked like they ought to be teaching Sunday school would steal your socks from inside your boots as you walked down the street.

The bus driver unloaded several suitcases and dropped off a couple of bundles of newspapers. Flower was his only new passenger. "Aboard!" he shouted, standing at the open door.

Lydia hugged Flower and said, "You don't need to write. It's just as well if nobody knows where you are."

Flower murmured, "I won't forget you, Lydia." She turned and held out her hand to Dave. "I won't forget you either, Sheriff. And I'll keep the promise I gave you."

He shook her hand, and left a roll of greenbacks in it. "You watch out for yourself."

He watched the bus pull away, holding his breath until the black smoke had drifted. He stepped up beside Lydia, whose gaze followed the bus. "You know she could get off that bus in Odessa and run right back where she came here from."

Lydia declared firmly, "She won't. She meant what she told you. You were right to trust her."

"Gettin' to where I don't trust anybody very far anymore," he admitted. "Sometimes I don't even like myself."

Lydia smiled and touched his arm. "You should, Mr. Buckalew. You're a kind and decent man. Don't ever change."

Her fingers dug in a little, and her eyes seemed to glaze. He thought she was probably reacting to Flower's leaving. She turned and hurried back down the street. He watched her as long as she was in sight. He brought his left hand up and rested it over the place where she had squeezed his arm.

165

12

The Widow England's

CAPROCK was the third boomtown in which Widow England's rooming house had opened its many doors to oilfield laborers needing a place to sleep. With each move, its rambling one-story frame structure was divided into sections, transported on a flatbed truck, then reassembled. The edges at which it was nailed back together were covered with strips of sheetiron to hide the irregular marks of the saw, and to make it less evident that the sections had settled at different angles that did not quite match. None of that mattered much in Ragtown, for expediency was prized over esthetics.

The place suited Slim McIntyre. He spent little time there anyway, except for sleeping. His only reservation was that it cost him a dollar a night—paid a week in advance—for a small, plain room that had a screened door but no window, a cot and mattress for his blankets and an ancient dresser to hold his few extra clothes. The dresser was missing one foot, victim of some long-forgotten accident, and a red brick was wedged beneath that corner to prevent a tipover. A bare light bulb hung from the middle of the stained sheetrock ceiling, for electricity had reached this part of Ragtown. A chipped white enameled washpan sat on top of a wooden applecrate that had a shelf built in to hold his towels. The only other item Mrs. England furnished was a Bible and a framed picture of Jesus to remind her roomers that though this was a heathenish boomtown, she and the Lord watched their every move. An empty cot filled what little space was left.

The landlady had promised to lower Slim's rent a little if another man came along to share his lodgings.

A windmill and small wooden tank provided water for the house, though the only indoor plumbing was in Mrs. England's personal living quarters at one end of the L-shaped structure. She rented out eight little rooms, all like Slim's, each having a single screened door that opened to the inside of the L, where she could observe the men's comings and goings and perhaps be aware of any departures from her rules of conduct.

The men who roomed there were either single, like Slim, or were married men whose families awaited them elsewhere. There were no facilities for cooking or the other necessities of family life. The thin sheetrock walls afforded none of the privacy that a married couple would have wanted, even if a woman were otherwise willing to put up with the Spartan accommodations.

In the night, Slim could hear the snoring of a tooldresser four rooms over. The men were expected to fill their washpans outdoors from a faucet suspended beneath the storage tank. A two-holer privy stood just beyond. For bathing, Mrs. England provided a small shower house, somewhat larger than a telephone booth, beside the windmill. Its sheetiron siding answered the demands of propriety by shielding the bather from public view. A steel barrel sat on top, the water taking what heat it might from the sun. It struck Slim as ironic that despite all the natural gas being flared off and wasted by the many torches that burned in the oilfields, no gas was to be had in Ragtown for heating water or cooking.

The sun was low on a Saturday afternoon as Mr. Birdsong stopped his nitro car in the dirt street beside the rooming house and Slim opened the door to get out. Birdsong gave the structure a moment's study. "Hardly fancy," he conceded, "but Mrs. England is a fine Christian woman, and I am told that her roof does not leak."

Slim shrugged. "I can't say one way or another. It hasn't rained since I took a room here."

"But some night it will, even in this desert, and you will be thankful for a solid roof over your head. I trust you will be ready for work Monday morning?" Not everybody in the oilfield would be.

"Yes sir, you can pick me up in front of the Teagarden."

"Bad business, taking all your meals in a restaurant. A sinful waste of money and ruinous on the stomach."

"I buy meal tickets now. That makes it cheaper. And Mrs. Whitmore's a good cook. A lot better than I'd be if I was cookin' for myself."

"Wasteful of your fortune, nevertheless."

Slim had learned that Birdsong was a widower, living alone in a small shotgun house near the edge of town. He prepared most of his own meals but had never invited Slim to share one with him, so Slim had no idea if the man was much of a cook. His spare frame suggested that he probably would not win prizes.

From the street, Slim had to walk around the end of the L and then turn back toward his own room. Mrs. England stood in her doorway, keeping watch as her roomers drifted in from work. She was a tall, plain woman in her fifties, friendly to a point but always holding something in reserve as if she might need room to back away in case a person failed to live up to her expectations.

She called to him and stepped out onto the narrow porch in front of the only entrance to her quarters. "Oh, Mr. McIntyre, you have company, a young man who said he is a friend of yours. He indicated that he might be interested in sharin' your room."

Slim was surprised to see Hap Holloway sitting on the wooden block that served as a step in front of his door. A roll of blankets and a large canvas bag sat on the ground beside him. "Thank you, Mrs. England."

She said, "He seems like a nice young man, a long way from mother and home. It's a pity he has had to suffer because he took up for the sanctity of womanhood."

Slim took a second puzzled look. Yes, it *was* Hap, all right. For a moment, he had thought she must be talking about someone else. "I wouldn't know anything about that, ma'am."

He walked toward Hap, the soft southern breeze cool against the day's sweat that had not yet dried from his shirt and underwear. He was tired, but a shower from that barrel atop the washhouse would soon put him back among the living. He extended his hand. "Howdy, Hap. What brings you . . ."

He stopped in midstride, for he saw that Hap's face was bruised, even swelling a little. He said, "You look like somethin' the cat wouldn't've drug in."

Hap stood up, bringing one hand to his face and pressing, then gingerly drawing it away. "Does it show that much?"

"It shows. You didn't try to get fresh with Tracy Whitmore again, did you?" Then he saw that Hap's knuckles were skinned and swollen.

"It was the Haskell brothers. I finally decided I'd better split the blanket with them fellers. By damn, cowboy, they'll hurt a man."

"I figured that out the first time they came into my view."

"We quit that pipeline job and drawed our time. Wasn't nothin' would do those boys but we ought to play a little poker. Thought they'd win my wages away from me, but they got awful touchy when it turned the other way. Accused me of cheatin'."

"Did you?"

"Sure I did. So did they. I'm just slicker at it, is all."

"What's that Mrs. England was sayin' about you takin' up for womanhood, or some such of a thing?"

"Oh, I might've stretched the story just a mite. Told her I had to fight a couple of old boys that was usin' bad language in front of a lady. I didn't tell her the lady was the queen of hearts. I got the notion she wouldn't take kindly to the whole truth, so I gave her the part of it that I thought she might like. It ain't as though I told a flat-out lie."

169

"You came awful close. Looks like you got all your worldly possessions with you."

"I was thinkin' maybe you'd like to have me move in and keep you company. The widder said with two of us here the rent would only be a dollar and half a day, total. Since you're already payin' a dollar anyhow, I'd be glad to throw in the other fifty cents."

Slim frowned. "I had to quit school in the ninth grade and go to work, but I learned enough arithmetic to know that half of a dollar-fifty is seventy-five cents."

Hap looked hurt. "I never thought I'd ever see two cowboys quibble over a quarter. But I reckon the whole world is goin' mad over money. You got the key to the door?"

"There isn't any key. There isn't any lock. You could've just opened the door and gone in."

Hap cheerfully accepted that as an invitation. He picked up the canvas bag and roll of blankets. "I hope the Haskell brothers don't find out about that. They'd be over here some night, checkin' out the boys' pockets."

"I never did understand how you could hook up with a pair like that. You know Sheriff Buckalew thinks they're probably the ones that robbed me."

Hap made no reply.

Slim said, "It was dark that night, but not so dark that you wouldn't've recognized somebody you know as well as you know those Haskells."

Hap felt of the flat mattress on the empty cot. "I wonder what jailhouse she bought this out of?" He dropped the blanket roll and the bag on top of it. "How come you decided to live under a roof like a human bein' instead of sleepin' out on the ground?"

"It came a rain one night."

"You could've slept in Ol' Man Birdsong's nitro shed."

"I'd sooner curl up in a rattlesnake den."

"Better this way," Hap said approvingly. "You've got all the comforts of home. Any room left in that dresser?"

Slim moved his own belongings into the top two drawers, leaving the lower two for Hap. "You never did say anything to what the sheriff thinks about the Haskell brothers."

Hap looked at the back wall. "They ought to put a window in

here. I'll bet this room gets mighty hot when we move into full summer."

For lack of a better answer, Slim decided that Hap had told him all he needed to know. He had laid a clean set of clothes on his cot when he emptied the bottom dresser drawers. He gathered up those and a towel. "I'm fixin' to take me a shower."

"Goin' to paint the town a Saturday-night red?"

"Not even a little bit pink. Lauralou Clive said she'd be in from the ranch tonight. Thought we'd eat supper together and go to the picture show."

"Must be nice to have a girlfriend who drives a car. Where do you-all go after the show is over?"

"She goes home to the ranch. I come back here."

"That's all? She just up and goes home? Ain't you ever brought her to your room?"

"No. This is no place for a girl like Lauralou. Anyway, Mrs. England would throw a conniption fit."

"A car is a fine place for a little rubbin' and squeezin' out where it's good and dark. Don't tell me you ain't . . ."

Slim said tightly, "Lauralou's a nice country girl. She wouldn't put up with such a thing."

"Maybe you just ain't tried hard enough. You might be surprised how good she really is if you gave her a chance."

Heat rising, Slim said, "I don't *have* to let you stay here."

Hap backed off a little, raising both bruised hands. "I didn't mean nothin' by it. I guess that's the difference between us. You figure they're all good girls till you find out otherwise. I figure they're not until they show me they are."

"Like Tracy did?"

Hap grinned. "She didn't leave me no doubt where she stood. Her and you are a lot alike. If I was you, Slim, I'd go shine up to Tracy. She's more your style. Both of them girls remind me of horses, kind of."

Slim saw no comparison. "Horses?"

"Tracy's like a good, honest workin' pony that'll take you where you need to go and do whatever job needs doin'. Lauralou's like a slick little racin' filly that shines on the track but wouldn't last twenty minutes out on rough ground."

"*You* take Tracy. She's got too sharp a tongue to suit me."

"That's just a show. Life ain't paved no easy road for her. She

171

puts on that tough act like somebody raisin' his fists in self-defense. Hard luck has hit her some bad licks."

"Lauralou's got her skinned on bein' pretty. Anyway, Lauralou's a ranch girl, and I'm a ranch boy. Kind of feels a little like bein' back home when I'm with her. Except I never knew any girl back home who looked quite that good."

Hap turned to emptying the canvas bag of clothes. "Ain't no use shinin' a light on a man who'd rather stay in the dark."

Somebody had already showered ahead of Slim, using up whatever warmth the water in the barrel overhead might have drawn from the sunshine. He went into the shower with his thoughts on Lauralou and the suggestions Hap had planted in his mind. He indulged in a little deliciously erotic fantasy until the shock of the cold spray jarred him back to the moment. Shivering, he finished the bath as quickly as he could. There was no drain, so the water ran out onto the ground, where it quickly soaked into the thirsty sand. Dry, he reached around a sheetiron partition where he hung his clean clothes to keep them from getting wet. He dressed and slipped into a pair of Saturday-night shoes for which he had squandered five dollars.

Hap viewed him with faint amusement when he returned to the room. "The downfall of the cowboy. First they fenced him in, then they taught him to bathe every Saturday whether he needed it or not. God knows what indignities are still to come."

"You ain't goin' to clean up?"

"Hell yes. Just waitin' for you to get through before I throw away my own self-respect. I got them Haskell brothers' money in my pocket. I'm goin' to get me some of old Preacher Perry's good stuff, and then I'm goin' down to Shemp Oliver's dancehall and wear a hole in my shoes, and then I'm goin' to see about gettin' a woman that knows how to earn five dollars the slow way."

"Mrs. England has got some strict rules. If you bring any whisky to this house you'd better have it all inside you, and even then it'd better not show."

"It'll all be in my belly, you can rest easy on that. I figure on drinkin' ever bit of it, except what some pretty woman may need to put her in the right frame of mind."

"Hap, you've got no shame."

"Never could afford it. Life's too short to be burdened down with guilt over doin' what the good Lord gave me the makin's for. Eat, drink and chase Mary, that's my motto." He took his clothes out to the shower house. Slim heard him shout when the cold water hit him.

Maybe that'll put your fire out, he thought. *It sure worked for me.*

Any such effect was short-lived. While Hap shaved over the washbasin he talked endlessly about the women in Shemp Oliver's dancehall and those at Jolene's. He seemed to know a lot of them by their first names. He knew chapter and verse about what they would and would not do and just how they did whatever they did.

Slim declared, "I don't know when you ever had time to work. Can't you talk about anything else?"

"I talk about what interests me. And nothin' interests me more than a good-lookin' woman."

They walked together toward the business part of town, Hap still discussing the merits and shortcomings of Jolene's girls. Slim tried to act as if he was not interested, though if his arm was being twisted he would have to admit that he was intrigued by the breadth of Hap's knowledge. Hap turned down an alley, catching Slim by surprise.

Slim pointed the direction they had been walking. "The Tea-garden's thataway."

"I'm makin' a detour first. Got to see a man."

Slim quickly realized Hap's destination. It was common knowledge that bootlegger Preacher Perry set up shop from the back of his blue Packard automobile about this time most evenings, in an open lot behind an oilfield supply company's pipeyard. Saturday was by far his best night for commerce. When Slim and Hap arrived at his place of business, Perry had half a dozen customers clustered around, pressing him to take their money. There were other bootleggers in town, but Perry was reputed to have by far the largest clientele. He was said never to shortchange his customers. He gave a full dollar's worth of hangover for a dollar spent.

Watching him, Slim could see that the little red-faced man enjoyed his work. He had a grin and a joke and a bottle for each person who tendered hard-earned money. Some got a very short sermon as well. Hap and Slim stood back until Perry was temporarily caught up.

Perry did not know Slim, but he gave Hap a hearty greeting: "Well sir, Brother Holloway, back so soon?"

"Soon hell. It's been more'n three weeks. They had me captive out on that pipeline job. I finally had to mutiny to get anything stronger than coffee to drink."

"I think you'll find this worth the wait." Perry reached into the automobile and brought out a large bottle. Slim judged it must be a full quart. "I trust you have the wherewithal?"

Hap reached into his pocket. "Now Preacher, you know I've never tried to beat you out of nothin'."

"You've begged and you've borrowed, but the Lord knows I never caught you stealing." Perry nevertheless counted the money. His gaze shifted to Slim. "And what's for you, brother? Plain shine, or had you rather have the imported stuff?" Imported from Mexico, he meant.

Slim shook his head. "I'm just here with Hap. I don't drink much."

"An excellent choice, even though it does my business no good. Half the world's ills can be traced to whisky."

Hap smiled. "Even good whisky?"

"Good whisky attracts bad drinkers. I would be pleased if every last drop in the world were suddenly to dry up forever. But it won't, and someone else will sell it if I don't. So I peddle whisky and preach temperance."

Hap told Slim, "He didn't come by the name Preacher for nothin'. He used to ride the circuit, poundin' the Bible and hammerin' against the gates of Hell."

Perry said, "And I would be doing so even yet, were it not that the world loves spirits more than it loves the Spirit."

Hap said, "Save me a sermon. I'll repent someday, when I'm as old as you are and can't have fun anymore anyhow."

A couple of tired-looking men in oily clothes had come up behind Hap and Slim. They laughed at Hap's remark. Perry asked them what would be their pleasure.

One said, "I come to buy me a half a pint, but I do believe that young feller's right. Enjoy while you can, because maybe tomorrow you can't. So make it a full pint." He winked at Hap. "First thing you know, people may start takin' Preacher's sermons to heart. Maybe you ought to stand around here and keep talkin' so Preacher won't sermon himself onto the dole."

Perry stared after the two men as they left. He frowned thoughtfully at Hap. "The gentleman may be right. The last helper I had quit me to go into business for himself. He was a knothead anyway. The Lord is certain to smite him. Am I to understand that you are at liberty?"

Hap said, "If you mean am I out of work, I am. Pipelinin' gets almighty hard on a man's back."

"You would find some heavy lifting in this job as well, on occasion. We sometimes have to transport the product in large containers."

"There's a heap of difference between liftin' bottles and liftin' pipe. I do believe I'm your man."

"You have been a good customer, Brother Holloway, so I know you can drink it. But can you leave it alone when it is time to work?"

"I've been fired for other things, but not for drinkin' on the job."

Perry's red face twisted as he considered the proposition. "That easy smile of yours should make you a good salesman. How about going to work right now? On a tryout basis."

Hap hesitated. "To tell the truth, I was fixin' to have me a night on the town. But . . ." He shrugged and looked at Slim. "I reckon the ladies'll just have to bear up under their disappointment." He held out his newly purchased bottle to Perry. "I reckon I'll have to sell this back to you."

Perry shook his head. "Sell it to the next customer. I see a couple of them coming now."

Slim grimaced. "It took me more than a week after I hit town before I found me a job. You stumble over one before you've even had supper."

"Talent, cowboy. You just got to have the merchandise that fits the market."

"Mrs. England is apt to throw you back out on the road before you get a chance to warm your mattress."

"I'd hate to see the poor woman distressed. Best thing is just not to tell her." Hap stuck out his hand. "Well then, go on to your supper and your picture show. And remember what I told you about women. If you never try, you never know."

Slim was relieved to leave Hap behind him. He had wondered how to ditch him gracefully. He would not have been surprised if

Hap had eaten supper with him and Lauralou and let Slim pick up the whole check. He did not care to share Lauralou's infrequent company with Hap or anybody else.

He found the Teagarden crowded as was usual for a Saturday night. His gaze roamed the mass of oilfield workers, searching in vain for Lauralou. He was always a little early, and she was always a little late, it seemed. He saw Tracy Whitmore, however. The waitress's gray eyes were fixed on him. She shrugged as if to tell him there was no vacant table and nodded toward one empty stool at the counter. He shrugged to tell her he would wait.

He must have spent twenty minutes standing at the door, watching others eat. Finally a couple of men finished their meal at a small corner table and stood up. There had been a time when Slim would have been courteous enough to let someone else have the table, but the hurly-burly of the oilfield had taught him that he who does not take care of himself is not likely to be taken care of. He moved quickly across the room to claim the place before someone else could.

Tracy took her time getting around to clearing his table. "Two glasses of water, I suppose?"

He wondered if he detected sarcasm in her voice or if he just expected it so much that he imagined it. "She'll be along pretty soon."

"She'd better be, or you'll have to go ahead and order. Mr. Schwartz doesn't like people holdin' tables on a busy night."

He thought about Hap's comparing Tracy to a good honest working pony. *Mule* might be more like it. He said, "One of these days I'm goin' to catch you smilin' at me, and the shock is liable to be fatal to both of us."

"Not likely," she said, and turned away to see after other customers. He watched her a minute, wondering how Hap could see anything in common between her and Slim.

The Dutchman looked Slim's way two or three times while he waited. Once the big man seemed about to leave his cash register and come to Slim's corner table. His ultimatum would be predictable: order or leave. But Lauralou showed up after a while, her smile shining like the sun on a new tin roof, her hair as golden as a Palomino. She paused in the doorway, her blue eyes searching while many eyes in the crowd turned toward her.

Lauralou made her way among the closely spaced tables,

176

brushing against the oilfield workers, begging their pardon but appearing to enjoy the attention they gave her. She reached out both hands for Slim to take them and turned her cheek, inviting him to kiss her. He sensed that many men in the room were watching, so he self-consciously gave her a quick peck, his face warm.

"You poor boy. I'm afraid I kept you waitin' much too long," she said.

He wished he could say something eloquent, like the florid dialogue subtitles in romantic movies, perhaps *A minute without the sight of your face is like an eternity.* But he could not bring himself to speak anything so golden. "Just a few minutes, is all. It wasn't nothin', hardly." Her blond prettiness made him tingle all over. He didn't know whether to grab and kiss her or to break and run. So he just sat there, staring.

He said, "What did you tell your daddy?"

"Nothin'. He hasn't been home since yesterday mornin'. Off somewhere on a drunk, I imagine. Wherever there's a rodeo or a high-stakes poker game. Or maybe a woman. Doesn't take much to make him leave the ranch. But I don't want to talk about Papa. I want to talk about you. What kind of excitement have you been up to all week?"

He did not understand her fixation on excitement, but he went along with it. He told her that he and Mr. Birdsong had shot three wells, one for Humble and two for Knox Anderson. He thought her eyes brightened a little at the mention of Anderson's name.

She asked, "What kind of a man is Mr. Anderson? Besides rich, I mean."

Slim shrugged. "I don't know that much about him. He's always around when we get to a well, but he takes his crews and leaves when we get ready to plant a charge. Nice feller, from what I can see." He wondered uneasily about her interest. "Middle-aged, of course. He's got to be a way over thirty, probably closer to forty. Why?"

"No special reason. I'm just curious why a man like him, with all that money, isn't married. Looks to me like the women would be standin' in long lines to get at him."

"You thinkin' about startin' a line?" he asked her, feeling a flicker of jealousy.

"Oh no, a man with all his background wouldn't look at a simple country girl. I'm just curious about people like him. We never used to have any of that kind around here. I can't help thinkin' what a catch he would make for some lucky woman who knows how to grab and hold on."

Slim would not pretend to know what there was about a man that would make a woman look twice. Except money, of course. From a few things Mr. Birdsong had told him, he gathered that many women did indeed set snares for the driller Anderson, but like a wise fox, he always managed to slip through without getting caught. Mr. Birdsong had indicated that Anderson once courted a woman but lost her to someone else, and now he took his women the way he took his whisky, casually, in moderation and without commitment.

He thought it best to change the subject. "What do you want for supper?"

"Whatever you're havin'." That always left the choice to him, and out of fear of looking cheap he had to order something pricey, a dollar's worth apiece, or even a dollar and a quarter.

Tracy Whitmore came over with menus under her arm. Slim did not need to look at the café's menu; he knew it by heart. Its only change since he had come to Caprock was a price rise penciled in on several of the items. Whatever shortcomings he might have in other ways, the Dutchman was a keen hand with figures.

"Steak and potatoes for both of us," Slim ordered.

Tracy gave Lauralou a quick study. "Had you just as soon have some greens as the potatoes, Lauralou? Looks to me like you might've put on a little weight."

Slim hadn't noticed it. She looked just fine to him.

Lauralou gave Tracy a cold smile. "The potatoes sound fine."

Tracy looked at Slim. "I ought to tell you, Mr. Schwartz raised the price of steak by twenty cents."

Slim mentally calculated what the extra forty cents would mean to him. That was almost as much as the picture show tickets would cost. He hoped Lauralou had not marked his hesitation. He told Tracy, "I can handle that."

"Suit yourself." Tracy gave Lauralou another quick glance and turned back toward the kitchen. The first time he had ever seen the two women together, Slim had sensed that neither had a nickel's worth of use for the other.

Lauralou said, "I wish there was another decent restaurant in this town."

There were other restaurants, and Slim went to them on occasion. They were hole-in-the-wall hamburger grills and chili joints, okay for himself but nothing to which he would take a girl like Lauralou. "Don't let Tracy get under your skin," he said. "I don't know what makes her so sassy."

"She's probably jealous."

"Of what?"

"Of me, because of you."

He shook his head. "She hasn't spoken ten civil words to me since I came to Caprock."

Lauralou nodded knowingly. "That's the first sign."

Slim noticed that as she went on talking to him about one subject and then another, her gaze returned often to Tracy.

Tracy brought the steaks after a while, each on a large platter with thickly sliced fried potatoes. She said to Lauralou, "Since you like potatoes so well, and you're not worried about your weight, I fetched you a little extra helpin'. Enjoy them."

"I will." Lauralou gave her that same cold smile again. "Tell me, Tracy, why I never see you anywhere except here. Never at the picture show or anywhere like that. Can't you get you a boyfriend to take you places?"

"If I ever wanted to go anywhere, I'm a grown woman and could take myself. Boyfriends are your department. I need one of those like I need a sore back. Catsup, either of you? Or maybe some hotsauce?"

Lauralou glanced warmly at Slim. "I have everything I need."

Slim felt his face flush. "Me too."

Tracy's tone was laced with sarcasm. "Fine. We like to see our customers get everything they want, and all they deserve. If you need somethin', just holler."

Every time Slim looked at Lauralou he found her staring speculatively at him. Uncomfortable, he tried to devote most of his immediate attention to eating the steak. He asked her, "Do you know what's playin' at the picture show tonight?"

"Somethin' with Clara Bow, I think. She's a sassy one too. Reminds me a little of Tracy Whitmore."

Lauralou waited while he paid the Dutchman at the cash register. As Tracy came out of the kitchen and looked toward them, Lauralou tucked her arm beneath Slim's. Slim sensed that many of the men in the room were watching. There weren't many girls around who had Lauralou's splendid blond looks. Being with her, he felt a little like a stud colt on exhibition at a horse show.

The streetlights were shining, and the Saturday night traffic was heavy as they left the restaurant. He turned left toward the movie theater, but Lauralou pulled him back. She said, "My car's parked up this way."

"It's not much of a walk to the picture show."

"Would it be all the same to you if we didn't go to the picture show tonight? Clara Bow always wins. This time I'd sooner go dancin'."

Slim felt a momentary panic. The first place that came to mind was Shemp Oliver's dime-a-dance joint. The girls all worked for Oliver. He couldn't take Lauralou there.

She seemed to know what he was thinking. "There's the Kit Kat out at the edge of town."

Slim had not been in the place. He knew it by reputation only, that it was a honkytonk where men sometimes took their wives but might as often take someone other than their wives. It was a place where Preacher Perry's batch-brewed beer found consistent and uncritical favor, and where a man not careful what he said or who he danced with could find himself nursing a broken jaw.

"I'm not sure you'd like the place."

"I've been there, and I like it. Crank the jitney."

The car, she told him, had been her mother's. It was several years old. Keeping the battery charged up and the tires aired gave her an excuse for driving to town every so often, one even her father could accept. That she usually did it on a Saturday night did not seem to bother him overly much, for by Saturday night he was usually either away somewhere himself or too far gone on Preacher Perry's bootleg to pay much notice. She drove up to the honkytonk, then pulled around in back of it to park, well out of sight of anyone passing by on the road.

As the motor stopped, he could hear jazz music coming through the open window of the building. She reached over and

180

touched his leg, catching him by surprise. "Doesn't that music make you want to get up and do somethin' wild?" she asked.

"I'm not much of a dancer," he warned her. "Ranch dances is about all I've ever been to, so I don't know the steps."

"You just keep up with me, Slim. I'll show you all the steps you need to know."

The building was a crude frame, like so many put up in the boomtown, with little attention to looks or permanence. It was covered with black tarpaper to keep wind and rain from penetrating between the rough planks that were its siding. Near the door, where a single large light bulb showed visitors the way, some of the tarpaper was peeling and hanging down, exposing the bare wood beneath. A sign was nailed beneath the light. It showed a black cat with suggestive feminine features and the name of the business: KIT KAT KLUB. A smaller sign gave notice: NO CHECKS, CASH ONLY.

That was no problem for Slim. He had no bank account anyway. His business with Mr. Birdsong had been strictly in currency. He wished only that it would last longer than it did. It seemed to him that in his cowboy days, when he *had* had a bank account, the money stretched farther.

A dour woman just inside the door took a dollar of it as a cover charge without any evident gratitude. She looked as if she could probably qualify for the steer wrestling in a country rodeo. "Find your own table," she said. "Any one that's empty."

"Yes ma'am," Slim responded.

Lauralou started tugging him across the edge of the rough pine-lumber dancefloor to a small table near the back wall. A couple of the dancers bumped Slim before he could get out of their way. They did not seem to notice, for they were caught up in the fast-moving music, played by a small band consisting only of a piano, a clarinet and a trumpet. The piano player sat on a thick red cushion and bounced up and down to the rapid beat.

It was nothing like the guitar and fiddle music to which Slim had danced in ranch barns. "I don't know if I can do this."

"Get a little beer down you and you can do anything," Lauralou said, smiling. "Don't be so self-conscious." She drummed her fingers on the table, keeping up with the rhythm.

A peroxided waitress in a short skirt and rolled-down stockings came to the table in a minute. Lauralou did not wait for Slim to order. She said, "Two beers."

The waitress eyed Slim with reservations. "It's cash only. In advance."

Slim gave her a dollar bill. The evening had whittled his savings more than he expected.

Lauralou said excitedly, "Don't you just love this place? It's so raw and plain, no show or pretense or anything. Just people drinkin' and dancin' and havin' a big time and not carin' what anybody else thinks." Her eyes widened. She pointed with her chin.

Slim saw the driller Knox Anderson on the dancefloor, stepping in a lively fashion with a lissome young woman Slim thought he might have seen through the window of Shemp Oliver's. Anderson seemed to be enjoying himself more than any roustabout in the place.

Lauralou said, "With his money, I guess he doesn't *have* to get married. Why buy a cow when you can get milk anyway?"

Slim blinked. He would have expected such a remark from a cowboy or a roustabout, but not from a girl. At least not the ranch girls he used to know.

The waitress came with a tray, two glasses and four bottles of beer. She set it all down with a clatter. "Beer's twenty cents a bottle. I figured you'd want this much anyway. When you want some more, just give me a whistle." She held two dimes in the palm of her hand. "You figured this for a tip, didn't you?"

Slim hadn't, but he did now. He would not embarrass himself in front of Lauralou by making an issue of it.

Lauralou poured one of the glasses almost full, the foam rising up and running over the edge while she giggled with delight. She sipped quickly to catch as much of it as she could. "Stuff's too good to waste," she said.

"Where'd you learn to drink beer?" he asked. Most girls he had known would rather be caught in their bloomers than to be seen with a bottle of beer.

"Preacher Perry keeps a lot of it stored in Papa's barn, where the law won't be apt to find it. But *I* know where it is."

She had finished her first bottle before Slim was half done with his. "Come on," she said, her voice turned a little coarse. "Let's kick up a few splinters."

The best he could say for his dancing was that he did not step on her feet much. Most of the time the beat of the music seemed to stay a little ahead of him. It was hard to concentrate on it when Lauralou kept her body pressed up tightly against him, her warm cheek to his, her perfume strong in his nostrils. He was glad the place was poorly lighted so everybody could not see the extent of his arousal. Lauralou could not possibly be oblivious to it.

When Lauralou finally tired, they returned to the table. She put away the second beer. He was still working on his first, so he shoved his second bottle over in front of her.

Knox Anderson and the young woman danced by the table and stopped. Anderson shoved out his hand. "Hello, Slim," he said. "Haven't seen you in here before."

"Haven't been before."

He spoke to Lauralou, calling her by name, which surprised Slim a bit. But after all, she did say she had been here before. Anderson introduced his dancing partner as Miss Smith.

When they danced away, Lauralou said crisply, "Smith. I suppose that's as good a name as any. Like as not, she's from that place of Jolene's."

"What would you know about Jolene's?"

"Just because I'm from the country doesn't mean I don't know what goes on in the world." She reached under the table and pinched his leg. "I'll bet I know as much as you do."

He bought Lauralou another beer and had a second one himself. Lauralou kept him on the dancefloor a lot, dancing as close as she could get and still allow them both to move. He felt he was getting drunk and knew the beer was only partially responsible for it.

Resting after dancing several numbers, he saw a new couple come in. He knew the man only by sight, for Mr. Birdsong had once pointed him out. His name was Victor Underwood, and he was a driller like Knox Anderson, except without Anderson's good luck, Mr. Birdsong had said. The old shooter had never gotten a nickel's worth of business from Underwood here because Underwood had not brought in a well that had any production to shoot.

Lauralou smiled wickedly. "There's father and daughter." She pointed at Underwood and the slight young woman with him, her head barely reaching Underwood's shoulder.

Slim wondered aloud. "She's his daughter?" It didn't seem reasonable that a man would bring a daughter to a joint like this.

Lauralou said, "Not really. She's his wife. But she looks more like his daughter. I can't imagine what she can see in an old booger like that."

The couple found a table near Slim's and Lauralou's. The woman smiled easily. She looked quite pretty in the dim light. Slim thought he could tell easily enough what Underwood saw in her, but he would have to admit that the other side of the equation must have something more to it than met the eye.

Knox Anderson and his date danced around the floor, and Anderson appeared to notice the Underwoods for the first time. He glanced uneasily at the woman in his arms and stopped dancing. He took her by the arm and led her to the Underwoods' table. Underwood stood up while Anderson introduced the woman who called herself Smith. Slim thought Anderson looked a little embarrassed. He figured it was because the Underwoods had found him with a woman who in all likelihood was a prostitute. It was not long before Anderson and his date left the honkytonk. The Underwoods sat in silence, staring at the closed door for some time before they finally got up to dance.

Lauralou took that as a cue to go out on the dancefloor again. She was unsteady, leaning to him for a considerable amount of support. She laid her head heavily upon his shoulder, her face warm as if she had a fever. They were midway through a second dance when she said huskily, "I think it's time to go."

Slim looked at the empty beer bottles on their table and wondered if she was in any condition to drive home. "Sounds like a good idea to me."

The fresh air felt cool and pleasant, carrying a hint of rain. Lightning flashed, and in its moment of brilliance Slim saw towering stormclouds rapidly moving in from the west. He held firmly to Lauralou's arm, for she stumbled stepping off of the little porch onto the bare ground. She swung around and grabbed him with both arms, holding him tightly. To his surprise, she kissed him, her lips soft and warm and insistent. He had a strong feeling of intoxication again, though he had drunk but two beers the whole evening.

She seemed not to want to move on. He said, "The car's yonderway." He turned her half around and held on to her while

184

they made their way through the darkness. "Looks like it could rain in a little bit."

He found himself in a dilemma. If she were unable to drive, he would have to drive her home, for he knew no place she could stay the night here in town. Then he would be stuck miles out in the country, for he would have no way to come back until she or perhaps Trinidad Suarez could bring him sometime tomorrow. If Douglas Clive came home, the scene was likely to be unpleasant. But he knew no alternative. He reached for the doorhandle.

She caught his hand and pulled it away. She backed herself against the automobile and drew him against her with a strength he would not have thought she had. She wrapped both arms around his neck and kissed him hungrily, holding until they had to stop for breath. She brought one hand up and rubbed it against his face, kissing him on the cheek, on the chin and finally on the mouth again. She found his hand and pressed it firmly against her breast. He thought he would melt to the ground like a used-up candle.

Struggling within himself, he managed to say, "We hadn't ought to be doin' this." He had much rather simply go along with it.

"Don't you like it?" she whispered.

"I like it a way too much. You've had a lot to drink. I'd be a yellow dog to take advantage of you now."

"You're not takin' advantage. I know what I'm doin'." She unbuttoned her blouse and moved his hand inside, holding it lest he draw it away. "Now tell me you want to quit."

"No, but if I don't right now it'll be too late."

He sensed a flare of impatience in her voice. She said, "I didn't think a cowboy or a nitroglycerin man would turn away from a little risk."

"*Somebody* had better."

"I didn't bring you out here to quit on me." She held him fiercely, as if afraid he might run away. She kissed him on the face, on the neck, moving his hand down from her breast to her thigh. She whispered, "We can do this better in the car."

Lightning flashed, but he was not sure it was real. His blood was racing, his face fever-hot. Had this been some dancehall girl, he would be past the point of turning away. But Lauralou . . .

"I can't," he protested.

185

She turned him around, pushing him against the car. She rubbed her body against him, her breath hot upon his neck as she pressed her cheek to his. She shuddered violently, clutching him with a frightening desperation. Slowly she began to ease, gradually pulling away.

"Well," she said finally, still breathing heavily, "that was better than nothin'. Crank the car."

He stood awkwardly, his blood running hot, his own breath short. One more word from her now and he would climb into the car with her, just as she had wanted. But for Lauralou the moment had passed. "Crank it," she repeated.

He turned the crank, and the motor caught. He started to walk around to the passenger side, but she pulled away. She drove twenty feet, then stopped and stuck her head out the window. She shouted back at him, "You're probably not much of a cowboy, either."

She drove away and left him standing on the dark back side of the honkytonk. The rain-cool wind whipped dust into his face.

13

The Ditch

SLIM SWAYED, not from the beer but from the emotional peak to which Lauralou had lifted him. She had carried him to the edge, then had left him aroused, frustrated and angry. He had felt arousal before, particularly dancing with a certain dark-headed girl back home who probably had no idea what was going on in his mind, and he had accompanied other cowboys more than once to houses like Jolene's which specialized in relieving that kind of tension. But never had anyone taken him quite so high and dropped him. His groin ached. It crossed his mind that a visit to Jolene's might ease his discomfort, but he mentally calculated how much the night had already cost him and dismissed the notion. Lightning flashed again. If he did not get to the rooming house before long, rain was likely to put his fire out and do it for nothing.

He set off walking toward the lights of Caprock to the south. Well past Ragtown, the Kit Kat Klub was isolated on the Odessa road, its secrets secure from casual view. Anyone sitting in a car parked behind the building might have seen what passed between Slim and Lauralou, but it was unlikely such a person would tell, for his or her own activities probably would not have stood examination. That sort of mutual silence shielded most of the honkytonk's patrons from gossip. It was self-regulation at a fundamental level.

As car and truck lights approached, he would stand at the side of the road and extend his thumb. No one stopped. The new shoes were but a passable fit at best, and they had already begun to pinch from the dancing. Walking made them worse. Slim suspected he would soon have a blister or two. But the smell of rain grew stronger, so he could not afford to stop and rest. The smarting in his feet served one constructive purpose: it took some of his attention away from his other frustration. He kept moving, mumbling to himself about the wily ways of women.

In the distance, he heard a persistent clanging of steel against steel as a roughneck crew on midnight *tower* tripped pipe in a derrick he could not see. He could also hear the chug-chug of distant engines as producing wells pumped black crude into wooden storage tanks. Gas-burning flares lighted the horizon, but the road was dark where he walked.

He had gone probably half a mile when he heard a whimpering sound he at first thought might be made by a lost pup. In the flashes of lightning, he looked in vain for an animal in trouble.

Then the sound became a voice, and the voice made words, though weak ones: "Somebody. Anybody . . ."

It came from the borrow ditch on the other side of the road, a little ahead of him. He called, "Where are you? Keep talkin'."

A sustained flash gave him time to seek out the source. A man lay at the bottom of the ditch. "Somebody come help me," the voice cried.

Slim half stepped, half slid down into the ditch, filling his shoes with sand. He knelt over the man. Another lightning flash showed him the track where the man had fallen off the edge of the road and landed down here. He asked, "Anything broken?"

He was hesitant about helping the man to his feet until he was satisfied that there was no broken arm or leg that might be worsened by movement.

"I don't think so. I just cain't git up."

As a precaution, Slim ran his hand down one of the man's legs, then the other. "Any pain?"

"I got pain in my head, not in my legs." The voice turned almost belligerent. "You goin' to help me or not?"

The man's breath told Slim all he needed to know about the reason for the difficulty. One hand still grasped a bottle. Slim felt a momentary disgust at a man who would drink more than he could hold, and his voice was a little curt. "Okay, I'm goin' to try and lift you up. You'll have to help me a little."

"Don't you spill my bottle." The voice was demanding.

So far as Slim could tell, the bottle was already empty. "Let's get you to your feet." It took three determined tries before he brought the drunk upright and managed to keep him from falling again. The man let the bottle go and tried to stoop to get it.

"Forget the damned bottle," Slim said impatiently. "You've had too much anyway."

"It's my bottle, and none of your Goddammed business!"

Slim reached down and picked it up for him. It was empty.

"See there," the man complained, "you made me spill it all."

Slim had encountered such people before, desperate for help until they got it, then demanding about the form it took. They were never satisfied, even with a gift. He considered letting the drunk slump back down into the bottom of the ditch to sleep it off. But the smell of rain was becoming stronger. This was not a country where it rained much or often, but occasionally when the clouds opened up they dropped a flood. A drunk could drown in this ditch.

They slipped and fell twice before he managed to get his burden up onto the road. The man complained, "Who are you, and why don't you leave me the hell alone?"

"You asked for help," Slim snapped, "and I'm givin' it to you."

"Aw hell," the man groaned. Slim stood back at arm's length, waiting for lightning to show him the man's face. When it did, he said, "You're Mr. Whitmore, aren't you?"

"I'm Autie Whitmore, and what's it to you?"

189

"I know Mrs. Whitmore, and your daughter, Tracy. They're probably worried about you. I'm goin' to get you home."

"You know my wife and daughter? Then you must know my son Benny too. He's a good boy, Benny is. Mighty good boy."

Slim's impatience ebbed, for Whitmore was talking about his son as if he were still living. Possibly this was why he stayed drunk, so he could sustain the pretense.

Slim said, "Come on, let's be gettin' you down the road."

"Yes sir, a good 'un, my Benny. Better boy never lived." He cried a little as reality briefly intruded. Slim managed to bring Whitmore's right arm over his shoulder and take a good grip on it. He walked in short steps. Whitmore staggered along with him, leaning heavily. He was a small man, but it did not take Slim long to tire under the weight. Now and then, a car or truck would approach, and Slim would put his thumb up hopefully, the bright twin beams paining his eyes. One by one, the vehicles passed without stopping.

They figure we're both staggering drunk, he thought.

At length, however, a car slowed before it reached them. Slim's hopes brightened. The car passed them, and the hopes flagged until it stopped and backed up. The lights blinded Slim as the driver got out and looked the pair over. A man's voice said, "Looks like you two might be in a little trouble."

Slim replied, *"He's* in trouble. I'm just tryin' to get him home."

"Why, that's Autie Whitmore. And didn't I see you a while ago at the Kit Kat, dancing with a nice young girl?"

"A nice-*lookin'* girl." Slim squinted into the glare, recognizing driller Victor Underwood.

Underwood asked, "What happened to the girl?"

"She decided to go home."

"And left you stranded?" Underwood grunted. "You must have taken liberties with her."

"No *sir.*" Slim had not considered that people would almost surely make that assumption. "We had a little disagreement, but it wasn't about anything I did." That, he figured, was explanation enough.

It seemed to suit Underwood. "None of my business anyway. Where did you find Autie?"

"Lyin' in the ditch back yonder a ways. It was lookin' like rain, and I couldn't just leave him there."

"You were right, young fellow. McGuire, isn't it?"

"Slim McIntyre."

"Oh yes. I had a student once named McIntyre, at the school of mines. He never could get the hang of calculus."

Slim didn't even know what calculus was. "Would you help me get Mr. Whitmore home?"

"Certainly. Let's put him in the back seat. Autie used to be a good man on a rig, when he could stay sober. I hate to see him in this condition." Whitmore seemed to have gone asleep, his arm over Slim's shoulder, his body a dead weight.

Underwood's petite young wife got out of the car and tried to help, but there was little she could do. Slim and Underwood managed to worry Whitmore into the back seat. Slim got in beside him and held him to keep him from sliding off onto the floor. "I don't know where he lives, exactly," he said.

Underwood shut the rear door and moved behind the wheel. "I do. I've hired him a couple of times for short-term help."

From what Slim had seen of Whitmore around Caprock, it seemed improbable that anybody could hire him for long at a time. Slim had known a few cowboys like him, looking for a bottle and a spree in town as soon as they managed to get a few dollars in their pockets.

Elise Underwood turned to look sympathetically at Whitmore, who was either sleeping or passed out. "The poor man. I can imagine how hard it must be for him to live with the memory."

From the little Slim had heard, Whitmore's addiction to whisky had not begun with his son's death. That had only intensified an existing condition. But he said, "Yes ma'am."

Underwood put the car into motion. It lacked several years being new, bearing out what Mr. Birdsong had told Slim about Underwood's difficulties in his quest for oil. Underwood asked, "Who do you work for, Slim?"

"Mr. Birdsong."

Mrs. Underwood exclaimed, "The shooter?" The tone of her voice implied pity. "Does your mother know the kind of work you do?"

"She died a long time ago, ma'am."

"I don't think she would approve, if she could know."

191

"It's a livin'. I was in bad need of a job, and that was the first one to come along. Mr. Birdsong treats me decent."

She turned to her husband. "I don't like to think of a young fellow like this foolin' around with all that dangerous stuff. Isn't there somethin' he could do on our rig, Victor?"

Underwood shook his head. "At least Mr. Birdsong can be trusted to pay him regularly. If we don't strike something before long . . ." He seemed eager to change the subject. He turned off onto one of the dirt streets into Ragtown. "You're a good Samaritan, Slim. A lot of men would have left Autie lying there."

Slim saw no reason to admit that he had entertained such an idea after feeling the sting of Whitmore's sarcasm. "I was brought up different."

"You were brought up well," Elise Underwood said.

He glowed in the warmth of her smile. It made up a little for the scalding he had taken from Lauralou.

Underwood slowed the car. At a corner, he began counting the tents on the righthand side. To Slim they appeared much alike, especially when the only light was from the automobile. They were all more or less variations on the one in which Hap Holloway had lived with the Haskell brothers.

"This is it," Underwood said, stopping. He got out and opened the rear door. "Careful with him now."

He and Slim managed to get the limp little man out and set his feet upon the ground, though Whitmore's legs seemed to be of rubber. He mumbled unintelligibly, his breath reeking of the whisky he had put away. Slim held him up while Underwood knocked on the tent's wooden doorframe. Slim heard a woman's anxious voice from inside. "Who is it?" She answered so quickly that he doubted she had been asleep. She had probably been lying awake, wondering where Autie Whitmore was.

"It's Victor Underwood, Mrs. Whitmore. We have Autie here."

By the sound of the footsteps, Slim knew the tent had wooden flooring, making it a little more civilized. A lamp was lighted, throwing a yellow-orange glow through the cotton canvas. In a moment, Flora Whitmore opened the door, holding an old robe closed with one hand. Her eyes were anxious as they sought out her husband. "Is he all right?"

192

Underwood said, "He seems to be. He had simply overindulged, from what we can see."

Slim thought that was a polite way of stating it, sparing Mrs. Whitmore's feelings. Underwood had a more polished manner than most of the people he had met in the oilpatch. Most would simply have said *drunk*.

Mrs. Whitmore set the lamp on a small table. "Bring him this way if you will, please."

Slim saw that blankets were suspended from rope to divide the tent into sections. Mrs. Whitmore pushed one of the blankets back to reveal a bed. Underwood said, "Slim, let's get the clothes off of him."

In a minute, they had Whitmore undressed and in bed. He had made little sign that he was aware. When he waked up in the morning he would probably have no idea how he had gotten here.

Mrs. Whitmore asked, "Where was he?"

Slim replied, "I found him out on the road." He saw no need to bother her with troubling details. "Mr. Underwood stopped and brought us in."

He became aware of another figure. Turning, he saw Tracy Whitmore standing in the lamplight, wearing a pink robe. "On the road?" Tracy said. "I thought you went out with Lauralou Clive. What were you doin' on the road?"

"Walkin'. Lauralou went home."

He could not tell what the expression on her face meant. She could have been laughing at him, or she could have been critical. Critical was more like it. She said, "I thought it was always the women who had to walk home."

Slim's face burned. He had no answer and did not try to invent one. He glanced quickly at Victor Underwood but saw no judgment in the man's face.

Mrs. Whitmore said quickly, "Slim and Mr. Underwood have done us a great favor." She reached out and took Slim's hand. "Thank you. Thank you very much."

He felt awkward. "It wasn't anything."

Mrs. Whitmore turned to Underwood. "And I thank you too, Victor. It hasn't been easy for any of us, what happened to Benny. But it's been hardest of all on Autie because he was there. He's felt responsible."

"Things happen in the oilfield, Mrs. Whitmore. There isn't anybody to blame. They just happen."

"I know. I just wish *he* knew."

Slim felt something touch his arm. It was Tracy's hand. Quietly she said, "I didn't go to hurt your feelin's, cowboy. I was just a little surprised that you could do anything to Lauralou that would make her go off and leave you."

His face burned again. He could not tell her it was what he did *not* do that had caused Lauralou to abandon him.

Underwood said, "We'd better go, Slim, and let these people get some sleep."

"Yes sir. Good night, Mrs. Whitmore . . . Tracy."

Tracy Whitmore caught his hands in hers. "Thanks, Slim."

He hurriedly left the tent.

The lightning flashed brilliantly now, followed by rolls of heavy thunder. Underwood said, "We'll take you home, Slim. Where do you live?"

Slim shook his head. "You and Mrs. Underwood better be gettin' on before it sets in to pourin'. I can trot it from here in just a little bit."

Underwood looked up at the threatening sky. "All right." He extended his hand. "Thank you for not leaving Autie."

The car had no sooner pulled away than raindrops began to pepper down. Slim decided he had been hasty in declining Underwood's offer to drive him home. He hunched his shoulders and started to walk. A voice stopped him.

"Slim!" The voice was Tracy's. The lightning showed her standing in the doorway of the tent. She was beckoning him. "You'll get soaked out there. Come in here out of the rain."

Hesitantly he retraced his steps. "It looks like it could rain all night."

"Then you can stay here all night. Mother wants you to. I want you to. You can have Benny's cot."

He was not sure he relished the idea of waking up in the morning under the same canvas as Autie Whitmore. But on reflection, he decided he would be gone long before Autie ever awakened.

"I'd be much obliged."

He stepped through the door into the lamp-lighted tent. The rain began to pelt against the canvas, and he was glad he was not outside, making a run for Mrs. England's rooming house. Tracy showed him the cot. She brought a blanket and draped it over a cotton rope, making a privacy partition of sorts. "Would you want some coffee or somethin' before you go to bed?"

"No thanks. Coffee might keep me awake."

She smiled, then stood on tiptoes and gave him a quick kiss on the cheek. "Thanks again for Papa. Sweet dreams."

She left him feeling anew a little of the arousal he had felt when Lauralou had driven off without him. *Damned little sleep I'm liable to get tonight,* he thought.

He was glad when Monday morning came and Mr. Birdsong appeared in his converted Studebaker to pick him up for the day's work. Hap Holloway had hoorawed him unmercifully about the fact that he did not sleep in his own bed and came home at seven o'clock of a Sunday morning.

"How did it feel, layin' Lauralou Clive down in that car? By damn, cowboy, I been wantin' to do that ever since the first time I seen her. And stayin' out all night . . ."

Slim had finally managed to convince Hap that Lauralou had left him after he declined to have sex with her.

Hap demanded, "But why the hell not? I mean, there she was, for God's sake, ready and willin'. What more could you want?" He seemed almost angry over an opportunity offered and refused, as if it were somehow his own loss.

"It just wouldn't be right."

"But you've done it with women before, ain't you?"

"That was different. I paid them. I never thought of Lauralou that way."

Hap stared at him in bewilderment. "You've got some damned strange notions about right and wrong."

"Maybe so, but they're *my* notions. I live up to them the best I can."

"I just wish I'd've been there. I'd give a hundred dollars . . ."

Slim said disgustedly, "You wouldn't have to."

Mr. Birdsong was humming to himself as they drove out to the magazine where he stored his explosives. "You seem to be feelin' awful good this mornin'," Slim said.

Birdsong was not given much to smiling, but he did now. "Rain, Mr. McIntyre, rain. You will not see much of it in this benighted part of our country, and when it does fall as it did yesterday morning, you treasure it as a jewel."

The rain, starting after midnight, had continued until about daylight Sunday morning. Most of it had soaked quickly into the sand, but on the harder ground some still remained in puddles. The ranchers should be happy, Slim thought. But he had not considered that their enthusiasm would be shared by oilfield people. To them, dry weather was no obstacle, though mud could be. He remarked on his surprise.

Birdsong said, "The air has a clean, washed smell to it, and the land is refreshed. The birds are singing, and flowers will bloom. Do you think that because my livelihood comes from beneath the ground I have no interest in what happens on top?"

"I guess I never studied on it one way or the other."

"I may never have told you, but I grew up on a small farm in Pennsylvania. I know the value of rain."

Birdsong had never talked much about his past. Slim knew little except that he had been a shooter for most of his adult life. "I always figured you come out of a city someplace."

"No, my forebears were men of the soil. But I was the third of several sons, so there was no land inheritance for me. I had to find my place elsewhere in the world. There was work in the oilfields, so I moved in that direction. I suppose you know that the oil had its beginnings in Pennsylvania?"

"No sir, I just figured Texas was the startin' of it."

"By no means. It began at a little place later called Titusville in Pennsylvania, not far from where I spent my childhhood. A man named Drake drilled a well some seventy or so feet deep and brought up oil just before the Civil War."

Slim knew more about the Civil War than he had ever known about the oil business. "My granddaddy was in that fight."

Birdsong sniffed. "On the wrong side, I would suppose."

"Well, the losin' side, anyway."

"My own father was a combatant in that affair. He hated every minute of it. When it was over, he returned to the farm, and he never left it again. Nor did I wish to, when my time came. But I knew something of the oilfields, for they were all around us when I was a boy. That is where I sought my fortune."

"I guess you never did find it."

"Why sir, I have had it all along. Most people think of a

fortune as money in the bank. But banks can close, and your money can be lost. No, Mr. McIntyre, a fortune is having a trade that you can always employ to earn your way. They may take away your money, but a man who has a trade need never want. His fortune is in his hands."

"I had a trade, punchin' cows."

"But too many others have the same trade, evidently. The market is oversupplied with cowboys. You should cultivate a specialty and become the best at it, preferably a trade that few other people find to their liking."

"Like shootin' oilwells?"

"That is one example. You do not find people tripping over themselves trying to break into this line of work."

"How did you come to be a shooter?"

"I had been working as a roughneck on drilling crews, and the market became overcrowded. An old nitro man offered me a position as his assistant, and I accepted, just as you did. I have always liked working with explosives. I suppose there is a touch of the anarchist in me. Even after all these years, I feel a special exhilaration when a shot goes off properly. Don't you have that feeling?"

Slim had to admit, "No sir, I break out in a cold sweat. Every time we fire a charge, I'm just glad to still be alive."

Birdsong seemed a little disappointed. "You have been good help, Mr. McIntyre, and I had hoped you would find the same pleasure in this work that I always have. But perhaps you are simply not meant to be a shooter."

"No sir, I reckon I'm not."

"A lot of shooters never get over their fear. Many I know become heavy drinkers because of it. I would not wish to see that happen to you."

Slim was uneasy about the direction the conversation had taken. "I ain't quittin' you, Mr. Birdsong."

"But you should, if that is the way you feel about it. The first time you see an opportunity to seize upon a job more to your liking, do not hesitate on my account. I can always find a new helper. Not as willing as you, perhaps, but I am used to a rapid turnover."

"I feel beholden to you."

"Nonsense. You have done all I asked of you and earned every dollar. I have been thinking about moving to another field anyway, one that offers me more shots than Caprock. Winkler County, perhaps, or Ward. But enough of that. We have to face up to the job at hand. We are going to shoot another well for Mr. Anderson today."

"Seems to me like we must've shot a dozen for him already. Looks like he'd be satisfied with the wells he's already got. I don't see how he can spend all the money he's makin'."

"You do not understand his type of man, Mr. McIntyre. The money is secondary to him. He loves the thrill of the hunt, the challenge of spudding in where no one has drilled before. He is a gambler, but he plays his game with drilling rigs and crews of men, with his skill and his nerve. If he loses, he walks away without tears. If he wins, his only thought is for the next game. He is a wildcatter."

"It's too fast a game for me."

"And for me. But I love to watch, and my trade gives me a chance to be a small part of it. When I was young I envied my older brother, who remained on the farm. I do not anymore. I have had a ringside seat at the greatest show I could ever have seen. I would not change places with any man."

They took an especially heavy load of nitro from the magazine. Birdsong said, "Mr. Anderson wants to give this one a big jolt."

This ought to do it, Slim thought. It was the heaviest load he had ever seen on Birdsong's Studebaker, and the largest number of tin shells. Birdsong seemed not in the least nervous about it. He was careful, as always, but casual as a rancher loading a truck with cattle feed. Slim felt the cold sweat starting as it always did when they set out across that uneven, sandy-bottomed trace toward the highway. Birdsong had assured him several times in the past that he had never lost a load of nitro on the road. That was self-evident, for otherwise Birdsong would not be here. But there was always a first time . . . and a last.

Anderson waited for them beside the wooden derrick as he always did, his necktie at half-mast. He shook hands with Birdsong and then with Slim. He had the easy, self-assured air of a man who knows where he is going and is on the right road to get there. "Say, Slim, I was surprised to run into you at the Kit Kat Klub Saturday night."

198

Birdsong's eyebrows tilted a little.

Anderson said, "And to see you with Lauralou Clive . . . Folks talk like she's quite some girl."

"She's full of surprises," Slim admitted ruefully.

Anderson turned to Birdsong. "This has been a jinx well from the start. I probably ought to've plugged the damned thing and gone on about my business, but it got under my skin to have it whip me. Had a man fall out of the derrick the second day and break an arm and a leg. We had a gas blowout that tore up half the rig. We lost our tools in the hole and spent three days fishing for them. And when we finally got to the Permian Lime we thought sure we had a duster. Then it started flowing by heads."

Slim had to ask, "Flowin' by heads? What does that mean?"

"It means oil rises to the top every so often. It's been happening about every three to five days."

Birdsong asked with concern, "When was the last time?"

"Saturday. I don't figure it's due again for another day or two, at least. But just the same, I wish you could've shot it yesterday."

Birdsong said, "Bad things happen to people who shoot wells on a Sunday." He frowned at Slim. "It can be dangerous business having a charge down in a hole when the oil commences to rise. It can bring the shells back to the top with it. If it throws them out onto the derrick floor, there is the devil to pay."

Anderson said, "I've heard stories about shooters catching the shells as they came out and holding onto them so they wouldn't explode."

Birdsong said, "So have I. But it would be like catching a thousand-pound greased pig."

Anderson started to leave. "I'll be over on Number Three if you need me." He winked at Slim. "You know how to pick the pretty women, cowboy. Give 'em hell." He drove away in his Packard.

Birdsong eyed the well with misgivings. "A jinx well, he called it. I've encountered those before."

Slim knew Birdsong's feeling about a Sunday job, but he was a little surprised that the shooter seemed to take this notion seriously. "You believe in jinxes and stuff like that?"

"I believe in the law of averages. When a pattern is set, it tends to repeat. But come along, let us be about our work."

Filling the shells one at a time, lowering them, hooking the next empty into line and filling it, they labored for several hours. They paused to eat their sack lunches. Gone was Birdsong's happy mood of the morning. As he ate, he kept staring disapprovingly at the well as he might stare at some person he felt was up to no good. At length he said, "So you were at the Kit Kat with a girl. I must say I am surprised."

"I was a little surprised myself. It was her idea."

"Married women might go with their husbands to such places, but decent young unmarried ladies do not."

"So I learned."

Birdsong regarded his assistant thoughtfully. "A young man's education is often costly and his pathway fraught with thorns." He left part of his lunch uneaten. "Let us get back to it, Mr. McIntyre. I have a feeling that the sooner we are through with this one, the better."

Slim had not satisfied his appetite, but he put away what was left. It would do for a midafternoon snack. "Yes sir."

They finished pouring up all the nitroglycerin they had brought to the well. Birdsong said, "I'm setting the timer short. Even if the well is not supposed to make a head for another day or two, I do not choose to take a chance. You can never be sure about one of these things."

He started the motor on the cable reel and began lowering the heavy string of shells. He was always a careful man, even when he appeared casual, but it seemed to Slim that he was more cautious than usual. Anderson had warned that the hole was a little crooked—rotary rigs had a tendency to drill them that way—and the torpedoes scraped against the steel casing at times. A spark was the most dangerous possibility. Birdsong slowed the descent to allow the shells to snake their way down through a couple of particularly bad bends, like a train moving around a curve, its individual cars out of alignment with one another.

The day was hot, but Slim felt cold, for when Birdsong was nervous, *Slim* was nervous. He wondered what they would do if the shells became stuck halfway down in that hole. There would be no way to get to the timer and shut it off. But Birdsong had a sure feel for the movement of the line, regulating the speed with a skill that years on the job had given him.

Slim became aware of a strange sound from deep in the hole, a low rumbling noise he had not heard before. He motioned anxiously to Birdsong, who stopped the line's descent and listened. The shooter's jaw went slack, and he rubbed an arm across his face. "My God, she's making a head."

"You mean the oil is comin' to the top?"

"Yes." Birdsong raced back to the reel and started the line running in reverse, pulling the shells back up, trying to outrace the oil coming from the bottom of the hole. "The only chance we've got is to get those torpedoes up here ahead of the oil, where we can control them," he shouted over the sound of the motor and the rumbling from the well. "Run yonder and grab that two-by-four. We'll wedge it through the bail of the first shell when it comes up. Then we'll try to hold them all down while the oil flows over them."

Slim had only a vague idea what he meant, but he grabbed a two-by-four about three feet long and raced back with it. He watched the line coming up from the hole. It was taut at first, indicating that the shells were moving faster than the oil. Then it went slack. Birdsong speeded the motor, but it could not catch up.

Birdsong shouted, "It's not going to work. Run! Run for your life!"

The older man set out sprinting across the pasture. Heart in his mouth, Slim jumped from the derrick platform and followed him, racing through the sand, the clutching thorny mesquite. "The truck," he exclaimed as he came up abreast of Birdsong, "What about the truck?"

"To hell with the truck! Just run, Mr. McIntyre."

Birdsong stumbled and went sprawling. Slim stopped and lifted him up. The shooter limped, and Slim slowed to stay with him. The old man shouted, "Don't wait for me! Go, damn it, go!"

Slim felt the wind from the blast before he heard the deafening thunder. The force of it thrust him violently forward. He fell hard, flat on his face. The rush of air felt as if it would rip all his clothes away. It drove sand against his skin like a million sharp needles. He felt himself rolling, choking on sand. He gasped for breath, but there was no breath. It was as if the blast had removed all the air.

The debris began to rain down around him, planks and pieces of iron and steel. He brought his arms up over his head to shield it while he drove his chin down into the sand. Something struck him in the middle of the back like the kick of a mule, and something hard and heavy fell across his legs. He wondered if they were both broken.

Suddenly then, there was silence, even more ominous than the noise. The debris had stopped falling. He tried to look up but had to rub sand from his burning eyes before he could see. Gradually forms took shape. What had been a wooden derrick was now just an oil-spattered skeleton, most of its timbers blown away. What was left leaned crazily, as if about to fall inward upon itself. He saw no trace of the Studebaker. All breath had been knocked out of him, and he felt a moment of panic before he began to force air back into his fiery lungs. With breath came voice. "Mr. Birdsong! Mr. Birdsong!"

He heard nothing at first. He found a heavy timber lying across his legs and expended a considerable effort in moving it away. He tried in vain to rise to his feet. His legs were not broken, but they pained him when he put weight on them. He crawled on hands and knees, looking around desperately. "Mr. Birdsong! Are you all right?"

He heard a moan and crawled toward it. He found Birdsong lying facedown. The cable reel from his truck lay across his back. "Lord Jesus! Mr. Birdsong!"

He did not know where he found the strength to move the reel, but he managed to roll it away. Birdsong tried to lift his head. His face was crusted with sand. Blood oozed from his mouth as he gasped for breath.

Slim had not cried since his father's death. He cried now.

Birdsong murmured, "Turn me onto my side, please. Carefully."

Slim tried to be gently. It was no use. Birdsong screamed in agony as Slim began to move him. Slim knew within reason that the man's ribs were shattered, and his back was probably broken too. To turn him would be to kill him. "You lie still, Mr. Birdsong. Somebody'll come directly."

He took a handkerchief from his pocket, raised Birdsong's head a little and spread the handkerchief to keep the old man's face out of the sand.

Birdsong asked in a tremulous voice, "Are you hurt, Mr. McIntyre?"

"No sir, not enough to count. Ain't nothin' broken."

"I'm glad. I've never killed an assistant."

"You just lie easy, Mr. Birdsong. You're goin' to be all right." It was a lie, and he nearly choked on it. "Mr. Anderson's sure to've seen the blast. He'll be along here any minute and get you to the doctor."

"Doctor?" Birdsong wheezed. "You can't even move me. No doctor could . . ." He broke into a fit of coughing, spitting up blood. Slim thought Birdsong was going to die, then and there. He watched helplessly, not knowing anything to do except hold the shooter's head up so he would not choke on his own blood. He prayed softly, the same thing over and over.

In a few minutes, Birdsong found his voice again. "In my room . . . you'll find papers. My will . . ."

"Don't be talkin' that way." Slim heard the roar of a car engine. He saw Anderson's Packard speeding across the thin two-rut trace that led to what was left of his well. "Help's comin' now. You just hold on."

Birdsong began coughing again. Slim sensed that the old fellow was rapidly losing what little hold he had on life.

Anderson braked his car to a stop. He and several men piled out. Slim waved his arm, and they came running through the sand. Anderson stopped short when he saw Birdsong lying facedown, blood soaking the handkerchief Slim had put beneath his face. "God in Heaven! You men, let's get him to the car."

Slim raised both hands. "You can't move him. He's broken all to pieces."

Anderson sank to his knees beside the shooter. "That well, that son-of-a-bitching well." His voice broke. "I wish to hell I'd plugged it."

Birdsong said weakly, "Mr. Anderson . . . I tried to tell the boy. There are papers in my room. A will . . . And listen . . ." He managed to raise his head a little, to look at Slim. "This is a good lad. He's hurt. He can't work for a while. There's money in my pocket. I want you to give him two hundred dollars of it."

Being the wealthiest man in the Caprock field did not make Anderson immune to emotion. A tear moved down his cheek. "I hear you, Mr. Birdsong."

Birdsong was quiet a moment. Then he said, "Maybe a hundred and fifty is enough." He seemed almost to smile. "It was such a pretty day . . ." And he was gone.

Slim sank to the sand and cried again.

Caprock's cemetery had been established before the turn of the century, but it had grown substantially since the oil play. Illness, accidents, sudden deaths that were no accident . . . a boomtown's toll was higher than most.

Slim was surprised at the number of people who turned out for the funeral. Birdsong's only relatives were back East, and it would take days for them to reach West Texas on the train, so the services did not wait for them. But Birdsong did not want for mourners. There were drillers, roughnecks, suppliers, merchants. Sheriff Buckalew was there, hat in his hands. Knox Anderson had stood up in the church and presented a eulogy, honoring a man whose skill and courage he said had helped to build an industry though Birdsong had shared in little of its wealth.

The description, Slim thought, could have fitted most of the men who had come to see Birdsong buried. They were, in the main, men of muscle and will who bent their backs to the labor of the oilfield, asking for little except a chance, dreaming dreams that would come to reality for only a few. And though they often cursed like muleskinners and lived a rough existence in the field, they bowed their heads in reverence as the minister said a final prayer for this man of their own, whose life had come down to a plain wooden box in a sandy grave far from the home of his boyhood.

Mrs. England owned a little coupe. Because Slim walked with difficulty and considerable pain, she had driven him to the church and then to the cemetery. She attended every service for an oilfield man whether she had known him or not. In a sense, she regarded them all as an extended family, praying for their souls even when she condemned their sins. "A good Christian man, that Mr. Birdsong," she remarked regretfully, turning to look back toward the place where a gravedigger waited to cover the coffin with sand. "So far as I know, liquor never touched his lips."

Slim said, "I've often heard him speak against it."

"It is not for us to question, but even so I sometimes wonder why the Lord so often takes the godly and leaves the heathen runnin' free."

Slim limped, his legs bruised black from the timber that had fallen across them. His back also bore a painful blue mark several inches across. "I don't know how come I lived and he died."

"You can be assured that the Lord spared you for some good purpose. He has a mission for you somewhere. Be watchful that you do not pass it by."

He heard a man's voice. "Slim McIntyre." Turning, he saw Victor Underwood and his pretty wife, Elise. He had noticed them in the church and again at the cemetery. They could not have known Birdsong very well, he thought, yet they had come to pay their respects. They exemplified the fellowship of the oilfields, like the brotherhood Slim had known among cowboys.

Underwood said, "We just wanted to express our sympathies."

Several people already had. Slim supposed that because none of Birdsong's relatives were here, as the man's only employee he was a survivor of sorts. "I'm much obliged." He turned toward his landlady. "Do you-all know Mrs. England?"

Both Underwoods did, slightly. Mrs. England spoke cordially enough to Elise, but her manner showed the reservation Slim had seen her demonstrate toward her roomers. She too probably had wondered about the disparity in the Underwoods' ages.

Underwood said, "I suppose you'll be looking for a job again, when you're well enough to work?"

Slim replied regretfully, "Yes sir, I sure will."

"Elise and I were both impressed by the way you helped Autie Whitmore when he needed it. If we hear of anybody looking for help, we'll send him your way."

Slim watched them walk toward their old car, arm in arm, as if both were young instead of only one. He felt a hand touch his arm and faced around. Tracy Whitmore stood there, her mother behind her. He had seen them standing with the crowd during the graveside service. Mrs. Whitmore dabbed a handkerchief to the corner of her eye. He doubted that the Whitmore family had known Birdsong any better than the Underwoods did. But they all belonged to the fellowship.

Tracy said, "I went to Doc Tolliver's yesterday evenin' to see about you. He had already sent you home."

Slim was surprised. "You went to see about me?" The thought that she had been concerned pleased him.

She said, "When I first heard about the explosion, I was afraid . . . *we* were afraid that you were gone too, like my brother Benny."

"The Lord must've been lookin' in my direction instead of Mr. Birdsong's. But I'll be doin' my runnin' in a slow walk for a while."

"I guess your job died with Mr. Birdsong."

"I'll get along. He left me a few dollars."

"Mr. Schwartz said you're welcome to come wash dishes at the café until you're up to heavier work. The job won't pay much of anything, but you can eat all you want."

"Tell him I'll be there tomorrow."

"Why, you can't hardly stay on your feet."

"I enjoyed all the idleness I could stand when I first came to Caprock. I'll heal faster workin'."

Tracy gave him a faint smile. "I'll see you there, then."

Mrs. England nodded approvingly as Tracy and her mother walked away. "I always like to see a young man show ambition."

Slim wondered how much ambition could be found in a dish-washing job. It was a long way down from the saddle.

Three

Big Boy Daugherty

14

Irish O'Dell

HE DID NOT RELISH the return to Caprock, but Turk Radke and Big Boy Daugherty had decided. One might try to reason with Boss, but one did not quarrel with him. One did not waste one's time even *trying* to reason with Radke. Irish's reconnaissance of several weeks ago had convinced the two men that Caprock was a going boomtown ripe for the harvest, especially since the Rangers and newly elected reform-minded local law enforcement had rendered their operations untenable in the Panhandle oilfields.

O'Dell drove his red Ford. Radke sat beside him, brooding, telling him how to drive, occasionally declaring his frustrations aloud. "Damn the Rangers anyhow! If people choose of their own free will to drink and gamble and whore around, what business do the Rangers have messing in it? This is supposed to be a free country. They ought to leave people the hell alone."

Irish had liked the climate better on the high plains. From what he had seen of Caprock and the country around it, it was a sandpit, more fit for centipedes and tarantulas than for people. He hadn't seen a dollar's worth of grass and trees, other than mesquites. But Boss maintained that money was greener than grass. Caprock had sounded to him like a place to generate that sort of scenery.

Irish had not told him or Radke about the highjacking he and Skinny had pulled on that rich driller—what was the name?—Anderson. They frowned on such independent activity because it might spoil the climate for bigger and better rewards. When the news had come about the Rangers killing Roscoe Poole, Irish had expected Boss to be upset. Instead, the big man had laughed, his belly shaking like a jar of clabber. Boss had never forgiven Poole for striking out on his own, free-lancing, jeopardizing the larger operation: "Served the fool right."

Irish had always suspected that it was Boss who got Poole sent to the penitentiary in the first place. A word in the proper ear, and Poole was gone.

To have told Boss and Radke about the Anderson holdup would have meant not only facing their wrath but splitting the take. Of course, there had been no take to split. That little redheaded Flower had evidently run off with it to God knew where. Skinny would gladly slit her throat if he could find her. Irish accepted the loss as he accepted a bad turn of the cards. There was compensation: he had taken pleasure in Flower's bed. She had just cost him more than most.

The money would have been small potatoes to Boss Daugherty, but for Irish and Skinny the robbery had looked like a fast way to pick up a few hundred bucks. What Boss and Radke didn't know wouldn't hurt them. Sooner or later, Irish intended to put together enough dough that he could set out on his own, letting Radke and Boss find somebody else to tend to their dirty work.

Irish glanced across at Radke's scowling face and wondered, as he often did, if the man might really be crazy. He could act that way sometimes, when he had greased the wheels and they didn't spin to suit him. Irish speculated that it might have been his upbringing in Hell's Half Acre. Once, drunk, Radke had told him about life in that part of Fort Worth when he was a boy. As the saying went, he had not been *brought* up, he had been *jerked* up by a weak-willed, whisky-soaked father who could never hold a job and by a violent, profane mother who sold herself on the streets. When she became too old or too ugly for the customers, she had become a madam of some prominence on the police blotters, selling younger women. She had knocked the boy Turk around like a punching bag. The neighbors always assumed his father had done it. Once, when Turk had shown up with his face bruised and swollen, several neighbors had called his father out into the yard and stomped hell out of him. Turk had told the story with a gritty satisfaction, for the old man had had it coming to him. He had no more backbone than a woollyworm, Turk said, letting the old lady get away with everything.

Turk had decided early that the way to get along in the world was to keep everybody afraid of him. Bust a nose or an arm, and you could count on holding people's attention. His paw never did learn that, he said, and people had always walked on the miserable son of a bitch. Maw knew. Turk had hated her guts, but he had to concede that nobody walked on her. She had usually been the first to strike a blow.

She had finally struck one too many. When she resisted being robbed, a pimp had beaten her to death with a tire iron. Looking at her broken body, Turk had been unable to raise a tear. He had felt only relief that he was free of her. He had almost wished he had been the one who had beaten her. Turk Radke had had but one use for women since. On occasion, when duty demanded that he put the arm on a woman, usually a prostitute, all he had to do was remember Maw.

The car was hot if Irish rolled up his window and dusty if he didn't. He compromised by leaving it only partially open, taking off his short-billed cap and rubbing sweat from his face onto his sleeve. He detested the sulphur smell emanating from the tall wooden derricks on both sides of the road. He had spent his boyhood in urban East Dallas. He had never yet seen an oiltown he considered fit for habitation. They were a means to an end, nothing more. He just wished that end would hurry up and get here. One of these days, he would go back where he came from and use all he had learned by working under Boss Daugherty. That bunch in Chicago who thought they were so shiny . . . they didn't have anything on Boss, and they didn't have anything on Turk Radke.

Boss had grown up as a farm boy on land that wouldn't make a living for a woodrat. He had gone only as far as the fourth grade, so he was a little slow at reading or writing words. But he was good at reading faces, and he had a natural aptitude with figures. Counting money, Boss could add sums in his head faster than a mechanical calculator could do it in a bank. He had a fondness for addition.

Irish had suggested setting up operations in Dallas and forgetting these dusty, smelly oiltowns, but Boss said there were already too many frogs in the Dallas puddle. He preferred boomtowns, where he could be the biggest frog.

Radke turned in the seat and looked out the back window for the second time in ten minutes. He said with a certain satisfaction, "The boys're still back there. I've been afraid they'd get stuck in the sand and we'd leave them behind."

Irish did not bother to look back. He knew the four-door Chevy would be trailing. None of the boys wanted to face Radke's anger if they kept him waiting on the streets of Caprock. He could lash out in unthinking violence when his blood was up. Irish tried to get him out of his dark mood. He said, "First thing I want to do is go over to Jolene's. She's got some good-looking women there. How about comin' with me?"

Turk frowned at him. "Can't you ever get your mind up past your belt buckle? The day you die, it'll probably be in a whorehouse."

"I couldn't pick a better place. You ought to try it yourself sometime. Those women can do a lot for you."

"Like the one you were so stuck on that time, the one that got her husband to back out on a job? She sure did a lot for *me*. Like to've gotten me sent to hell. But she paid for it."

Irish chilled a little, his face pinched in the pain of the memory. Yes, he had hungered for that woman, more than any he had ever known, and he had known a lot of them. He would have gone to hell and back for her if she had come to him of her own free will. When he had finally taken her at Radke's order, it had been an empty, galling experience, for she had given him nothing. He could as well have been making love to a dead woman. In a way, he supposed, she *was* dead, in spirit.

Her eyes kept coming back to him when he was least ready. None of the several men he had killed had ever haunted him. He seldom gave them a thought. But this woman he had taken . . . those hazel eyes had set his soul afire and would not leave him alone.

A dog trotted along in the narrow bladed road. It evidently had not yet heard the car. Radke sat forward, suddenly excited. "Speed up. Hit that little son of a bitch."

Irish was startled. "What the hell, Turk?"

Radke grabbed the wheel, trying to steer the car toward the dog. The animal looked back over its shoulder and cut quickly toward the ditch. Irish fought to regain control and almost put the coupe off the road. Yelping in fright, the mongrel scurried up the other side of the ditch and raced under a barbed wire fence to the security of a mesquite thicket.

Irish struggled to bring the car back up where it belonged. He seldom dared raise his voice to Radke, but he did so now without thinking. "Good God, Turk . . ."

Radke muttered, "I always hated dogs. Why the hell didn't you run over him like I told you."

"And tear up a good automobile? Maybe get us both killed?"

"When I was a kid, they'd come up and lick everybody else's hand. They'd just try to bite mine." Radke sat back in sullen silence. Irish said nothing more. Radke could be dangerous when he was like that. All the more reason Irish wanted to get away from him one of these days.

To the sides of the road, sandhills glistened in the sun, and a warm wind sent skiffs of sand riffling along the tops of the dunes. Distastefully Irish ran his tongue across his teeth, imagining he could feel the grit. He was strongly tempted to chuck all this and head back to where people knew what pavement was. This place had better pay off pretty good. It probably would. He would have to give Turk and Boss credit for being able to squeeze a handsome profit out of these miserable boomtowns where less imaginative men might turn up their noses. Their technique was simple enough: control the biggest bootleg operation, the biggest whorehouse, the best dancehall and honkytonk. After a couple of object lessons administered in the right places, the rest of what they wanted usually fell into line without too much difficulty, too many bloody noses or broken bones. Boss had a simple approach to the local laws, too: buy them off, scare them off or have them killed. One way or another, he got the job done.

It was the Rangers who sometimes caused him trouble, who were finally making it so hot that Boss was moving out of the Panhandle. They could not be bought, and they didn't scare worth a damn. Nobody in his right mind ever killed a Ranger. If the courts didn't administer retribution, the Rangers administered their own. They had long memories and a long reach.

Every booming oilfield Irish had ever seen had a Ragtown, and Caprock was no exception. The first sight of one always caused him to shiver, thinking of the discomfort ahead. A casual passerby, looking at Ragtown's tents and shacks, might assume there weren't twelve dollars of real money in the whole put-together, but Boss had taught Irish that this was not so. Most of the men who lived there were employed in the oilfield, rough-necks drawing maybe five dollars a day, drillers as much as ten to fifteen, other jobs somewhere in between. The work was hard and sweaty and mean; and when it was done, a lot of these men were looking for something to drink, a woman to fondle and maybe crawl in bed with.

The secret to financial success, Boss always said, was to have for sale what people wanted to buy; it didn't take a college education to figure that out. The less the competition, the better the sales. Taking care of the competition was Turk's job, and Irish's and the rest. They were good at their work.

Driving down the main street, still well short of the stone courthouse, Irish started looking for a parking place by the curb or in the line of cars parked in the middle of the wide but unpaved thoroughfare. "What time you got, Turk?"

Turk frowned at his pocketwatch. "Damned near one-thirty."

Irish complained, "I told you we ought to've stopped and had dinner in Odessa."

Turk touched a button, and the watch played a little tune. He had taken it off of an unconscious bootlegger just before he pitched him onto a flatcar and watched the train carry him far away where he would not provide competition to Boss's enterprises. "I wasn't ready in Odessa. I'm ready now."

During his and Skinny's visit, Irish had found that the best café in town was the Teagarden, owned by a big Dutchman who seemed to have run a bluff on a lot of people. Irish found a parking space by the curb a few doors from the Teagarden and pulled in. The Chevy drew past and parked in the center of the street. Irish got out and stretched, stiff from the long trip. He waited on the curb for the four men from the Chevy to walk across the dirt street and join him and Radke.

They were Skinny and Frenchy and Grat and Sarge, a grim-eyed lot afraid of nobody much except Turk and Boss. They did what they were told, when they were told, and saw to it that nobody messed in Boss's interests more than once.

Skinny disliked Caprock as much as Irish did. He said to Radke, "I don't see why Big Boy sent us on ahead. When'll he be comin' down hisownself?"

Radke scowled. "He'll come when he's good and ready. And don't you ever let him hear you call him Big Boy. He hates that name. Call him Boss, or better still, call him Mr. Daugherty. Otherwise he's liable to throw you down, sit on your head and fart in your face."

That image seemed to bother Skinny more than a little. "I didn't mean nothin' by it. Thing is, I always feel better when I know he's close around."

Turk was half a head taller than Skinny. He leaned over the little man, his face clouded with threat. "I'm here. What's wrong with *me?*"

Skinny sweated. "Nothin', Turk. Nothin' at all."

Having reestablished an authority that had never been in doubt, Radke looked at the restaurant. "No use working on an empty stomach. We'll eat first, then get started on business."

The café was full. Several men stood along the inside front wall, waiting for tables to clear. At a table on the north wall, four laborers finished eating and moved toward the big man at the cash register. A young waitress began stacking dishes. She had served Irish several times when he and Skinny had been here before. She was not the prettiest girl he had ever seen, by far, but she was female, and therefore he was interested.

A group of men who had been waiting started toward the table. Radke overtook them, his companions just behind him. "You'll have to wait," he told a tall roustabout who seemed to be leading the others. "That's our table."

The roustabout drew himself up to his full six feet and doubled his fists. "Like hell! We was here first."

Radke had a way of introducing himself to a town so that people knew who he was from then on. He brought his knee up and gave the roustabout a sharp jolt where it would hurt the most. When the man bent over in pain, Turk grabbed his ear and gave it a hard twist. "Wash the oil out of your ears and you'll hear better next time."

Skinny and the others moved to appropriate the table. Irish heard sounds of anger among men scattered about the room. The waitress declared indignantly, "Those men have waited their turn. You've got no right to buck the line."

Frenchy, who had served time in Angola for being an inept safecracker, reached out to pinch her and got his hand jabbed smartly with the business end of a fork. He jerked it back in surprise and sucked on it, trying to stop the blood.

Irish laughed to himself. He had always heard that Frenchmen knew how to finesse women, but this one was as inept in that department as he had been in his first chosen line of work. Frenchy's temper was quick, like Radke's. Irish stepped between him and the girl to head off retaliation. "Sweet thing," he said, smiling at the waitress, "you'll have to pardon my Louisiana friend. He only knows how to handle alligators."

Crisply she said, "Tell him the next time he tries to handle *me*, he'll think an alligator took a bite out of him."

Irish watched the big man at the register for sign of fight. He had seen the Dutchman carry two men out, one under each arm, and throw them into the street. Schwartz walked toward the table, his face tinged with red. He stopped a little short, looking over the men who had seated themselves.

Radke stepped in front of him. "You got something to say, say it to me."

The Dutchman appeared to recognize the type of men he was up against. He met Radke's eyes for only a moment, then looked down. Boss had always said Turk could win more fights with his eyes than most men could with their fists. He said with Turk it was like a snake charming a rabbit before he swallowed it whole.

The Dutchman said, "Go on, Tracy. It'll be all right this time." He turned back toward the cash register, his broad shoulders sagging a little.

Irish could see satisfaction in Radke's eyes, though he had never seen the man betray his feelings with a smile. Against a bunch like this, the Dutchman's bluff manner had crumbled. Irish thought he could read Radke's mind. He was considering adding the best restaurant in town to Boss's other acquisitions. It would be easy.

He saw that the crowd's mood was surly, but most of these men had been around the fields long enough to recognize the caliber of muscle Radke had about him. They might surge forward in a mass, but individually they weren't going to do a damned thing. Once again, Radke had established his authority from the start.

The waitress still glared indignantly. Irish saw a threat of violence in the way Radke stared at her. He did not want to see the girl hurt. "Sweet thing," he said quickly, "how about clearin' this table?"

Defiantly she declared, "Clear it yourself!"

Radke nodded at the man seated across from him. They brushed the remaining dishes and utensils off onto the floor with a clatter and a crash. The girl jumped back in dismay.

A young man who had been sitting at the nearby counter quickly slid from his stool and moved toward them as if he meant to fight. He limped heavily. It was bad luck to hurt a cripple, but Radke would do it and not give it a thought. Again Irish stepped into the way. Calmly he said, "Looks to me like you've already got one busted leg, friend. You don't need another."

The girl moved quickly to take the young man's arm. "It's all right, Slim."

"Ain't neither," the young man declared angrily. "Nobody's got a right to treat a woman thataway."

Irish let his gaze rove quickly over the room. He saw the crowd's ugly mood and sensed that there was fixing to be a battle if this went any further. Oilfield workers might stand for a lot of things, but not physical abuse to a woman or a cripple. It was time to show his hole card, before Radke or one of the others lost his head and did something that might leave somebody hurt or dead. He swept back his coat to let everybody see the pistol in his shoulder holster. He said nothing but let the sight of the artillery speak for him. It was eloquent, for the crowd cooled quickly.

Irish turned his attention back to the girl. "How about it, sweet thing?"

The Dutchman came with a broom and a metal dustpan. "Go on, Tracy. I'll get this."

Turk Radke's eyes had the color of lead bullets, and about the same degree of warmth. Irish could read the cold calculation in them as the big restaurant owner humbly swept up the broken dinnerware. Persuading the Dutchman to share his take with Boss should present little difficulty. One down. They still had the bootlegger, the whorehouse, the dancehall and the honky-tonk to go.

Radke and his five men took their time eating what the wait-ress grudgingly slammed down upon the table. Irish watched the faces and did not care for what he saw. Skinny, a tenement rat from somewhere back East, slow with his thinking but quick with a knife. Irish had not intended to hurt the driller Anderson after they had robbed him. Skinny had done that on his own, for the pleasure of it. He liked to see people bleed. Frenchy, of a violent temper and poor judgment. Grat, who had come out of Hell's Half Acre with Radke, sharing his contempt for the world but not Radke's fire. And huge, dumb Sarge, with his scarred wrestler's face and arms that could twist steel bars or crack a man's ribcage like a walnut. Boss and Radke had chosen them for strength and ruthlessness, not for brains. Men who thought too much were not likely to accept orders without question. Irish wondered sometimes why Boss and Radke had tolerated him so long. Of all these and the rest who would be following soon with Boss, Irish was the only one who ever listened to an order and then asked *why?* Even he did not do it often.

Done, the men got up and waited for Radke to pay the bill. Radke stood at the cash register, silently staring the big Dutch-man down before he pushed the check forward. "Looks to me like the girl's not any better at arithmetic than she is at being a waitress. She's overcharged us."

The Dutchman quickly ran down the figures, following them with the point of a pencil. "The sum is correct." His eyes came up reluctantly to Radke's.

"I say she figured three dollars too much."

The Dutchman wanted to argue but would not. "Very well."

He scratched off the original total and wrote a new one. "You men are passing through?" His voice sounded hopeful.

Radke shook his head. "We like it here."

Irish felt the hostile stares of the crowd following him and the others as they walked out of the restaurant. It was an uncomfortable feeling, but he knew Radke had a purpose. He had made an impression, and the word would spread quickly. A good start was half the job. By the time Boss got here, the ground would be plowed and planted.

Skinny stood picking his teeth and looking speculatively up and down the street as if counting money. "What next?"

Radke said, "We'll get rooms for us and Boss. What's the best hotel in town, Irish?"

Irish knew the ratty little place he and Skinny had used would not suit Boss for a minute. "There's a big stone one down in the older part of town, across the street from the courthouse. Cattlemen's or Stockmen's or some such name." He had tried for a room there before but had been told none were available. He had not made an issue of it because he and Skinny had been here simply to case the town and not to make themselves noticed. Radke, however, was ready to be noticed. He got into the red coupe while Irish cranked it.

The hotel had the solid look of old cattle money, like the stone courthouse itself, predating the oil boom. Beside a seeping water tank out back stood the whitewashed wooden tower of a windmill, its cypress wheel turning gently, squealing a little in its need for a greasing. Windmill towers spelled stability and permanence, but they looked like dwarfs against the tall oil derricks that spelled quick money. Irish O'Dell had little liking for either tower, but he could tolerate them for the cash, just as he tolerated Boss and Radke and the rest.

He stood at the curb, staring up at the second-floor windows that faced out onto the street. Boss always favored a southeast corner room where the windows were most likely to admit a cooling breeze. His bulk made Boss a man who took a lot of cooling. Irish saw that the windows were open, which meant the rooms were occupied.

Well, if he knew Turk Radke, they were fixing to have a new set of tenants. Radke strode through the open front door with the air of a bank examiner or a tax collector. He found no clerk at the counter. He had expressed hatred for those little bells that hotels always seemed to furnish for summoning a clerk. He banged the flat of his hand demandingly upon the countertop.

A slender middle-aged man in white shirt and bow tie appeared quickly from a room in back. "Here, here!" he said indignantly. "We have some day sleepers."

"Looks to me like the clerk is one of them," Radke retorted. "We've come to get rooms."

"There are no rooms to be had," the clerk said stuffily. "You may put your name on our waiting list if you choose, but I cannot say how long it might be before we have a vacancy."

Radke pretended he had not heard. "We want three rooms, including the one right over us here, on the southeast corner."

"Out of the question. I told you, sir, all of our rooms are occupied. The southeast corner room is permanently rented to a drilling superintendent for Gulf Oil."

Radke looked towards the stairs and nodded. "Frenchy. Grat. Sarge." Frenchy led the other two up.

The clerk said, "I told you . . ."

"I heard. But you're fixing to have a vacancy."

Irish heard fists banging on a door, a sudden rush of angry voices and the rumbling noise of a scuffle, quickly ended. Big Sarge came down the stairs, one hand firmly gripping the collar of a portly middle-aged gentleman whose face was crimsoned. Frenchy appeared at the balustrade, throwing down a couple of suitcases, some shoes and a pair of high-laced boots.

Radke smiled coldly at the clerk. "See there? I told you you were about to have a vacancy. Now, show me your register."

The clerk watched him sullenly while he signed *Edmund Daugherty and associates.* Radke said, "What're the numbers of those other two rooms?"

For just a moment, Irish thought he saw a glint of triumph in the clerk's eyes. "I don't think you want them both. One of them belongs to Sheriff Buckalew."

Radke let the pen slip and make a large ink blotch on the register. So far as Irish knew, he had never encountered this complication before, a sheriff living under the same roof. Boss was not going to like it one bit. But there was no backing down. This was the best place in town, and Boss always insisted upon the best. As for the sheriff, he would soon find himself either in

Boss's pocket, on the road or under a tombstone in that cemetery Irish had seen just over the hill.

Radke said, "We'll take two rooms on the other side. Are you going to see that they are cleared, or will we?"

The clerk turned the register around and for the first time saw the name Daugherty. He looked as if he had swallowed a fly.

"I'll take care of it."

Radke turned to Irish. He came as near smiling as he ever did. "All right. We've got work to do."

15

Moonshiners

HAVING SPENT the final years of his adolescence under Prohibition, Hap Holloway was not without some knowledge of moonshine, but he had never helped operate a still before. He stared at Preacher Perry's elaborate contraption with admiration bordering on awe. While the red-faced Preacher hummed a hymn, Hap fed mesquite wood at a slow pace into a blaze beneath the smoke-darkened copper mash barrel.

Preacher broke off the hymn to say, "One must be careful not to let the mash come to a boil, but simply allow it to make steam and come to fruition in the Lord's good time."

The cooking mash floated at the top of the sugar-and-water

222

mixture within the large barrel. As steam rose, it passed through a pipe at the barrel's top and moved noisily down into the next unit in the line, called a thumper. Beyond that it went into a coil barrel filled with water to cause the steam to condense. At the bottom of this barrel, it dripped from the coil into a crock jar. Hap's job at the moment was to keep the fire going at the proper level while Perry watched the crock lest it overflow and waste that prime stuff in the sand. Perry tasted the corn liquor periodically but sparingly, checking it for flavor and strength, pouring it into a mixing barrel, because one batch might come out stronger than another. Mixing it gave the end product all the semblance of consistency demanded by a thirsty oilfield clientele. The only time Hap had seen Perry take a drink of his own whisky was in this tasting.

"Impure, this stuff could blind a man," Perry admonished, "or give him the jakeleg. Too strong, it could kill him. I would have no such blight upon my conscience."

From someone else, Hap might have taken this for hypocrisy, but Preacher meant it. He held much the same paternalistic view toward his whisky customers as he once had held for the members of his flock when he had been a practicing man of the cloth. He offered toward some of his less scrupulous competitors the same rebuke he once had visited upon those who mocked the Word. He remained a true believer in the biblical teachings, but he saw no sin in good corn whisky.

Hap said, "Seems almost sacrilegious, cookin' this stuff in the daytime. I thought good moonshine was only made by moonlight."

"The time of the cooking has nothing to do with flavor but only with the vigilance of the local authorities. Smoke can be a giveaway in some places. Fortunately, Sheriff Buckalew does not concern himself with such trivial matters."

"What if the Rangers was to come to town?"

"There is so much black smoke around from oil burning in the fields that no one is likely to notice the pale bit this mesquite throws off. Anyway, we are far from Caprock."

That was the by-damn truth, Hap thought. Perry had located his still at a weathered old homesteader shack on one end of the Douglas Clive ranch. It was at least eight or ten miles from town. Back at the turn of the century, Perry had told him, the state had thrown much of this sand country open for homesteading, offering up to four sections to anyone who would stay on the land for three years. Most of the homesteads had been too small to furnish a living from cattle and the land too poor to farm. The homesteads would either be consolidated or sold to neighboring ranches at the end of the prove-up period. Clive and his predecessors on this land had used the frame shack to store feed. Now, for a share of Perry's profits and all the moonshine he could drink, Clive allowed Perry its use to make and store his corn liquor, put up in oak barrels until it had aged enough to make it fit for sale.

Men aged quickly in the oilfields, Perry said. So did corn liquor.

Water for the mash came from a windmill one of the previous landowners had put up for the benefit of his cattle. The water was pure and sweet and cold, pumped from a depth of seventy or eighty feet beneath the sands. Sure did make good whisky, Hap thought. A shallower old hand-dug well was nearer the house, but it had been allowed to deteriorate, its circular stone wall crumbling. Remnants of a well rope hung in threads from the rotted windlass. When the fire was going well, Hap walked over and looked into the deep pit. He could see a reflection of the sky on a little water, but mostly the bottom appeared to be only wet sand, some thirty feet or so down.

Perry said, "You'll find these old homesteads all over this country. They're a sad remembrance of those who came before us and starved to death trying to raise a crop on land the Lord never intended for the plow."

Hap commented dryly, "They ought to've tried corn."

Beyond the windmill, beyond a badly sagging set of working corrals, Hap could see what once had been an attempt at a field. It was a sandy wasteland now, blown out in places to the red hardpan, growing only a pitiful scattering of poor weeds. A hundred years from now, he thought, it would probably look no better. Like a bird fouling its own nest, man sometimes made an unholy mess out of the home Nature had provided him. He watched a long-legged jackrabbit making its way among the weeds, seeking sustenance. Poor pickings even for a rabbit.

He saw dust on the two-rut road and turned, suddenly worried. "Company comin'. You don't reckon the Rangers . . ."

The thought of being arrested by the Rangers made his stomach queasy. They were known on occasion to give a man a "cowboy shampoo," clubbing him over the head with a pistol barrel. And he thought often of the night in Oliver's dancehall when a Ranger had blown hell out of a man wanted for murder. Sheriff Buckalew was firm but wouldn't hurt anybody who didn't need hurting. The Rangers were another matter.

Preacher Perry seemed unworried. "It's just Clive. Probably come for more money. A true Philistine, that man. He can never get quite enough, either of money or of whisky."

Clive's Ford sedan was black, but the roads had given it a dirty gray color that in Hap's opinion matched the ranchman's personality. From what Hap had seen of him in town, he seemed perpetually in an ill humor, like maybe his feet always hurt him, or he had a boil on his butt. Hap remembered that Slim McIntyre had come to Caprock expecting to go to work for Clive. Slim might not know it, but failing to get that job had probably been one of the luckiest events of his life. Between Clive driving a man to do more work than ought to be expected of two, and his daughter Lauralou flaunting her body at him, a cowboy could go crazy on that ranch.

Clive drove up faster than a man ought to and set his brakes abruptly, sending dust fogging over the still. Perry tried futilely to cover the crock jar that held half a gallon of fresh whisky. He muttered, "May the Lord protect us from fools."

Hap had seen a chuckwagon cook take the double of a rope to a cowboy foolish enough to ride up too close to the wagon, and the horse hadn't raised half as much dust as Clive's automobile. "The Lord must love fools," he said. "He sure gave us aplenty of them."

Preacher responded with a shrug. "Perhaps He will give them more brains in the next life." He did not condescend to go out and meet Clive; he let Clive come to him.

The rancher slammed the car door and stumbled as he turned. Though the day was barely more than half-done, he appeared already on his way to being drunk. He moved with uncertain steps toward the still. "Good mornin', Preacher."

It was two o'clock in the afternoon, or perhaps a little later. Clive walked to the crock jar, stuck a finger in and tasted. "Ain't too bad," he said.

"I am glad you approve," Preacher replied. Hap knew that was about as near to an out-and-out lie as Preacher ever came. The bootlegger didn't give a damn what Douglas Clive thought. The arrangement between them was strictly business; mutual admiration had no part in it.

Preacher said, "My woodpile is wearing kind of low. Could you get that young Mexican of yours to drag up some more mesquite?"

"I ain't got him anymore. I fired his chili ass," Clive said.

"What did he do?"

"Nothin'. It was just an attitude I could feel comin' on. Let a Mexican stay on a place too long and he gets to thinkin' it's his."

"He has a family, doesn't he? What'll he do now?"

Clive snorted. "It ain't no worry of mine." He stuck his finger into the jar again, taking another taste. "So I reckon you'll just have to drag up some more wood yourself." He gave Hap a moment's critical study. "This boy ain't too good to do a little wood-haulin', is he?"

Next to digging postholes, cutting wood was one of the jobs Hap had dreaded most in his cowboying days. But hating the chore had not excused him from it.

Frowning, Clive turned back to Preacher Perry. "I expected you to come by the house this mornin'. I've got a payment due today, ain't I?"

Preacher glanced in the direction of the afternoon sun. "The day is far from over. I planned to go by this evening, after we finish running this batch."

"I need it now. I'm fixin' to go on a little trip. I'd like to have three hundred dollars."

"Three hundred dollars?" Hap knew by the darker red surging into Preacher's round face that he would be cussing a blue streak if he were not a pious man at heart. "I don't see where I owe you that kind of money."

Hap had not paid much attention to the car, assuming that Clive had come alone. Now, turning away from the growing argument that was no business of his, he saw Clive's daughter, Lauralou, in the front seat. He had watched her in town numerous times and let his imagination run free and wild, but she had never given him more than a toss of her head, a silent rejection. Probably figured him for an oilfield roughneck without enough money in his sock to show a girl a good time. That would have been on the mark more often than not. Well, what the hell? Nothing ventured, nothing gained. He would give her another chance. Since he had started working for Preacher, his pockets were jingling more than they used to.

He walked over to the car and touched his fingers to the brim of his once-proud cowboy hat, long since reduced by the ignominies of the oilfield. Her blond good looks took his breath a little. He did not understand how Slim McIntyre could have said no to all that ripeness when it had been offered so freely.

"Howdy, Lauralou."

She gave him a cool study. "Am I supposed to know you?"

"I know *you*. I'd like to give you a chance to know me."

"Is there any reason that I should?"

"Well, I'm a friend of Slim McIntyre's."

Her face flushed a little. "I don't know who you're talkin' about."

"Yes you do. Slim's a good old boy, but in lots of ways he's just a rank amateur. Me, now, I've been around the track. You wouldn't go off and leave *me* standin' back of no honkytonk. No ma'am, you'd be takin' all I could give you and beggin' for more. Me and you, we could be bosom friends. I'm ready to start any time."

"You go to hell!"

"I expect I will, eventually. But while I'm here I want to spread joy as wide as I can. All you got to do is ask."

"I'll ask you to leave me alone."

Douglas Clive hollered at him. "Hey, you, what you doin' over there?"

Hap tipped his hat again. "Keep smilin', Lauralou. See you in town sometime." He turned to face Clive, who stood with hands on his hips, looking angry enough to fight. He evidently had not won his argument with Preacher.

Clive declared, "You have no business with my daughter."

"Just tryin' to be sociable, is all."

"There is no call for you to be sociable with us. She don't have nothin' to do with oilfield trash. And that goes for moonshiners too."

Stung, Hap felt his skin prickling. "Then what do you bring her to a place like this for?"

"Where my daughter goes is no concern of yours."

Remembering what Slim had told him, Hap thought, *It had better be a concern of yours, a big one.* Liked excitement, she had told Slim. Seemed like the kind of excitement she was looking for stood a good chance of making a grandfather out of Douglas Clive before he was ready for it. Or her either.

Preacher pointed his round chin toward the mash barrel. "I think you need to be putting some more wood on the fire."

Hap realized Preacher was trying to remove him from harm's way. He turned his back on Clive and did as he was told. He didn't want to be messing up on this job and losing it; he had never had one that paid so well and required so little heavy lifting. He busied himself with the wood, then walked over to look in the crock jar. It was almost to the point of running over; Clive's arrival had distracted Preacher. Hap brought an empty jar to place beneath the drip spout and emptied the full one into the mixing barrel.

Turning, he saw another car coming up the road. He thought of the Rangers again, but he didn't remember that he had ever seen a Ranger drive a red coupe. "More company, Preacher. What is this, a railroad station?"

Perry squinted worriedly. "Somebody you know, Clive?"

Clive seemed suddenly nervous. "I wouldn't want anybody to find me here. It wouldn't look right."

"Too late to run now," Preacher said coolly. "It's one of your creditors, perhaps. Your sins have found you out."

Three men climbed from the coupe. They were strangers to Hap. No, on second thought he believed he had seen the driver in town a few weeks back, maybe at the dancehall, or perhaps at Jolene's. A tall, dark-complexioned man who looked as if he might once have been a football player, he wore a short-billed cap and also a coat, unusual at this time of year. With him was a dried-up little guy with a sharp face that made Hap think of a rat, or maybe a possum. The third man quickly drew Hap's attention. He had a cold, hard appearance. None of the three looked as if they had ever taught Sunday school.

The wind momentarily swept the driver's coat back and Hap glimpsed a pistol in a shoulder holster. His heart skipped as it occurred to him that they might have come to pull a highjacking.

Bootleggers were notoriously good targets for highjackers because they usually carried a lot of cash.

The third man moved ahead of the other two, his step purposeful, his manner that of a man in full control of all he surveyed. His narrow-eyed gaze ran swiftly over the still, over Hap and Clive, settling on Preacher. He made what might have been a flicker of a smile, but it was cold as January. Hap shivered again.

The man said, "You're Preacher Perry."

Preacher did not seem cowed. On the contrary, he was a bit testy. "I am *Mr.* Perry. I have not preached the Gospel in many a year. I am still a firm adherent to its teachings, though. One of its teachings is respect for the property of others, and this, sir, is private property."

The man did not respond for a moment. He walked over to the old well and peered down into it. He said, "You could drop a man in there, throw a little dirt over him, and nobody would ever find him." He glanced up at Perry as if inviting him to consider the implication. Hap could not see that Perry was troubled. His was not a business for the timid or weak.

The man said, "You may think you have a secret place here, Mr. Perry, but all I had to do was ask a few questions around town." He gave Preacher a moment's grave contemplation. "We believe in private property too. The fact is, we represent a man who has a reputation for making investments pay off quite well."

"If you want to buy some of my product, fine, but this is the factory. I prefer to do my business in town."

The driver spoke up. "I bought a bottle from you the last time I was in Caprock. You were doin' a brisk trade."

"One will always do good business if he offers a decent product to a public ready and willing to buy. I try always to give my customers their money's worth."

The cold-eyed one said, "You could charge them a lot more money and get it."

"I have competitors, sir. I sell the best quality, but many of my customers will settle for second best if they can get it cheaply enough."

"Competition can be controlled, Mr. Perry. That's where my friends and I fit into the picture. We've decided that what you need in your business is some good partners."

Perry gave Clive a critical glance. "I already have one more partner than I need."

The man turned his attention to Clive. "And I suppose you'd be Clive. As I heard it, you own this land."

Clive drew himself up into a belligerent stance. He reminded Hap of a rooster spreading its feathers for one more bluff before it turns and runs. "I don't see where that's any of your business."

The cold eyes touched Hap. Hap turned up both hands and said, "I just work here."

The stranger seemed to dismiss Clive and Hap without further thought, swinging back to Perry. "My name's Turk Radke. That mean anything to you?"

Perry reacted to the name as if he knew it, but he demanded, "Is it supposed to?"

"Maybe you've heard of Edmund Daugherty."

Perry flexed his hands. He began to look nervous. "You mean Big Boy?"

The man frowned darkly. "Mr. Daugherty gets red in the face when he hears that nickname. I would not use it again, were I you."

"I never heard him called by anything else."

"Then at least you know of him. You know he is a man who gets things done."

"I know he's a thief and a murderer and an abomination in the sight of the Lord. I take it you are one of his disciples."

"You could call me his lieutenant, like in the army. Or weren't you ever a soldier?"

"I was, and proud to say it."

"You can look upon Mr. Daugherty as the captain. He draws up the plans. I'm the lieutenant who takes the soldiers to carry them out. The good-looking gentleman with the cap is Irish O'Dell. The little man is Skinny. He may look small to you, but he has talents that make him as large as the next man. It is not a big army, but it knows how to get things done. Mr. Daugherty, now, he figures to be your partner. We're here to make the arrangements."

"I'd as soon make a covenant with the devil."

Radke stepped close to Preacher Perry, leaning toward his face. Hap held his breath. Perry began to sweat heavily. Radke pointed his index finger at Perry and punched it firmly several times against the bootlegger's ample stomach. Radke's voice dropped so that it was a strain to hear him. "When I was in France, whisky man, I saw a soldier jam a bayonet into a kraut soldier's belly. Spilled his guts on the ground. Made the damnedest mess you could ever imagine, like a bloody bundle of snakes squirming in the grass."

Perry said nothing. His hands trembled, yet he did not seem ready to give in. Radke crooked his finger and beckoned the smaller man. "Show him your knife, Skinny."

The little man took a long knife from his pocket. He opened the blade and pushed it against Perry's stomach.

Radke said, "You being a veteran like me, I'd hate to see Skinny do to you what that soldier did to the kraut."

Perry made a whimpering sound as the blade poked inside his shirt. Skinny thrust upward, and two buttons popped off. He did it again, slitting the shirt open to the collar.

Radke smiled coldly. "You mentioned the devil, whisky man. Skinny could send you to him right here and now, real easy."

Skinny brought the knifepoint up against Perry's throat.

Hap could not restrain himself. "For God's sake, Preacher, he's fixin' to kill you!"

Perry tried to stand up to the fear, but he could not. He began to wilt. "Wait. Wait." When Skinny removed the knife, Perry's hand went up to his throat. He trembled as he stared at a tiny smear of blood on his fingers.

"You ready to talk a little business?" Radke asked.

Perry nodded, beaten. "What does Daugherty want to pay me for a share?"

"Pay? He doesn't pay, you do. He just wants a percentage for taking care of the competition and seeing that you can charge what your whisky is really worth. Anybody hollers, we fix them. Anybody doesn't pay, we collect. You just take care of the work. Boss and I take care of the worrying."

He turned to Clive, hands on his hips. "We go on using your place just like the whisky man's been doing. You get your share, and you don't raise any squawk."

Clive could not move. A drop of sweat hung suspended at the end of his nose.

Radke fixed Hap with hypnotic eyes. Compared to him, the

Haskell brothers could have been ordained into the ministry. "And you, boy? Are we going to have any trouble with you?"

Hap shakily repeated, "I just work here."

Radke turned back to Preacher Perry. "Don't you forget that Mr. Daugherty owns an interest in this setup now. If there's one thing Boss and I can't abide, it's a thief."

Holding the knife close to Perry's face, Skinny snapped the blade shut with one hand. The noise was like a period at the end of a sentence.

Radke showed them his back, as if to demonstrate confidence that neither Perry, Clive nor Hap had the nerve to make any move against him. Hap had been so hypnotized by Radke that he had not noticed the one called Irish moving to Clive's automobile. Lauralou Clive watched the tall man, her blue eyes big and frightened.

O'Dell leaned through the rolled-down window and spoke. "There now, sweet thing, there's nothin' for *you* to be scared of. I'm partial to good, clean country girls. What's your name?"

Her answer was so quiet Hap could not hear it.

O'Dell said, "I don't remember that I ever knew a Lauralou before. Your daddy and us, we're partners now, so you keep a lamp in the window. I'll be seein' you." His hand moved to touch her cheek. "Maybe even tonight."

Skinny had kept his eyes on Perry, Hap and Clive, the closed knife in his hand. Hap sensed that the little man hoped one of them would give him an excuse to reopen the blade. Hap had no such intention, nor did Preacher or Clive.

Radke said brusquely, "Come on, Irish. We've other business."

O'Dell smiled at the girl. "Don't forget, sweet thing. A lamp in the window."

In a minute, the coupe was back on the two-rut trace, headed toward town. Douglas Clive had the washed-out look of a man who had just lost breakfast and dinner. Preacher Perry staggered over to the shack and slumped down on the wooden step, his knife-cut shirt half-soaked with sweat, a thin ribbon of blood still seeping from the shallow cut Skinny had inflicted upon him.

Hap brought him a cup of whisky from the mixing barrel. "I know you're not a drinkin' man, Preacher, but it looks to me like a time when religion needs to be spiked with a little whisky." He took a sip himself before handing it over.

Perry was silent, trembling. Hap said, "It's a good thing you gave in. He might've gutted you like a catfish."

Perry downed half the whisky from the cup. "I knew one or two like that in the war. No blood in them, just ice. No fear and no remorse. The devil's own."

Clive cried, "You got me into this, Preacher. What're we goin' to do?"

Preacher gave him a withering glance. "We've fallen into the clutches of Satan's minions. For now, we can only do what they tell us to."

"Can't we fight them? Can't we do somethin'?"

Perry just shook his head.

Hap said disgustedly, "I didn't see you fightin' them any. Nor me neither. The only one I see bleedin' is Preacher. At least he stood up as long as a man could."

Perry took another sip of the whisky. "They need us. That's what will keep us alive and on our feet. We've got to keep them needing us until the Lord shows us the way."

Lauralou got out of the car and walked to her father's side. Her eyes were still wide from excitement. "Who *were* those men, Papa? I never saw anybody like them in my life."

Hap said, "If you're lucky, you never will again."

But he saw something besides fright in her eyes. He had a chilling suspicion that in some perverse way she had enjoyed being a witness, had enjoyed being touched by a gangster named Irish O'Dell.

Girl, he thought, *Slim McIntyre was lucky to get away from your daddy. He was even luckier to get away from you.*

Preacher Perry bowed his head. Hap heard him ask quietly, "My God, hast Thou forsaken me?"

16

Trouble
at the Teagarden

VICTOR UNDERWOOD had waited for two hours in and around the cramped Caprock telephone office, trying to get a call through to the Panhandle town of Borger. He would sit awhile in the hot little frame building where the waiting area offered only two wooden straight chairs beside the open screen door, in front of the service counter. When one chair became too hard, he would try the other, then walk out to pace the narrow front porch, wishing to hell Brady would answer his call. In deference to the operator, he did not smoke indoors. Outside, he would strike a match on the sole of a lace-up boot and light his pipe, but today he took no pleasure in the tobacco's sweet flavor.

After an eternity, he heard the telephone operator shout to him through the screen. "Mr. Underwood, your party is ready."

He hurried through the door. She silently pointed to a wall telephone. It had a wishbone hook for the black receiver, and he had to turn up the mouthpiece, for the previous customer had been a little woman about five feet tall. "Hello! Is that you, Brady? Victor Underwood here . . . No, things are not going as well as I would want them. How is it up there?"

He stood in foot-tapping impatience while Brady told him about the miserably hot weather and the wind and the dust, and about his mother-in-law's long and irritating visit. Underwood only half listened, thinking how much it was costing him to let Brady run through his litany of complaints. When Brady paused, Underwood seized the opportunity. "I have not received my royalty check for the production from that Number Four well. It should have been here a week ago. I need it, Brady."

For a minute, he could hear only the crackling of the long-distance line, and he thought the connection might have been broken. He was about to call out to the operator sitting at her cable-cluttered switchboard when Brady's reluctant voice said, "I hate to tell you this, Victor, but that well has played plumb out. All it's done for the last three weeks is suck air."

Brady could not have hit him harder if he had been in the telephone office swinging a club. While Underwood struggled for words, Brady went on apologetically, "You know it never was much more than a stripper. I've seen more oil leak out of a T Model Ford. Looks to me like we'd just as well haul down the rig, pull the pipe and plug the hole with a stump."

"Maybe if we were to shoot it . . ."

"We did. All we got was dust. Sorry, Victor, but that's the breaks in the oil game. We'll just have to postpone our plans for gettin' rich. Maybe the next one . . ."

Underwood found himself sweating heavily. It would seem the telephone company could afford to put a few fans in this place, the rates they charged. A game, Brady had called it. Dice offered better odds. "There may not be a next one. I've been spending that royalty on the well I'm drilling here. Without it . . ." He glanced uneasily at the operator. She seemed to be busy with her switchboard, but he suspected she was taking in every word. It was bad enough being broke; for everybody in town to know made it worse.

He lowered his voice. "I've exhausted all my credit down here. Do you think there might be someone up there . . ."

Brady replied regretfully, "I'm afraid not, Victor, not without gilt-edged collateral. I'll bet you're borrowed up to the eyebrows on your equipment."

"That and a bit more."

"I wish I could help you, but I'm in pretty deep myself. Losin' this well has hurt me as much as it has you."

I doubt that, Underwood thought sourly. Brady had partnered him on some drilling enterprises that had come to but little payoff. Most of that little pay had always seemed to go to Brady.

Brady said, "I'll buy out your interest in the rig and the pipe, for whatever good that might do you. I have to warn you, though, it won't bring much. That kind of equipment is a drug on the market up here."

Brady would probably send Underwood the least amount he thought he could get away with. Good old Brady. "All right. Do the best you can. As quickly as you can."

At best, that meager return probably would keep him drilling no more than another couple or three weeks on Number Three Stringfellow. He was considerably short of the pay zone, if there was to be one at the bottom of that hole. His old cabletool rig was ungodly slow. If he could afford a rotary like Knox Anderson's . . .

"Goodbye," he said, and hung up the receiver, giving the crank a twist to signal the operator that the call was finished.

It was a wasted motion, for her switchboard was no more than ten feet away. She came to the counter without removing her headphones and figured his charges on a pad of yellow paper. He paid reluctantly, for every dollar spent elsewhere was a dollar that would not go toward making hole out on Henry Stringfellow's ranch. He didn't have many of those dollars left.

He walked out onto the porch and stood, letting the wind touch cool against the sweat beneath his shirt. He dreaded telling Elise, though he knew she would shrug it off and ask him what he wanted for supper. He wondered sometimes if she realized how bleak things could become for them. He wondered also how he was going to tell the crew. Tough as things had sometimes been, he had never missed making the payroll. He would make today's, out of his savings. But after that . . .

He watched a hunched-over man in oil-stained clothes, shuffling unsteadily down the street. He recognized Autie Whitmore. Autie survived these days on what his wife and daughter earned at the Teagarden and on odd jobs he could pick up here and there. Nobody trusted him on a drilling crew anymore. For a fleeting moment, Underwood saw himself in Autie's place. The thought was bitter. But he would feel no better off than Autie if he had to go to work for one of the major companies and be regarded with contempt as an overeducated flunky, subject to orders from people lacking half his training and field experience.

Why couldn't I have been lucky, like Knox Anderson, instead of so damned smart? He gave himself to a minute's speculation on where he might be today if he had remained in South America. Considerably richer, no doubt. But South America had hastened the death of his first wife, Mary. And had he stayed there, he would not have come to know Elise. He would not trade Elise for a forest of pumping wells.

It struck him that he had not eaten anything since breakfast, and very little even then. It was now midafternoon. His stomach burned from the acid of stress—it often did—but he needed to put something in it. He started toward the truck, then decided to leave it standing where it was. It drank gasoline like Autie Whitmore drank whisky. The Dutchman's Teagarden was only a couple of blocks. Perhaps the exercise would work off some of his frustration.

He moved along the wooden sidewalk, immersed in his troubles and paying scant attention to the people he passed. He became aware, however, of three men coming out of a poolhall and walking toward him side by side, taking up the sidewalk. A faint tingle began along his spine, a vague recollection of another time and place. Two of the three seemed somehow familiar. He thought he had seen them when he was drilling up near Borger. If these were not the same ones, they were the same type, thugs who gravitated to the busy oilfield towns like vultures. But unlike vultures, which waited patiently for something to die, this kind sometimes hurried the process along.

He sensed that they intended to crowd him off into the street, probably for no better reason than to show they could do it. At another time, he might have yielded ground, but he had already tasted enough gall for one day. A stubborn anger kept him walking, holding to a straight line. He felt three pairs of eyes sardonically challenging him. He squared his shoulders and met the outside man head-on, tensing so that his body went rigid as a fencepost, ungiving. The thug walked into him and bounced off against the man next to him. They both cursed, but Underwood was in no mood for compromise or apology.

The three faced around, fists clenched, and moved toward him. He quickly realized that his action had been foolhardy. But instead of ganging him, they abruptly drew away, turning and walking on down the street. He wondered if his dark mood could have made him look that menacing. Then he sensed a presence behind him. He recognized the voice of Sheriff Dave Buckalew.

"I admire your spirit, Mr. Underwood, but I have to say that I wonder about your judgment."

"It was a damnfool thing to do, Sheriff, but I had a lot on my mind. Those three looked like the smallest of my problems."

"They could've been the biggest one real quick."

"You don't know my biggest one."

"I could guess pretty easy. I suspect a lot of drillers have got the same problem right now."

"That could be." Underwood searched Buckalew's face for reproach but found none. He found instead a grimness, a simmering anger that he sensed was not directed at him. "Something wrong, Sheriff?"

Buckalew studied him a moment, his eyes half-closed. "That Indian called Choctaw, is he still workin' for you?"

"Yes, he is. Why?"

"I haven't seen him in town for a while."

"He hasn't forgotten about that chain you keep on the courthouse square. As long as he stays at the rig, he keeps out of trouble."

Buckalew seemed pained to ask, "Was he at the rig all last night?"

"Yes. He hasn't been off the location in weeks. Why?"

"I had to ask. The reason I had him on the chain was the big fight he had with Ox, that bouncer from Jolene's."

"I remember. But I don't understand the question."

"A drillin' crew found Ox this mornin', facedown in a slushpit north of town."

"Dead?"

"As dead as he'll ever be. Looked like somebody had beaten him real bad, then held him down in the oil and mud until he drowned."

Underwood felt a chill. He had no truck with Ox and his kind, but that was a grisly way for any man to die. "I won't say that Choctaw wouldn't kill a man. I won't even say he never has. But if he did, that wouldn't be his style."

"I never seriously thought so, but I had to ask. No, I think it was probably your three friends yonder, or some of *their* friends."

Underwood had to turn and look. He was gratified to see that the three had passed out of sight. "You didn't make any effort to arrest them."

"I spent all mornin' huntin' around out there, tryin' to find some kind of evidence. They didn't leave any." Buckalew looked exasperated. "I hate to admit it, Mr. Underwood, but I was almost hopin' they'd try to whup up on you. Ever since that bunch hit town, I been watchin' for some excuse to show them the county's hospitality."

Underwood shivered, fully realizing what could have happened had the sheriff not been watching the three. "I'm just as happy you didn't get that privilege at my expense." He wiped a soiled handkerchief across his face. "I think I've seen a couple of those men before, in or around Borger."

"I wouldn't doubt it. From what I heard, Borger had a plentiful sufficiency of them until the Rangers sent a few to glory."

Underwood remembered all too well. The mobsters had run over the honest business people and subverted many of the officers. When they became so bold as to murder a prosecuting attorney, an infuriated governor declared martial law and sent the Rangers to administer rough justice. The Rangers were more interested in results than in constitutional restrictions, and they forced an exodus of the shady element that brought cheers from most of the general population.

Underwood said, "I was about to go into the café for a bite to eat. You look as if you need a little nourishment yourself. Join me?"

"Draggin' Ox out of that slushpit kind of taken away my appetite. But I'd be pleased to drink coffee with you."

They walked into the restaurant together. At this off hour, in midafternoon, its customers were few. Underwood chose a table by the window where he could look out on the people and the traffic in the dusty street. He saw two men at a corner table. They looked to be of the same caliber as the three he had met on the sidewalk. As before, he was sure he had seen them elsewhere. Both of them fixed a hostile stare on Buckalew.

"Friends of yours, Sheriff?" he asked quietly.

Buckalew returned the two men's hostility. "They're part of the bunch. One of them's called Turk Radke. He's the righthand man to Big Boy Daugherty, so I'm told. They call the other one Frenchy. Either one of them would skin his mother for the hide and tallow."

"I knew of Daugherty in the Panhandle fields. I tried to tend to my own business and avoid his sort. Is he here?"

"He's comin', looks like. He's sent some of his henchmen on ahead. I'm afraid Ox was meant for an object lesson."

"Why Ox? I thought he was one of their kind."

"I can't get Jolene to tell me much, but it appears they're tryin' to muscle in on her business. I heard a rumor that a couple of them got rough with her. Ox stomped on them pretty good and threw them out into the street. Last night there was a commotion outside of her place. Sounded like a bad fight. Ox went to see about it, and he never came back."

Underwood frowned. He had been in a lot of oilfields, and he had seen this pattern more than once. He had hoped he would not see it in Caprock. "What can you do, Sheriff?"

"Just keep watchin' like a birddog, hopin' to catch them at somethin' I can salt them away for."

Underwood shook his head, pitying the lawman. Buckalew was a likeable sort, still basically a cowboy despite the badge he carried and the responsibility he bore. He had probably been just what this town and county needed in a sleepier time when the biggest excitement of the year was cattle-shipping season. But he was floundering in turbulent waters that could easily drown him, especially if mobsters like Daugherty were moving in.

"Do you ever think about going back to ranch work?"

"All day every day and half of every night. But if I was to turn my back on this place now it'd be like a cowboy quittin' in the middle of the fall works. I wouldn't be much of a man."

"You'd be a *live* man. Daugherty and his kind are not to be trifled with. They'd kill you in the blinking of an eye."

The grimness of the sheriff's face showed that the thought was not new. "I wasn't brought up to be a quitter."

Underwood could understand that. He considered his financial troubles, the well he intended to finish if he had to tie a crowbar to the end of a rope and work it by hand. *Neither am I,* he thought.

Tracy Whitmore came out of the kitchen with a pot of coffee. She filled the men's cups and took Underwood's order for a plate lunch. He noticed that the thug Frenchy watched her intently, undressing her with his eyes. As Tracy returned to the kitchen, she made a wide detour around the man's table, not offering to fill his cup or Radke's. Evidently she had already learned to avoid Frenchy's reach. Underwood felt a quick anger, picturing Elise caught in the same predicament.

"If there's ever anything I can do to help you, Sheriff . . ."

"You're a driller. Fightin's not in your line."

"I worked in South America. We carried pistols, and more than once we had to fight off bandits who wanted to rob the crew. These men are a different brand, but bandits just the same."

A young man came out of the kitchen, wearing a wet apron and leaning on a cane. Underwood recognized Slim McIntyre, the cowboy who had worked for the shooter Birdsong. He saw a smile pass between the cowboy and Tracy. Underwood had never considered Tracy a pretty girl, certainly not like Elise. But she glowed as she looked at McIntyre, and the glow transformed her.

The sheriff noticed too. His eyes brightened, his grim mood easing. "Now, there's a sight to bring out the sunshine on a cold winter's day."

Underwood let memory drift. He thought of Mary, long years ago, and Elise in recent times. "Everybody's felt that way once, if he's been lucky. Haven't you, Sheriff?"

Something came into the lawman's eyes, a fleeting sadness. "Once." He took a quick sip of his coffee.

"I'm luckier. I've been blessed twice."

Buckalew's gaze settled on Tracy, but Underwood had a feeling he was seeing someone else. The sheriff asked, "Can the second time ever be as good as the first?"

"It won't be the same. But yes, it can be as good."

McIntyre noticed Underwood and Buckalew. He seemed a little embarrassed, being caught in his admiration of Tracy. He moved toward them, walking with only a trace of a limp. "Evenin', Sheriff . . . Mr. Underwood."

Underwood extended his hand, and McIntyre took it. "Are you here for a late dinner, Slim, or an early supper?"

McIntyre shook hands with Underwood. "I'm washin' dishes here till I'm in shape to go out and find me a real job again." He looked back toward Tracy, who stood in the kitchen door. He gave the two thugs in the corner a suspicious study, then limped back toward Tracy.

Underwood suspected his plate lunch was getting cold in the kitchen while Tracy visited with the cowboy, but he said nothing. She remembered after a little and brought it, along with the coffeepot.

Underwood said, "I saw your father at a distance a while ago. How has he been?"

"About the same. Some good days, some bad." The tone in her voice told him more than her words.

"I hope you'll give him my best regards."

"He'll be glad you asked." She started back toward the kitchen, carrying the pot.

Frenchy hammered his empty cup upon the table and demanded, "Hey, sister, how about a little service? I'd like some of that coffee too."

She glared at him. "Maybe when you start payin' for it."

"I'm a partner here, sort of. You'd do well to remember it."

Reluctantly she went to his table and poured from the pot.

He gave her a sly grin and said, "Why don't you stick your finger in it? Make it sweet enough that I won't have to use no sugar."

She replied in a cutting voice too low for Underwood to make out the words. Frenchy said something else. She raised the pot and poured the hot coffee over his head and down his collar. He squalled loudly and grabbed her hand. Underwood and Buckalew jumped to their feet, but Slim McIntyre was nearer and quicker. He took two long strides, swung the cane high and brought it down across the thug's right hand so hard that Underwood heard the wood crack. Frenchy shrieked in pain and jerked back his hand, grabbing it with the left.

"My fingers!" he cried. "You broke my fingers!"

Slim took what was left of the cane and hooked it around the back of the man's neck, giving him a savage jerk. "You ever touch Tracy again, I'll break more than your fingers!"

Buckalew quickly intervened, pushing between the two, taking hold of Slim's cane. "Let's see your hand," he demanded of Frenchy. When the man extended it, Buckalew squeezed it roughly. Frenchy cried out again. Buckalew kept squeezing the fingers while the thug cringed. "They're not broke," he said, "but they ought to be. Pity he didn't bust your head." He turned to Tracy, who clung to Slim, her face flushed. "You talked like this man owes you. How much?"

"I don't know, exactly. The whole bunch has been comin' in here to eat. I always give them a check, but they never pay. I keep tellin' Mr. Schwartz, and he keeps tellin' me to forget about it."

Turk Radke intervened, his eyes cold. "We have an arrangement with the Dutchman. It's our business, and his."

Buckalew said angrily, "The Dutchman's not here, so I can't ask him. But I think you owe this young lady a tip for the trouble you've caused her." He caught Frenchy by the front of his shirt and gave him a rough shaking. "Pay the girl."

The man dug a roll of bills from his pocket and painfully peeled off a dollar. Buckalew gave him another shake. "That ain't near enough." Frenchy peeled off several more bills. It was evident that his fingers hurt him. "You've got no right . . ."

Buckalew's eyes narrowed. "I'm sheriff in this town, and I'll do any damned thing I decide to. I've decided that if I ever catch you in this café again I'll put you on the sunny end of that chain at the courthouse, down by the ant bed, and let you sweat for about a week." He took Frenchy's shirtfront in both hands and gave the man one more good shaking. "Do you understand me, punk?"

Frenchy mustered a tentative defiance. "Big Boy'll have somethin' to say about this when he comes."

"You tell your Big Boy that he's not a bit too good for that chain, either." Buckalew shoved the man away from him. Frenchy stumbled backward and almost went down. Buckalew said to Tracy, loudly enough that Frenchy had to hear, "You let me know if he comes back anymore. I'll break that other hand."

Radke had stood back, silently watching, his gray eyes smoldering. "You wear big boots, Sheriff. But I don't think you'd want to die in them."

Buckalew turned on him, bristling. "You threatenin' me?"

"I'm just telling you." He turned on the cowboy. "And you, pearl diver, you've got a payment coming to you. Nobody does to one of my boys what you did just now."

Frenchy scurried to the door ahead of Radke, turning to seek out Slim with hating eyes. "You, boy, next time I see you, you won't be needin' a cane. You'll be needin' a stretcher."

Tracy was tight lipped, clutching Slim's arm. Underwood thought she was less frightened than angry. So was Slim, who said, "I could've taken care of him by myself."

Buckalew said, "I don't doubt it. But it's not just him you've got to worry about. It's the others that come along behind him."

"They were just makin' big talk. I've heard big talk before."

Underwood put in, "This your first boomtown, Slim. You don't know about people like that. You don't know about Big Boy Daugherty and the men he keeps around him."

"All I know is that I ain't standin' by and lettin' nobody abuse Tracy." Slim put his arm around Tracy's shoulder.

The sheriff said, "Mr. Underwood is tryin' to tell you that these gangsters' whole operation depends on gettin' the town buffaloed and keepin' it that way. You just whupped one of them, and they can't afford to let you get away with it."

Slim glanced at Tracy, then back to the sheriff. "I'm not fixin' to run."

"I wouldn't tell you to run, exactly, but if I was you I'd walk awful fast. They killed a man last night. You're liable to be the next one."

Slim's eyes went wide at talk of a killing. He looked down at Tracy. "But I've got no job. I don't have anywhere to go."

Buckalew said, "I've got no job for you, but I've got a piddlin' little ranch where you can stay until things cool down. House isn't much, but the roof doesn't leak water and the stove doesn't leak coals."

Underwood put in, "I know where it is, out next to Henry Stringfellow's. It's not far from my rig. I could take you out there with me."

"I wouldn't want to bum off of anybody. I've always earned my way."

"You could give my horse some ridin', check on my cows for me," Buckalew said. "Unless you want to come down and stay at the jail with me, this town won't be safe for you."

"I spent a night in your jail once, Sheriff. I don't fancy that notion atall."

Tracy gripped Slim's arms. "Please, Slim, do what they're sayin'. I don't want you hurt."

"It'd still be runnin'. I don't like the taste of it."

The lawman said, "You'd like the taste of their brass knucks a lot less. They beat Ox half to death last night, then drowned him in a slushpit."

Slim looked down at Tracy. "You really want me to go?"

"No." She blinked rapidly. "I don't want you to go, but I'd rather have you out of my sight and safe than here where I'd be dreadin' every minute that they'd do somethin' awful to you."

Reluctantly Slim nodded at Buckalew and Underwood. "I'd be much obliged, then. I'll have to go by Mrs. England's and put my stuff together, what there is of it."

Underwood picked up half of the broken cane. "You'll need to get another of these too. This one won't be any good to you."

Slim shook his head. "I was fixin' to throw it away."

Underwood looked at his plate lunch, only a little of it eaten. The excitement had robbed him of appetite. He tried to pay Tracy, but she waved his money away. "Thanks for takin' Slim away from here."

She turned back toward the cowboy, who stared sadly at her. The sheriff jerked his head at Underwood as a signal for the two of them to go outside and leave the young couple alone. Underwood glanced back once. They were in one another's arms. He felt guilty for having seen.

Buckalew looked down the street in both directions. Underwood knew he was watching for any of the Big Boy mob. Buckalew said, "You're a Yankee, ain't you, Mr. Underwood?"

Underwood was taken aback. He had not thought of himself in that way for a long time. "I guess I am."

"My old granddaddy fought the Yankees in the War Between the States. But he'd've liked you."

"My father was in the same war. He wore the blue. But I believe he would have been proud to call you friend. I know *I* am."

17

A Further Education

SLIM McINTYRE felt as if he were being rushed, given no chance to consider. Allowed a little more time, he might have elected to stay in town and stand the risk, for he did not know how long it might be before he saw Tracy again. But the account of Ox's violent death had been a stomach-turner, and he could see that Sheriff Buckalew's concern was real. Slim knew nothing about the gangster element beyond stories he had read and a couple of movies he had seen. Gangsters were supposed to exist in cities back East somewhere; he had not considered that they might reach out into a town like Caprock, right here in West Texas. It was true that somebody—almost surely the Haskell brothers—had tapped him on the head for thirty-three dollars

247

his first night here, but he did not regard them as gangsters of the kind the newspapers told about. They were petty thieves who should be swinging picks and shovels on some road gang, their ankles locked to a good stout chain.

Mrs. England had already heard about the murder; news like that penetrated even closed doors like dust from a west wind. She left the tiny porch of her L-shaped rooming house to follow Slim, the sheriff and Victor Underwood to Slim's cracker-box room. She wrung her hands in indignation. "Lord knows, I don't hold with that man Ox and his kind, nor with the tainted women in that house down there. I pray every night for the Lord to shine His light upon them and cause them to cease their wicked ways. But I would not wish that kind of a death off onto no-body." She fastened a demanding gaze on the sheriff. "Who you reckon done it?" Her eyes implied that he should have solved the case by now.

Buckalew took no offense. "You've lived in other boomtowns, Mrs. England. You've probably heard that Big Boy Daugherty's thugs have moved in on Caprock. I expect your guess would be about the same as mine."

Her gaze turned with sympathy toward Slim. "And now they've made a threat against this fine young man. I declare, I don't know what the world is comin' to. I wish the Lord would rise up in His wrath and smite the heathens hip and thigh."

Victor Underwood said, "I would not be surprised if one day He sends the Rangers in here to do His work."

The sheriff looked as if he had bitten into a sour apple. "He won't need the Rangers. They're my job."

Underwood said, "I've been to too many oilfield funerals, Sheriff. I don't want to go to yours."

It did not take Slim long to pack, for his accumulations amounted to little. Mrs. England brought him a paper sack of sugar cookies and homemade bread. She watched regretfully as he looked about the room to be sure he had left nothing. She said, "I'm sorry to lose you, but I'm sure the sheriff and Mr. Underwood are right. And I'm proud of you, takin' up for Mrs. Whitmore's poor defenseless girl."

"Poor maybe," Buckalew said, "but not defenseless. She scalded that thug like you'd scald the bristles off a hog."

"And what about the girl? You reckon they're liable to try and do somethin' against her?"

That thought had haunted Slim from the first, one reason he had not wanted to leave town. But Underwood told Mrs. England what he had already told Slim. "They want this town to be afraid of them, but they don't want it angry enough to rebel. They know that most working men just want to do their job and mind their own business. If the mob muscles in on the bootleggers, nobody pays much attention. They can take over a house like Jolene's. They can kill a man like Ox because most people consider him beyond the pale anyway. But if they did something to a driller's daughter like Tracy they would have a howling mob of roustabouts smashing their doors down."

"I wonder what it *would* take to wake everybody up," Buckalew said.

Slim pitched his belongings into the wooden bed of Underwood's truck. He tried to shake Mrs. England's hand, but she embraced him in arms strong enough for a wrestler. He would have settled for the handshake. She said, "You and that splendid young Hap Holloway . . . what would the innocent women here do without you and your kind to take up for them?"

The mention of Hap Holloway and innocent women in the same breath brought a quizzical look from the sheriff. Slim would have to explain the connection to him someday, but this was not the time. Mrs. England had been kind to him, if overprotective, and he had rather leave her illusions intact. She was still waving as the truck pulled around the corner. Sheriff Buckalew followed in his black car.

Underwood avoided the main street, so Slim was robbed of a final chance to see the Teagarden and perhaps be lucky enough to wave at Tracy. Slim lamented, "I feel like a dog that's bein' whipped away from home."

"It's better than being buried here."

Slim slumped against the door, glumly watching Ragtown pass by, and the oilfields that began at the edge of town. He remembered the road; he had traveled it with Trinidad Suarez, going to the Douglas Clive ranch his first full day in Caprock. He had been out this way several times with Mr. Birdsong to shoot wells, but he had never been as far as Underwood was taking him. "I don't like the idea of bein' a burden on Sheriff Buck-alew."

"You'd be a burden on his conscience if something happened to you."

Slim watched the oil derricks thin out, then disappear as the truck cut across a corner of the Clive ranch. From things Hap had told him, he knew that Hap and Preacher Perry ran a boot-leg still out here somewhere. Hap had indicated that Clive not only knew about it but took a percentage of Perry's income, part in cash and part in merchandise. Slim had tasted moonshine, most of it barely drinkable, but he had never seen a still. Well, if Clive couldn't get himself an oilwell, maybe the next best thing was a contraption that pumped whisky. Oil from a well had to undergo considerable refinement before it could be put in an automobile. Preacher Perry's whisky was ready to drink right out of the barrel.

He doubted that Underwood was aware of all this. Slim took him to be dedicated to business, without much time or patience for the kinds of distractions to which so many around Caprock seemed devoted. But he had seen the man's young wife. He supposed Underwood didn't spend *all* his time on business.

They came to a wooden gate that bore a small and peeling wooden sign proclaiming in modest letters *Henry Stringfellow*. Slim got out to open the gate, then saw a couple of horsemen pushing a bleating flock of sheep along the other side of the fence toward a set of net-wire pens a hundred yards beyond the gate. Underwood cut the engine, for they would have to wait a bit. Slim stood beside the truck so the sheep would not so easily see him and perhaps turn back on the riders. Both horsemen were Mexican. When the dust dropped momentarily, Slim rec-ognized one as Trinidad Suarez.

The sheep passed slowly. They were mixed ewes and lambs, many of the lambs tending to drop toward the rear, the ewes bleating, turning periodically, looking anxiously for their trail-ing offspring. Underwood got out of the truck. He and Slim walked to the fence together.

Slim said, "Howdy, Trinidad. Remember me?" He extended his hand over the fence.

"Sure 'nuff," the young man responded, breaking into a smile of recognition, teeth shining a pearl white against the dust that coated his face. He shook Slim's hand.

"I thought you was workin' for Douglas Clive."

Trinidad turned serious. "Mr. Clive, he fired me."

"What for?"

"Another cowboy, he comes along lookin' for work. Mr. Clive, he tells me he is tired of Mexicans."

Son of a bitch, Slim thought. "So now you're workin' for Mr. Stringfellow?"

"Not for pay. But Mr. Stringfellow, he is a kind man. He says for me to come stay on his ranch until I find another job. He lets us live with my wife her brother, Miguel." He pointed toward the other man, who had gone on.

Slim nodded toward the sheep. "But you *are* workin'."

"I do not feed my family Mr. Stringfellow's groceries and sit doing nothing. I am a poor man, but I am not a beggar." He lifted his hand in a semblance of a wave and rode on after his brother-in-law and the sheep.

The gate swung easily, not sagging and heavy like so many. That was a mark of good caretaking and bespoke a man who took pride in what he owned, even if it *was* a sheep outfit.

Slim perceived that the air was somehow different, and not just from the dust or the sheep. It carried no smell of oil. The sulphur had been so pervasive in Caprock that he had become accustomed to it and forgot it existed. Its absence here, far from developing fields, was noticeable.

When Slim climbed back into the truck, Underwood pointed westward. "The sheriff's place is that way. If you look hard, you might see the top of his windmill in the distance."

Slim could not. The dust from the sheep had drifted into his way. Underwood pointed toward a wooden derrick a mile or mile-and-a-half away. "We'll go by the rig first. I think you'd enjoy a good meal cooked by someone else before you have to begin subsisting on your own."

Having shot many wells with Mr. Birdsong, Slim no longer stood much in awe of the tall derricks of steel or wood. He had even become able, within limits, to judge the financial status of the drilling company by the caliber of the equipment. Studying this rig as they drove up to it, he guessed that Underwood's was what the oilfielders called a "poor-boy" operation. Most of the

251

equipment he could see showed the scars of age and heavy use, like the chugging old truck. Somehow the picture did not quite fit a man of obvious education and culture like Victor Underwood. But stories told around Caprock had assured him that even well-educated oilmen could go broke if the breaks didn't favor them, just like good cowmen could when weather held hot and dry and the cattle market turned sour. Many would argue that college-trained geologists had no better success rates in locating good wells than self-trained "creekologists" who trusted intuition and experience.

Slim was surprised at the plain tarpaper-covered shack where Mrs. Underwood waited on the step in front of the door. Seeing the Underwoods in town, he had assumed they would live much better than this. The small and simple structure stood atop a set of heavy skids, which reminded him of a sled. He had seen feed sheds larger than this crude frame shelter.

Elise Underwood's brown eyes were warm. She met her husband halfway, embracing him as if they had been apart for a week. Slim supposed a woman could get awfully lonesome living in such a little shack, miles from anybody except family and working crew. He remained near the truck, not wanting to intrude.

Underwood hailed him. "You remember Elise."

Slim removed his oil-stained old cowboy hat and bowed slightly. "I sure do. Mighty pleased to see you again, ma'am." Her smile warmed him and made her look even younger than he remembered her.

"Slim is going to stay at Sheriff Buckalew's place for a while." Underwood did not explain. Slim guessed he tried to shield his wife from unpleasantness. Perhaps her small shoulders were too thin to carry the weight of trouble.

But trouble was in Underwood's face. "Elise, I've brought bad news. The Number Four well up north has stopped producing."

Her smile faded as she saw the worry in his eyes. "How badly are we hurt?"

"Badly enough. I'm going over to the rig and talk to the men. Perhaps you'd better not come."

Slim saw in her eyes a determination that surprised him. He had figured her for a fragile flower who might wilt under stress. She said, "Whatever involves you, involves me. I'll come."

"The men may swear a little."

"I grew up in the oilfields. They won't say anything I haven't heard before."

Underwood frowned, doubting. Slim wondered if he also had figured his wife for a fragile flower. Underwood started toward the rig, carrying a badly worn leather briefcase under his arm. Elise took several quick, short steps to catch up with him. Slim fell several paces behind, for it was not any of his affair.

He recognized old Henry Stringfellow's car parked near the derrick. Underwood had told him the rancher visited almost every day, checking on his progress toward or retreat from a fortune. Stringfellow stepped down from the rig floor to the ground. Underwood shook the sheepman's hand.

Stringfellow spoke some pleasantry to Elise, then strode out to meet Slim, offering his hand. "I remember you, cowboy. I found you and Trinidad givin' a poor pony a double load one day."

"I imagine the pony was as grateful to you as I was."

The rumbling and clanking of the machinery was overpowering. Slim watched the huge walking beam pumping up and down. Each downstroke dropped a sharp, heavy bit to the bottom of the hole, gradually chipping away at whatever rock, gravel or compacted sand was down there. A tall man with several days' growth of gray-sprinkled whiskers held his hand on the well rope, letting it ride up and down with each stroke. Mr. Birdsong had said a good driller could tell by the feel of the rope what was going on at the bottom of the hole, no matter how deep. It took a long time for a man, however willing, to become a good driller.

A large, dark-complexioned man stood nearby. He looked strong enough to wrestle a bull to the ground. By his high cheekbones and the shape of his face, Slim wondered if his ancestors not many generations back had possibly done that very thing to the buffalo.

Underwood spoke to the driller, who nodded and signaled to the Indian. In a minute, the machinery was shut down, though Slim could still hear the hiss of a steam boiler beneath a sheet-iron-roofed section beyond the rig floor. The driller hollered loudly enough to scare cattle a quarter mile away, "You-all come on over. Mr. Underwood wants to talk to us."

Underwood's dour expression showed that it was not something he *wanted* to do. Three more men came out of a distant large tent from which a stovepipe projected. Light gray mesquite smoke curled upward. One man had a flour-sack apron tied about his middle.

Mr. Birdsong had told Slim that a typical cabletool outfit was made up of a driller and a tooldresser. If it worked two tours a day, that was four men, plus sometimes an extra roustabout or two to take care of whatever might come up, like fetching fuel for the boiler or helping handle pipe.

Underwood's reluctant gaze moved from one man to another and back to his wife. He said, "I've brought the payroll." The others smiled, but Underwood did not. "The rest of my news is not so good. You know that I've depended on a well up north for operating costs here. That well has dried up."

The smiles faded. The driller arched an eyebrow. The men seemed to be guessing ahead of Underwood; they had probably encountered similar situations before. Oilfield work was precarious, financially as well as physically.

"I don't know when I can pay you again after today. The best I can do is to promise that I will pay you as soon as I am able, or to offer you an alternative proposition." Underwood waited a moment for reactions to pass. "I have faith that there is oil on this ranch. The formations tell me it *has* to be here. I have enough money left to continue to feed you. If you will stay with me and work for board, I will give each of you a share in the lease."

Nobody spoke, though Underwood paused long enough to give them the opportunity. "I will be honest with you; it will probably not make any of us rich. But if we can bring in even a middling good well . . ."

The tall driller said glumly, "That's a mighty big *if,* Mr. Underwood. We've already drilled two dusters on this place. So far this well has looked just like the other two. I'm afraid we've got about as much chance of strikin' oil here as we'd have of strikin' Irish whisky."

The cook said, "If I was a young bachelor, Mr. Underwood, I'd stay and gamble along with you. But I've got a wife and two kids in town. They can't live on prospects."

The Indian stood silent and still, revealing nothing by his expression.

254

The driller said, "We hate to leave you in this shape, Mr. Underwood. But you can see how it is."

Underwood gave each of the men a moment's study, then shrugged in resignation. "I have no hard feelings. Come on down to the cook tent, and I will pay you off."

Elise Underwood had listened silently, but her face had colored. She raised her hands and said firmly, "Wait a minute now, let's don't be so quick. Most of you have worked with Mr. Underwood before. Has he ever treated you any way but fair?"

The driller said, "Nobody's goin' to argue with you about that, Mrs. Underwood. He's always shot square with us."

She took her husband's arm. "He's an oil man, and he says there's oil under this ground. If you'll stay with us, we'll find it, and it'll be worth more to you than any wages you could earn workin' for somebody else."

The driller said sympathetically, "But we've got families, and they have to eat *now.*"

The three men turned away toward the kitchen tent. Underwood gave his wife's hand a squeeze and followed. Only Elise and the Indian remained on the rig floor. She looked up at him, for he towered far above her. Her voice betrayed emotion she was trying hard to control. "Aren't you goin' for your pay too, Choctaw?"

"No ma'am. I've got no wife and no kids. I've got nowhere in particular to go and nothin' in particular to do."

She touched his hand, and he stiffened in surprise at the gesture. "You're a good man, Choctaw. But you and Victor can't drill this well all by yourselves."

"We can if we have to."

Slim and the old sheepman waited on the ground just off the rig floor. Elise gave Stringfellow a forlorn smile. "I don't suppose you'd like to learn the drillin' trade, Uncle Henry?"

He knocked ashes from his pipe. "I've spent too many years around sheep to learn anything that new." He turned to Slim. "What about you, cowboy? You would appear to be an easy learner."

"Me?" Slim tried to think of excuses. He looked up at the tall wooden rig, imagining himself climbing all the way to the crown block more than eighty feet above. The thought was scary. He grabbed at the first thing that came to mind. "They've lost their cook."

Elise Underwood said, "When my father was alive, I sometimes cooked for crews he worked on. I can do it again. Choctaw and Mr. Underwood can teach you what you need to know."

Slim felt the Indian's stern gaze burning like sunlight through a magnifying glass. Choctaw said dubiously, "I've met a lot of cowboys. Most of them were too dumb to learn any other trade."

Henry Stringfellow had evidently built a good rapport with the drilling crew. He grinned. "A smart Indian ought to be able to train one of them, though."

Choctaw grunted. "We'd still be shorthanded to run two *towers.*"

Stringfellow said, "Trinidad Suarez has been wishin' for any kind of a job. He'd be a willin' student."

Choctaw looked to be near rebellion. "My daddy brought me up to be a warrior, not a schoolteacher."

Stringfellow gestured toward the derrick. "Ain't much call these days for a warrior. There's a right smart call for oil."

Choctaw's gaze settled on Slim again, hard. "There's experienced men in town lookin' for a job. They wouldn't need no trainin'."

Elise said, "But they'd want a regular paycheck. Mr. McIntyre here has already volunteered to work on faith."

In truth, Slim had not volunteered to do anything, but entreaty in the woman's brown eyes stopped him from saying so. He *did* need a job. One that might or might not eventually pay off was better than not having one at all. At least he wouldn't be taking advantage of the sheriff's generous nature.

"Yes ma'am," he said, biting back his misgivings. "I'll stay if you want me to."

The crew came out of the cook tent and retrieved their belongings from another that had been their sleeping quarters. In a few minutes, they climbed into an old Chevy coupe parked on the far side of the rig. They disappeared in a fog of dust on the two-rut road toward town, a dozen miles away. Victor Underwood stood alone by the tent, watching until they were out of sight. When he walked back to the rig, his steps were slow and his shoulders hunched. He looked as if he probably hurt all over.

"I swore I'd drill it by myself if I had to, but that was wishful thinking. We need a crew."

Elise placed her hands on his arm. "Choctaw is stayin'. He can drill well enough to spell you. Mr. McIntyre says he's ready to go to work. Uncle Henry is goin' to bring that Mexican, Trinidad. And I'll do the cookin'. So you see, we *have* a crew."

Underwood blinked in astonishment.

"That's a persuasive young woman you've got there, Victor," Stringfellow said.

Underwood gave her a doubting look. "But you, cooking . . ."

"You know I've done it before. I was pretty darn good if I can say so without braggin'. We've got too much at stake here to let a few small obstacles stop us."

"Money is no small obstacle."

"I've spent most of my life gettin' by without it. Daddy always said it wasn't havin' too little that made us poor. He said we were poor for wantin' too much. All I want now is to see us finish that well."

Underwood stared as if he had never seen her before. "I don't know what to say."

She tiptoed up to kiss him on the cheek. "Don't say anything. Just come with me to the cook tent and let's see what-all I'll need to fix supper."

Henry Stringfellow mused, watching the couple walk away, "My late wife, God bless her, wasn't much bigger than that. The strongest women I ever knew came in small packages."

Choctaw observed, "So does dynamite."

Stringfellow turned toward his car. "I'll fetch Trinidad in the mornin'. He's out helpin' Miguel doctor soremouth sheep. Even an oil derrick ought to look good to him after that."

When the old rancher drove away, Choctaw faced Slim, his huge hands on his hips. Curtly he declared, "I'll bet you never even been on a drillin' floor. I'll bet you don't know the difference between a calfwheel and a bullwheel."

Slim knew one was bigger than the other. "I worked awhile for Mr. Birdsong, the shooter."

"Shootin' is one thing. Drillin' is another. You'd better learn what everything is and what it's for, so when me or Mr. Underwood tells you to do somethin' you'll know what we're talkin' about."

Choctaw pointed out the walking beam, which supported the drilling cable and would eventually pump the oil if the well came in. He showed Slim the calfwheel, which raised and lowered the steel casing, and the larger bullwheel, which regulated the length of the drill bit's fall and pulled the bit from the hole when it needed sharpening. He warned him to stay clear of the massive bandwheel that worked from a long belt connected to the steam engine in the rear and gave power to the walking beam.

"Fall into that," he declared sharply, "and the world'll be short one more dumb cowboy."

Slim said, "I don't remember that I ever met you before, but you act like you're mad at me about somethin'. What is it?"

Choctaw gave him a minute's hard study. "I knew cowboys when I was a kid. Always acted like they was the lords of the earth. Thought they had to whip any Indian that didn't step off the sidewalk for them. Well, they never whipped *me.*"

Slim could see why. Choctaw was one of the biggest men he had ever seen in terms of muscle. "I'll step off the sidewalk any time you want me to."

Choctaw glanced back over his shoulder. "Another thing: Mrs. Underwood. There's been one or two thought because she's younger than Mr. Underwood that she might be lookin' for a young man to give her somethin' her husband couldn't. I've been obliged to correct their thinkin'."

Slim said, "Such a thought never entered my head. Anyway, there's a girl in town . . ."

"You keep thinkin' about that girl, then, and maybe me and you'll get along."

Slim wondered if Elise Underwood realized she had a guardian. After watching and listening to her a little while ago, he doubted that she needed one.

Underwood returned from the kitchen tent and shook Slim's hand. "I promise, you won't be sorry." Then he said to Choctaw: "We still have daylight. Let's be making hole."

The machinery began clanking and chugging again. Slim asked, "What do you want me to do?"

Underwood had his hand on the drilling line. "Show him the boiler, Choctaw. It probably needs some wood."

258

Choctaw took Slim to the rear of the unit, where he could hear the hiss of steam from a boiler sheltered beneath a sheetiron roof. He showed Slim a stack of cut, dried mesquite wood, then opened the fire door. "You'll have to keep enough wood in here to hold the steam up, but not enough to get the pressure too high. Been boiler men killed for not watchin' the pressure."

The gauge had red numbers beyond a certain point. Choctaw stuck his finger against its glass case. "The pressure ought to stay between there"—he moved the finger—"and there. That's what keeps everything runnin'. When you're not tendin' the boiler you can help out on the rig floor. And when you're not doin' either one, you can be out gatherin' and choppin' wood to keep that stack in good shape. And the woodpile over by the cook tent." He turned to go but stopped again. "It don't pay a man to have too much idle time on his hands way out here. He gets to thinkin' about things that he oughtn't. You keep busy, cowboy."

Choctaw wasn't much taller than Slim, but he probably outweighed him by close to a hundred pounds. Watching him walk away, Slim recalled the stories he had read and the picture shows he had seen about cowboys and Indians. The cowboys had always won.

This damned sure isn't any picture show, he thought.

18
Jail Time

SHERIFF DAVE BUCKALEW awakened suddenly from his nap, jarred by a loud noise out on the street. He got up and walked to his hotel-room window. Evidently a truck hauling a load of drilling pipe had made a sudden stop to avoid hitting a car, and a chain had snapped, dumping several strings of pipe onto the ground with a considerable clatter. He saw no sign that anyone was hurt or that anybody was about to get into a fight over the accident. They didn't need him down there. He thought about returning to the bed, for he badly needed the sleep, but he was wide awake now. His dresser clock showed it to be three-thirty in the afternoon. He had hoped to sleep until supper, for he had been up all the previous night, chasing pipe thieves around the oilfield. They had gotten away from him, dodging along the rough back roads without lights. Had the truck down on the street not borne the clear markings of a major oil company on its door, he would have gone down to check it out, just in case.

His attention was drawn to a familiar red Ford coupe pulling up to the curb beside the hotel. He felt a churning of frustration in his stomach as he watched Irish O'Dell alight from it. A girl climbed out on the passenger side. O'Dell took her arm. Dave thought she might be some dancehall girl trying to earn a little extra on the side until he took a second look. He was surprised to recognize Lauralou Clive.

He had heard and dismissed a rumor that O'Dell was playing around with Lauralou. As little use as he had for either of the Clives, father or daughter, he felt a twinge of disappointment. Lauralou had long struck him as reckless in her constant quest for excitement, but he had not considered her so lacking in judgment that she would become involved with a felon, even one with O'Dell's good looks and dashing manner. The pair disappeared from his view. He knew they were coming into the hotel. In broad daylight. He would not have been surprised had she been one of the short-skirted women who followed the oil booms for whatever they could get, but this was a hell of a way for a hometown girl to act.

He tucked his shirttail into his britches, then stopped to yawn. He was not in a good humor to begin with, and seeing Lauralou with Irish O'Dell was enough to start him cursing under his breath. He stepped out into the hall and waited at the top of the stairs, his stomach sour.

O'Dell and Turk Radke and their bunch had settled in a set of rooms along the hotel's front, where they could watch the main street. Dave had briefly considered finding lodgings elsewhere, but decent rooms were hard to find in crowded Caprock. Anyway, leaving would have been capitulation of a sort, and be damned if he was going to let them have that satisfaction. Living under the same roof with the Daugherty mob was a little like spreading his blankets near a rattlesnake den. But he could observe their comings and goings to some extent. Sooner or later, he might catch them committing a jailable offense. Up to now, they had managed to conduct their deviltry—and there had been quite a lot of it if rumors were to be believed—out of his view.

Watching Lauralou ascend the stairs with O'Dell, he could easily see why men might lose their heads over her. She had a filled-out figure and a sensuous way of moving that he might find hard to resist if she ever tested him. Rumors said she delivered all that her manner promised, when she wanted to.

Lauralou did not see him until she was almost at the landing. Startled, she missed a step and would have fallen but for O'Dell's firm hold on her arm. Her face flushed.

Dave ignored O'Dell. "Howdy, Lauralou. I'm surprised to see you here, and I'm surprised at who you're with."

Lauralou did not meet his eyes.

Dave asked, "Does your daddy know where you're at?"

She did not answer. O'Dell said jauntily, "Always the good and watchful sheriff. Tell me, Buckalew, do you take an interest in what every grown woman does in this town?"

"I guess I don't quite see Lauralou as a grown woman. She's still a schoolgirl to me."

"She's been out of school a long time."

"A pity, because she's got a lot to learn."

O'Dell smiled wickedly. "She's an apt and willin' pupil." He led Lauralou down the hall, pushing a door open and taking her inside.

A minute later, three men came out of the room, grinning and snickering until they saw Dave. Quickly sobered, they passed him and went on down the stairs. One was the rat-faced little thug called Skinny. Another, his hand wrapped, was Frenchy, who had made bold with Tracy Whitmore and gotten his fingers cracked. The third was a huge, fight-scarred man who looked as if he could lift a horse. Dave had heard them call him Sarge. He had also heard that Turk Radke had tried to force Sarge upon Jolene as a replacement for the late Ox. Making him the new bouncer would give the mob a set of eyes and ears in Jolene's house to be certain they received their share of everything she took in. He could also watch for prospects who seemed to have more money on them than was good for their health. So far, from what Dave had heard, Jolene was still holding out against everything Radke demanded. Dave watched the three, his hands itching to hit something. Frustration had a sour taste, but there was nothing he could do.

One day, damn you. One day.

He went back to his own room to pick up his wallet, his keys, his pistol, his hat. He walked to the window again and looked down upon the street, where the busy truck and auto traffic kept dust rising and falling. For the thousandth time, he visualized Caprock as it used to be, quiet and dull. He wished he could turn back the calendar. Times, the battlefields of France seemed almost preferable. At least there he had usually known what to do. There the enemy had been something he could see, something tangible he could shoot at. Here they were under the same roof with him, yet they were like wraiths he could sense but not quite see, feel but never quite touch.

There had been a time when he had never bothered to lock his room, but that time was past. He gave a resentful glance toward the room into which O'Dell had gone with Lauralou. He started to descend the stairs, changed his mind and walked down the hall as quietly as his boots would let him. He stopped at the door to listen, half hoping he might hear something, perhaps a cry for help, that would give him an excuse to break in and drag O'Dell off to jail. But it was a forlorn hope. Lauralou didn't want any help. She had entered that room of her own will. Whatever she was doing now, behind the door, was of her own choosing. He was mesmerized for a moment, yielding to an erotic imagination. Then he grumbled under his breath about his momentary lapse, chiding himself for weakness. *Watch it, Buckalew, or you'll wind up joining the rest of them.* That thought came more and more often.

He found lanky Waddy Fuller standing in front of Shemp Oliver's dancehall. Waddy strode several steps to meet him. He pointed a thumb toward the dancehall door. "You been tellin' me to keep an eye on them thugs. They come out of the hotel a little bit ago and made a beeline for the dancehall. I just seen them take a bunch of money away from Shemp."

Dave's hopes rose for a moment, then ebbed even before he asked, "Did you see them point a gun at him?"

"Nope, they don't have to. We both know they've got the Indian sign on him."

Dave chewed at his inner lip while he studied the dancehall.

263

"If they've thrown that big a scare into him, he won't tell us anything. But I reckon we ought to go and ask him anyway." He walked into the room, where the chunky Oliver was wielding a broom like a weapon, attacking the settled dust as if he had just declared war. He was so absorbed in his anger that he did not notice Dave and Waddy until Dave spoke. "You want to tell me about it, Shemp?"

Oliver swung around quickly, bringing up the broom to defend himself before he recognized Dave. "Tell you about what?"

"Waddy saw Daugherty's boys take some money from you. I've got plenty of room in the jail if you'd like to tell me somethin' I can hang on them."

Fear quickly eclipsed the anger in Oliver's face, fear that Dave could smell like the garlic on the man's breath. "I've lived in a Daugherty town before. If they was to think I'd been talkin' to you I could find myself floatin' facedown in a slushpit like Ox, or layin' out in the mesquite brush with a bullethole between my eyes. I doubt there'd be many people cry at my funeral. *You* wouldn't."

Dave would have to admit that Oliver had a point. He had never brought himself to develop any respect for the man. He had a cowboy's fine contempt for the exploitation of the girls who danced in this place, earning so little that some turned to part-time prostitution to make their drab lives a little more bearable.

"So you'll just keep knucklin' under and payin' whatever extortion they want from you?"

"Beats hell out of sudden death." A knock sounded at the back door. "I got business to attend to." He leaned the broom against the wall and walked toward the back as the door opened. Preacher Perry stood there. Oliver jerked a thumb in Dave's direction, and both men held their silence.

Dave turned to Waddy. "Let's go." He stopped on the plank sidewalk, still watching through the window. He saw Hap Holloway carrying in cases of beer for Oliver to sell to thirsty dancers. "Waddy, you ever tried any of Preacher Perry's bootleg suds?"

Waddy shook his head. "Nope. You want me to?"

"I doubt you'd like it much. It tastes like it needs to be run through the horse one more time." He jerked his head. "Come on, let's go around back and see if we can get Preacher to talk to us."

They walked down the side of the dancehall and waited until Oliver had finished paying Perry. When Oliver went back inside and closed the door, Dave stepped out into the alley, into Perry's view. The portly bootlegger eyed him with misgivings. Though Dave had always tolerated his business activities, there was never any telling when a lawman might decide to start upholding the federal prohibition laws, or taking a cut.

"Howdy, Preacher," Dave said pleasantly. "How's business?"

"It has been better."

"Before you had to start splittin' with the Daugherty gang?"

Perry looked back suspiciously at Hap, who was putting empty cases into the trunk of the automobile. "Someone must have been talking to you, Sheriff, someone the good Lord shorted on judgment."

"I wish somebody would. You know I've never interfered in your business as long as you didn't raise a commotion. But I've been hearin' things. I have an idea they've got your head wedged in a vise."

Perry began sweating, looking both ways down the alley. He gave Hap another quick glance. "Hurry up, boy. We have work to do." Perry walked around the car and opened the door on the driver's side.

Dave shifted his attention to Hap, who was trying to stack the cases so they would ride easier. "How about you, Hap? You got anything to tell me?"

Hap shrugged. "All I do is work here." But trouble was in his eyes, as it had been in Oliver's and Perry's. Hap looked at the ground and said quietly, "You know the Haskell brothers I used to run with? You might want to go talk to them."

Perry's anxious voice called, "Hurry up, Hap. We have deliveries to make."

"You'd better go pretty quick, Sheriff. Else you'll miss them." Hap climbed into the car beside Perry and slammed the door. Dave ducked his head to avoid the dust as the car sped down the alley.

Waddy said, "The way people keep wantin' to not talk to us, you'd think we smelled bad or somethin'."

"There's a bad smell around here, but it's not ours, and it's not just oil in the air. We're drivin' out to Ragtown."

He had visited the Haskell brothers' tent so many times in the course of one investigation or another that he could have driven straight to it in the dark with the lights off. Until lately, just about any time an offense was committed by parties unknown, the Haskells had been his first thought. Now, in comparison to the new crowd in town, they seemed almost benign.

The tent was stained from dust and rust and rain, for it had seen service in oilfield towns before Caprock. Chances were that it might see service in others even yet, for boomers were highly mobile, following the scent of oil wherever it might lead them. The Haskells were not boomers in the sense that they spent much of their time working in the fields. That was only an occasional necessity when they found the pickings lean in their more favored pursuits of gambling, highjacking and general confidence games.

He stopped the car in front of the tent and stepped out. He could hear conversation, actually more like an argument, going on inside. He nodded for Waddy to follow him, and he pushed through the flap without announcing himself.

One of the brothers quickly declared, "It wasn't us. Whatever it is, somebody else done it."

"A guilty conscience hollers before anybody accuses it."

Both brothers looked as if they had been run over by a team of oilfield mules. One's face was streaked with red where cuts had been treated with Mercurochrome or iodine, and blue from bruises where there were no cuts. The other had one eye swollen and dark, his lips split and double their normal size. A front tooth was chipped. Both men moved stiffly, obviously hurting.

Dave said, "Looks like you boys've been used pretty hard. Want to tell us about it?" He noticed two cheap suitcases lying open on canvas cots. The brothers had been packing what few clothes they owned.

The brother with the swollen lips tried to say something, but he could not bring out the words plainly enough to be understood. The other said, "I don't see where we owe you any favors, Buckalew. You always been buzzin' around us like a horsefly lookin' for a place to bite. Well, next time somethin' turns up stole around here, you'll have to hunt somebody else to blame it on. You'll be sorry to know we're fixin' to leave."

"I'm brokenhearted. Before you go, you want to tell me who did this to you?"

Haskell shook his head. "Nosiree. You'd have us testifyin' in front of a jury, and when we left the courthouse there'd be somebody lookin' to drown us in a slushpit, like they done Ox. I don't see no reason we ought to be totin' your load for you. You never done nothin' for *us.*"

"It was Turk Radke or some of his boys, wasn't it? Maybe that big bruiser Sarge?"

The brothers looked at one another. The one who had done the talking said, "I ain't sayin' it was or wasn't. But there's a new bunch moved into town, and they don't want any piss-ant competition from the likes of us. They said next time they'd get *mean.* Me and Bo, we never did like the climate here anyhow."

"I've been hopin' to get somethin' solid that I could use to put Radke and his bunch away."

"Not from us you ain't. This town ain't seein' nothin' more of us except our shirttails. We're gone." Haskell closed his suitcase. His brother Bo followed his example. "I'll tell you one thing, Sheriff. We're just a couple of dogie lambs compared to that bunch. Them's wolves, hungry ones." He moved to the tent flap, then paused. "You know anybody goin' to Odessa? We sure would like to hitch a ride."

"Me and Waddy'll haul you out to the edge of town. You can thumb it from there."

They carried the two beyond the city limits and stopped. As the brothers alighted from the car, Dave said, "You boys ever come back to Caprock, I'll throw you in jail."

"What for?" Haskell asked.

"For hitchikin'. You know it's against the law."

Waddy turned to watch the Haskells through the rear window as Dave backed the car around and started toward town again. "Good riddance. Them boys've been like a boil on the butt."

Dave grimaced. "I'm afraid we've swapped a boil for a cancer."

He drove the rest of the way in silence, face creased with trouble. He found an open spot by the curb near the front of the hotel and cut the engine. He sat, frowning in thought. He could feel Waddy's gaze and knew what Waddy wanted to ask him. He answered without waiting for the question. "I don't know. We've just got to keep watchin' and hopin' we'll see somethin'. Or maybe somebody'll get tired enough of bein' stomped on to come tell us what we need to know."

Waddy sat to full attention. "I wisht you'd looky yonder."

Irish O'Dell and Lauralou came out of the hotel. Lauralou had her arm locked possessively around O'Dell's waist. Her face seemed to glow. O'Dell just looked tired.

Waddy let a small whistling sound escape his lips. "You don't reckon . . ."

"I reckon."

"What some of the hometown boys wouldn't give . . . And me to." Waddy hastened to add, "If I wasn't already a happily married man."

Dave watched the couple pull away in O'Dell's red coupe. Lauralou was sitting as tightly against O'Dell as she could without getting into his lap. He thought of Douglas Clive. Surely Clive must know. Some fathers around here would be hunting for O'Dell with a shotgun and not worrying about the consequences. Clive was probably just immersing himself a little deeper in a bottle.

Waddy said, "Don't seem right, him comin' in here and takin' up with one of our own girls."

"I'm not sure who was doin' the takin' up." Dave got out of the car. "If you don't have anything else to do, Waddy, you can go check the jail and then mosey on home to supper. I'm goin' up to my room. Got some thinkin' to do."

Waddy sometimes knew his limitations. "I wouldn't be much help to you there." He started up the street.

Dave was about to enter the hotel when he saw Skinny and Frenchy walking to meet Waddy. He watched. They blocked the sidewalk, as they had done with Victor Underwood. Unlike Underwood, Waddy hesitated, then stepped down into the street to let them pass. Dave shook his head.

He waited until the two were almost ready to enter the door, then moved in front of them in silent challenge. They glared at him, but they moved aside. Dave walked through the door first. He felt a glow, winning even so small a triumph.

In his room, he ruefully surveyed his face in the mirror and remembered that he had not shaved today. There had been a time when he had prided himself on better self-discipline. Half the men in the oilfield did well to shave twice a week, including Sunday. He was succumbing to too many of their careless habits, he thought. He lathered his face over the small washbasin and sharpened his razor on a leather strap. His hands were not quite steady, and he nicked himself once. He blamed it on loss of sleep. One of these times, he was going to slip off to that little homesteader house on his ranch and stay for three or four days, doing nothing except sleep and eat.

As he walked down to the Teagarden for supper, he thought of Waddy eating peacefully at home with Annabelle. He wouldn't trade places with Waddy, for Annabelle would have to come with the deal, but there were times when he could not help envying his deputy a little. Surely enough, the café was crowded and noisy. Men stood in line, waiting for a place to sit. He considered going on up the street to the Elite hamburger joint, but he didn't think a hamburger fried on an overgreased grill would rest easy on a stomach already riled.

Tracy Whitmore spotted him standing in the doorway, trying to make up his mind. Beckoning, she pointed toward the kitchen. He followed her there. She said pleasantly, "Crowd's pretty heavy tonight, Sheriff. You're welcome to take supper in here if you don't mind standin' up."

"I'm much obliged." He acknowledged Mrs. Whitmore. She stood in front of the wood range, frying thick-sliced potatoes in deep, hot lard. She nodded back, pushing futilely at a single curl that kept falling over her sweat-beaded forehead.

He asked Tracy, "Heard anything from your cowboy?"

"Just a note is all. Mrs. Underwood brought it by. Four or five lines to tell me he's doin' all right. I don't suppose he's much at writin' letters."

"It probably takes all his attention, learnin' his way around a drillin' rig. He's a rank tenderfoot in that line. Oilfielders call them beetles, or some such of a thing."

"Weevils," Tracy corrected him.

Her smile took the edge off what had been another calf-slobbers kind of day. He could not help comparing her to Lauralou. He would admit that Lauralou was by all odds the better-looking. If a man was looking for excitement and didn't know any better, he would pick Lauralou. Dave remembered seeing Slim McIntyre with her several times. But excitement always faded. He hoped Slim had the good judgment to hang onto the silver and let the tinsel go.

He asked, "Has that Frenchy feller been back in here givin' you trouble?"

"No. I've seen him stop in the door two or three times, like he intended to come in, but he's always turned away. I guess you ran a good bluff on him."

"It wasn't a bluff."

If Frenchy needed a woman he could spend his money at Jolene's like other men did. Dave wouldn't voice such a thought where Tracy or her mother could hear it, of course. Respectable women didn't know much about that murkier side of oiltown life, or ignored it and pretended they didn't know. Dave accepted that attitude. It kept the lines distinctly drawn, eliminating a lot of uncertainties about what to say and where to say it.

Tracy filled a plate for him. He held it in one hand and ate with the other, leaning against a cabinet for support. He had eaten many a chuckwagon meal leaning against a wheel when his legs were too sore or stiff for him to squat on the ground. The food tasted the same.

Tracy said worriedly, "I guess anybody could find out where Slim is at if he wanted to bad enough."

"That rig's a long way out in the country. Frenchy and those other ginks strike me as bein' too citified to go to that much trouble unless there was money in it. But if they were to catch Slim in town where it's handy . . . He'd better stay put for a while."

"That means I won't be seein' him."

"This won't last forever, I promise you."

"What're you goin' to do?"

"I wish I knew."

The town was relatively quiet that evening, so Dave managed to get to bed early. At one point, he awakened to a shuffling of feet in the hallway, a rattling of loud conversation, the thumping of suitcases or boxes set down roughly upon the floor. He grumbled to himself, wishing people would have more respect for the weary. The racket died down, and he drifted back to sleep.

He was up soon after daylight. He felt his face and decided a shave could wait. Maybe tonight. He looked out the window as he almost always did early in the morning, wondering if it might rain today. It seldom did, but his ranch upbringing kept him wishing it would. He brushed his teeth, dressed and walked down the stairs to start another day in what could still be a nice little cowtown if they had just left it the hell alone.

The desk man, Albert, was already on the job, his black bow tie a throwback to gentler days when this hotel had catered to ranch families, cattle buyers and during court sessions to out-of-town lawyers and judges. Albert had always been an officious type, protective of his dignity and that of the hotel. His transition to the boomtown atmosphere had been as unwilling and incomplete as Dave's. Dave had not liked him much in the beginning because of the man's superior airs, but he valued him now as a vestige of a better time.

"Beautiful morning," Albert said.

"They usually start that way. What worries me is how it'll end up."

"This one did not begin very well, I'm afraid. They awakened me after midnight. You have some new neighbors. The man himself, and a couple more of his worthy associates."

Dave stared out the open front door. He could feel this day going to hell in a hurry. "Big Boy Daugherty?"

"The very one." Albert's lip curled in disdain.

Dave glanced up the stairs. "How did he look to you?"

"Do you remember that cattle buyer who used to come in here from Fort Worth, tracking cow manure across the floor and never once hitting the spittoons?"

"I do."

"I would not be surprised to learn that Mr. Daugherty is his long-lost brother."

Dave heard footsteps on the stairs. He stepped back through the open door into Albert's room so he could see and perhaps remain unnoticed. Frenchy and big Sarge strode into view, both grim faced. They did not speak to Albert, nor did the desk man speak to them. Dave walked back into the small lobby and watched through the window while Sarge cranked O'Dell's red coupe.

"Looks to me like they're fixin' to carry bad news to somebody. Maybe I ought to go see who." Dave went out, started his black car and followed the red coupe at a discreet distance.

He was surprised to see it pull up in front of Jolene's place. Even granting that these men seemed to have a perpetual appetite for that sort of thing, he thought it unusually early in the morning to be making a special trip. He parked and sat, watching the two men rattle the locked front door. In a minute or two, a woman appeared, a shadowy figure on the other side of the glass. From the men's gesturing, he assumed they were arguing with her. The door finally swung inward, and the two went inside. Dave got out of his car and followed.

Quietly he pushed the door open and stepped into the lobby. The heavy odor of perfume hit him. It was in strong contrast to the faint sulphur smell of oil which perpetually hung over the town.

He could hear voices down the hall, in Jolene's office. He started to move in that direction, then stopped as he saw the woman called Lydia standing halfway up the stairs, watching him questioningly. He put a finger to his lips and pointed toward Jolene's office. He moved to its open door, the carpet silencing his steps.

He could hear Jolene's angry voice. "I told you before, I don't need any partners, and the only protection I need is from you!"

A deep voice he took to be Sarge's said, "You don't have your man Ox no more. I heard he wasn't much of a swimmer."

Dave knew Frenchy's voice. It was higher pitched than Sarge's but no less threatening. The difference was that between a Bowie knife and a stiletto. "We been patient with you too long, Jolene. Boss come in last night. He was awful peeved when we told him you was still holdin' out on us. He told me and Sarge to fetch ourselves over here first thing this mornin' and not come back till we got the job done."

Jolene declared, "You'll get damned hungry, sittin' here waitin'. You can tell that old lard bucket there'll be snow six feet deep on the Fourth of July . . ."

The sentence was interrupted by a sudden footstep, a gasp of surprise and pain.

Dave swung through the door, hand on the butt of the pistol. Frenchy had Jolene's arm twisted almost to the point of breaking. Sarge stood watching, huge hands on his hips.

Dave shouted, "Hey!" Frenchy swung around in defensive reflex. Dave whipped his pistol from its holster and swung it as hard as he could, slamming it against Frenchy's knuckles. Frenchy doubled over, crying out as if mortally wounded. Slim McIntyre had already cracked the same hand.

Sarge just stood there, too surprised to move. Dave swung the pistol around to cover him. He always carried an empty in the cylinder to prevent an accidental firing, but Sarge wouldn't know that. The big man raised his hands. "I ain't heeled, Sheriff. You don't need to be a-pointin' that thing at me."

Lydia had rushed into the room behind Dave. Jolene held her arm, face twisted in pain.

Frenchy remained bent over, gripping the hurt hand close against his chest. His voice was little more than a wheeze. "You've broke it. You've broke it all over again!"

"I damn sure hope so." Dave glanced at Jolene. "You all right?"

She felt of the arm as if fearing it might be broken. She looked more angry than frightened. "I'll be all right. If you'll fetch me my baseball bat and leave me with that little bastard for a minute, you'll see how us Cajuns square up our debts with one another."

"Don't tempt me." Dave looked at the whimpering Frenchy, then at Sarge. "You two are under arrest."

Sarge blinked in disbelief. "We're with Boss Daugherty. Where we come from, that means nobody messes with us."

"You ought to've stayed where you come from."

The big man's breath would stun a dog. "All we done was try to buy us a little pleasure. She said it was too early in the mornin' and jacked up the price. Wasn't no real harm done."

"I heard enough to know that's a lie. We'll let a jury decide what to do about it."

Jolene showed misgivings. "A jury?"

"You want to stop Daugherty, don't you?"

Jolene sat down heavily in the chair behind her desk. Lydia stood beside her, one comforting hand on Jolene's shoulder. "Cases have a way of never comin' to trial when Daugherty's men are involved."

"We've got a chance now to put a halter on two of them, at least."

"If you're lookin' to me to testify, Buckalew, you can forget it," the madam said.

"You've always been a brave woman, Jolene. I don't see anybody else resistin' their extortion like you have."

"Resistin' extortion is one thing. Testifyin' against them is another. As far as I'm concerned, nothin' happened just now."

Sarge made a dry grin. "You ain't only a good-lookin' woman, you're a smart one." He turned to Dave. "Why don't you take a lesson from her and go mind your own business?"

Dave backed away from Sarge's breath. "I don't need her testimony. I'm witness enough, if that's how it has to be." He looked at the other woman. "What do *you* say, Lydia?"

He had not noticed until now the way her hazel eyes were fastened upon Frenchy. He saw loathing there.

Frenchy blinked, staring back at her. "Lydia! I think I know you." He blinked again. "Hell yes, I remember you."

Her voice was edged with hatred. "And I remember you. I remember what you did to me, all of you."

Frenchy demanded, "Does Irish know you're here?"

"I've made it a point to stay out of his sight." She turned to Dave. "Yes, Sheriff, I'll do it. I'll be glad to testify."

Jolene reacted with alarm. "Lydia, you can't . . . You could get yourself cut up, maybe killed."

"This man Frenchy and the others . . . they already killed me a long time ago."

Frenchy's face twisted. "You wait'll Irish finds out. He's hunted the whole country for you . . ."

Fear flickered in Lydia's eyes, but her hatred overcame it. "He can't do worse to me than he's already done."

"Turk Radke can. At least you're still breathin'."

Dave motioned with the muzzle of the pistol. "Go on. Out into the lobby." To Jolene he said, "I wish you'd call my deputy, Waddy, at his house and tell him to hurry over here. I could use his help gettin' these two to the lockup."

Jolene didn't even know Waddy's last name, which Dave took as a compliment of sorts to Waddy. He told her Waddy's number. She called central and in a moment said, "Mrs. Fuller, I need to talk to Mr. Fuller, please." There was a pause, then, "Tell him it's Jolene." The next pause was much longer. Waddy finally came to the telephone, and Jolene relayed Dave's message. When she hung the receiver back on its wishbone cradle, she said, "I'm afraid you'll have to explain to that woman, Buckalew, or your deputy'll be sleepin' by himself tonight."

"Won't hurt him," Dave said. "I've done it all my life." He tried to watch Frenchy and Sarge, but he kept being drawn back to Lydia. She had seated herself in a chair across the room and was staring at the wall. The turmoil in her eyes told him she was reliving an old horror. He felt helpless, wanting to help her but knowing no way.

Jolene was looking at Lydia too. "You'd better not stay here anymore. Irish'll come lookin' for you. Maybe Radke too."

Dave knew Jolene was right. "Where can she go?"

"I don't know. Irish won't hurt her, but if Radke wants her there's no way you can stop him short of puttin' an armed guard on her door twenty-four hours a day. She needs to get out of this town."

Waddy arrived, looking considerably downtrodden. "Dave, you've got me in a right smart of trouble with Annabelle."

"I'll straighten it out. Right now we've got these men to take to jail. Bring the cuffs."

Frenchy whimpered when Dave snapped them on his wrists. "I've got to see a doctor. I think you broke my hand."

It was turning a dark blue where the pistol had struck. "It's a long way from the heart. Let's be goin'."

He put the two in the back seat of the black car. He doubted they would try any violence against him or Waddy, not here in the street where somebody could see and bear witness. They would depend upon the influence of Big Boy Daugherty or the muscle of Turk Radke to free them.

Jolene stood on the front step, watching anxiously. "What about Lydia?"

"I'll be back directly," Dave promised. "We'll talk."

Waddy cranked the car, then got in on the passenger side, turning to watch the two prisoners in the back. Dave pulled away from the curb and headed for the jail.

Frenchy kept complaining. "Damn it, Sheriff, this hurts like hell. I got to have a doctor."

Sarge demanded, "You goin' to let Boss know where we're at? He won't leave us sittin' in your cracker-box jail."

"I'll let him find out in his own due time. I want you two to enjoy the county's hospitality long enough to get sick of this town."

He considered putting them on the chain, where the warm sun might cook some of the meanness out of them, but they would be too visible there. Daugherty and Radke would learn too soon what had happened to them. Dave wanted time. He and Waddy locked Frenchy and Sarge into separate jail cells, slamming the steel doors as hard as they could. Dave had found long ago that the heavy sound of a cell door closing had a salutary effect upon many men. It probably was not new to these.

Sarge complained, "We ain't had breakfast yet."

Frenchy whined, "You got to do somethin' about my hand."

Sarge seemed to have no sympathy for Frenchy and his problem. "I always eat three eggs. Sunny-side up. And plenty of ham. Lots of fat on it."

Dave said, "Waddy, I'll phone Doc Tolliver to come over and look at Frenchy. You go fetch them some breakfast from the Teagarden."

"What should I bring?"

"Hotcakes. That's the cheapest."

"What about Annabelle?"

"I'll explain to her when I get time. Right now we've got more important things to worry about."

"Not to me they ain't."

Dave had just as well have put the pair on the chain for all the good it did to hide them indoors. The doctor had just declared Frenchy's hand bruised but not broken when Turk Radke strode into the jail, fists clenched, his eyes cold. "I heard you got a couple of my boys in here."

Dave had seen Radke several times in the hotel and on the street, but this was the first time the man had been this close or had spoken to him. He resisted a strong impulse to step back, as he might from a bristling wolf. "How'd you find out so quick?"

"We have eyes in the backs of our heads. I want them out."

"But I want them in, and it's my jail." Dave sensed more intelligence in Radke than in most of the henchmen he had seen, such as Skinny, Frenchy or Sarge. He also sensed more menace in this man than in Irish O'Dell. Lydia had said O'Dell could smile at a man and kill him. Dave doubted that Radke even knew how to smile.

276

Radke looked around with contempt. He sniffed the air. "I never saw a jail that didn't stink."

"It's the class of prisoners we get. There's room for you too, but I don't think you'd elevate the society much."

"I want to talk to Frenchy and Sarge."

Dave would have denied him if he could have thought of a legal reason. He made a quick search and found no weapons on Radke. "Go ahead, but don't you stay long."

Radke was still talking to his henchmen when Waddy finally arrived with the men's breakfast. Dave knew Sarge would tell Radke about Lydia, if he hadn't already. "Waddy," he said, "you lock up your pistol out here, then go feed them. I've got to be movin'."

"Where to?"

"Back to Jolene's."

"Seems to me you spend a lot of time at that place anymore. When you goin' to talk to Annabelle?"

"First time I get the chance."

"I hope it's before dinner. Else I'll be eatin' with the prisoners."

19

Hard Cases

DAVE FOUND Jolene and Lydia surprised at his quick return. He said, "Things've moved faster than I figured. Radke's already talked to Frenchy and Sarge. Lydia, he knows by now that you've said you'd testify against them."

Jolene's eyes were grim. "You'd better pack up and leave town, girl. I don't want your blood spilled all over this carpet."

Regretfully Dave had to agree. "I hate to lose you as a witness, but I'd hate worse seein' them hurt you. And they will."

Stubbornly Lydia declared, "I've run far enough already. I said I'd be here to testify, so I'll be here."

Jolene retorted, "You're liable to be too deep in the ground to

278

talk to anybody. Get out of this town. Get out of this business. You never should've been in it in the first place."

"I have Turk Radke to thank for that. I want to see him pay, him and the rest of them. Irish too. Maybe Irish most of all, because he could've helped me and didn't. He joined the rest of them instead."

Jolene shrugged, asking Dave by her expression to think of a better argument. Before he could come up with anything, the front door opened. Dave stepped out of the office to look. "Speak of the devil," he muttered. He had not thought Irish O'Dell would be here this soon.

O'Dell strode directly to the office, giving Dave a quick glance that said to get out of his way. "Lydia!" he exclaimed.

Lydia took an involuntary step backward and stopped against the wall. "Irish!" Despite her brave talk, Dave saw fear flicker in her eyes. "You stay away from me!" she said in a breaking voice that betrayed her.

O'Dell lifted a hand as if he wanted to reach out and touch her. "I been lookin' for you, Lydia. God, you don't know how long. Every oiltown in Texas and Oklahoma, just about. I was half afraid you weren't even alive anymore."

Lydia looked to Jolene, then to Dave, her eyes asking for help.

O'Dell saw where her gaze settled. "Sheriff . . . Jolene . . . I've got a lot to tell this woman. Would you leave us alone? I won't hurt her. I won't even touch her if she doesn't want me to."

"I *don't* want you to," she declared. Her eyes begged Dave not to go.

Dave told O'Dell, "Anything you want to say, you'll say it with me standin' here."

O'Dell hesitated, uncomfortable. "Lydia, I never thought I'd ever go huntin' for any woman, but I've hunted for you. I'd give anything to take back what I did."

Her fear faded as rapidly as it had risen. Her reply crackled with hatred. "So, you remember what you did to me?"

"Every day and every night, I've remembered. When I try to look at another woman I see your face instead of hers. You've haunted me like some kind of a ghost."

Dave said dryly, "I've seen you with Lauralou Clive. You didn't look too haunted."

279

"A substitute, that's all, and not much of one. Lydia, I'll make it up to you, all of it."

"This? What you and Radke and the others turned me into? You couldn't even begin. I just want you to leave me alone."

"You haven't left *me* alone, not a day, not a night. It'll be different this time. I'll leave Boss and Turk. I'll take good care of you. I'm not lettin' you stay here"—he gave Jolene a hard look—"in this kind of a place."

Jolene said caustically, "You've taken to religion kind of late, don't you think?"

"I can change. *She* can change." He turned toward Dave. "You goin' to give me any trouble, Sheriff?"

"I will if you touch her."

"Just about every small-town law I ever saw had a price. I wonder what yours is."

"You couldn't even start to pay it."

O'Dell's eyes locked with Dave's for a moment. Dave saw in them not the cool deliberation he had found there before but a wildness, even an obsession. "I've found her now, and nobody's keepin' me away from her anymore. Not Boss, not Radke, and not you, Buckalew."

Dave moved between O'Dell and Lydia. "You've had your say, and she's havin' no part of you. So get on along, and don't you be comin' back here." He put his hand on the pistol at his hip.

O'Dell looked past him at Lydia. "I'll be comin' back soon as I can pack up a little stuff. I'll be comin' to get you and take you away from this place." He turned on his heel and strode out. Dave heard the door slam hard as the man left.

"He meant it," he said to Lydia. "I'm afraid the only way I'll stop him will be to shoot him." That thought brought him no pleasure. "You'd better get your things together. I'll take you to the train in Odessa."

Jolene said eagerly, "I'll help you, Lydia."

Lydia did not move. "I've got somethin' to tell you, Sheriff, somethin' I should've told you the day they found Ox."

Jolene turned, suddenly frightened. "No, Lydia!"

Lydia had a determined look in her eyes. "I know I promised you, Jolene, but I've got to break that promise." She turned grimly toward Dave. "I saw them that night. I was at my upstairs window, lookin' to see who was raisin' a ruckus in the street. Ox went out to quiet them down. I saw Turk Radke knock him to the ground with somethin' . . . a tire iron, likely."

A tear ran down Jolene's cheek. "Lydia, they'll kill you. They'll have to, now."

"Ox went to his knees the first time, but he looked like he still had fight in him. Radke hit him a couple more times, then he and Skinny dragged him off to a car."

Dave felt a chill. "You're sure who they were?"

"They walked by a lighted window. I saw their faces."

Dave looked accusingly at Jolene. "You could've told me about this yourself."

Lydia said, "Jolene didn't see it. I was the only one. I promised her not to tell, but after seein' Irish just now, I knew I had to."

"Was he there that night?"

"I don't think so. At least, I didn't see him." She looked down. "I almost wish I had, so you could put him away."

Dave walked to the front window, fretting. "Now I *have* got to get you out of town. They'll come after you for sure when I charge Radke and Skinny with murder." He felt a prickling along his back, a need to be moving. It seemed an hour before the two women came back down the stairs, each carrying a cheap suitcase. He held the door open while they walked outside, then he took the suitcases and put them in the back seat of his car. He cranked the engine while the women embraced each other.

O'Dell had taken his red coupe from where Frenchy and Sarge had left it parked. Though he did not see the car, Dave had a strong sensation of being watched. A chill played on his spine.

Jolene did not wave as the car pulled away. She stood on the small porch, her arms folded. Dave suspected she was crying a little, inside.

He said, "A strong woman, that Jolene."

"She's been like a sister to me, and sometimes a mother. They'll give her trouble, Mr. Buckalew."

He wished he could tell her otherwise. "She's tough."

"Not always. You know she's got a daughter?"

"I saw a picture on her desk once."

"The girl's bein' raised by her grandparents over in Louisiana. For all she knows, her mother is dead. Jolene has kept it that way. She acts tough, but I've seen her cry."

"It's a hard life, I suppose."

281

"You can't begin to know."

"You could get out of it."

"I've tried."

"You can try again. When you get on the train you can go back to where you came from and start over."

"After what I just told you about Radke and Skinny? What about my testimony?"

"You wouldn't live to deliver it. I'll just have to find somethin' else to hang them for."

She sat in silence awhile. "It's not easy, puttin' a life like this behind you and actin' like it never happened."

"Any harder than goin' on with it?"

She did not reply.

He was suspicious of a black car that pulled into the street a few lengths behind him. He could not see who was driving it. Probably some oilfield worker, totally innocent, but Dave could not shake the idea of being watched. It was getting so he didn't trust anybody anymore.

After a few minutes of silence Lydia declared, "I said I'd be a witness for you, Mr. Buckalew. I'll keep that promise. Do you know a place where I could hide out until you need me?"

He demanded, "Are you sure? It'll be dangerous."

"What can I lose? They already took my life once."

He remembered the offer he had made to Slim McIntyre when the cowboy needed to stay out of sight. "I know of a place. You'd be all by yourself a long way out in the country, and it has mighty few of the town comforts. But you'd be safe. Radke and his bunch wouldn't have any idea where to find you."

"I wouldn't mind bein' by myself for a while. It would give me a chance to think."

He looked in the rearview mirror. He could see a black car, but he was not sure it was the same one. Most of the cars in town were black, seemed like. "We'll start out toward Odessa, just in case. When I know we're clear we can switch off onto some oilfield roads and double back."

Several miles out, the traffic thinned to a point that all he could see behind him was a pipe truck. He turned off across a ranch cattleguard and onto a rough two-rut road that oilfield vehicles had beaten across the sand and shinnery and through the mesquite brush. Lydia glanced at him questioningly but said nothing, pressing her hands against the dashboard as the car hit a rough spot. The road was crooked and the going slow, but eventually he turned into a better one that had enjoyed the benefit of a county roadgrader in the not-too-distant past.

"At least we know nobody has followed us," he said in a roundabout way of apologizing. They had skirted part of the oilfield, where the smell of oil and gas lay heavy. The road passed near enough to a couple of tall gas flares that he could feel the heat and hear the roar of the flames that burned off the unwanted and dangerous by-product of the oilwells.

"Makes you wonder how hell must be," he remarked.

She said darkly, "I already know."

He turned into a more familiar but less-traveled road after a while. He had left the oilfield behind, though a single isolated derrick stood some distance out in front. "A wildcat," he said. "Bein' drilled by Victor Underwood."

The name meant nothing to her, which did not surprise him. A man who had as pretty a little wife as Elise Underwood should have no reason to become acquainted at Jolene's place.

The twin-rut road thinned to a point that it was at times almost imperceptible amid the grass and weeds, the shinnery and low-growing mesquites. She remarked, "If somebody really wanted to get lost, this would be the place."

"That's the whole idea." He came to a barbed-wire fence, two extra-tall cedar posts marking the location of a wire gate. "My ranch," he said, "if you want to call it that."

He stopped the car and got out. A long cedar stake attached to a chain, one end slipped through a wire loop, held the gate closed. He opened it and laid the gate on the ground, beyond the wheel ruts. He drove the car through, then got out and closed the gate behind him. "It's not but a little four-section place," he told her as he drove on. "Not big enough to make a livin' on. A homesteader took it up twentysomethin' years ago. Managed to stay just long enough to prove it up and get title from the state. He was glad to sell it to Henry Stringfellow for a little of nothin'. And Uncle Henry sold it to me when I got back from the war. Didn't cost much, but it isn't worth much."

The road circled around a mesquite thicket and over a low hill. Ahead stood a windmill and a small frame house built in a box-and-strip style that had gone out of favor twenty years ago. The house had once been painted white, but most of the paint had long since flaked off. A couple of whiteface cows stood in the road. Dave honked the horn, and they moved aside for him. A young calf ran and bucked alongside the car, playing with it until the mother bawled her misgivings.

It was the first time Dave had seen Lydia laugh. For a moment, the worry and the weight of hardship seemed to slip away from her. She looked younger than he had thought. She said, "We had a few cattle on the farm when I was a girl. I always loved the calves. I wished they would never grow up."

"If they didn't, there wouldn't be much reason to keep cows. The calves are the only thing that bring in money, and sometimes not near enough. That's why I've held onto the sheriff job."

"You can't keep on bein' sheriff forever, can you?"

"When I first bought this place I had notions that in ten years I'd be a big ranch operator. But the outfit's still the same size it was to begin with, and it doesn't show any signs of gettin' bigger."

He stopped in front of the house. "It doesn't look like much from outside. I'd better warn you, it won't look any better on the inside. But it's got a good roof on it."

He opened the front door for her. There was a keyhole under the knob, but he had never seen the key. Nobody locked doors this far out in the country. "I'm afraid it needs a good sweepin' and moppin'. I just get out here once or twice a week to take a quick look at the cattle. Sometimes I fix me a meal and sometimes I don't. Been a month since I've stayed all night."

The house had just two rooms, the largest a kitchen with an old iron cookstove, a table and chairs and a lumpy couch that had been left by the original homesteader. An open door showed the tiny bedroom, the spring bed covered by an old patchwork quilt Dave's mother had made twenty years ago.

He watched Lydia as she turned slowly, giving the place a long study. He could not blame her if she changed her mind. "I can still take you to Odessa and put you on the train."

"No, this'll be fine. Needs a little air, though." She raised a window and propped it with a stick, recoiling a little as the breeze lifted dust from the sill and put it into her face.

He said, "There's some canned goods here, some flour, some

coffee. I couldn't stop for extra groceries in Caprock while you were with me. If anybody had been watchin', it would've been a dead giveaway that I wasn't takin' you to the train." He picked up a dry bucket from the small cabinet. "There's no indoor plumbin', and no electricity, of course. I've got a pretty good stack of stovewood cut out back yonder."

He carried the bucket to the windmill, where a spigot was placed at about waist height on the pipe, just below another pipe through which the mill pumped water out into a concrete live-stock trough and, farther away, an open surface tank dug into the ground. He rinsed the bucket, then filled it and carried it inside. From a stack of wood in the back he gathered an armful, cut to stove length, and took it in to fill the woodbox beside the stove. He started a fire for Lydia and watched her prepare the coffeepot.

"Don't be fixin' for me," he said. "I'll be goin' on. I'll come back this evenin' and bring enough fresh grub to carry you for several days."

He heard a horse nicker and went to the door. A sorrel with three white stocking feet stood in front of the small wooden barn, tossing his head. "Ol' Red wants his feed. I always put out a little for him whether I intend to ride him or not. That way he'll come to me when I want him."

"I'd almost forgotten how pretty a horse could be."

"Can you ride?"

"I grew up on a farm, remember?"

Dave pointed toward the Underwood derrick, whose top was barely visible over a line of mesquite trees. "If anything happens and you need help, it's maybe a mile and a half as the crow flies to that well yonder. It's a right smart more by the road. Don't you hesitate to go there if you need to. The Underwoods are good folks, and they'll help you."

"I'll be all right."

"I know you will. But just in case . . ."

He walked out to the barn. Lydia patted the sorrel horse on the neck while Dave went inside and brought out a half bucket of oats to pour into a wooden trough. The horse eagerly thrust his nose into them, quickly eating them all and licking up the last grain. Lydia watched, fascinated. "This takes me home. I've wished a thousand times that I'd never left."

"You can still go back."

"It wouldn't be the same, ever again."

"Maybe not, but it could be good if you'd let it."

Lydia followed him to the car. Opening the door, he turned. "You sure you'll be all right out here by yourself?"

"You don't know how long I've wished I *could* be by myself."

"It isn't much, but it's the best I've got."

She placed her hand on his arm. Her hazel eyes stared at him in a way that he could not turn from her. She stepped back, finally, to let him leave. "You go ahead and file your murder charges, Sheriff. When the time comes, I'll testify."

"You know the risk. Are you sure?"

"I'm sure. And, Sheriff . . ." She gave him a small smile. "This is a fine place."

If Radke or O'Dell or any of the other Daugherty men had watched him leave town, they would know how long it should take him to drive to Odessa and return. He could not afford to be back in Caprock too soon. He left his little ranch and picked up the wheel ruts that took him to the Underwood well. Nearing the site, he heard a rhythmic thumping as the walking beam raised and dropped the drilling bit, chipping away at ancient layers of sand and rock deep in the blackness, perhaps two thousand feet down. He understood the physical process but not the mentality that allowed men to probe far into the crust of the earth in search of unseen wealth. He could only imagine what must have been in the mind of the first man who had tried. He must have appeared a madman to those around him. Perhaps there was a madness in it even yet. It appeared so to him, sometimes.

Victor Underwood stood on the rig floor, his hand on the rope that moved up and down in the drilling pipe in concert with the rocking of the walking beam. The big man called Choctaw was stripped to the waist, sweating heavily as he sledgehammered a new point onto a white-hot drilling bit next to the forge. Slim McIntyre, using a set of wrenches, held the long bit steady for him. Dave watched the sweat-soaked young cowboy with a touch of pity. Slim had probably never worked this hard on a cow outfit. No matter what doubts Dave might have about the search for oil as a fit and proper endeavor, he would give the oilfield

286

laborers credit for strength and determination. They worked like plowhorses.

Underwood shut down the drilling operation and gave Dave a wave of recognition. Dave stepped up to the edge of the drilling floor. "Don't be quittin' on my account."

Underwood wiped his face with a kerchief. "It's time anyhow. Elise should just about have lunch finished. You'll eat with us won't you, Buckalew?" He pointed his thumb toward the cook tent.

Dave tried to think of a good reason not to, but all he could see in his mind was the long waiting line at the Teagarden. "I wouldn't want to put you out none."

"There's always plenty."

Choctaw finished his work with the sledge and turned, wiping his bare arm across his brow in a futile effort to remove the sweat. "I hope you ain't lookin' for me, Sheriff. I ain't been up to nothin' but hard work."

Dave said, "I'm not lookin' for anybody. I was just out to my little place yonder and thought I'd see how things are goin' with you-all. You fixin' to make Uncle Henry a rich man?"

"Either that or I'll make myself a very poor one," Underwood said.

Dave looked down into the slushpit where cuttings from the well were spilled. "Any sign of oil yet?"

"We aren't deep enough. We still have a few hundred feet to go before we reach the most likely structure. It can be a slow and frustrating process."

Dave watched Slim McIntyre flop his unbuttoned shirt, trying to fan his sweat-beaded skin. "Slim, you about ready to head back to cow country?"

Slim blinked sweat from his eyes. "Soon's I get rich."

Trinidad Suarez came up, dragging dead mesquite for the steam boiler. He began chopping it into proper lengths to feed the flames that powered the drilling operation.

Dave asked, "You don't mind that he's a Mexican?" Some people would.

Underwood shook his head. "He works as hard as anybody. It took him a little while to get over his nervousness about all the machinery, but he did. Choctaw and Slim get along with him fine, and his wife helps Elise with the cooking."

287

"His wife is here?"

"She didn't want to stay at Henry's without Trinidad. The family lives in a tent, yonder." He pointed.

Dave said, "I wish that little place of mine was big enough that I could pay a hand. I'd hire him myself."

Underwood smiled. "Not until I finish this well, I hope."

"I'm afraid I'll be an old man with all my hair in my ears before that place gets any bigger."

By the time the men had finished washing what grime and grease they could from their hands, Elise Underwood came out of the cook tent and shouted, "Dinner!" To Victor Underwood, with his Yankee upbringing, it was lunch. But to Elise, brought up in Oklahoma and Texas, it was dinner.

Dave held back until the working men had all been served before he took a plate. In cowcamps it had been part of the unwritten chuckwagon etiquette that the working hands ate first, and anyone else who happened to be around brought up the rear. He could not help staring at the tiny Elise while she spooned out large helpings of food to her husband, to Choctaw and to Slim. Somehow she looked too fragile to be living out here like this, cooking for a crew. But here she was, and if she had any misgivings about her place, he saw no sign of them in her cheery, outgoing manner.

Trinidad motioned for Dave to go ahead of him. In a lot of places, a Mexican would be expected to eat last and carry his food to some place apart. Dave demurred and told Trinidad to go ahead. He felt the dark brown eyes of Trinidad's wife studying him with a measure of doubt. He reasoned that past treatment had probably given her cause enough. A small girl clung to the Mexican woman's thin leg, her large black eyes shy but curious about the stranger who wore a pistol on his hip.

Slim asked at length, "You seen Tracy, Sheriff?"

"Ate breakfast at the Teagarden this very mornin'. She looks fine, just fine."

"She always does. Did she send any message?"

"She didn't know I'd be out thisaway. Fact is, I didn't either." Buckalew considered telling why he had come but decided against it. A careless word in town by any of these people might be all the mob would need. He did not know Elise Underwood well enough to predict what her reaction might be to a woman from Jolene's staying at such close proximity to her camp. She might take it in stride, but on the other hand . . .

He finished his meal and carried his plate, coffee cup and utensils to a tub which awaited them. "I'm much obliged, Mrs. Underwood, Mrs. Suarez. Best meal I've eaten in a long time." Food always seemed to taste better in camp than in town.

He shook hands all around and wished Underwood luck on his well. "I hope you make Uncle Henry a happy man. And yourselves as well."

He took the trouble to circle around and drive into Caprock on the Odessa road for the benefit of Radke and his bunch, if they were watching. He pulled into a parking place near the front of the hotel and climbed the stairs. At their head he confronted a burly little man he had not seen before. The man said, "Been watchin' for you, Sheriff. Boss wants to see you."

"Boss? You mean Big Boy Daugherty?" He figured this man had arrived with Daugherty in the night. He had the shifty-eyed look that Dave had seen in others of that organization.

"*Mr.* Daugherty. He don't like bein' called Big Boy. He don't appreciate people makin' fun about his size."

"Sensitive son of a bitch, isn't he?" Dave started up the hall toward his own room.

The man hurried along behind him. "Hey! I said Boss wants to see you."

"But I don't want to see him, except maybe the south end of him as he leaves town."

The burly man dropped his chin, frowning. "Boss ain't used to bein' kept waitin'."

"The experience'll be good for him. Keep him humble." Dave proceeded to his room. He made it a point not to look back. He heard a few uncertain footsteps as the thug started following him, then stopped. Dave had observed that, with the possible exception of Turk Radke and Irish O'Dell, Daugherty chose his assistants for brawn rather than brain.

He heard a door close down the hall as the thug went back to report his failure. He could hear heavy footsteps and a deep, growling voice raised in anger and disbelief. Curiosity chewed at him like a dog on a bone. A man who could provoke so much apprehension must be worth seeing, but Dave did not intend to put himself at the beck and call of any felon who happened into town, even one as infamous as Big Boy Daugherty. He went to his room and lay down on his bed to rest, his boots just off the edge so they would not soil the spread. He closed his eyes and thought of Lydia, of the way she looked in his little ranchhouse.

That pleasant flow of thought was interrupted by a knock on the door. He did not get up. "Who's there?" he shouted, suspecting that he knew.

"O'Dell," came the answer. "O'Dell and Radke."

Slowly, to let them know he was not impressed, he arose from the bed, stretched, then opened the door. O'Dell and Radke stood in the hall, the thin Skinny a couple of paces behind them. Dave did not invite them in. "Well?"

Radke's arms were folded, his eyes belligerent. "Boss sent word over here while ago. He wants to talk to you."

"And I sent word back that I don't have anything to talk to him about."

"You ain't coming?"

"I ain't comin'."

Radke glowered. Irish O'Dell said, "Boss can be a right generous man when he feels like it. You'd be doing yourself a favor if you listened to what he's got to say."

Dave was strongly tempted, just to have a look at the man. But he replied, "When he gets ready to say goodbye to this town, that's when I'll want to listen to him."

Radke's gray eyes smoldered. "You've got two of my best boys in the jailhouse. How long you intend to keep them there?"

"Till they stand trial."

"For talking a little tough to a whore? Hell, that's about the same as a traffic ticket. These oilfield towns are full of trash like her. It ain't like she was a regular citizen."

"She's a citizen *here.*"

"Bail, then. The least we can do is go the boys' bail till time for their trial."

"Judge Potter'd be the one to set bail."

Radke dug into his trousers pocket and came up with a roll of bills as large as a man's fist, held together by a rubber band. "Boss and me want them out. How much do you think it would take to make you see your way clear?"

Dave swallowed. He would guess that Radke held enough cash in one hand to buy a small ranch. The sight of that much money held him in fascination for a moment. He forced himself to look away from it and bring his gaze back to Radke's frowning face. "I told you, it's up to Judge Potter."

Radke growled, "I never saw a John Law that wouldn't listen to reason if you put enough money in his hand."

"I hear the Rangers didn't listen. I hear they ran you and Daugherty and all your bunch out of the Panhandle."

Radke's brow furrowed with anger. "They didn't run us out. Nobody runs us out. The boom just fizzled, and we decided to find a livelier place."

"There's other towns on the boom besides Caprock, places where it won't get so hot and the sand won't blow."

Irish O'Dell said, "Boss has already taken a likin' to Caprock. He says there's nothing quite as pretty as a place where the oil derricks stand thick as East Texas pine trees. A man won't notice the sand in his shoes if there's money enough in his pockets."

Dave wondered if Radke and Daugherty knew about O'Dell and Skinny highjacking Knox Anderson. He suspected that had been a free-lance operation. If so, it wouldn't hurt to stir up a little dissension. "Speakin' of money in somebody's pockets, Radke, there was a driller got held up for his payroll here a few weeks ago while O'Dell and Skinny were in town. I had a notion it was them."

Radke glanced at O'Dell with suspicion. Skinny looked at the floor, his face darkening. O'Dell said quickly, "He questioned me and Skinny about it at the time. But it wasn't nothin' to do with us." He made it sound convincing. Dave supposed he had had considerable practice at lying.

Dave said, "Odd thing about that robbery, O'Dell. We found the money hidden underneath a hotel down the street. Same hotel where you and Skinny were stayin'."

Radke growled, "Our boys have orders not to pull stuff like that." Suspicion lingered in his eyes.

Skinny said in a clipped voice, "It wasn't us."

Radke looked back at him, not believing. Then his gaze returned to Dave. "What about those two boys of mine? It ain't like they'd bothered some decent woman. You know the law won't do much to them for roustin' the likes of Jolene."

Dave's hand dropped to his pistol. He drew it from the holster. "It'll do a right smart for murder."

291

Radke's jaw dropped. "Murder?"

"You and Skinny. You killed a man called Ox. I've got an eye-witness."

Radke's eyes were suddenly wild. He reached up toward the place where he usually carried a shoulder holster, but he had left it in the room. "What witness? Who?"

"You'll see when your trial comes up." He thrust the pistol forward, almost into Radke's face. He moved so quickly that he took the men by surprise. "Come along, Radke. You too, Skinny. I'm chargin' both of you with murder."

Radke froze, looking to O'Dell for help. O'Dell was not armed either. He said, "Don't worry, Turk. Boss won't let you stay in there long."

Dave patted Skinny's pockets for weapons. He found only a long knife, which he pitched back through the open door into his own room. It clattered across the floor. "You-all start walkin'."

O'Dell's hands were at shoulder height. "What about me?"

"I've got no call on you right now. When I have, you'll be seein' me."

O'Dell followed the men to the stairway. "Buckalew, just a minute."

Dave expected him to demand the identity of the witness. Instead, O'Dell declared, "You took Lydia away."

Dave saw no reason to deny it. "I did."

"You took her to Odessa. I suppose you put her on the train. Where'd she go?"

"I didn't watch her buy a ticket."

Dave saw genuine pain in O'Dell's eyes. "I wanted that woman, Buckalew. I'd've taken her out of that place and given her anything she asked for."

"You helped put her into that place, or one like it. I gave her a chance to get out."

"That woman's my business, and mine alone. You get in my way again, Buckalew, and they're liable to have to hold a new election."

Dave held his gaze to O'Dell's, trying to stare him down. It was a draw. "You won't be votin' in it," he said, and marched his grumbling prisoners down the stairs.

The sun was setting when Dave reached the little ranchhouse. He had intended to leave town much earlier but had been called out into the oilfield to investigate the theft of a truck. The truck was found abandoned, stuck in the sand, its motor burned up in an attempt to force it free. Whoever had taken it had left the scene afoot. At such times, Dave wished he had a horse handy; he could have followed the tracks. To attempt it in a car would only get the car stuck as thoroughly as the truck.

Lydia held the screen door open while he brought in two sacks of groceries and set them on the narrow cabinet top. "I've still got one more to fetch from the car." He paused and looked around in surprise. He could not remember that the little house had ever appeared so clean. She had swept and mopped it out, corner to corner. The cabinet and table, thinly covered with sand every time he came here, were wiped spotless.

"This doesn't look like the same place," he told her, smiling in pleasure.

"A little work helped the day pass," she said, trying to shrug it off but pleased by his compliment. She began to empty the sacks. He had brought canned milk, eggs, bacon, beef, potatoes, coffee and canned goods of various kinds.

He said, "This ought to hold you a few days. I don't know what you like to read, but I brought you some magazines. You can't clean house *all* the time."

"This must have cost you considerable."

"You're a witness, so you're a guest of the county." He would argue with Judge Potter about it the next time the commissioner's court went over the bills.

"I'll start us some supper," she said, and began putting small pieces of kindling into the Majestic iron stove.

"I'd best be gettin' back. It'll be dark pretty soon."

"You've got to eat. I'm not too bad a cook. You can bring that other sack in while I start the fire."

He had told himself all the way out here that he would stay no longer than necessary to deliver the groceries, but that notion quickly evaporated. He found himself in no hurry to leave. "I didn't bring that chuck out here to eat it myself."

"There's enough here for an army, and I don't eat much."

That was probably so, he thought, judging by her slender figure. In a fresh dress, in the quiet of this isolated old house, she looked different from the woman he had first met at Jolene's, somehow younger even than the woman he had brought here this morning. She looked as if she might have spent her life here, in this house or one like it. She could be a farm or ranch wife, if someone were seeing her for the first time. She looked as if she might fit in the company of Elise Underwood.

He went to the barn and fed the sorrel horse, which had seen his car and had trudged up from the pasture to bum a bait of oats. He caught the smell of mesquite smoke from the chimney and turned to stare at the house. He had never seen a woman in it before. Her presence put a strangely different cast on the place.

He carried in the last sack of groceries and set them on the table, taking them out of the sack piece by piece, then putting them away. He enjoyed working alongside Lydia in close quarters, bumping against her without really meaning to. He stepped back. "I'm afraid there's just room for one cook in here."

"You don't need to apologize because the house is small. I grew up in one not much bigger. And there was a bunch of us."

The coffee was ready, so he poured a cup and sat at the table, out of her way but where he could watch her. Each time she looked in his direction, he was drawn by her eyes. A man could drift away and die happy, he thought, just looking into the depths of hazel eyes like those.

It was dark outside by the time supper was ready. The smell of fresh hot biscuits reminded him of old times in other ranchhouses, of quiet and peaceful times that it seemed he would never see again. She set down a platter of fried potatoes and steak, and a bowl of hot red beans taken from a can because there had not been time to prepare them from scratch. She said, "It's a rushed-up job, but I hope it tastes all right."

"Smells fine," he said, waiting for her to start, even as she waited for him. After a moment of uncertainty he passed her the platter. "After you, ma'am."

She made a tentative smile, appreciating his deference. They ate in awkward silence, trying not to stare at each other. It was a lost effort. Done, she put down her knife and fork and sipped at her coffee. "Why do you look at me that way?"

"I guess it's your eyes." He was astonished to find himself

294

speaking so freely. "I've never seen any like them. Well, maybe once."

"When was that?"

"A long time ago, over in France."

"A French girl, then?"

"A French girl."

"Were you in love with her?"

He was a while in answering. "Yes, I was."

"What became of her?"

"I came home. She stayed behind."

"Maybe you should've brought her with you. Or sent back for her."

"I should've, but I didn't."

"Why not?"

"I was young. I was chuckle-headed enough that I listened to just about everything people told me. They said all the French girls were cheap, that I'd be ashamed of her and myself both if I brought her home."

"Because you'd slept with her?"

He paused, surprised that she saw through him so easily. "They said a girl who'd let you go to bed with her wasn't worth much. They were older than me, most of them, and I didn't have any better sense than to believe them."

"So you listened to them and set your feelin's aside."

He stared at the floor. "I left her cryin' at the train station. I tried to tell myself I was doin' the right thing. It was the biggest mistake of my life."

Her eyes were sympathetic. "You could've gone back, or sent back for her."

"I did send for her, but it was too late. There'd been a bad flu epidemic in her village. Marguerite was gone." An old ache came up in him, and a swelling in his throat. He arose from the chair and went to the door. He took a handkerchief from his pocket and blew his nose in an attempt to cover. "Dust out at the barn must've got to me." He stared into the night. "It's a slow, mean road in the dark. I'd better get started."

When he turned, she was standing in front of him. "You might run off of the road and get stuck in the sand. You'd have a long way to walk." She placed a hand on his arm. "You'd do better to wait till mornin'."

"You know what people'd say."

"You just told me what happened when you listened to what people said." Her fingers gripped his arm. "Stay, Dave." Those large hazel eyes stared up at him, warm, asking, melting away whatever reservations he harbored. He leaned toward her, and she came into his arms.

She said, "I'm not blind. I've seen the way you've looked at me. You're a good man and a kind one, Dave Buckalew. A woman like me doesn't often find that sort of kindness in a man."

His face flushed hot as he leaned down to kiss her and felt her respond, pressing her body against him. He felt himself giving way to a long pent-up hunger. "Lydia, I didn't bring you out here for this."

"I know. I wouldn't have come with you if I thought you did." She kissed him again, then turned, taking his arm and leading him toward the other room.

Waddy would have to stay in the jail tonight, guarding the prisoners. Dave would not be back to spell him.

Irish O'Dell had had a hollow feeling deep in his gut from the moment he had returned to Jolene's and found Lydia gone. He had given way to a moment of desperation and had shaken Jolene so hard that she staggered when he turned her loose. All she would admit was that the sheriff had taken Lydia to Odessa to catch the train. She claimed to have no idea where Lydia had gone. Under the circumstances, she had said, it was better that she not be told.

It had been Irish's intention to put Lydia into the red coupe whether she wanted to go with him or not and hustle her away from town, away from this part of the country, maybe even out of Texas. He would take her far enough that Boss Daugherty and Turk Radke would never find them.

Leaving Jolene's, he had raced up the road all the way to Odessa, hoping to overtake Buckalew, to kill him if that was what it took to get Lydia away from him. But he had seen no trace. They had moved too swiftly for him. She could have taken a westbound train toward El Paso or an eastbound toward Fort Worth. The man at the ticket counter said he had sold a lot of tickets to a lot of women, bound for too many destinations to remember.

Irish had returned to Caprock like a whipped hound with its tail between its legs, his heart on the ground. He would lie awake many sleepless nights now, wishing, wondering, aching like a man with a cancer gnawing at his innards.

He watched the tall, lanky deputy sheriff reluctantly unlock a cell door and let Turk Radke out. Waddy Fuller declared sullenly, "Sheriff Buckalew sure ain't goin' to like this."

"It makes no difference whether he likes it or not. You've got your orders from the judge. Now, turn the rest of them loose too."

Irish knew better than to expect gratitude from Turk Radke. Radke grumbled, "It took you long enough. Where the hell you been?"

"It took that old judge a while to come around to my way of thinkin'. He finally set bail at five hundred apiece on you and Skinny and a hundred on the other boys."

"I suppose Boss told you to slip the old man a hundred or two for himself, like he always does?"

"I didn't have to. Judge was scared enough that he caved in without it. Saved Boss his money."

Radke was displeased. "Boss always likes to give them something. They sometimes get over being scared, but they don't ever get over being bought."

"I can go back."

Radke waved him off. "There'll be another time. We ain't convinced Sheriff Buckalew yet."

"No, and we're not goin' to."

Radke nodded darkly. "Boss never did like killin' a lawman, but I think this is one time he'll have to change his mind. You want the job?"

O'Dell swallowed, taken by surprise. "I don't believe I do." He watched Skinny and the other two leaving their cells. "Turk," he said quietly, "you didn't believe what Buckalew said about me and Skinny and that highjackin', did you?"

He saw the answer in Radke's deep frown. Radke said, "You know the way Boss feels about you-all doin' things on your own. He'd stomp hard enough to rattle the whole hotel."

O'Dell had as soon crawl into a hole with an angry old badger as to face the huge man's wrath over a piddling little job that had been pretty much of a waterhaul anyway. "I don't see why you have to say anything to him about it."

"Maybe I won't, if you'll think a little more on taking care of Buckalew."

Irish weighed the options and did not like either one. "I'll think on it."

20

Another Chance

S LIM McINTYRE was gratified at how quickly he learned the basic operation of a cabletool rig and the various tasks associated with it. He learned the difference between the bullwheel and the calfwheel, between the Sampson post and the headache post. He learned to fire the boiler and keep it running, to ram and sledge a new point onto a drill bit. He learned how to bail out the hole when the mud at the bottom became thick enough to impede the dropping of the bit, then run a bailer of fresh water to the bottom and release it without muddying the sides and risking a cave-in. He learned how to set casing, its diameter decreasing as the hole deepened.

At various times, he worked both the day tour with Underwood and the night tour with Choctaw, alternating as he was needed. On a small crew like Victor Underwood's, a worker had the opportunity to learn all the jobs rather than a single specialty. It was more than an opportunity; it was a necessity. In his off hours, when he was not on his cot in the sleeping tent, he often pitched in to ease the workload on the others, just as Underwood and Choctaw often spelled one another without regard to whose tour it was. They were not working for hourly wages. In a sense, they were all partners in the enterprise.

The only job Slim had not tackled was the drilling itself. A good driller had a special touch. Not even Choctaw, with his years of experience on cabletool rigs, made any claim for expertise on the drilling line. Though circumstances required that he handle that responsibility now, Slim could tell that he did so with reluctance. When Underwood was not sleeping, he was usually on or near the rig floor during Choctaw's tour, watching, worrying.

It was hot, noisy work, the steam engine at the far end driving the heavy bandwheel that powered the machinery, the pitman rod's eccentric course driving the walking beam. The strike of the bit echoed a slow, steady rhythm from the depths of the hole. Slim could see intense concentration in Underwood's face any time the sounds changed, or the feel of the drilling line indicated something different was happening at the bottom.

Underwood kept a log that told him every formation through which the bit passed as it hammered its way down toward China, toward either failure or glory. Slim did not understand the terminology scribbled in the book, but it was important only that Underwood did. The driller frequently compared this log to the ones from the two failed wells, watching hopefully for any deviations that might indicate a better outcome.

Underwood did not talk much. Slim would try to read his eyes, to gauge the driller's mood changes from hopefulness to apprehension. He thought he saw more of apprehension. He understood the stakes. This well was Underwood's last chance at independence.

Elise Underwood's moods were easier to read because they varied little. Despite her small frame, she exhibited a boundless energy, and she sang a lot. If she shared any of her husband's misgivings, she did not betray them to the crew. Slim doubted that she betrayed them to Underwood, either. Her brown eyes were drawn to her husband when he was within sight. They appeared warmly content.

Slim often wondered how she and Trinidad's wife, Gabriela, got along so well together, for Gabriela's English was broken and poor, and Elise Underwood seemed to know no Spanish beyond *bueno* and *adiós*. But they laughed and used sign language in cooking meals for the working men, in cleaning the cook tent and in watching after the little girl, Manuela. Everybody on the crew kept an eye on the child, for there were a dozen ways she could be hurt or killed around a drilling rig. She had learned one valuable lesson for herself, burning her hand on a steam line. The heat of the boiler made her keep her distance from that, even when her father was stoking it with mesquite. Other hazards she might walk into included spinning wheels and moving belts, and not least by any means the slushpit into which the bailer dumped its cuttings and mud each time the bottom of the hole was cleaned. After a few misadventures, she had learned what was off limits, the same way Slim, as a ranch child, had learned not to climb a windmill ladder or to crawl around the horses' legs.

Raising children on a drilling location was not ideal, but Choctaw said economic realities forced some families to do it. He seemed particularly drawn to the brown-skinned child and often put her on his knee to play horse. Slim asked him once why he had never had a family of his own. Choctaw did not reply. Slim saw Choctaw gazing often toward Elise, though the Indian would quickly shift his attention in another direction when he realized he was being observed.

Trinidad Suarez proved himself a willing worker on the rig, though, like Slim, he had been a cowboy all his life. He had come to this job knowing even less about it, for Slim at least had the prior advantage of having worked around wells with Mr. Birdsong. Trinidad had an extra handicap, the language. His English was better than his wife's, but it did not prepare him for the peculiar nomenclature of the oilpatch.

Choctaw said some drillers would not hire Mexicans because of the language problem. An order misunderstood at a critical moment could lead to disaster.

The isolation of this rig reminded Slim of ranches on which he had worked, seldom going to town and seldom seeing anyone except other members of the crew. The only company dropping in were Uncle Henry Stringfellow, who rarely missed a day, and Sheriff Buckalew, who swung by on his way to or from his little ranch. Slim had never been to the place, but he could see the top of Buckalew's windmill to the west, beyond a range of dunes.

Isolation on a ranch had never bothered Slim much, but it was different here. Perhaps it was the strangeness of the oil-drilling atmosphere, to which he was not yet completely accustomed. More likely it was something else.

He sat on a bench outside the cook tent one evening after supper, staring westward across the sand and mesquite toward the red glow of a summer sunset. He heard someone walk up behind him but did not turn until he heard Elise Underwood's voice. "Pretty, isn't it?"

"Sand and mesquite? I never thought of them as pretty, especially."

"I meant the sunset, but it all goes together. It's a good country if you accept it for what it is and don't waste it wishin' it was somethin' else."

"I suppose."

"But you're wishin' you were some*where* else?"

"In a way. Or wishin' somebody was here."

"Maybe you ought to take the truck in some night and see her."

"I've thought about it. Sheriff says he wishes I wouldn't. Mr. Underwood too. They're afraid I'd run into trouble. But I'm half a mind to go anyway, trouble or not."

"Don't. I'll fetch Tracy out here when she has a day off from the Teagarden."

Slim could have kissed her, but of course he *would* not. Smiling broadly, he said, "I'd be much obliged. I don't know how I could ever repay you."

"You've already paid me, standin' by Victor. He needs you, all of you. We've got to bring this well in."

"What if it don't make a well, Mrs. Underwood? What will you-all do?"

"We don't even think about that. It *has* to make a well. So it will." She went back into the tent.

Choctaw came out with a tin plate in his hand, mopping up

302

brown molasses with a buttered biscuit. "What was that all about?" he demanded suspiciously.

"She just promised to bring Tracy Whitmore out to see me."

"Autie Whitmore's daughter? What's she to you?"

"I can't say for sure. I know we like one another."

A small grin crossed Choctaw's round face. "I always had a suspicion it was Mrs. Underwood you was interested in. So there really *is* a girl in town."

"I told you once."

"People been known to lie. Cowboys especially." Choctaw sat down on the bench, his weight causing Slim's end of it to rise a little. He mopped up what was left of the molasses and shoved the final bit of biscuit into his mouth.

"Pretty sunset," he commented.

"Same thing *she* said."

"Indians notice things like that. Did you know Mrs. Underwood has got a drop or two of Cherokee in her blood?"

"Nobody ever said."

"She's from Oklahoma, like me. Everybody in Oklahoma has got a little Indian blood, or claim they do." He gazed at the sunset. "Us Indians, we're brought up close to nature."

"You think cowboys aren't?"

"Never got to know any of them well enough to tell. Never wanted to. We're natural enemies, cowboys and Indians."

"I never wanted to be an enemy to you."

"Then let's smoke a peace pipe, us two. Since you're a Texan, we might even pull that Mexican Trinidad in on it."

"You got a pipe?"

Choctaw pulled a sack of Bull Durham tobacco from his pocket. "All I got is the makin's. I reckon a cigarette will have to do."

Slim had heard of blowouts, but he had not seen one. When Uncle Henry Stringfellow brought a report one day about a blowout that had torn up part of a rig near Caprock, Slim asked Underwood what caused it.

The driller replied, "When the earth's crust was being formed or being buckled and twisted by the pressures from beneath, sometimes air or gas was trapped in small pockets, like large bubbles. Now and then a drilling bit will puncture one of these pockets. The release of pressure is usually slight, but sometimes it may be enough to blow all the tools and occasionally even the casing from the hole.

"You know about the explosion that killed Autie Whitmore's son. That was gas. When it came up, a spark or something set off the fire. Most often a blowout in this part of the country is only a release of trapped air. It may bring up mud and rocks, and perhaps the drilling tools. But if there isn't any gas, there shouldn't be a fire."

"How do you know one's comin'?"

"You don't. But if you're standing over the hole when one starts, you'll know it. It's a little like being at the muzzle of a shotgun when the trigger is pulled."

Slim learned more than he wanted to know about blowouts one afternoon when, though off duty, he was helping Trinidad worry a worn bit into the forge for reshaping. Underwood stood in his usual place, his hand on the drilling line as the walking beam drew it up and dropped it. A newly forged bit had been lowered more than two thousand feet into the hole. It was past two-thirds of the way to the pay zone, if there was to be one. Choctaw had wandered up from the sleeping tent, yawning.

Slim heard Underwood shout, "Blowout!" The drilling line went slack, some of it coming up from the hole amid a shrill whistling noise. Slim froze, remembering the way he had seen Mr. Birdsong's line start snaking out when a rising head of oil had lifted his nitroglycerin shells. He remembered the panic that had set him to running. This time he was paralyzed in place, watching mud spew from the casing. His heart hammered.

Underwood shouted, "Get off the floor!"

Slim felt Trinidad grab him, bodily dragging him from the platform and down into the sand. "I'm all right," he protested.

Turning, he saw that Underwood was down, floored by a shower of mud and rocks that rattled the wooden rig and pounded against the sheetmetal roof of the shed that housed the engine.

"Good God!" Choctaw cried. "Let's get him out of there."

Slim found his feet and turned to help as the Indian rushed onto the platform. Underwood's legs were entangled in the drilling line that had spilled back out of the hole. The spewing mud thinned, but the whistling continued as a million years and more of trapped air found release through the well's narrow opening.

The driller's right leg was broken. He cried out when Slim and Choctaw and Trinidad tried to pick him up and extricate him from the twisted cable. All four men were coated in mud so thick it was impossible to see what color their clothing had been.

Elise Underwood rushed from the cook tent. She watched a moment, her face blanched. But she did not tolerate the shock for long. Seeing the men's uncertainty, she took charge. Her voice, normally soft, gained a steel edge. "We've got to get him to town without jarrin' him any more than we can help. Slim, you and Trinidad bring me that sheet of plywood out yonder." She pointed to a scrap pile. "Choctaw, there's a bottle of whisky in the house. You'll find it in the kitchen cabinet. And don't . . ." She did not complete the sentence, but it was clear she meant that he was not to drink any of it. She knelt beside her husband and tried to brush the mud from his face, not caring how much of it she got on herself. "Lie still, Victor. We'll get you to town as quick as we can."

Slim and Trinidad brought the strip of heavy plywood, a two-foot-wide remnant from a full sheet. Elise ordered, "Lay it down right there, next to Victor. It'll do for a stretcher."

Trinidad's wife stood back out of the way at the edge of the platform, her black eyes wide. Elise said, "Gabriela, please bring me a cloth out of the cook tent. Wet it and squeeze it out so I can wash Victor's face." She made a squeezing motion with her hands. The Mexican woman went running.

Choctaw brought the bottle of whisky. Its seal was still unbroken, for Underwood was not much of a drinker. Choctaw uncapped the bottle and handed it to Elise. She cautiously lifted her husband's head. "No matter how careful we try to be, what we do is goin' to hurt. So drink some of this, Victor."

He hesitated. "The well . . ."

"The well's not goin' anyplace. It'll still be here when we get back. Drink. Drink plenty."

Slim asked, "Hadn't we ought to try to splint that leg before we move him?"

Elise looked up. "Do you know how?"

Choctaw declared, "I do if he don't. Come on, cowboy. Let's be gettin' it done. You and Trinidad hold him."

Slim had never seen anyone set a broken leg. His stomach was queasy as he watched the big Indian. Underwood gasped, almost falling into unconsciousness. Elise cradled his muddy head on her lap and talked to him in a quiet voice while Slim and Choctaw made splints from two pieces of one-by-four, padding them with cuptowels out of the cook tent and tying them with cotton rope.

All three men carefully lifted Underwood while Elise slid the plywood beneath him. She said, "Trinidad, you go start the truck. Choctaw, you and Slim carry Victor and put him up in the bed of it."

Slim had ridden in the truck enough to know that its springs were shot. Victor Underwood was in for a rough ride. Trinidad had the truck running by the time Choctaw and Slim reached it and lifted Underwood up onto the open bed. They slid the plywood sheet up against the cab. Elise climbed up after them. "Trinidad, you stay and shut everything down. Slim, you drive the truck. Choctaw, you help me hold Victor as still as we can."

Choctaw objected. "It's goin' to be rough back here. You ought to ride up front."

"This is my husband. I belong here with him. You men do what I told you!"

There was no ignoring the imperative in her voice. Elise Underwood, too small to weigh a hundred pounds, had taken firm command.

Slim drove slowly and with care, easing into the poor two-rut road's many bumps and potholes, trying to shake Victor Underwood as little as possible. He kept looking through the cracked rear glass. Elise sat with her back braced against the cab, her husband's head in her lap. She was bent over him, comforting him the best she could. Choctaw sat on the edge of the plywood sheet to keep it from sliding around in the bed of the truck. One hand gripped the sideboard.

When Slim hit a deep rut while looking back at his passengers, Choctaw yelled angrily, "This ain't a horse, cowboy. Keep it on the road!"

Uncle Henry Stringfellow met them in his old black car. With one look at the mud-drenched men he sized up the situation and wasted no time on foolish questions. "I'll drive ahead of you and open the gates," he shouted at Slim. He roared off in a cloud of dust. When Slim reached the gate that led into the Clive ranch, Stringfellow was holding it open, waving him through. In a minute the old rancher passed him, rushing to beat him to the next gate.

After the last one, he pulled alongside the truck and shouted, "I'll go on ahead and have the doctor ready." Then he was gone.

Only as he drove into the tent-and-shack city that was Ragtown did Slim begin to consider his personal risk in coming to Caprock. Sheriff Buckalew had told him that Judge Potter had freed Frenchy on bail despite an assault charge. He had said, "That Frenchy's got a hard reputation. You'd better stay out of town."

Now here he was, in town again. Driving along the busy street, he found himself watching for Frenchy.

He saw Henry Stringfellow's car parked in front of the doctor's office. As Slim pulled the truck in against the wooden sidewalk, the rancher stepped out onto the porch. The doctor followed. He did not seem as concerned as Slim thought he properly should, but blood spots on the man's white apron showed that Victor Underwood was not his first accident patient for the day, nor was he likely to be the last. Oilfielding was risky work.

Slim climbed hurriedly into the bed of the truck to help. Choctaw said, "You'll have to excuse our stretcher, Doc. It was the best we could find on short notice."

The doctor shrugged. "I've had them carried in here on everything from sheetiron to a section of windmill ladder. We'll have to get those muddy clothes off of him and wash him before we can do much." He led the way to an examination table.

Slim and Choctaw eased Underwood from the plywood sheet. He groaned a little but staunchly withheld any other expression of his pain. The doctor removed the splints and cut away the trousers. Elise held her husband's hands, which went white-knuckled as the doctor felt of the leg.

"Who set this bone?" the doctor demanded gruffly.

Choctaw replied guiltily, "It was me."

"You did pretty well. If you ever decide to study medicine, I'll endorse your college application."

Not many times had Slim seen Choctaw smile as he did now. "Have to get out of the fifth grade first."

The doctor gave the leg another examination. He looked at Elise. "It's already set as well as I could do it. If you want it X-rayed, you'll have to take him to Odessa."

Elise squeezed her husband's hands while she pondered.

Underwood answered for her. "We'll trust you, Doctor. Do whatever's the fastest. I've got to get back to drilling."

The doctor frowned at him. *"You* won't be doing any of that for a while, my friend. You're going to be flat on your back."

"But I can't be. We've got to bring in that well."

"No man is indispensable. Let your crew do it."

"Choctaw's the only one besides me who can drill. Can't you fix me so that I can keep working?"

"Is an oilwell worth being crippled the rest of your life? A hundred of them, maybe, but not just one. You be still now."

The doctor held a cone over Underwood's face and administered ether. He told Elise, "I'm going to put his leg in a cast that'll keep him off his feet for a long time. I hope *you* understand, because he probably won't."

She said grimly, "Do what you have to. He's worth more to me than all the oilwells in Texas."

The doctor said, "He ought to mend all right if he'll give himself time. He needs to consider his age."

Elise said, "That's something I've never done."

"You've probably helped to keep him young. I wish I'd seen you first. Maybe I wouldn't be such an old codger now." He gave Slim and Choctaw a quick glance. "If you men would like to go out back and wash some of the mud off of you . . ."

Henry Stringfellow said, "I'm goin' down the street. One thing I never could do is sit around a doctor's office. Reminds me how old I am."

The mud had dried and caked. Slim and Choctaw shook and rubbed as much of it from their clothes as they could, then washed themselves. Afterwards, waiting in the parlor, Choctaw drew thoughtfully on a crooked Bull Durham cigarette rolled in brown paper. "Times like this, I wisht I'd made more out of my life. I've had lots of chances to drill. Just never wanted the responsibility. Thought all I wanted was to do my job, draw my pay and drink however much whisky it'd buy."

Slim stood at the window, looking out onto the street. He could not see the Teagarden from here. He had it in mind to walk down there and see Tracy. To hell with Frenchy and the rest of that bunch. A thought struck him. "Tracy's daddy is a driller."

"He drinks like I do, only more. I can shut it off. He can't."

"He could if he was stranded way out yonder and couldn't get ahold of anything."

"You'd have to tie him to his bed at night. He'd walk all twelve miles to town for a shot of whisky."

"Maybe if he knew how important it was . . ."

"The only thing important to a drunk is the next drink. Believe me, I've been there."

Elise came into the room and slumped wearily into a wooden chair. She said, "I dread when he wakes up and realizes he can't move around."

The door opened. Knox Anderson stepped in. Elise gave him a thin smile. Slim recalled whispered rumors about her and Anderson. He had given them little credence.

Anderson strode across the room, his hands thrust forward. Elise took them. He said, "I just ran into Henry Stringfellow. How's Victor?"

"It's a bad break. It'll be a while before he can do much."

"How about you? Are you going to be all right?"

"However Victor is, that's how I'll be. I'm afraid he'll be in a bad way when he comes out from under the ether and realizes he can't finish drillin' the well."

"How much deeper does it have to go?"

"Victor doesn't know, exactly. He figures another six or seven hundred feet."

"Don't you worry your pretty little head about that well. I'll take one of my rotary rigs out there. We'll have it finished before you know it. No charge. Just for old times."

Her eyes brightened. "You'd do that for us, Knox?"

"You know I would. You don't even have to ask."

The momentary joy left her, and the light dimmed in her eyes. "You're a true friend, Knox. But I can't let you do it."

"Why not?"

"If you'll think about it a little, you'll know why. Everything Victor has done, you've done bigger and better. No matter how hard he's worked, he's never been able to catch up to you. You've won every game."

"Not every game, Elise. Not the most important one."

"All the more reason, then. Can't you see how it would hurt his pride if you had to come in and finish that well for him? And he'd think you'd done it for me, not for him."

"So the well just sits there, idle?"

"No, it'll get drilled. I've still got a crew. We'll finish it, them and me." Elise turned toward Slim. "I overheard you talkin' about Autie Whitmore. Do you think you can find him?"

"More'n likely. But I don't know if he'll be in shape to work," Slim said.

"Find him. We can *get* him in shape."

Choctaw frowned. "You sure you want him?"

"I need him. And I think maybe he needs us."

Slim asked, "How're you goin' to pay him?"

"Like we're payin' you and Choctaw and Trinidad. On hope."

"What if he doesn't want to come for that?"

Choctaw pushed to his feet. "He'll come. I'll tote him under my arm if I have to."

Elise said, "Choctaw, you watch out for Slim, in case he runs into those men the sheriff talked about. I doubt they'll give him any trouble as long as you're there."

Knox Anderson marveled. "Elise, do you really think you can pull this off?"

"My daddy was an oil man. My husband is an oil man. I never heard either one of them ever say *quit*. Your damned right we can do it."

Anderson kissed her on the forehead. "Don't ever let anybody say Victor Underwood isn't a winner. He won the best prize of all." He turned to Choctaw and Slim. "Come on, men. Let's go find Autie."

Slim wished he had a chance to clean up, to change out of the mud-streaked clothes before Tracy saw him. But he walked into the Teagarden just as he was, Choctaw and Anderson trailing behind him. The place was almost empty, for it was not yet time for the supper rush. Two roustabouts sat over coffee and pie. Tracy had her back turned, wiping an adjacent table.

Slim called, "Tracy!"

She turned. In her surprise at seeing him, she threw the damp rag to one side. It almost landed in one of the roustabouts' pie. "Slim! What're you doin' here?" She made a couple of quick steps toward him, then saw Choctaw and Anderson and remembered herself. She stopped and studied him. "You look like you've been sloppin' hogs."

"We had an accident out on the rig. We're lookin' for your daddy."

"Oh, I thought . . ." She covered a little disappointment. "Have you looked for him at the house?" She called it a house, though it was only a large tent.

Slim moved closer, wanting to touch her but deterred by the presence of other people. "No, the first thing I thought of was to see you . . . to ask you."

"What do you want him for?"

"Mr. Underwood got hurt. Mrs. Underwood needs a driller."

"Nobody's hired Papa as a driller since . . ." Her eyes misted. "Well, you know the shape he's in."

"Maybe it's time somebody gave him another chance."

They stared awkwardly at each other until Choctaw declared, "Cowboy, we got business to attend to. You goin' to kiss that girl or not?" He gave Slim a shove toward Tracy.

Mrs. Whitmore stood in the kitchen door, wiping her hands on her apron. "Tracy, why don't you bring Slim back here for a piece of pie while I talk to these gentlemen?"

Choctaw said, "Make it chocolate. That was always my favorite."

Mrs. Whitmore smiled as Tracy led Slim past her. "I'll get these gentlemen something. You visit with Slim for a bit."

In the kitchen, Tracy turned. "What flavor do you like?"

"I didn't come in here for pie."

"That's fine, because the pie's all out yonder anyway." She moved into his arms.

As Tracy had said, they found Autie Whitmore in the tent that the family called home. Well on the way toward being staggering drunk, he tried to focus his eyes on the three men who pushed into the tent. He fastened upon Slim. "I know you, don't I? Where'd you fall into all that mud?"

"Sure you know me, Mr. Whitmore. I'm Slim McIntyre. I'm a friend of Tracy's. And that's Choctaw, and Mr. Knox Anderson. We've come to get you."

"Get me? For what?" He shrank back defensively against a bureau. "I ain't done nothin'. You-all leave me alone."

"Mr. Underwood has gotten himself hurt. We need you for a driller on his rig."

"I ain't a driller no more. How'd he come to get hurt?"

"A blowout."

"Like what killed my boy? And you want me to go out there?" He looked as if he would jump and run if his shaky legs would let him.

"This was just an air pocket, no gas and no fire."

"I ain't goin'." His eyes looked wild. "You-all can't make me."

Choctaw moved forward, towering over Whitmore. "You ain't listenin'. The cowboy said we need you, and you're goin'."

Anderson touched Choctaw's shoulder. "Just a minute. Mr. Whitmore thinks we're threatening him."

"I am," Choctaw said.

"But we don't have to do it that way. We can talk this over in a friendly fashion, man to man. He'll see it our way when we give him a chance. I have some good Kentucky bourbon outside in my car." He walked out of the tent and was back in a minute with the bottle. He broke the seal. "The real stuff, pre-Prohibition. You have the privilege of the first drink, Autie."

Whitmore surveyed the men with suspicion but took the bottle. His Adam's apple bobbed as he downed a couple of big swallows. His face twisted with pleasure. "That *is* the real stuff. None of that backyard hooch." He handed the bottle back to Anderson. "But I still ain't goin'."

Anderson offered the bottle to Choctaw, who was tempted but shook his head. "You know how it is with me and whisky. If I start, I won't quit till I'm on Buckalew's chain. I'll wait outside." He left the tent.

Anderson took a drink and passed the bottle to Slim. Slim swallowed a sip but tried to make it look like more. Whitmore's eyes followed the bottle. When Anderson offered it back to him, he accepted it willingly, took a strong drink and handed it to Slim. Slim faked a swallow and passed the bottle to Anderson, who did not fake.

After a time, the bottle was nearly empty. Whitmore had a death grip on it and was singing discordantly. Anderson's necktie was at half-mast and his face flushed. His voice was only marginally better than Whitmore's.

Choctaw walked through the door and watched the two men for a minute. He eyed Slim critically. "You all right, cowboy?"

"I'm fine. I'm not sure about them."

Whitmore's voice trailed off, and he slumped forward in his chair, asleep. Anderson reached carefully and took the bottle from his fingers just as it appeared about to slip to the floor. Just enough whisky was left in it for one good drink. He handed the bottle to Slim. "I think he's ready to go with you now. When he wakes up out yonder, he'll be needing that drink."

Choctaw said severely, "He's had his last drink till we finish that well."

Anderson pushed to his feet and grabbed at the tentpole for support. Choctaw caught and steadied him. "I think you better stay here and rest awhile, Mr. Anderson. That chocolate pie must not agree with you."

"Good idea. I ought to know better than to eat pie on an empty stomach." He sat down heavily on Whitmore's bed. "You tell Elise . . . Mrs. Underwood . . . that I hope she brings in a gusher, and it pumps a thousand barrels a day."

Slim and Choctaw carried Autie Whitmore out to the truck. He was a hundred and fifty or sixty pounds of dead weight. They got him situated in the front seat. Slim said, "I better take a look at Mr. Anderson before we go."

He went back into the tent and found Anderson stretched out on Whitmore's bed. Slim picked up the bottle from the floor, where it had fallen. The last of the whisky had spilled out. He paused, looking at the wealthiest man in Caprock, and at the moment probably one of the drunkest.

Slim said, "Mr. Anderson, you're a gentleman. I'm pleased that I got to know you."

"You-all just see that you finish that well for her . . . for both of them."

"We'll do that," Slim promised. "You watch and see."

As Slim started the truck down the dirt street, Autie Whitmore slid over against Choctaw, dead to the world. Choctaw grumbled, "A cowboy and an Indian, a Mexican and a drunk. The poor woman's got herself one hell of a crew."

Four

The Reckoning

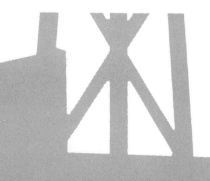

21

A Showdown

DAVE BUCKALEW had decided that if he could not do anything else to Big Boy Daugherty's henchmen, he would try to drive them crazy. He had lost a shouting match in old Judge Potter's courthouse office and law library over the release of Radke and Skinny, Frenchy and Sarge on ridiculously low bail. The judge had hunched in a leather-covered chair in front of his rolltop desk and avoided meeting Dave's eyes. "You wouldn't tell me who your murder witness is," he said defensively.

"It's a matter of safety," Dave replied. "I can't until the trial comes up."

"Then it's just your word that you even *have* such a witness."

"My word has always been good around here."

"This isn't just a little petty cattle stealing, or the highjacking of some oilfield pipe. This is murder. I want to see that witness myself, or at least know his name."

"You will, when it's time."

"That isn't enough. The bond stands."

If the judge had been a younger man, Dave might have floored him, even at the cost of his badge. But he could see fear in the old jurist's eyes. He doubted that Daugherty's men had bribed him; the judge had a long record of honorable service. They had probably frightened him half to death.

"Let me put them back in jail, Judge. Set the bail high enough for me to keep them there. Then they can't hurt you."

"The jail's not big enough for all of that mob. Even if it was, I'm sure Daugherty knows where to get more. All we can do is hope he'll find the rewards too small for his appetite and leave us."

"It's not all *I* can do," Dave declared sternly. As he turned to leave the judge's cramped office, Potter called, "Dave, remember you're supposed to uphold the law. Whatever you do, keep it according to the statutes."

"I may write a few statutes of my own."

He began following Daugherty's men when other duties did not busy him elsewhere. Sometimes he did it overtly, so they knew from the start that he was dogging their steps. Other times he moved surreptitiously, revealing himself when he felt the moment was right for a surprise. Often he sent Waddy Fuller on similar errands of silent harassment.

Waddy did not quite see the logic. "They ain't goin' to do nothin' when they know we're watchin'."

"That's part of the idea. If we can keep them on their left foot all the time, we might cut down on Daugherty's business. Maybe he'll decide to move where the pickin's come easier."

Dave took particular pleasure in breaking up a floating gambling operation. There had been gambling in Caprock before, but it had not often resulted in violence, and it had not been run by Daugherty's people, so for the most part he had left it alone. The first time he found Daugherty's set-up he smashed several slot machines with the back side of an ax. The rest—mainly poker and crap games—would simply shift from one site to another each time he found it and shut it down, for cards and dice were much easier to move than slot machines. But at least he had the satisfaction of harrying Daugherty's gamblers, of keeping their nerves rubbed raw.

O'Dell and Skinny often traveled together. Dave tried to make himself their third shadow. Several times he broke up their attempts to collect money from various people in town such as Shemp Oliver or the Dutchman or Jolene. He drove up behind them as they were talking to the bootlegger Preacher Perry where he usually set up shop on a back street to peddle his moonshine. Perry had money in his hand, but at sight of Dave the pair climbed into O'Dell's red car and pulled out, leaving Perry standing there holding a wad of greenbacks.

Dave leaned toward the open window of his black county automobile. "Save your money, Preacher."

"They'll be back," Perry said dejectedly.

"So will I. When you people have had enough and are willin' to help me, we'll do somethin' about it."

Perry appeared to have lost weight. Dave suspected old P.P. wasn't eating much these days. Probably had a perennially upset stomach, perhaps an ulcer. Perry stared obliquely at him. "Sheriff, how much schoolin' did you have?"

"Went most of the way through the tenth grade. Why?"

"Didn't get past the sixth myself. But I learned to count. I don't count but one of you. Maybe another half if I include that deputy. There's a baker's dozen of *them* around town."

"You're not figurin' the badge. It counts for several."

"A Ranger badge might, but you're just a county sheriff. If they ever decide to, they'll eat you for breakfast. You've chosen a hard way to serve the Lord."

Dave drove around until he picked up the red car again. Skinny was driving. At sight of Dave behind him he almost ran up against a parked car, then swerved sharply back into the dirt street. He drove a few blocks, saw that Dave was going to stay with him, then turned back to the hotel. Dave got out of his car as they left theirs. Skinny was trembling with anger and frustration. O'Dell's eyes bespoke a sardonic humor.

"Don't you ever sleep, Sheriff? Missin' sleep can make a man start havin' hallucinations."

"Don't you ever get the notion that *I'm* a hallucination. There's no rest for the wicked, not in Caprock."

Skinny took a step toward him, then stopped and muttered, "Can't even go to the toilet without some John Law a-watchin'." He approached the hotel door with dread. Dave suspected O'Dell and Skinny would catch hell from Daugherty for showing up without the payment from Preacher Perry. Maybe if he badgered them long enough they would kill each other off. But that was too much to ask of Providence. Providence needed help.

He waited in the hall after O'Dell and Skinny went into Daugherty's room. He heard a deep, gravelly voice raised in anger and Skinny's wailing reply. Dave chuckled and leaned against the wall, filling in with imagination the scene he could not see beyond the door. Presently the door opened and a chastened Skinny came out into the hall, followed by O'Dell. Dave stepped away from the wall, letting them see him. Skinny muttered, "Goddamn you to hell!" and turned back into Daugherty's room. O'Dell followed, shaking his head.

In a moment, tall Turk Radke came out. He stopped two paces short of Dave, his gray eyes smoldering. He wore a shoulder holster, but no pistol was in it. He was not giving Dave an excuse to arrest him again. "Buckalew, what would it take to get you off of our tails?"

"Leavin' my jurisdiction'd do it."

"Boss is a stubborn old bastard when he gets his mind made up."

"I'm a stubborn bastard too."

"He's also a patient and calculatin' man, up to a point." His eyes narrowed. "Me, I never had more than a nickel's worth of patience, and you've used up about four cents' worth of it."

Radke retreated into Daugherty's room. Dave waited until he decided nobody was coming out for a while, then started down the hall toward his own room. He was unlocking his door when he heard footsteps on the stairs. He turned and waited.

Lauralou Clive came up and stopped for a moment, one hand on the rail, the other gripping a handkerchief. She did not look in Dave's direction. Hesitantly she went to the door of the room where O'Dell slept. She knocked timidly but received no response. She knocked again, harder. She waited a minute, then moved down the hall to Daugherty's door.

Dave could hear a man's voice from inside. Lauralou responded, "It's Lauralou Clive. I'm lookin' for Irish."

The door opened slightly. Dave could not see a face, but he could hear a man's voice. "Irish ain't here."

"I think he is," Lauralou argued. "Tell him I've got to see him."

"I told you Irish ain't here. I'll tell him when he comes back."

The man started to close the door, but Lauralou pushed her body against it and shouted through the opening. "Irish, I've got to talk to you."

Lauralou had her arm inside the door. The man forced it out and shoved the door to. Dave could hear the turning of a key in the lock. Trembling, Lauralou turned back toward the stairs, her head down.

Dave caught her by surprise. Her blue eyes filled with tears as she tried to focus on his face.

"Any way I can help you, Lauralou?"

"Not unless . . ." Her voice went bitter. "No, there's nothin'." She moved past him and descended the stairs, wiping her eyes with the handkerchief.

Dave had never wasted much respect on either Lauralou or her father, but he could not help feeling sorry for her. He suspected he knew her trouble; it was a logical consequence of what she had probably regarded as a bold adventure. He could not ease her burden. She had made her own bed. With O'Dell's help.

He heard a brief quarreling in Daugherty's room. To his surprise, Irish O'Dell came out and strode briskly after Lauralou. He hurried down the stairs without giving Dave a glance. He took Lauralou's arm. "Come on, sweet thing. We'll go for a drive." Dave stared after them a minute, wondering if O'Dell might be about to do the right thing for once.

He washed his face and felt the stubble scratchy against his hand. He decided to shave, lest some new driller in town mistake him for a roustabout and try to hire him. He was wiping away the last remnants of lather when he heard a knock. Opening the door a little, he saw Skinny's thin face and hating eyes.

"Boss wants to talk to you."

Dave had already been down this road once. He had never yet seen Boss Daugherty, though they lived on the same floor. He had heard his booming voice giving commands, and he had heard the floor creak under the man's weight as Daugherty had paced back and forth. Many a time Dave had left his door ajar, hoping in vain to satisfy his curiosity with a glimpse of the old bandit in the hallway. But stubbornness won out over curiosity. "He's got two good legs. Let him walk over here and talk to *me*."

"Boss don't move around much. He likes to set in one place and let people come to him."

"Like a big fat spider waitin' in his web?"

The sarcasm went over Skinny's head. He had a mission, and he stuck to it. "I was sent to fetch you."

Dave decided Skinny wouldn't move from his door. "When I finish washin' up."

"Boss don't care if you're washed or not. He wants you."

"I'm gettin' damned tired of hearin' what Boss wants. Tell him I'll be there when I'm ready." He turned his back on Skinny but prudently watched him in the mirror over his lavatory. Skinny waited a minute in frustration, then turned away.

Dave finished wiping his face and put on his shirt. A tingle of anticipation ran through him at the prospect of seeing Boss Daugherty face to face at last. He started for the door, reconsidered and strapped his pistol belt around his waist. He doubted they would attack a sheriff in a hotel in the middle of town, but with people like Radke and Skinny he could not be certain of anything. Most of Daugherty's men did not appear the kind to invest much time or energy in thought; they would act on impulse or order. Skinny had a look that said he would have no compunction about slipping a knife between Dave's ribs. Lydia had said when Radke flew into a rage he was capable of anything, and the man's flint-hard eyes indicated that her judgment of him was sound.

Dave did not knock. He simply walked in, slamming the door behind him. He had smelled a rattlesnake den more than once. This was one. Skinny was standing at a window, his back turned. He spun around. Frenchy jumped up from his chair, turning it over. Turk Radke sat on the edge of a bed, giving Dave a sullen stare.

A table was laden with food . . . steak, mashed potatoes, beans, biscuits, a pot of coffee. At the table hunched the largest man Dave had ever seen, a mountain of flesh. He guessed

Daugherty might easily weigh three hundred and fifty pounds. The man's right hand was poised in midair, holding a fork on which a chunk of steak was impaled and dripping gravy. His round and puffy red face was distorted by a mouthful of food which he chewed with the placid demeanor of a cow chewing her cud. He attempted to speak, but his voice was muffled by the food in his mouth. He swallowed, his thick throat bobbing. He washed everything down with a long sip of coffee and laid aside the fork with the steak still on it.

His voice was deep and resonant. "So you're the cowboy law that's been givin' my boys a wall-eyed fit. You don't look as scary as they've made out. You look like just another ol' country boy to me."

Dave noticed that the man's feet beneath the table were bare except for dirty white cotton socks. A pair of outsized old brogan shoes lay on their sides where he had carelessly kicked them off. The laces had been pulled out of them for comfort. Daugherty's shirt was sweat-darkened around the armpits and unbuttoned halfway down the front, exposing white underwear, part of a hairy chest and a little of his distended belly. Daugherty's hand resembled a ham as he motioned with it. He talked in a slow, country-raised drawl. "Drag you up a chair and set yourself down. Me and you, we got things to talk about."

Dave did not move. "I don't know what they could be."

"I like to be friendly to the local laws wherever I go. Eliminates a lot of misunderstandin'."

"I think we understand one another. I'm tryin' to run a clean county. You've dirtied it up."

"Clean?" Daugherty snorted and shoved the forkful of steak into his mouth, talking while he chewed. "You got bootleggers, confidence men, illegal gamblin' . . . you got whores and highjackers."

"I do the best I can, just me and one deputy."

"What you need is some friends that can help you keep all that mischief under control. Now, these things are naturally goin' to come to a boomtown. Since you can't stop them, the next best thing is to have somebody that can at least keep them in line and runnin' smooth. That's where me and my boys come in. We've had aplenty of experience."

Dave's voice was caustic. "So I've heard."

323

A false smile forced its way across Daugherty's broad and pliable face. "I always been one that favored law and order. Especially order. And I feel like good lawmen is poorly paid. I'm always willin' to help make up for it . . . call it a bonus."

Dave said dryly, "Call it a bribe."

"Ugly word, *bribe*. I like *bonus* better."

"I don't think people here would look at it your way."

"People!" Daugherty snorted. "Most of them are too busy takin' care of their own business to care. All we do is to levy sort of a sin tax. In return we keep things runnin' smooth and peaceful and no trouble to the law. Me and my boys, we don't allow no smalltime grifters and highjackers. We got ways of dealin' with them so they don't stay long or ever come back."

"I already saw one example. I carried the Haskells out to the county line. They were in an almighty hurry to leave."

"Proves my point. They wasn't no loss to society, was they?"

"I wouldn't want to trade a pair of coyotes for a pack of wolves."

Daugherty grunted. "I can tell that people have poisoned your mind against me. Fact is, I think me and you have got a lot in common. You look to me like one that was brought up in the dirt. You never had no silver spoon in your mouth."

"My folks were shirttail ranchers with nothin' but a toenail hold, and they eventually lost even that."

"Same as me, except I growed up on an East Texas farm, lookin' a pair of mules in the butt from daylight to dark. We was so poor us kids ofttimes had to hunt possums to put meat on the table. Ever eat possum, Buckalew? It's nigger food. People in town called us white trash. *Pore* white trash. Well sir, the *pore* part was sure right, but we wasn't trash. I made up my mind that I was goin' to get richer than any of them high-nosed planters and merchants, and I done it. I could buy and sell them all if I was of a mind to."

"Now you're tryin' to buy *me*."

"I'm just tryin' to get you to see it my way. I can help you, and you can help me. Us ol' country boys ought to stick together." He finished the steak and picked up a piece of apple pie, squeezing some of the filling out upon his thick fingers.

Daugherty's eyes were almost hidden behind the folds of

flesh, but Dave sensed their determination and cold power. He recoiled a little, as he would recoil from a snake.

Daugherty demanded, "What is it you want out of life, Buckalew? Good car, a house in town? I hear tell you're a bachelor. A man with money can fix that up in a hurry. What is it you really want?"

Dave did not know why he told him. "A decent little ranch, some good cattle, a few good horses. Some peace and quiet. Mighty little I've had since the oil came in."

"You could have all that. Wouldn't take you long to get enough money to buy you a nice place of your own. I ain't talkin' about no penny-ante stuff. As for peace and quiet, just give me the high sign. You could set in the shade and take your ease."

Dave was momentarily tempted, remembering the roll of bills he had seen in Radke's hand one day. But the moment passed. He remembered what Lydia had said, that Daugherty was like a big fat tick, swollen with blood sucked from the helpless. "Keep your money. I've got no use for you or for these thugs you keep around you."

Turk Radke's eyes carried a chill. "Now listen, you son of a bitch . . ."

Daugherty said sharply, "Turk, you know I never did like to listen to a dirty mouth. I won't have that kind of talk." He turned back to Dave. "As a boy, I never did even cuss the mules. Didn't believe in it. Still don't. My mama seen to it that I was church-raised." He licked the apple filling from his fingers. "About these murder charges you filed on Turk and Skinny . . . I ain't seen no evidence."

"You'll see it at the trial."

"Word comes to me that you're supposed to have a witness. Where's he at?"

"In a safe place. I wouldn't want any accident to happen."

"It could be worth a right smart to you if you was to forget where that witness is stashed. You could tell the judge you've decided the witness was mistaken. Folks tell me the deceased—what was his name, Ox?—drowned in a slushpit."

"After bein' beaten half to death. He had aplenty of help in his dyin'."

Daugherty's eyes showed a little more through the heavy padding of flesh. They reminded Dave of pigs' eyes. "Your witness see all that?"

He started to say *she* but caught himself. "My witness saw enough."

"From what I heard, that Ox wasn't no loss to the community. I've seen a many of his kind killed in one boomtown and another. Folks never did make much fuss."

"Caprock is different."

"You still got some old-fashioned notions, Buckalew. The world don't put much stock in them anymore. The dog with the biggest teeth gets the bone. The rest just get chewed up. I always had a strong set of teeth." Those half-hidden eyes seemed to peel Dave away layer by layer. "I do wish we could find a way to work together, two old country boys. Ain't really much difference between us."

"There's a world of difference. If you can't see it, there's no use us talkin' to one another."

Daugherty's puffy face wrinkled like a prune. "No, I reckon there ain't. An almighty shame, it is. I always liked a man who stood up for what he believed—as long as he wasn't standin' in my way. Well, Buckalew, you go on and play by your rules. I'll play by mine." His voice dropped ominously. "If I was you, I wouldn't be startin' no continued stories." He picked up his cup, sipped and frowned, putting the cup back down. "Coffee's gone cold."

Like the conversation, Dave thought. He backed out of the room, watching all the men, especially Radke. Not until he was in the hall and had closed the door did he pause for a deep breath. That room still made him think of a rattlesnake den. It even smelled like one. He found himself shaking.

He was in his office that afternoon when the telephone rang. He recognized Doc Tolliver's voice. "Dave, I think you'll want to get over here pretty quick." Doc was not often given to excitement, but his voice was urgent.

"What's happened?"

"I've got a patient you may want to talk to. I don't know if she's going to make it, so don't waste any time."

A woman, then. Dave thought of Lydia and felt a moment of alarm but dismissed that idea. She was safe at the ranch. "I'm on my way." He met his deputy coming up the courthouse steps. "I'll be over at Doc's if you need me, Waddy."

Waddy nodded. "I been watchin' the hotel like you told me. Ain't none of that gang come out since dinner. Looks like me and you got them scared."

Dave made a wry smile. "Sure we have."

It would not have been a long walk to the doctor's office, but cowboy's upbringing had taught him that a man didn't walk when he could ride a horse. He had no horse here, but the car served to uphold tradition.

He found Hap Holloway sitting in the outer waiting room. He had never known Hap to be sick except in the aftermath of overindulgence. Blood spotted the young man's clothes, and blue blotches marred his swollen, freckled face. Dave demanded, "What got you all bruised and bloodied up?"

Hap was unnaturally grim. "The bruises came from a little disagreement over a hand of poker. The blood ain't mine. It's Lauralou Clive's." He pointed toward the inner door. "Doc said tell you to go on in."

Dave found Lauralou lying on an operating table. A sheet covered her to the bare shoulders. Her face was a ghostly white. The doctor and a nurse leaned over her, the nurse wiping the girl's face with a dampened cloth. The doctor glanced up at Dave. "I don't know if I got the bleeding stopped or if she simply ran out of blood."

"What happened to her?"

"An abortion. A bad job of it. Holloway out there said he found her lying in an alley, wrapped in a blood-soaked blanket. My guess is that whoever did the operation thought she was dying and didn't want to be caught with a woman's body on his hands. He just bundled her up, hauled her off and dumped her like a dead cat."

Dave was always suspicious where Hap Holloway was concerned. "What part do you reckon Hap played in it?"

"None. If he had, why would he bring her in? He's a wild sort of a boy, but not that wild." The doctor shook his head. "She's not the first woman I've had brought to me this way. Perhaps you can get her to talk. She hasn't told me a thing."

Dave moved close. "Lauralou, it's Sheriff Buckalew. Can you hear me?"

She blinked, and her eyes moved, but she did not answer.

He said, "Won't you tell me who did this to you?"

She turned her head and looked at him a moment, then closed her eyes. He feared she was dead until he saw the sheet move with her breathing.

He said to the doctor, "Somebody's got to tell her daddy."

The doctor frowned. "He already knows. The telephone operator called around and found him drinking at the Kit Kat. He came, took one look at her and got sick all over the floor. He left here like a whipped dog."

"Probably drownin' himself in whisky," Dave guessed. "He's as bad as Autie Whitmore." He gave the girl a long study. "She got any chance?"

"I've called Odessa. They have equipment over there to give her a blood transfusion. We'll be leaving with her in a few minutes. We'll save her if we can."

"Try hard, Doc. She's like Hap, I guess. Not all bad, just got too much vinegar for her own good."

He went back out into the waiting room, where Hap sat twisting his old hat around and around. Hap asked anxiously, "Is she still amongst us?"

Dave said, "She is, for now. How did you happen to find her?"

"I seen the blanket first. I taken a second look, and there she was. Whoever throwed her there probably thought she was already dead."

Dave studied Hap's eyes for any sign that he might be lying. He saw none. "How come you in that alley in the first place?"

"I was makin' a delivery for Preacher Perry."

"Bibles, no doubt."

Hap shrugged. "If that's what you want to call it."

"I didn't know you were acquainted with Lauralou."

"I wanted to be, but she never would give me a second look. Had her sights set on a higher level."

"She missed her target with Irish O'Dell. You have any idea who could've operated on her?"

"That sort of thing is out of my territory. I never put a girl in shape to need such as that . . . I don't think."

Dave's stomach burned with futility. There had been a time when such a thing would not have happened in Caprock, or if it had, he would have known just where to turn. But now, with all these thousands of people he didn't even know, people who didn't seem to care about anything except taking their share of whatever was here and moving on . . . there were days he just wanted to chuck the whole mess . . . let them go ahead and make a jungle out of it. Like now.

"Those bruises," he said, "you want to tell me about them?"

Hap shrugged. "Feller said I was cheatin'."

"Were you?"

"Not as good as he was. He taken the whole pot."

Dave suspected it had happened in one of the floating games, but he knew Holloway had told him all he was going to. "Can I take you somewhere, Hap?"

"I'm goin' to help Doc carry Lauralou to Odessa. She can have some of my blood if she needs it."

Dave was reluctant to give the devil his due, but he said, "You did the right thing this time. I wish you could make a habit of it."

Hap blinked. Without guile, he asked, "What did I ever do wrong?"

Dave walked out onto the porch and down to the black car with the sheriff's symbol painted on the door.

He saw a parking place near the Teagarden and pulled in. He found the café empty except for a couple of coffee drinkers. Tracy Whitmore came out from the kitchen, smiling. "What'll it be, Sheriff?"

"You got anything for a sour stomach?"

The smile left her. "Hope it wasn't somethin' Mama cooked."

"No, it's just this job. Sometimes I see things happen here that spoil my digestion."

She fetched a spoon and a bottle of something with a drug-store label. It looked like a mixture of clabbered milk and to-bacco juice. She said, "Wildcatters call this their dry-hole remedy."

He shuddered at the taste. "Ought to be poured down a hole . . . a deep one." He was glad she didn't ask him any questions. He didn't feel like talking about Lauralou. "What do you hear from Slim McIntyre?"

"Mrs. Underwood took me out to see him Sunday, him and Papa. You'd be proud of Papa. He hasn't had a drink since he's been on that rig."

They were probably posting a guard on him at night, Dave

329

thought, but he would not say so. "That's fine. How's Victor Underwood?"

"Not happy. He's got his leg in a cast. Can't move around much, can't help with anything. But the drillin' is goin' good. Papa says they're about down to the pay zone, if there is one."

"Let's hope it's there. The Underwoods could stand some good luck for a change."

"So could Papa," Tracy said. "Maybe he'd feel better about himself if he could bring in a good well. It's been a long time."

He heard someone shout his name. "Dave!"

Waddy Fuller stood in the doorway, eyes wide with excitement. "Seen your car out there. They want you at the hotel, quick. Looks like there's fixin' to be somebody killed!"

Dave trotted for the door. "What's happened?"

"It's Douglas Clive. He's got a gun, and he's tryin' to call out Irish O'Dell."

Dave cursed. For a moment he was tempted to leave things alone. Clive and O'Dell deserved each other. But he sprinted toward the car. "Crank it, Waddy." He barely gave Waddy time to jump in after the car started. He sped up the street, pressing against the horn and wishing he had a siren. The county had not seen justification for the expense.

He left the car in the street, motor running. Albert, the desk man, was standing outside, on the walk, gesturing wildly. "Upstairs, Sheriff. Hurry!"

Drawing his pistol, Dave took the steps two at a time. He could hear Waddy coming up behind him, unable to match the pace. Past the head of the stairs, in the center of the hallway, Douglas Clive stood with a Colt revolver in his hand, his arm hanging straight down. Farther along, O'Dell stood beside Big Boy Daugherty's door. His hand rested on the stock of a pistol still in its shoulder holster. "Back off, man," he said brittlely. "I've got no wish to kill you."

Clive was turned in such a way that he could see Dave without taking his eyes from O'Dell. "You stay back, Sheriff. This isn't your affair."

"The hell it's not. It's my town. Give me that six-shooter, Clive."

"You can have it when I've finished what I come to do." The

man's face was flushed a deep red. He swayed a little from drinking. "You don't know what he did to my little girl."

"I do know. I saw her just now, down at Doc's."

"Then you know why I'm fixin' to kill this man. He's the one got her in that fix. He's the one killed her."

"She's not dead. With luck, she'll live. You raise that pistol, though, and *you'll* be dead. You haven't got a snowball's chance in hell." He extended his hand. "Come on now, give me the gun."

"He used her like some whore. He knocked her up and turned his back on her. He ain't fit to live." He started raising his arm, bringing up the pistol.

O'Dell jerked his own pistol from its holster and brought it into line, aimed at Clive.

Dave shouted, "Don't do it, O'Dell. I'll send you up for murder."

O'Dell appeared tense, sweat on his forehead. "I don't want to. But if I have to, it's self-defense. You can see that."

Dave pondered the chance that he could jump Clive and knock the pistol aside before the ranchman could fire. It was poor. The possibility was strong that he might even take O'Dell's bullet. "Clive . . . don't!"

Clive's arm moved with painful slowness, raising the revolver. His eyes were riveted on O'Dell, and on O'Dell's pistol pointed straight at him. Clive began to tremble. The arm stopped halfway up.

Dave thought of a rabbit, charmed by a snake until it was paralyzed. That was Clive. The ranchman began to shake violently, sweat beading his face. He made a cry of futility and fear, then dropped his arm. Dave jumped to grab the revolver before Clive could change his mind.

O'Dell still held his pistol, aimed at Clive. Dave shouted at him, "Hold your fire. It's over."

Clive was on the point of collapse. He had stood at the brink and looked into the chasm. He shook uncontrollably and cried like a child. Dave put himself between the two men and turned Clive around, facing away from O'Dell. "Waddy, take Clive downstairs, quick." Waddy grasped the ranchman's arm and hustled him toward the stairs, apprehensively looking back over

331

his shoulder in O'Dell's direction. O'Dell lowered his pistol, but he did not put it away.

Dave had forgotten his sour stomach. In the aftermath of crisis, it forcibly exerted itself again. He wished for a support to lean on but did not want to show weakness to O'Dell, and to the other men who crowded into the hallway from Daugherty's room. Big Boy himself stood in the doorway, filling it with his bulk. His trousers hung like a bag, and his feet were clad only in white socks.

Skinny declared, "You ought to've killed the son of a bitch."

Dave wondered which he was talking about, Clive or himself.

O'Dell holstered the pistol and walked toward Dave. Coldly he said, "I could easy've shot you, Sheriff, and claimed it was an accident while I was defendin' myself."

Dave shuddered, realizing the man probably could have gotten away with it. Most people in the oilfield would have thought it too bad, and many would have attended his funeral. Then they would have gone back to their own business, leaving O'Dell and Radke and Daugherty to theirs. Daugherty was frowning. Such an unfortunate accident would have suited his purposes. Perhaps O'Dell's failure to take advantage of the opportunity would give the overweight gentleman a good case of indigestion. That thought made Dave's stomach feel better.

Dave asked O'Dell, "Why didn't you when you had the chance?"

"It would've been messy. Too many questions and too much red tape. If I ever take care of you, Sheriff, it'll be neat and clean and no damned questions to answer afterwards." O'Dell looked back at Daugherty and the men around him. His voice dropped to a level Dave could barely hear. "Can we go down the hall a ways and talk, just the two of us?"

Curious, Dave said, "I see no objection." He let O'Dell walk ahead of him, and he kept a watchful eye on the men slowly working their way back into Daugherty's room. Most of them looked disappointed that the show was over without a shot being fired. It had been like a circus without a tiger.

O'Dell stopped at the head of the stairs. He looked behind him, seeing that nobody could eavesdrop. "I didn't ask for what happened just now."

"You did, the first time you touched that girl."

"She did everything but beg out loud for it. You'd've done the same thing if she'd thrown herself at you."

Dave was glad she never had. "I wouldn't've left her to face the trouble all by herself."

"I took her to somebody who's supposed to be able to take care of things like that. I didn't know he'd butcher her up and then throw her away. Believe me, he's fixin' to get his wick trimmed good and proper." He shrugged. "It isn't Lauralou I want to talk about. It's Lydia. I got to thinkin' about you sendin' her out of town."

"She wanted to get away from you. All of you."

"Right after that you filed those charges on Turk and Skinny. Boss said you told him you have your witness put away in a safe place. All of a sudden it's come to me that Lydia is your witness."

Dave's heart jumped. He hoped he did not betray himself with his eyes. "What gave you a notion like that?"

"I just put two and two together. It added up to Lydia. And you know where she's at."

"Even if I did, I'd tell the devil before I'd tell you."

"I want that woman, Buckalew, but I don't want her dead. Turk and Skinny wouldn't let her live a minute if they knew. You better do somethin' about those charges, and tell her to forget anything she saw. If you bring her back here to testify, they won't let her live long enough to take the oath."

He turned and started back toward Daugherty's room, then stopped for a moment. "One more thing: you keep that coward Clive off of my back. Next time I may have to kill him."

Dave was shaken by how accurately O'Dell had guessed. Now that he had gone that far, it would probably not take him long to find out about Dave's ranch and to make another educated guess. Lydia had to be moved. His back tingled with urgency.

He walked downstairs, looking for Waddy and Clive. Clive was on his knees at the edge of the sidewalk, heaving. Waddy said with exasperation, "He's been at it ever since we came down. I wouldn't think he'd have anything left."

"When he gets done, take him over to the jail and let him sleep it off. Don't lock the door on him, but be damned sure he doesn't get ahold of a pistol again."

He saw a movement at a second-story window and looked up.

Irish O'Dell stood in Daugherty's room, watching him. He felt the prickling again, stronger than before.

He could not leave Lydia on that ranch another night.

He cranked the black car, drove it to a gasoline station and filled the tank. With a long look behind him into a sinking sun, he set out through the oilfield, then across the Clive ranch. Somewhere along the way he picked up a thorn and felt the car pull sharply to the right as a tire went down. Muttering impatiently, he stopped to remove the tire. He rolled up his sleeves, glancing nervously toward the west. The sun was about to slip behind a rising bank of clouds that looked as if they might carry rain. At this rate it would be dark by the time he reached the house. He took off his pistol belt, folded it and laid it on the seat to be out of his way while he added another patch to many on the tube. Finished and in a hurry to be going again, he carelessly pitched the pump onto the floorboard. As he paused to open the gate onto Uncle Henry Stringfellow's land, he could see the distant wooden derrick where Victor Underwood's crew was drilling. It was too far to hear the engine. He drove onto the two-rut road that led to his own place, adjoining both Clive's land and Uncle Henry's. He opened the final wire gate and honked the horn as he traversed the last couple of hundred yards, letting Lydia know he was coming.

She met him at the door, smiling with pleasure and surprise. She walked out to meet him as he cut the engine. "Dave! I didn't expect you again so soon. You just brought me groceries yesterday." She came into his arms.

He hugged her, then stepped back, putting aside his wanting of her. "I didn't know yesterday what I know now. I've got to move you."

Fear leaped into her hazel eyes. "They know I'm here?"

"Not yet, maybe, but they won't be long in figurin' it out. This time I *am* takin' you to Odessa and puttin' you on the train."

"I've liked it here, Dave. I hate to leave."

"And I'd want you to stay if things were different. Let's go and put your stuff together."

Reluctantly she went ahead of him to the front door. He lighted a lamp while she put her clothes into the same cheap suitcases she had brought here. In the kitchen, she paused, opening a cabinet.

334

"Forget the groceries," Dave said. "You won't need them on the train."

"Surely I have time to fix you a little supper."

A little supper, and then some talk, and then whatever the mood and the moment brought . . . he knew how it would be. He touched her cheek, wishing. "Not this time. I won't feel easy till I see you on that train."

She gripped his arm with both hands, her eyes sad. "If you think it's best . . ."

"I do." He picked up her bags and carried them to the door while Lydia blew out the lamp.

The horse had wandered up from the barn. Lydia paused to pat it on the neck while it nuzzled her. "We've gotten to be good friends. I'll miss him."

Dave swallowed, watching her with the horse. Nothing about her seemed any longer to suggest that she had ever belonged to a place like Jolene's. He had become used to her being here. She and this little ranch seemed to fit together like a hand and a soft glove. "He'll miss you feedin' him every day. Maybe another time . . . sometime."

But he knew it was unlikely she would ever return. For her own safety, he would forget about her being a witness. He would put her on that train and not let her tell him where she was going. Only in that way could he be assured that O'Dell or Radke would not find her.

She said, "I only regret that you didn't have a milk cow. When I was a girl I milked a cow every day, sometimes two." She turned away from the horse. "Out here was almost like bein' home again."

"There's no reason you can't go home, if that's what you want."

She tried to smile. "Thanks anyway, Dave, for the dream."

He wished he knew what to say. He wanted to tell her that someday when Daugherty and Radke and O'Dell were only a bad memory, she might come back. But other memories might stand in the way. He could not lie to her about that, and even if he tried, she would know better.

"You'd best be gettin' in the car, Lydia," he said.

A man's voice spoke behind him. "Yes, get in the car!"

Dave spun, his stomach cold. He knew the voice before he saw the face, and the pistol in Irish O'Dell's hand. O'Dell stepped from behind a corner of the house. Lydia cried out.

O'Dell let a smile flicker and die. "I got to thinkin' what a good idea it would be if I followed *you* for a change, Buckalew." He motioned with the muzzle of the pistol. "Raise your hands way high, to where they won't get you in any trouble."

Lydia brought one hand up to her throat, trembling.

O'Dell looked at the darkened house. "Mighty convenient. Dumbest thing I ever did, takin' you at your word that you'd put her on the train and shipped her away somewhere." He pointed the pistol toward the car. "Get it started, Buckalew. Me and Lydia have got places to go."

Dave's feet would not move. He felt a fool, not having realized that O'Dell might follow him. "If you take her to town, they'll kill her."

"I'm not takin' her to Caprock. I'm clearin' out of here, takin' her to where they won't find us. And you won't either."

"How'd you get here? I don't see your car."

"Left it by the gate and walked in. That's where I'll leave yours, with the ignition wires cut. Now go start it."

Dave remembered he had laid his gunbelt on the car seat before patching the tire. "I'll have to turn on the switch."

Lydia stood beside the car, her face ashen with dread. "Down, quick," Dave whispered to her. He slipped the pistol from its holster and turned.

O'Dell was too quick for him. Dave saw O'Dell's weapon spit flame. The bullet struck him like the blow of a sledge. He slammed back against the car, stunned. He tried to bring his own pistol into line but could not move his fingers. Helplessly he let the pistol slip from his hand. Lydia screamed as Dave slid down the side of the car, the ground rising up to meet him.

O'Dell sounded far away, as if in a well. "Damn fool, I didn't come here to kill him."

Dave sensed Lydia kneeling, touching him, crying his name. Though a blur, he saw O'Dell lift her to her feet. "Climb in the car like I told you," he ordered her. "We're gettin' away from this place."

He felt O'Dell drag him free of the automobile and drop him again to the ground. "Don't carry on so," O'Dell said to Lydia. "They'll probably raise a monument to him. *Killed in the line of duty,* or some such thing. Beats hell out of bein' killed by some drunk in a car wreck."

O'Dell started the engine and switched on the lights. Dave heard the door slam and the automobile pull away. He tried to rise up, but he could not. The wound in his shoulder was fiery as a forge. He could not even bring a hand up to touch it. He felt as if he were falling slowly, slowly into some deep, dark hole.

In his mind, he was calling, "Lydia! Lydia!" But the only sound that came was a groan.

After a time—he had no idea how long—he felt something touch him. He thought it was probably the horse, drawn by curiosity. But he heard Lydia's voice. "Dave! I thought he'd killed you."

She began trying to lift him. "Dave! Dave! You've got to get up. We've got to get away from here."

His head seemed to be spinning. He tried to bring it to a stop, to make sense of what was happening. "Lydia?" He was not sure whether he spoke the name or merely thought it.

She said, "There was a tire pump on the floorboard. When he tried to pull me out to get in his car, I hit him with it. I hit him two or three times. I left him unconscious, but he won't stay that way long."

He wanted to ask her why she hadn't gone ahead and killed O'Dell, but the words would not come. She kept trying to lift him. "Come on, Dave, help me!"

The desperation in her voice brought him strength from somewhere. He found his legs and one arm. The other felt limp and dead except for the fire in his shoulder. With her help he managed to get to his feet, though his knees kept trying to buckle.

She brought his arm around her thin shoulders. "Lean on me. We've got to get away from the house. He's liable to be back here any minute."

He fell once to his knees and brought her down with him. She pulled back to her feet, drawing him up. "Come on, Dave. You can make it. Out into the brush yonder."

Through a haze, he could see car lights moving toward the house. "It's him." Lydia's voice was determined. "We've got to move faster. He thought you were dead. He'll know different when he sees you're not where he left you."

She took him into the mesquite. "Ease down now. Rest for a minute till we see what he does."

He could hear O'Dell calling for Lydia, cajoling, then threatening, then cajoling again.

Dave's vision was blurred, but he could see that O'Dell was driving the car in a circle, trying to pick them up with his headlights. The car stopped, and O'Dell jumped out, shouting. Dave's heart quickened. "Run, Lydia. Don't let him get you."

Lydia's hand tightened on his arm. "I think he caught a glimpse of the horse out by the barn and thought it was us. Come on, let's move while he's on a wild goose chase."

Dave did not know how he managed to keep his feet. The heavy sand pulled at his boots. She was straining to hold him up. "Lydia, leave me. He won't find me here in the dark. Strike out for Underwood's well. They'll help you."

"He left your car by the gate. If we can reach it . . ." She tugged at him. "Come on, Dave. It isn't that far."

They struggled through the sand, running into bushes they could not see in the dark. They came in a while to the barbed-wire fence. Lydia said, "It's not much farther now."

Dave had to stop often. She raised her skirt and tore away a large section of her slip to press against his wound. The bleeding had slowed but not stopped. Moving, a hundred yards seemed a mile. But finally he thought he could see the dark shape of his car. "We're almost there," Lydia said.

She pushed him down into the sand and dropped flat beside him. He could see the car lights leaving the house, moving in their direction. Lydia's fingers tightened desperately on his arm as O'Dell stopped at the gate. Dave saw the man walk in front of his headlights, and he thought O'Dell might be coming out into the sand. But he heard a hammering sound, metal beating against metal. Shortly a door slammed, and O'Dell's car pulled away, its lights shining against the brush that lined the side of the road. It disappeared around a bend, and there was only darkness.

Lydia waited a while before she raised up. "I'm afraid he fixed your car so we can't use it. But I'll go see."

She was gone several minutes. When she returned, he could hear discouragement heavy in her voice. "He smashed the spark plugs and cut the wires. We're stranded."

"He'll come back," Dave said. "He'll bring help to hunt for us in the daylight."

"We can't afford to sit here and wait for him. We'll have to keep goin'."

Dave's legs seemed to be of lead. His head was spinning again, and the wounded shoulder was afire. "I won't make it," he said weakly. "You'll have to go it alone."

"The horse. Maybe I can catch the horse." She left him.

He lost track of time and probably consciousness. He knew only that she returned tired and frustrated. "He wouldn't let me get close," she said, breathing heavily. "Irish spooked him."

Dave thought of the movies he had seen in which the horse came to the rescue of the cowboy. If he managed to survive this ordeal he might never go to a movie again. "Help me get a little farther from the house. Then you head for that well."

She supported him through the gate and two or three hundred yards into the brush on the other side. He reached such a point of exhaustion that she was carrying and dragging him. "Enough," he rasped. "This is as far as I can go."

His throat was parched. He was beginning to fever. He would give a month's pay for a cup of water. "Go on now. Go to Victor Underwood's crew."

She clung to him. "No. I'd get lost and wander around in a circle. There's no moon, no stars. I'm stayin' with you."

He did not know how long he lay there before a light rain began. She tried to cover him with her own body, to keep him dry.

The coolness of the rain seemed to ease his fever. He thought he felt a little stronger. The rain stopped. Lydia shivered from cold, and he held her, trying to give her some of his warmth. He felt her slip away into a fitful sleep. He kept holding her with his good arm.

The distant noise of an engine intruded upon his consciousness, and Lydia awakened with a start. "Irish!" she said, her voice frightened. "There are his car lights."

"He's brought help. Soon as they can see, they'll find our tracks." Anxiety tingled like an electric shock. "I can't outrun them, but you can if you'll start now."

"We've got time before sunup. You can travel some more, Dave. I know you can. Come on, try."

He protested, but she lifted him to his feet. The shoulder had gone almost numb while he lay in the sand, but now the movement brought new pain, new bleeding. He managed to move one foot, then the other. Soon he was walking, though Lydia had to support much of his weight.

He told her, "You can't hold me up all the way to Underwood's well."

"Don't you die on me, Dave Buckalew. I'll get you there alive if it kills both of us." Her stern voice told him he was wasting his time arguing with her. He quit trying, saving his energy for the traveling. The darkness seemed heavy enough to reach out and touch. They stumbled at times into the clutches of unseen mesquite bushes, thorns tearing at their clothing, gouging their skin.

He could feel a cool mist on his face. That helped relieve some of the fever, the burning of his parched throat. He trusted his sense of direction to carry them toward the well, for the cloud-darkened sky left him nothing except instinct to go by. He could hear Lydia breathing heavily, though she would not admit fatigue.

Darkness began to fade under the influence of a sunrise hidden by the heavy clouds and the thin veil of mist. Urgency gave him strength. It was not yet full daylight, but O'Dell should be able to see well enough now to find their tracks. Even city-raised thugs should have no trouble following the trail they had left in the sand.

The mist began to lift, but not enough. In vain he looked for the wooden rig. It was somewhere ahead of them. He could hear a heavy rumbling sound coming from it, but he could not tell how far away it might still be.

Lydia kept looking over her shoulder. After a time, he heard her gasp. "My God, yonder they come!"

He turned. The fever had clouded his vision, but he knew Lydia had not imagined them. Hope deserted him. "Leave me, Lydia. Run!"

She led him around a shoulder-high mesquite. "Lie down," she said. "Stay low. I'll lead them away from you."

"No, Lydia," he cried. "They'll kill you!"

"They did that a long time ago." She caressed his cheek, then leaned down and kissed him, tears in her hazel eyes. "Thank you, Dave. For just a little while, you brought me back to life again." Then she was gone, running, angling away from the path they had followed. He heard a distant pistol shot and saw movement, three vague figures running in the direction Lydia had taken. But he could see nothing of her. She was lost to him in the mist and the heavy growth of mesquite.

Tears came in a burning flood, and with them a black despair.

22

Thunder in the Earth

IRISH O'DELL dreaded facing Boss Daugherty. He had made up his mind that if he found Lydia he would simply desert the big man and Turk Radke. He didn't need them anymore; he could probably thrive as well on his own. He would go to some distant city as he had long wanted to do, taking Lydia with him. She would resist him at first and try to run away from him, but she was bound to come around when she realized that in a strange city, far from anyone or anything she knew, she was dependent upon him.

He had declared many times that he feared no man on earth, but in bleak and secret moments he knew that was a lie. He feared Turk Radke, who was dangerous when he was in an even temper and deadly when he went into one of his frenzies. He feared Boss, for reasons he had never comprehended. Boss never carried a gun. Boss was too old and fat and slow to catch any man determined not to be caught. At best he waddled along in an awkward walk. But there was something in his eyes, or perhaps back of his eyes, that put a shiver down O'Dell's spine when Boss was displeased. Angry, Daugherty radiated a black malevolence that caused men to back away from him instinctively, as they might back away from a mad dog. Irish could no more stand up to Boss's power than he could stand against a moving truck.

Irish had often been tempted to leave. He had stayed because the attraction of the money was stronger than his hidden dread of Radke and Boss. Now he had something he wanted more than money, or did have until she had hit him over the head and run.

Boss would be mad as hell. He would demand to know why Irish had gone alone. The fat man would never understand that Irish had suspected Buckalew might lead him to Lydia, and he did not want the boys to kill her. They would. Certainly Radke and Skinny would, the moment they knew or even suspected she was the sheriff's witness against them. Maybe if he took a couple of the other boys he could handle them. He had always been able to make Frenchy and Grat see things his way. With their help, he could find Lydia and escape.

If Boss had ever loved a woman in his life, Irish had seen no sign of it. He had never known Daugherty to take one into his bed, though he assumed Boss had done so in his younger days. Boss seemed to care strongly only about food and comfort, about money and about the power to run things his own way. He never allowed feelings for people to stand as an obstacle. Boss had liked Buckalew in some odd way Irish had not fathomed, but he would not be pleased at the idea of the sheriff's being wounded and yet surviving. That presented a new and potentially potent threat to Boss's organization. He thought Boss could sign a death warrant for his own mother if someone showed him a profit in it.

Daugherty raised up from his couch when Irish opened the door. The springs made a groaning sound. Growling like an old and overfed bulldog, Boss fastened an accusing stare upon Irish and spat a brown stream into his stained coffee-can spittoon.

"Where you been?" He became aware of the dark bruise across the side of Irish's head and a deep cut that had run blood down into the collar. "Looks like somebody taken a baseball bat to you."

"Somethin' like that. I'm not sure what it was."

"I hope you done better to whoever served you so poorly."

"She knocked me out. When I came to, she was gone."

"She?" The growl coarsened. Anger arose in the fat man's eyes. "You and your women. Couldn't be the one that was bangin' on the door for you this mornin'. I hear tell she's got herself in a real fix, liable to die. Bad business, Irish. I swear, women are a bigger downfall for you boys than whisky is. I wisht you'd get your mind up out of your britches and leave them alone."

It was time to forget about maneuvering and cut right to the bone. "Boss, I need help. I shot Sheriff Buckalew."

Boss's jowls quivered in surprise. "Not in front of a crowd, I hope."

"It was out in the country. There was just one witness."

"Good. You taken care of the witness, didn't you?"

"I'm afraid not. Looks like I didn't even kill Buckalew. I thought I had, but when I went back he was gone. He couldn't have left without help. It was her."

Boss's wide mouth twisted. "Her?"

"Lydia. You remember . . . wife of Jim Benedict, the two-bit grifter Turk put away that time up by Borger."

Boss growled again. "I remember. Another piece of bad business. You been huntin' her like a crazy man ever since."

"I found her. She was workin' at Jolene's. Sheriff's been hidin' her out in the country."

"A woman from Jolene's? Now, why would Buckalew do such as that?" As Irish feared, Boss quickly found his own answer, for he had an intuition that could sometimes be frightening. "She was his witness, wasn't she? She was his witness, and you knew it all along."

"Not all along," Irish said defensively. "I just figured it out today. Seems like she saw somethin' the night Turk and Skinny suckered Ox out of Jolene's place and took care of him."

Boss's face turned the color of raw sausage. "And you let her get away? If you had half the sense God gave a gray mule, you'd've taken some of the boys with you."

"They'd have killed her."

"As sure as you're standin' there. You wouldn't be in the fix you're in now, and you wouldn't be draggin' us into it with you."

Irish imagined he could feel the heat rising from Boss. He moved back half a step. "They can't get far. I busted up his car to where it won't run. I want to be out there waitin' with Frenchy and Grat when daylight comes. Won't take us long to run the two of them down."

"It'd better not. Do the job right this time, and plant them deep enough that they won't never be found."

"I don't want her killed, Boss. It took me too long to find her again."

"The world is full of women. You can buy a dozen of them for a hundred dollars."

"This isn't just *any* woman."

"She's sure not. She can send the boys to the electric chair, and maybe you too. I want you to take Turk and Skinny with you. They'll finish the job if you ain't got the stomach for it."

Irish felt as if he had swallowed rotten meat. "I'd rather take Frenchy and Grat."

"You'll do like I tell you. You'll take Turk and Skinny." Daugherty's eyes seemed almost to disappear between rolls of flesh. That was when the facade of the harmless old country boy fell away and he always appeared most dangerous. "Irish, you've growed a way too big for your britches. This outfit got along good before ever I knowed you, and it can get along good without you. I hear tell somebody found an Indian skeleton out in them sandhills the other day. Probably buried for a hundred years till the wind uncovered it. They could find *you* out there after a hundred years."

Boss turned away from him and shouted, "Turk! Skinny! You-all come in here!" Skinny hurried from the next room with the submissiveness of a mongrel dog called by its master. "What you need, Boss?"

"Is that knife of yours good and sharp?"

"It always is, Boss."

Daugherty gave Irish a murderous stare. "I want you to go

find Turk and fetch him in here. I got a job of work for you-all to help Irish with."

Irish turned away, seething but helpless as Skinny hurried out into the hall. His hand moved toward his shoulder holster and stopped.

Boss snarled, "Turn around, Irish, and look at me."

Irish could not resist the command. Daugherty's eyes had gone cold. "I know what you're thinkin', Irish. But you ain't got the guts to shoot me. Even if you did, have you ever tried to shoot a fat hog?"

Irish shook his head, for voice would not come to him.

Boss growled, "It's the hardest thing in the world to kill one. A bullet won't hardly go through all that lard. About the only way is to hit him right between the eyes. You couldn't look me in the eyes and do it, Irish. At heart you're as yellow as a drunk's liver."

Irish could not meet that withering gaze. Whatever resolve he had mustered left him like water draining from a broken bucket. He looked at the floor and knew that Boss had him, as he always did.

For the last couple of days, Slim McIntyre had watched Autie Whitmore become increasingly agitated. Each time the bailer was run into the hole to clean it, Autie would examine the cuttings, squeezing them between his fingers, bringing them to his nose and sniffing at them. Slim asked no foolish questions aloud but hoped Autie would tell him something. All he got was a silent frown and once a muttered, "Damn it, we ought to be there by now."

But late yesterday afternoon he had thought he caught a fleeting smile, at least as near a smile as Autie ever allowed to escape. The little driller sent Trinidad to bring big Choctaw from the sleeping tent and held up a handful of mud for him to smell. Choctaw betrayed no expression.

"Keep makin' hole," was all he said.

Slim smelled of the mud himself. He didn't know what he was supposed to be looking for. It smelled like just about all the other mud he had seen in his life, except perhaps danker. It had been down there a long time. This whole operation smelled like mud, not oil.

346

Autie stepped down from the platform and walked over to talk to Victor Underwood. Choctaw and Trinidad had carried Underwood out in his chair and set him in the shade of the wooden rig to watch the drilling. Twice since they had brought him home from the doctor's, he had tried to get up and walk on the cast. He had fallen both times. Slim had feared he would rebreak the leg, but the cast must have been solid, for the only casualty was Underwood's pride. He seemed finally reconciled that he could be only a spectator to the work on his own well.

Autie Whitmore had been a surprise to Slim as the days had passed. When he had waked up that first morning on the rig he had shouted and cursed about being shanghaied, drugged, tied and kidnapped, forced into slavery. He had started trudging off through the sands, following the dim ruts that wound their way across the pastures toward distant Caprock. Slim had wanted to run after him, to bring him back, but Choctaw had caught Slim's arm. "Let him go," he had said.

"We went to a lot of trouble to get him out here," Slim protested.

"Let him walk awhile in the hot mornin' sun. Give him an hour with the head he's got on him and he'll sell his soul to the devil for a drink of water. I've been there."

So Slim and Choctaw and Trinidad had gone about cleaning the rig floor, muddied so badly by the blowout. After a couple of hours, Choctaw had looked up at the sun, already hot at ten o'clock. "I'll start the truck while you fetch a jug of water, cowboy. It's about time to go reel in the fish."

Trinidad had smiled knowingly, his white teeth shining. He had stayed at the rig while Slim and Choctaw went bumping down the rough road. Slim could see Autie's tracks in the sandy ruts. The farther he went, the more the tracks betrayed a weaving pattern.

"Slow down," Choctaw said. "We don't want to run over the ill-tempered little son of a bitch."

Autie Whitmore sat on the road's high center, in a place where wind had scoured sand out of the ruts on either side. He was slumped in misery, his face nearly purple, his shirt soaked with sweat. He said nothing as Choctaw got out of the truck and handed him the jug of water. He took a sip and scowled.

"What I need is hair of the dog."

"That dog is dead," Choctaw said. "There won't be another one till we finish the job."

Whitmore drank half the contents of the jug. Choctaw said, "The truck goes back to the well. You want to ride, or you want to keep walkin' towards town?"

Autie stared resentfully at the Indian. "I got any choice?"

"Sure you got a choice. Ride to work or walk to Caprock. Work's a damn sight closer."

Autie gave Slim a share of his resentment. "I don't know what my daughter sees in you. When I tell her what you-all done to me . . ."

He climbed into the truck, holding the jug as if it were a pet pup. He spoke no more until they returned to the rig. He stood at the edge of the platform and morosely studied the stage of the cleanup. "Hell of a mess you got here, is all I can say. How you expect a man to work?"

"With everything he's got," Choctaw declared.

Autie had done that, Slim would have to admit. As he gradually sweated the whisky out of his system, the little man had thrown himself into the job with a will Slim had not expected. He had thought they might have to do everything short of using a whip. He could not say Autie had worked cheerfully, for the driller seldom compromised his dour expression. But he worked steadily and with a growing confidence as one day led to another and the hole deepened under the relentless pounding of the bit. For Autie it was a chance at redemption.

It was much more for the Underwoods. As Victor Underwood's leg began to heal and he showed more strength, he insisted upon being carried out each day from the flimsy little frame house he shared with his wife. Elise Underwood was like two women. One was a quiet and tender nurse who attended quickly to every need she saw or imagined in her husband. The other was a firm boss who watched every operation on the rig floor and did not hesitate to take charge if she perceived any shortcoming. She no longer wore a dress; she wore muddy dungarees two sizes too large, and heavy work boots made for a man. She was quick to grab hold of the bailer, to run the bullwheel or even to take the drilling line when Autie or Choctaw from time to time needed to walk off into the mesquite. Slim wondered how a woman so small could generate so much energy and harbor such steel determination.

Now the sun had slipped almost to the horizon as Autie talked to Underwood, letting Underwood smell the mud on his hands. Slim was frustrated that nobody explained anything to him. He looked at Trinidad. The Mexican only shrugged, for he had even less experience at this line of work than Slim. Slim turned to Choctaw. "What is it?"

"Maybe nothin'," Choctaw said. His expression indicated that was his final word. He went to the forge, ramming a new point on the bit that had just come up from the hole.

Normally they switched drillers after supper, but tonight Autie went back and lighted the yellow-dog lamp. With Choctaw standing by, he kept drilling until the bailer brought up the smell of something different. "Gas," he said. He moved quickly to put out the lamp and motioned for Slim to carry it off some distance from the platform. "We'd best shut her down till daylight."

Even then, nobody told Slim nothing. He could only read the tense look on Underwood's face, the hopeful expression in Elise's.

Something was about to happen. Or nothing, depending upon their luck.

He was awakened before daylight by the noise Autie made, grumbling to himself as he put on his clothes, crusted with dried mud. "Ain't nobody got any interest in finishin' this job? Sleepin' till the mornin's half-done. I never seen such a triflin' crew."

Usually it took both Choctaw and Slim to get Autie to quit his canvas cot when it was time for a change of tour. The sun as yet was nowhere in sight.

Choctaw rolled over on the sleeping tent's only steel cot. He considered canvas too flimsy for his size and weight. "If that oil's there atall, it's been there for a million years. Another hour or so won't make much difference."

"Every hour we waste is another hour I got to wait to have a drink."

Choctaw grunted. "Better for you if we was out till winter."

"Just because Indians can't handle their liquor . . ."

"And you can?" Choctaw retorted. "Come on, cowboy," he

said to Slim, "this old turkey buzzard ain't goin' to let us rest noway."

Because it was earlier than usual, Elise and Gabriela had not yet arisen to start breakfast in the cook tent. To escape from Autie's grumbling, Slim built the fire under the boiler. They had put it out last night after the first hint of gas. To light it now carried some risk, but without steam nothing would move. Autie and Choctaw tinkered around on the rig floor. A brief rain had peppered down on the tent sometime during the wee hours. Now Slim found the wood damp. He liked the smell of it even though it complicated his job. He studied the early-morning sky, an old cowboy habit. Though he could barely feel it on his face, mist still clung in the air. He could not see more than a quarter mile. Perhaps it was going to rain again.

Slim and Trinidad carried Victor Underwood and his chair to the cook tent for breakfast. Everyone was in a talkative mood, though the conversation skirted around the one subject Slim was most interested in. No one spoke of the well and its proximity to the pay zone. He wondered if it might be some sort of superstition among oil people, like the one among ranch folks that if you predicted rain too openly you were likely to chase it away.

Autie quit talking when they started the wheels to turning, the walking beam to rocking up and down. He held to the drilling cable as if it were a lifeline, his face tense and expectant. He seemed to be listening for something, feeling for something. The line rose and fell, rose and fell. An hour, then more.

Slim watched Autie's face change from hope to doubt to despair, then to hope and despair again. Autie turned once to Victor Underwood and declared a sense of surrender. "Any time you want to shut it down, just say the word. There ain't a damned thing down there."

Underwood looked glum, but he said, "Keep punching, Autie."

Henry Stringfellow drove up earlier than usual, as if he had sensed something. The old ranchman talked to Victor Underwood a moment and put out his pipe. He moved his roadster back some distance from the well. Elise Underwood came out of the cook tent and stood beside her husband's chair. She clutched his hand, then moved up onto the platform with the men.

Slim saw it in Autie's eyes first, a sudden widening, a moment of doubt followed by conviction. Then he heard it, a slow rumbling deep in the hole, rapidly becoming a rolling thunder. He saw the drilling line go slack, as it had before the blowout.

Autie declared, "She's a-comin' up. I don't know if it's salt water or oil, but she's bringin' the tools up with her. Clear the floor!"

In his mind's eye Slim could see the heavy drill bit flying out of the hole and landing on top of his head. He stepped hastily down from the platform. He said, "Trinidad, let's carry Mr. Underwood back a ways."

Underwood protested, "I'm fine right here," but Slim thought caution was the better part of valor. Elise followed behind Slim and Trinidad and her husband, her face flushed with anticipation.

Slim had watched from a distance as other people's wells had come in, but this one was in his lap. He was not prepared for the noise that assailed his ears almost to the point of pain. He held his breath, expecting at any second to see oil gush from the rim of the casing and explode up past the crown block.

It seemed to take forever. He began to think it was like thunder that promises rain but brings only wind, and he looked down, steeling himself for disappointment.

The sound changed, somehow, and so did the smell. He heard an exultant shout and looked up. He saw oil . . . black, beautifully, wonderfully black . . . rising to the crown block and beyond against a cloudy morning sky. Elise Underwood squealed with delight and threw herself across her husband. His arms went around her, and he almost rose up from the chair in his excitement.

Autie Whitmore danced up and down in the heavy black spray, flapping his arms like a rooster. He turned his face upward to let the oil splatter him from ear to ear. "I knowed it! I knowed it all the time!"

The sulphurous odor was heavy, almost stifling. After the first heady moments of joy, Slim began to worry about the waste. He turned to Choctaw. "Hadn't we ought to be doin' somethin'?"

Slim had never realized how wide the big Indian's mouth was

until he saw him grinning as he had not see him grin before. "We'll give it time to clean the hole out." He slapped Slim across the shoulder so hard that Slim almost went down. "I never saw a cowboy with more than fifty dollars in his pocket. How does it feel?"

Slim's clothes were half-soaked. "Oily. Stuff smells pretty bad, don't it?"

"It never smells when you own a piece of it. But better not spend your money just yet. It's seldom as good as you think it's goin' to be."

Trinidad Suarez stood with his wife and little girl on the other side of the well, beyond most of the spray. They seemed bewildered, perhaps even awed, trying to figure out what this would mean to them.

Choctaw said, "You can't judge a well by the way she blows in. When she settles down she could make a thousand barrels a day, or she could sputter out like a burnt match. At least Mr. Underwood was right about the formation. Now he'll be able to get money to drill another. One well ain't the world, but it's a start."

Slim could not keep his eyes from Elise and Victor Underwood. Blackened from head to toe, they hugged and laughed and kissed like two excited schoolkids.

Uncle Henry Stringfellow walked up to Slim and Choctaw, his dead pipe in his hand. "Looks like I'm finally goin' to be a smart rancher."

Choctaw beckoned by crooking his finger. Slim followed him, wading through a loblolly of oil. Together they turned the control head while the flow diminished, dropping down below the crown block and finally shutting off altogether. Slim's exuberance subsided along with the oil. He wiped his hands futilely upon his drenched trousers. "How'll we ever wash all this stuff off of us?"

Choctaw said, "You never will. It soaks to the bone. You've got the mark on you now, cowboy, like a tattoo. I'll bet you never punch another cow the rest of your life."

Elise Underwood stood behind her husband's chair, her arms around his neck, her cheek pressed against his. "You were right all along, Victor. You did it!"

"*You* did it," he corrected her. "You and these good friends."

352

He raised his oil-blackened hand. Choctaw took it, then Slim, then Trinidad. "It's part yours. You own a share in it, all of you."

"You'll need it all to drill more wells," Choctaw said. "I've kind of enjoyed the gamble. Put my share into the next one, if you don't mind havin' a damned Indian for a partner."

Underwood smiled. "I don't see any damned Indian. I just see an Indian, and a good friend."

Slim said, "I'll gamble along. With this one behind us, the odds ought to be better the next time."

Trinidad and his wife talked quietly in Spanish. He said, "Gabriela likes this oilwell. She would like another one."

Elise kissed the oil-blackened faces of Choctaw and Slim then put her arms around Trinidad and Gabriela, hugging them together. "Thank you. Thank all of you."

Uncle Henry Stringfellow had stepped up onto the blackened platform, looking at the capped well, grinning as if he had just received a five-inch rain. He stiffened, then pointed with the stem of his pipe. "You-all looky yonder. I think that's a woman out there."

Slim saw a movement in the mist, shapeless at first, then materializing. "It *is*. Looks to me like she's runnin' towards us."

Uncle Henry claimed exceptional eyesight, trained by counting sheep's legs as they ran by him and then dividing by four. "There's somebody after her."

Slim saw one man, then two, afoot. He heard a shot.

The woman was at least two, perhaps three hundred yards away. The men were gaining. Slim realized they would catch her before she could reach the well, or shoot and kill her if that was their purpose. Without thinking, he set out running toward her, shouting to get their attention.

Behind him he heard Choctaw's voice. "You ain't even got a gun!"

He missed a step, then kept going. He realized he could do nothing if they were determined, but perhaps they would back away when they saw there was a witness. Choctaw was far behind him, yelling, "Slow down! Wait for us!" But Slim feared for the woman. If he hesitated, they might kill her, then retreat before he was close enough to see their faces. The sand tugged at his boots and made every long step a challenge.

He saw a third man trailing fifty yards behind the others,

353

struggling to catch up in the deep sand. The man in closest pursuit of the woman was small and thin. His feet did not sink so deeply. Slim recognized him as one of the thugs who had come into the Teagarden every day to eat while he was washing dishes there.

The second man was taller and stronger-looking. Slim thought he remembered them calling him Irish. He heard the man shout, "No, Skinny! Let her go!"

But Skinny seemed grimly determined. The woman stumbled on an exposed mesquite root and sprawled in the sand. As she attempted to push to her feet, Skinny caught up with her. He grabbed a handful of her hair and jerked her head back. Slim saw the flash of a knife in the man's hand. He wanted to yell, but his throat was choked in horror.

The other man shouted, "Skinny, don't!"

Skinny raised the knife. The woman screamed. The one called Irish threw an arm about Skinny and spun him around. Skinny plunged the knife into Irish's stomach. A pistol cracked. Skinny doubled over. The pistol fired again, and Skinny fell backward, quivering in the sand. The woman crawled quickly away from him on hands and knees.

The third man, still some distance behind, fired a pistol. Slim knew how vulnerable he had let himself be, but he had come too far to stop. He picked up Irish's pistol, which had fallen to the ground. He was half afraid it might be so packed with sand that it would explode, but he brought it up and sighted along the barrel. He did not have to fire. The man turned and went running, dodging among the mesquites. Slim freed a pent-up breath and lowered the pistol.

The woman sobbed softly. Her dress hung in strips where mesquite branches had caught her. What was left of it and a pink slip beneath were crusted with wet sand. Her hair was wet and stringy, full of sand and twigs and thin mesquite leaves. She looked as if she had been roped and dragged.

He dropped to one knee beside her. "You're safe now, ma'am. They hurt you?"

"They would've," she said tightly. She breathed hard from the running and the fright. Her gaze went to Irish, who sat with one leg buckled under him. One hand held the red-stained knife. The other pressed against his stomach, blood seeping between

354

his fingers. Slim had seen the same look in Mr. Birdsong's face in the last moments of the old shooter's life. He shuddered, remembering.

Incredibly, the man was trying to laugh. It was a husky, rattling sound. "Big joke on Skinny. Big joke on Boss, too. He meant Turk and Skinny to kill you and me both, Lydia. I wish I could see his fat face when he finds out." He coughed up blood. "You tell them, Lydia." He looked at Slim. "You too, friend. Tell them I said it was Turk Radke and Skinny that killed Ox."

The woman moved closer to the dying man. Some of the terror lingered in her eyes. "Irish, why did you stop Skinny?"

Irish's voice was labored and thin. "Because I love you, Lydia. Forgive me?"

She was a moment in answering. Her voice was bitter. "I'll thank you for stoppin' Skinny. But forgive you, after what you did to me and to Dave? You'll walk into hell without that comfort."

Irish looked disappointed. The light faded from his eyes. He slumped over into the sand. Something about those dead, staring eyes made Slim's stomach queasy. He reached down and closed the lids. Reluctantly he walked over to Skinny's twisted body and felt for a pulse but knew by the gray look of the man that he would not find one.

Choctaw and Trinidad had come up in time to hear Irish O'Dell's final words. Choctaw held a rifle that Uncle Henry always carried in his car. He fired at the fleeting man but missed by a considerable margin. Slim flinched at the shot.

Choctaw said defensively, "I didn't have a bow and arrow."

Slim knelt by the woman again and pointed to the well. "Think you can make it, ma'am? If you can't, we'll carry you."

"I'm all right." Worriedly she declared, "You've got to go help the sheriff."

"Mr. Buckalew?"

She pointed. "He's back yonder in the brush. Wounded bad."

A dozen questions ran through Slim's mind, but they had to take a back seat. Choctaw said, "Me and Trinidad'll go. You help this lady get to the well."

The woman said, "That was Turk Radke who ran away. Be careful of him. He and Skinny were after me because I was the sheriff's only witness. Now you're witnesses too."

Choctaw said grimly, "I never had no use for Ox, but that was a hard way for any man to die, beaten half to death and drowned in a slushpit. Come on, Trinidad, let's go find the sheriff."

Slim remained shaken. Mr. Birdsong's was the only violent death he had witnessed before, and that one had been accidental. Nothing in his experience had prepared him for this spectacle of two men killing one another. He wanted to look away, but some morbid fascination kept drawing his gaze back to them. "I'd better get you out of here, ma'am. You sure you've still got it in you to walk?"

She looked anxiously in the direction Choctaw and Trinidad had taken. "I'm all right. I just hope Dave . . . Sheriff Buckalew is."

Slim still had O'Dell's pistol in his hand. He found the safety and set it, then put the weapon in his pocket. He helped Lydia to her feet. "Lean on me if you need to."

She took his arm but carried her own weight. He said, "With this oil all over us, we must've looked kind of scary."

She shook her head. "Not compared to Irish and Radke and Skinny. I was never any gladder to see somebody."

"You live in Caprock? I don't remember I ever saw you."

She was a little slow to answer. He figured she was still short of breath. "I never got out much."

"I don't understand how you came to be so far out here."

"They wanted to kill me for what I'd seen. The sheriff hid me on his ranch."

"He could've brought you to us. We'd've watched out for you."

"He didn't want to put anybody else in danger. I don't think he told a soul, not even his deputy."

From the little Slim had seen of Waddy Fuller, he could understand that.

Autie Whitmore and Uncle Henry walked out fifty yards to meet Slim and Lydia. Elise was not far behind them. She grasped both of Lydia's hands. "You poor thing. Let's get you to the house and get some of that sand washed off of you." Her own face was black with oil, her hair soaked.

The old sheepman's eyes were filled with concern. "I couldn't rightly see just what was happenin' out yonder, but I heard shootin'. Where's Choctaw and Trinidad?"

356

Slim told him what little Lydia had said about the sheriff. Stringfellow satisfied himself that the woman was not hurt. "It's a long ways if they've got to carry him. I'll run my car up Dave's road and honk the horn. They can bring him to me."

Autie said, "Sheriff's always been decent to me. I'll go with you."

Lydia said anxiously, "Radke is still loose out there somewhere. He'll kill anybody who gets in his way."

Slim took Irish's pistol from his pocket and offered it to the rancher. "Just in case."

Uncle Henry was hesitant. "You may need it yourself."

Elise said, "Victor has a rifle in the house."

Stringfellow accepted the pistol. He and Autie trotted ahead to his car. Victor Underwood still sat in his chair next to the frame shack, where Slim and Trinidad had placed him when the well had started to come in. Trinidad's wife and little girl stood beside him. Underwood watched as Elise and Gabriela hustled Lydia into the house. The little girl followed, bubbling with curiosity.

Her curiosity was no greater than Underwood's. Slim told the driller what he knew. It was not enough to answer all of Underwood's questions, but it did not answer Slim's either. Underwood frowned in thought. "Anything strike you odd about that woman?"

"Everything about this strikes me odd."

"That fellow Ox was a bouncer at Jolene's. I know, because Choctaw had a terrible run-in with him once. How did that woman witness what happened to Ox unless she was there, at Jolene's?"

Slim's eyebrows went up. "You mean she's . . . naw, she couldn't be." But he had to think about it a little. "She didn't seem like that type. I mean, the way she was worried about the sheriff, like he meant more than just protection."

Underwood made a thin smile. "You're a young man, Slim. There's a lot in this world you haven't seen yet."

He heard a car being cranked on the other side of the house. Underwood's jaw dropped in surprise. "That's mine," the driller declared. "Who . . ."

"Radke!" Slim declared. He grabbed a short length of steel pipe that lay near the platform and sprinted around the corner.

He saw Radke rushing to get into Underwood's car. Brandishing the pipe, Slim made a run at him. Radke drew a pistol from his pocket. Slim gave him no time to bring it into line. He swung the pipe and brought it across the man's hand in much the same way he had struck Frenchy that time in the Dutchman's café. Radke shouted in pain and anger and dropped the pistol. But he grabbed the end of the pipe and gave it a sharp twist that wrenched it from Slim's hands. He raised it over his shoulder and swung it as if it were an ax. Slim scrambled to get out of his way.

Roaring in rage, Radke rushed after him. Slim felt his heart jump, for the tall man could brain him with one blow. Slim circled, hoping to pick up the pistol Radke had dropped. Radke seemed to outguess him. He reached down for the weapon and brought it up. For a second Slim stared into the tiny muzzle. It looked as big as a courthouse cannon. Radke jerked the trigger, and Slim braced himself for the impact. Nothing happened. Whether from sand or whatever reason, the pistol had jammed.

Radke rushed again, raising the pipe. Slim ran around the corner of the house, looking desperately for something he might use to defend himself. A short piece of two-by-four lumber lay in a pool of oil beside the blackened platform. Slick, it almost slipped from his fingers as he grasped it. He managed to bring it up and deflect a savage swing of the pipe. The impact knocked the timber from his hands.

As Radke brought the pipe up for another blow, Slim saw no alternative but to move in close, to try to block the move. He drove his fist into the man's hard stomach with all the strength he had. It was like punching a tire that was fully inflated. It yielded but little. Radke's strong arms closed around him. Slim gasped for air. He felt as if his ribs were being crushed. Radke heaved him away, and Slim felt himself sliding on his back along the oily ground, into the edge of the slushpit.

Radke picked up the length of steel pipe and raised it again. Slim brought up his arm but knew it would not keep the man from smashing his skull.

He heard a woman's voice cry out. "Radke!"

The thug hesitated, holding the pipe ready to swing. Lydia stood on the front step of the house, a rifle braced against her shoulder. Flame leaped from its barrel. Radke went stiff, dropping the pipe. The rifle fired again. Radke took a long step, tripped over Slim and sprawled facedown in the slushpit's pool of muddy water and oil. He shuddered and went still.

Lydia walked past Underwood, carrying the smoking rifle. Slim was so shaken he did not attempt at first to get up. He looked at Lydia, then at Radke. He tried to swallow, but his mouth and throat were so dry the effort brought pain.

Lydia stood beside him, staring at the man in the pit. Tears trickled down her cheeks.

Slim managed to say, "Thanks. He almost had me."

She did not reply. She stood there, sobbing quietly. Slim got to his feet and put his hands on her shoulders. "Don't cry. I know it must be a hard thing to kill a man, but you had to do it."

Her hazel eyes looked at him through tears. "Hard? I owed him that. It was the easiest thing I ever did."

23

Arm of the Law

IT BOTHERED SLIM to see the lifeless Radke lying half covered by a slick mix of oil and mud. But he was a while in working up the nerve to drag the body out onto dry ground and cover it with a piece of oil-blackened tarp that had been tied on the west side of the derrick to keep the afternoon sun from blinding the driller. Hiding the corpse did not help much; Slim could not forget for a minute that it was there. He took comfort in the fact that it was Radke's and not his own.

He washed as much of the oil as he could from his face and hands and changed into a reasonably clean set of clothes without the benefit of a thorough bath. Everything around the rig was black and gummy. The sulphur odor was heavy and commanding.

Hearing Uncle Henry's car, he left the tent. He saw Lydia rush out of the little frame house ahead of the other two women and run to meet the automobile. Uncle Henry had barely brought it to a stop before she opened the back door and cried, "Dave?" The sheriff made a futile effort to climb out. She put her arms around him, burying her face against his neck. Slim watched, a little surprised despite what Underwood had told him.

Choctaw and Trinidad and Autie walked to the edge of the slushpit. Choctaw lifted a corner of the tarp, looked a moment and let it drop back into place. "We heard a couple of shots. We didn't know what to expect when we got here. Looks like you taken care of things all right, cowboy."

"Wasn't me," Slim said, pointing toward Lydia. "It was her."

Choctaw and Trinidad looked at each other. "From what the sheriff told us, I reckon she had a right," Choctaw said.

Autie added, "I seen him over in Caprock. He was the number-one bully of the whole outfit. High time somebody done him in."

Uncle Henry honked the horn and leaned out of the car. "This man needs to be got to a doctor. Somebody want to go with me and open gates?"

Slim trotted to the car. He needed to get away from this place for a while. He didn't intend to come back until somebody hauled the bodies away.

Elise Underwood looked in at Lydia and the sheriff, her eyes soft. "Some of us'll follow along. Don't bother to shut the gates."

As Uncle Henry turned the car around, Slim twisted to look at the sheriff. He was pale and drawn, hunched in exhaustion and pain. Lydia clung to him. Watching her, Slim could not imagine her in a place like Jolene's.

Uncle Henry said admiringly, "That young woman led them away from Dave. Saved his life and like to've lost her own."

Slim had no difficulty accepting that. "She saved mine too." He told Uncle Henry about Radke.

The rancher said, "I seen a red coupe parked up there close to the pasture gate. He must've figured it was too far to go back for it." He glanced at the sheriff in the rearview mirror. "Well, Dave,

361

there's three of Daugherty's bunch you won't have to worry about anymore."

Buckalew's voice was almost too weak to hear, and it carried a tone of defeat. "You don't kill a snake by cuttin' its tail off. I reckon you folks'll have to call the Rangers in. I'd just as well give up my badge."

The rancher frowned. "The community wouldn't want you to do that."

"The community? Most of them figure to make their dollar and get out . . . that's all it means to them."

Uncle Henry had traveled far enough from the well to feel safe in lighting his pipe. He puffed thoughtfully. "Maybe."

On the final stretch as they neared Caprock, passing through the developing oilfield, Uncle Henry leaned forward, studying a rotary rig that had spudded in on a new drilling pad next to the road. "I'm goin' to stop here just a minute. Yonder's a man who ought to be told about all this."

The rancher honked the horn. A man with rolled-up sleeves and a tie at half-mast turned in response. Slim recognized the driller Knox Anderson. Stringfellow said, "You-all sit tight. This won't take long."

Anderson waved jovially and stepped in front of the car when Uncle Henry brought it to a stop. Stringfellow got out. Anderson grinned at the oil on the rancher's clothes. It meant the Underwoods had finally made a well. It would have been easy for Anderson to be resentful, to wish that Victor Underwood would fail. Slim had known people who could not tolerate others' success.

Stringfellow said a few words, and Anderson's face fell. Anxiously he peered in at Buckalew. "My God, I never thought they'd go that far. There's a phone at the Gulf company office. I'll let Doc Tolliver know you're coming, then I'll follow after you."

As Anderson stepped aside, Uncle Henry hit the accelerator. Looking back through a trail of dust, Slim saw Anderson trot to the edge of the platform to confer with some of his men, then sprint toward his own automobile. Uncle Henry said, "Dave, I know you've got your reservations about oil men, but they're good people mostly. Victor Underwood, Knox Anderson . . .

in *my* cowboyin' days we'd've said they were men to ride the river with."

Slim heard no reply. The way the sheriff lay heavy against Lydia's shoulder, he suspected Buckalew had lost consciousness. He felt a renewed anxiety, and he prayed softly, as he had prayed for Mr. Birdsong.

Uncle Henry pushed hard on the horn, honking pedestrians and town traffic out of the way. As he pulled in at the doctor's office, Tolliver and Hap Holloway hurried out to meet the car. Bootlegger Preacher Perry stood on the low porch. Hap opened the car's back door, and the doctor leaned in. Brow furrowed, he felt the sheriff's wrist. Slim hurried around the car to help. The doctor backed away. "I can't feel much pulse. You-all carry him up into the operating room. Hurry!"

There was no time for friendly greetings between Slim and Hap. Each took one of the sheriff's arms around his neck. Buckalew was a dead weight. The doctor hurried up the steps while Perry held the door open. Uncle Henry offered Lydia his arm. Slim wondered if the rancher realized what she was, and if it would make any difference to him. His guess was that it wouldn't. Stringfellow seemed to meet life head-on, taking it for what it was and accepting with good grace what it was not.

They stretched Buckalew upon a long, narrow table that had a pad on it about as thin as the mattresses in his jail, though this one at least was covered by a white sheet. The doctor ripped the shirt open. He removed a wadded piece of a woman's slip, stiff with dried blood. He glanced at Lydia. "Good thing you stopped the bleeding, or he would have been dead long before now."

Lydia was white-faced. "Will he live?"

The doctor shook his head. "I don't know."

Tolliver's nurse pushed up a small table with alcohol bottle, pan, bandages and surgical instruments. The doctor looked at the other four people. "You've done your job. Now it's time for mine. If you wouldn't mind waiting outside . . ."

Uncle Henry took Lydia's arm and led the way. In the outer room, Slim shook Hap's hand. He noticed that a dark bruise half circled one of Hap's eyes. "What got ahold of you?" He touched a swollen spot on his friend's cheekbone.

Hap flinched. "Don't ever play cards with somebody who is bigger than you are and cheats."

"How'd you happen to show up just when we needed you?"

"Preacher brought me over here to see if Doc had heard anything about Lauralou."

"Lauralou?" Slim blinked. "Somethin' happen to her?"

Hap explained about the botched abortion. "They think she'll pull through, but she's all messed up inside. Never will have any babies." He rubbed his arm. "Still kind of sore where they stuck that big needle. They pumped a tubful of my blood into her."

Slim remembered his brief infatuation with Lauralou and tried not to dwell on the disillusionment that had ended it. "Seems like she went through a lot more punishment than she had comin' to her. I guess her daddy is with her?"

Hap said, "He's been sittin' in the Kit Kat with a bottle welded to his mouth. Lauralou's over in Odessa all by herself. I'll borrow Preacher's car tonight and go see about her."

This surprised Slim. "I didn't know you were interested in Lauralou."

"I guess I always was, from a distance. Now we're blood kin, if you want to look at it that way."

Slim thought he should warn Hap that she was likely to hurt him. When she recovered and whatever momentary gratitude she might feel had spent itself, she would probably revert to her true nature. But he doubted Hap would be receptive to that kind of admonition; *he* had not been. Some lessons were not transferable; each man had to learn for himself.

He studied Lydia, who sat apart from the men, her head down, her hands clasped as if in silent prayer. He sensed a sincerity in her that he doubted Lauralou would ever understand. His mind drifted to Tracy Whitmore. She would be pleased about the well, and the fact that it had been her father who brought it in. Perhaps now Autie could live for the future instead of slowly killing himself over the past.

Trinidad held the screen door open for Elise Underwood and Choctaw. Elise immediately seated herself beside Lydia and squeezed the woman's hand. "Any word?"

Lydia shook her head but did not speak, nor did she look at Elise, who said, "He's a good strong man. He'll be all right, you'll see."

In a few minutes, Knox Anderson entered the room. He asked no questions, for he saw the answer in the faces. He smiled awkwardly as he recognized Elise. "Uncle Henry told me your well came in. I'm glad for you and Victor. To be honest, I wasn't sure you could do it."

She tried to respond to his good will, but the mood in the room was too tense. "I told you we would. Someday, Knox, you'll learn to trust my judgment."

"I never questioned it but once. You and Victor proved me wrong that time. Where is Victor, anyway?"

Elise said he had remained at the well with Autie and Trinidad's family. His cast would make it difficult for him to ride in a car, and anyway, someone needed to stay until some kind of law showed up to see about the dead.

Preacher Perry might be a bootlegger now, but he had never put all of his past behind him. "I'm ashamed when I think of the times Buckalew asked me for help and I was afraid to give it to him. This might not've happened if I had." His voice firmed. "I would suggest that we all join hands in a circle and do some strong talking to the Almighty." They stood up and stretched their arms, clasping hands. Perry bowed his head. "Dear Lord, there's a man in yonder in bad need of Thy blessing. He's a good man we can't afford to be losing. I believe Thou art too merciful a God to be wanting to turn us over to the Philistines even though we are a wicked people who have too often slighted Thee for spiritous liquors and the sins of the flesh. This is a man who has tried to serve Thy people and gotten damned little help from us in return, so we ask that *Thou* would help him, Amen."

Uncle Henry Stringfellow chewed on the stem of a cold pipe, his face agitated. "You were right, Preacher, about us not helpin' him much. In a way, this town put him where he is."

Slim argued, "It wasn't the town that shot him. It was Irish O'Dell."

The rancher said, "But it's a town that's tolerated O'Dell and Radke and Big Boy Daugherty and the rest. It's a town full of people too busy to stop and stomp a snake as long as the snake's just bitin' somebody else. I wish Dave could wake up and find out the town was waked up too."

Choctaw put in, "There's three snakes layin' out yonder that won't ever bite anybody again."

Stringfellow said curtly, "But except for Lydia, the town didn't have anything to do with it. Big Boy Daugherty is still sittin' over yonder in the hotel, milkin' this community any way he wants to, and nobody but Dave Buckalew has lifted a hand."

Knox Anderson agreed. "Daugherty pulls the puppets' strings. But if you take the puppets away from him one by one, pretty soon he wouldn't have enough for a show." He turned to Uncle Henry. "I'm as guilty as anybody. I've been too busy with my own worries to pay attention to Daugherty. I don't even have any idea how many men he has working for him."

Hap Holloway said, "I can tell you pretty close. One time and another, most of them have given me and Preacher some grief." He counted on his fingers, his lips moving silently. "Take away the three that's gone, you've still got ten, maybe twelve that go out here and do his dirty work . . . collect his percentage, run his gamblin' operation and such. That's not countin' a few small-time pickpockets and highjack artists that pay him protection to let them operate."

Choctaw declared, "We could get us a bunch together and go rush that hotel like the cavalry used to charge my ancestors."

Anderson said, "And probably get some good men killed. I remember how it was in France when we went over the top and charged the German lines. It would be better to outflank Daugherty than to run at him straight-on."

Hap offered, "This time of the day, they're generally scattered out doin' whatever Big Boy's payin' them for. We might pick them off one or two at a time, like pullin' the legs off of a spider till he can't walk anymore." he elbowed Slim. "What do you say, cowboy? You game?"

Slim felt misgivings. A lifetime of ranch work had trained him for hunting cattle, not for hunting men. But he could not back away from the challenge without looking as Douglas Clive must have looked, caving in to Irish O'Dell. He swallowed his anxieties. "I'll do what I can."

Anderson nodded in satisfaction. "I've got some rough and ready roustabouts down at my pipeyard who would probably be tickled to get in on this." He paused. "One other thing: nobody but us knows the sheriff is hurt, and that three of Daugherty's men are dead. Daugherty's probably sitting in that hotel room right now, wondering. It'll be better to keep him wondering as long as we can."

Hap took out his pocketwatch. "It's gettin' on to dinnertime.

Wouldn't surprise me if we was to find one or two of them down at the Teagarden, feedin' their faces on the Dutchman's grub." He looked at Slim. "You're probably itchin' to say howdy to Tracy anyway."

"I'd figured on goin' as soon as I could. I *didn't* figure on fightin' my way in."

Hap rubbed his hands in anticipation. "Oughtn't to be no fightin' to it, hardly, if we work it slick enough. I got a notion Tracy can help us."

Slim protested, "No sir. I don't want her gettin' hurt."

"She won't. She'll set the trap. We'll spring it." Hap had to turn his face up to look at big Choctaw. "You look like just the man we need." Then glanced at Trinidad. "How about you, Pancho?"

"The name is Trinidad. Yes, I will go. The *cherife* has been a good friend of mine."

Knox Anderson said, "Just don't get yourselves killed. I'll be along as soon as I can with some help."

Hap declared, "If it goes smooth enough, the only help we'll need is a truck to haul them away in. And maybe you ought to fetch along that deputy, Waddy, so everything'll stay about half-legal."

Hap set out down the street afoot. Slim took long strides to catch up to him, wondering what Hap had on his mind. He said worriedly, "We don't even have any guns."

"Man carries a gun, he gets to wantin' to use it. It's generally the wrong people that get shot."

The four of them entered the Teagarden . . . Slim, Hap, Choctaw and Trinidad. The place was building toward its noonday rush. Slim let Hap look around for Daugherty's men. His eyes were on Tracy, coming out of the kitchen with a tray of food. She set it on a table where four laborers were seated. Just as she started to put the plate lunches in front of them she saw Slim. She spilled half a cup of coffee, on the floor, fortunately, and not on one of the customers. Apologetically she finished serving the men, then made her way among the tables to Slim. She was too self-conscious to hug him in front of so many people, but she gripped his hands.

"I'm tickled to see you, Slim, but I wish you weren't in town. If Frenchy should find out . . ."

"I'm hopin' he does." He wanted to kiss her but would not embarrass her. He squeezed her hands and let go.

She rubbed two fingers under his chin and brought them away with a black smudge. He had not done very well washing all the oil off. He and Choctaw and Trinidad had changed clothes, but some of the oil and particularly its smell still clung to all of them. "Did the well come in?" she asked hopefully.

"Sure did. You daddy was the one punched it through."

"I'm glad. Maybe now we can quit worryin' about him so much."

Hap had no interest in oilwells. "Tracy, there's two of Big Boy Daugherty's men at that table yonder. See them?"

"Of course I see them." Her face twisted with contempt. "They eat like horses and never pay. Mr. Schwartz feeds them to keep from havin' this place smashed up some night."

"You go tell one of them that there's a man waitin' at the kitchen door who's got somethin' for Big Boy Daugherty."

"I didn't see anybody back there."

"We'll be back there. You just go tell him."

Tracy gave Slim an anxious look. "Don't you know the kind of men those are?"

Hap said, "Don't worry about Slim. I'll take care of him."

"You? Just look at your eye. You can't even take care of yourself."

Slim said, "Go ahead, Tracy. It's somethin' that needs to be done."

Tracy assented, reluctantly. "All right, but if you both get killed don't come cryin' to me about it."

The four of them started around the building. Choctaw paused to lift a length of oil-stained rope from the bed of a parked truck. "You know how to hog-tie a calf, Trinidad?"

"All my life."

They reached the back door. Hap opened it and said, "You-all stand off out of sight. They know me, so they'll probably think I'm here to make a payment for Preacher. Whichever one comes, I'll lead him out." He stepped inside.

Slim stood with his back against the wall. He glanced at Choctaw, who was rubbing his hands. Choctaw said, "You want to take him, cowboy?"

Slim was not keen on the idea, but he would not stand back and look the slacker. "You just watch me."

He heard voices inside the door, one of them Hap's. Hap said, "We got it outside. Come on, and we'll give it to you."

In his nervousness, Slim almost lunged at Hap, who walked out first. The man who followed was a short, burly-looking fellow with a flattened nose, probably broken in some long-ago fight for the wrong cause. Slim threw his arms around him and wrestled him to the ground. Surprise gave Slim an edge, but that did not last long. The man quickly found an angry strength and was about to break free when Hap and Choctaw jumped in to help.

Choctaw pulled the man's thick wrists together behind his back. "Tie him, Trinidad."

The Mexican quickly took several wraps. Choctaw pulled the man's legs up, and Trinidad tied them close to the hands. Then he cut the rope, saving what he had not used.

Hap was breathing heavily but was exhilarated. "I ain't had so much fun in a month. We better get him out of sight before the other one comes lookin' for him."

Slim pointed to a three-holer toilet, made of lumber framing and sheetiron. In the noon sun, it would almost be hot enough in there to boil water. "That'll hold him."

The burly henchman cursed as they dragged him across the bare ground and into the stifling toilet. "It stinks in here," he cried.

Hap said, "Don't breathe and you won't smell it." He closed the door and set the wooden bar that would hold it shut.

They waited awhile for the second man's curiosity to get the better of him. At last Hap said, "Looks like I've got to go fetch him. You-all be a-watchin'."

In a minute, Slim, his back to the wall, heard a loud commotion in the kitchen. Hap came flying out through the screen door, a tall, angry man on his heels, shaking his fist and cursing. Slim made a lunge and missed. The man caught Hap and had both strong hands around Hap's throat when Choctaw threw a big arm around his neck and choked him loose. He wrestled the man to the ground. Slim jumped on to help hold him while Trinidad made the tie. Hap's face had a bluish look, and he rubbed his throat while he gasped for breath.

369

A wide-eyed Tracy came out the door, followed by her puzzled-looking mother. She watched the tying of the thug, then looked at Holloway. "Are you all right, Hap? I thought he was fixin' to kill you."

Hap tried to answer but could not. He was still choking.

Slim asked, "What did he say to make a man that mad?"

Tracy colored. "He'll have to tell you. I won't." She went back into the kitchen, explaining to her mother what the excitement was about.

Preacher Perry came into the alley as they dragged the second thug to the toilet and shut him in. "Knox Anderson is wondering where you-all are. He has brought some roustabouts and a truck."

Slim nodded toward the toilet. "We've made a start." He turned to Hap. "I wish I knew what you said to get that feller so het up."

Hap had regained his breath, though his voice was still husky from the choking. "I just told him that I'd heard some of the girls over at Jolene's snickerin' about him. I told him they had a funny name for him over there. He didn't think it was near as funny as I did."

"What name was it?"

"See if Tracy'll tell you. It sure turned her face red."

Slim decided he could wait. "Where next?"

Hap pointed up the alley. "They're runnin' a floatin' poker operation in the back room of Shemp Oliver's dancehall. Craps too. Shemp don't like it, but there ain't been a damned thing he could do."

Slim asked, "Is that where you got your shiner?"

Hap grimaced. "Yep. Feller named Grat watches over the game. Him and that gambler beat up on me with a billy club that Shemp uses to keep peace."

Slim had avoided the dancehall, not for moral reasons so much as frugality. He was the first to enter the back door, his eyes taking a minute to accustom themselves to the interior after the bright sunshine. Half a dozen men were seated around a table, cards in their hands. Slim surmised that the room was one Oliver used to store his beer and bootleg whisky, for an ample supply was stacked along the walls.

The players appeared to be oilfield workers except for one

who wore a white shirt and a loosened necktie. No one paid much attention to Slim. He recognized Grat, sitting in a leaned-back chair, sipping beer from a brown bottle and watching the game. Slim had seen the man several times, eating at the Dutchman's.

Grat finally gave him some notice. "You want to join the game, dishwasher?"

"I'll be takin' a hand in a minute," Slim said.

Trinidad and Hap walked in. Grat saw Trinidad first and set the beer bottle on the floor. "Hey, you, we don't allow no damned Mexicans in here. Vamoose!" Then he saw Hap. "Holloway, we throwed you out of here once." He came up with a billy club. As he started forward, Hap turned and moved briskly to the back door with Grat in close pursuit. By the time Slim got outside, Choctaw had Grat down on his stomach, pressing the billy club against the back of his neck, pushing his face into the alley's sand.

Trinidad was making the tie. "Pretty soon," he said, "we need more rope."

Hap took pleasure in the way Choctaw manhandled the thug. "How does that alley dirt taste to *you*, Grat?"

Slim asked Hap, "What about the gambler in yonder? Is he one of Daugherty's men?"

"I don't think so. I think he just gives Daugherty a cut to let him play. He's as slick a bottom-dealer as you'll see."

Slim followed Hap back through the door. Hap stepped up to the table where the poker game was taking place. He watched a minute or two, until the gambler raked in a pot. Loudly enough that no one could miss hearing, Hap said to Slim, "Did you see how smooth he pulled that card out of his sleeve? Ain't many can do that and not get caught."

An angry hush fell over the room. The gambler's face flushed as he became aware of sudden hostility among the players. "He's seein' things, boys. I don't have anything up my sleeves."

It was a lost cause. In an angry rush the roustabouts piled on him, knocking him and his chair backward to the floor. Slim could hear the impact of fists against flesh and bone, the gambler's plaintive cries for help, then for mercy.

Hap moved toward the door, a satisfied smile spread across

his freckled face. "Come on, cowboy. They're doin' fine without our help."

Outside, Slim said, "I didn't see him pull a card out of his sleeve."

"I could've been wrong."

Knox Anderson waited in the alley with half a dozen tough-looking roustabouts and a truck that had tall wooden side-boards. In the bed of the truck stood a couple of thugs who appeared to have been run over by it, or by something else of comparable size, their faces battered, their clothing torn. They were complaining loudly about having rights. Anderson said, "The boys picked up a couple of them on the street." He watched two of the men lift the hog-tied Grat up into the truck. "Preacher said you have a couple more."

Slim pointed to the toilet.

Hap said, "There'll probably be one comin' out of Shemp's in a minute, soon's the boys get through teachin' him the Caprock rules of poker."

Oliver's back door opened, and two brawny oilfield workers pitched the well-chastised gambler out into the alley. His nose had been bloodied, his face bruised, his shirt torn into strips. One of the roustabouts asked, "Does this one go, Mr. Anderson?"

Anderson said firmly, "He goes."

Shemp Oliver stood in his door, watching in a mixture of puzzlement and anxiety. "We'll pay like hell when they come back."

Preacher Perry moved up beside him, looking pleased. "They're not coming back."

Uncle Henry Stringfellow brought an apprehensive Waddy Fuller into the alley as the roustabouts were hoisting the gambler into the bed of the truck. The two prisoners who were not tied began protesting loudly about the right of due process. Waddy worried, "I sure do wish Dave was here."

Stringfellow asked, "If he was, what would he do?"

"He'd haul them down to the jailhouse." Waddy brightened, having come up with his own answer. He drew himself up to his tallest and stiffest lawman stance and followed as the truck moved down the alley. The roustabouts retrieved the two from the sheetiron toilet and hoisted them up with the others.

Tracy came out the back door of the restaurant. She stared in momentary disbelief at the truck with its cargo of Daugherty men, then beckoned to Slim with a quick motion of her hand. "Two more of them just came in to eat."

Three of Anderson's roustabouts stepped forward. "We'll fetch them. That'll just about make us a truckload." They followed Tracy into the rear of the restaurant. In a minute Slim heard a commotion from inside, and a chorus of cheers. The roustabouts came out, dragging two disheveled and bewildered men Slim recognized from his dish-washing days. Dutch Schwartz had one of them by the collar. Several oilfield workers spilled out the door, cheering Schwartz and the roustabouts on, volunteering their muscle to whatever remained of the job.

Anderson raised both hands to get their attention. "We'll deliver these to the jail, then we'll start a sweep of the places where Daugherty's boys are known to hang out."

"What about the hotel?" somebody shouted.

"We'll leave Big Boy Daugherty for last."

Most of the crowd followed Anderson and his roustabouts and the truck. Tracy came to Slim's side and studied him critically. He realized his shirt had been torn. She said, "Looks like there's more than enough men now to take care of them. You could stay out of it."

"Job's not over yet," he told her.

Hap put in, "The biggest one of them all is Sarge. They made Jolene take him on as a bouncer. He's even stouter than Ox was. Liable to take several of us to whip him."

Choctaw knotted his fists. "I whupped Ox. Well, I fought him to a draw, anyway. I reckon I can handle this Sarge. You-all comin'?"

Slim gave Tracy a hug. "Comin'."

Tracy clutched his arm. "Do you really need to go to Jolene's?"

Hap said, "Don't you worry, Tracy. I'll see that whatever he does down there, he doesn't get any fun out of it."

Slim had never been inside Jolene's place, though curiosity had tempted him. He let Choctaw and Hap go in first, for they seemed comfortable with it. Trinidad hung back, stopping at the door.

373

Hap told him, "You watch the outside. This is no place for a married man."

Trinidad seemed pleased at being excused. "If you need me, I will be here."

The first thing that struck Slim was the heavy odor of strong perfume. The second was that the two young women seated on a davenport were not as pretty as he had imagined they would be. One was twenty pounds too plump, her rolled-down garters pinching into heavy legs. The other showed a slight gap between her front teeth.

Hap seemed to know them both. "Howdy, Mae. Howdy, Peaches. My, how you both sparkle!"

Sparkle? Slim felt disappointment. He had assumed that anything so popular would come in a better-looking package.

He had never seen Jolene except from a distance, on the street, but he recognized her as she stepped from a room just down the hall. She gave the three men a quick looking over and settled her gaze on Hap. "Kind of early, ain't it? Even for you." She seemed to be laughing inside, at some joke of her own.

Hap bowed slightly. "I regret to say that we've come on business, Jolene. We've come lookin' for Sarge."

Jolene's expression turned quizzical. "What could you possibly want with Sarge?"

Hap motioned toward Choctaw. "This man has come to stomp the whey out of him."

A gruff voice came from down the hall. A huge man appeared in the doorway Jolene had used. "Somebody lookin' for trouble out here?"

Slim decided Sarge was larger even than Choctaw. He wished they had brought some of Anderson's roughnecks.

Hap seemed to have the same thought, seeing the two men together. "*Are* we lookin' for trouble, Choctaw?"

Choctaw seemed unimpressed. "I can whup him."

Jolene's expression turned to alarm. "If you-all are goin' to fight, take it outside. I'd sooner have two buffalo bulls a-loose in here."

Sarge frowned at Choctaw. "I don't know you, do I?"

"You'll know me when we get through." Choctaw opened the door and motioned for Sarge to go ahead of him. On the sidewalk, Sarge turned and rushed. Choctaw took two long steps to meet him. Slim thought Jolene had expressed herself well. He had never seen two buffalo bulls fight, but he doubted they could hit each other much harder than Sarge and Choctaw.

He watched, fascinated, as the two big men struggled and grunted and sweated, trying to wrestle each other to the ground. Sarge was by all odds the larger, but he had not indulged in the hard physical labor to which Choctaw was accustomed. Slim was not sure which was the strongest. They went down on the walk and rolled out into the dirt street, Choctaw on top for a moment, then Sarge. Both men had fists like sledgehammers, and they used them to the same effect. Traffic stopped. Drivers got out of their cars and trucks to watch the spectacle of these two huge men thrashing and tumbling in the middle of the street.

Slim smelled Jolene's perfume and turned. She stood just behind him and Hap and Trinidad. She said, "I wonder if you boys know what you're doin'? I've been wishin' for somebody to come along and do this to Sarge, but I dread seein' what happens to you when Big Boy sends his troops out."

Hap said, "Don't you fret, Jolene. By tonight, Big Boy's goin' to be the lonesomest man in town."

Slim lost track of time, but he suspected the fight went on for the better part of ten minutes. Before it was done, the two combatants were moving slowly, first one and then the other raising an arm, a fist, as if it weighed a hundred pounds. Choctaw's stamina, reinforced by hard work, finally won out. Sarge lay on his back, chest heaving. He waved one hand to beg for peace because he had no breath left to speak. Choctaw was astraddle of him, his clothing shredded, sweat cutting ribbons through the dirt on his bloodied face. He gritted through the pain: "Hap . . . go fetch the truck."

Slim helped Choctaw to his feet, the big man's weight almost bringing him down before the Indian got his balance. Hap and Trinidad dragged Sarge out of the street and up into the wooden sidewalk so the traffic could move. Jolene seemed pleased as she looked down upon the fallen bouncer. "First time one of Big Boy's bunch has ever looked good to me."

As Hap left, Slim said, "I want to go see about Sheriff Buckalew."

Choctaw seated himself on the middle of Sarge's back. "You

375

go ahead, cowboy. Me and Trinidad will stay and watch out for Sarge till Anderson's truck comes to haul him off."

Slim found Elise Underwood and Lydia sitting side by side in the doctor's front room, still waiting. Their faces told him they had received no word. Uncle Henry Stringfellow had returned to wait with them. The old rancher asked Slim, "Things still goin' all right out yonder?"

Slim said, "Fine. I'd hoped by now you'd have some good news in here."

"The doctor hasn't been out," Elise said.

Lydia gave Slim a glance but said nothing. Slim sat down across the small room from the women and tried to read a newspaper, but he gave up and put it back on the endtable.

After a time, Doc Tolliver came in, wiping his hands on a towel. He smelled strongly of alcohol and ether. He should be a good poker player, Slim thought, because his face betrayed no hint of his thoughts. He surveyed the two women, the two men, and said, "Everybody should have so many friends."

Lydia's face was lifted hopefully to him, silently begging. He stopped in front of her. "The bullet came out all right. He won't do much sheriffing for a while, but he'll show his scar to his grandchildren some day."

Tears welled into Lydia's large hazel eyes. She whispered something Slim could not hear. Elise took her hands. "I told you."

The doctor said to the women, "He'll be a while coming out from under the ether, but you can go in and sit with him if you'd like to."

Elise said, "Lydia?"

Lydia stood up and started to follow the doctor but stopped. "No. I don't belong there. I'd best go back where I *do* belong."

Elise took her arm. "He'll be askin' about you."

"Just tell him . . . no, there's nothin' to tell him, except that I thank him for lettin' me know how to live again, even for a little while."

She pushed the screen door open and stepped out on the porch. She hesitated a moment, then moved down to the sidewalk. Elise started after her. "Lydia . . ." But she halted at the door.

Uncle Henry's eyes were sad. "You know where she's goin', don't you?"

"I know. But she doesn't belong there."

"Not many do. Life doesn't always ask us what we deserve. It gives or it doesn't. It sets us on a road, tells us to walk it and locks the gate so we can't turn back."

He faced Slim. "Ain't much we can do here. Let's go see how Knox and the boys are comin' along."

Slim stopped as he reached the street. He could see Lydia, walking in the direction of Jolene's.

He said, "I wonder what it takes to unlock a gate."

24
Redemption

THE SWEEP by the roustabouts gathered more candidates
for the jail than Hap Holloway had predicted. Standing
outside the iron-barred cells, Slim counted sixteen. The men
had picked up three or four who were not part of the Daugherty
organization but nevertheless made their living by the sweat of
other men's brows. "They've gathered a few sheep with the
goats," was the way Hap Holloway put it, then added, "but when
shippin' time comes, you send them all anyway."

Slim knew that one was still missing, besides Big Boy Daugherty himself. He did not see the man called Frenchy, the one
whose hand he had struck with his cane at the Dutchman's.

Knox Anderson said it shouldn't matter. "When he sees

what's happened to the rest of them, he'll leave town anyway." He turned to the tall, thin deputy. "I'm afraid we'll have to do something about your overcrowded jail."

Waddy stared at him, not comprehending. "You want me to shoot some of them?"

"Not a bad idea," Anderson said, "but impractical. I'm afraid you don't have enough real evidence to hold these men. If Dave Buckalew had been able to prove anything, he would have jailed them already. You'll have to turn them loose as soon as a lawyer shows up. And one will. They always do."

Hap was outraged. "After all the trouble we went to in catchin' them? I'd rather shoot them."

Anderson said, "I suggest that we load them all onto the back of my truck and haul them to Odessa. I'll phone ahead and hire a couple of boxcars. We'll ship half of them east to Fort Worth and half of them west to El Paso, under seal. That will scatter them pretty well."

Waddy Fuller was astounded at the boldness of the idea. "Is that legal?"

"No," Anderson admitted, "but they haven't let the niceties of the law be any obstacle to *them*. I've seen other boomtowns ship out their undesirables this way."

Hap said, "I'm glad Dave Buckalew never thought of this. He's considered me undesirable ever since I've been here."

Anderson sent one of his roustabouts to bring the truck. Waddy Fuller unlocked the cells and ordered the prisoners out. They were forced to walk through a gauntlet of Anderson's men and climb up into the truckbed. Some grumbled, but not very loudly, for the roustabouts made a show of being there on serious business.

Though his action probably was no more legal than the deportation, Waddy deputized Anderson and the roustabouts who were to accompany the Daugherty men to Odessa. He made a stern speech to the prisoners on the truck. "You-all are damned lucky we're so kindhearted, lettin' you get out of this town in one piece. But if any one of you ever shows up in Caprock again, it's goin' to be open season on you, like on quail." He patted the pistol on his hip. "This is the law talkin' to you."

The truck pulled away, followed by Anderson and a couple of

carloads of roustabouts firmly committed to seeing their cargo safely to Odessa and freighted out according to plan.

Slim reminded Waddy, "The biggest one is still left, at the hotel."

Waddy frowned. "We ought to've waited with the truck and shipped him with them."

"No, he'd get them organized and be back here before the dust settled. It's like with cattle; one or two old outlaws can turn the whole bunch wild. That kind, you rope and tie down and separate from the herd."

Waddy Fuller was not celebrating over the prospect. He repeated something Slim had heard him say several times today. "I sure wish Dave was here."

Slim asked, "If he was here, what do you think he'd do?"

Waddy considered. "He'd walk right in and put the cuffs on that old warthog." He added hopefully, "He'd probably take some help with him."

Slim said, "I'll go with you." He was curious about Daugherty. As much as he had heard the name, he had not seen the man. Not many people in Caprock had. He looked around at Hap, at Choctaw, at Trinidad. "We'll all go with you." He turned on his heel and started toward the hotel. He could hear the others hurrying to catch up. A nervous Waddy was at his side as they walked into the small lobby. The desk clerk looked up from his ledger, surprised at the invasion.

Waddy asked, "Albert, is Big Boy Daugherty in his room?"

"He's always in his room." The clerk wrinkled his nose to show his disdain. "About the only time he ever leaves it is to go to the toilet down the hall."

Slim asked, "Has he got anybody with him?"

"Not that I know of. It's an odd thing. Generally his men are coming and going all the time. Today they've been going out and not coming back."

"We've noticed that. I wonder if he has?"

Albert said, "As a matter of fact, he's come to the balustrade two or three times in the last hour or so, asking me if I have seen any of his *boys*. He's been walking the floor too. I can feel it shake all the way down here." He looked wishfully at Waddy Fuller. "It would be too much to hope that you're about to relieve me of my star boarder."

Waddy replied, "That's kind of what we had in mind." He looked around to be sure he did not go up the stairs alone. Slim moved up to one side of him, Hap the other. Choctaw and Trinidad followed.

Waddy was about to knock on Daugherty's door. Slim said quietly, "If I was you I'd stand to one side. What if he was to shoot through it?"

Waddy swallowed. Such a thought had not occurred to him. He stood at the side of the door and stretched his arm. From inside came an anxious voice. "Who is it? Is that you out there, Turk?"

Sweating, Waddy turned the knob and flung the door open, then stepped quickly back out of the way. No shot was fired.

"Who's out there?" the anxious voice asked again.

Waddy worked up his nerve and stepped inside. Slim and the others followed him.

Slim had not known just what Big Boy Daugherty would look like. He had heard he was a large man, and he had expected him to look fierce as a lion. What he saw was an incredibly fat old man with his shirt unbuttoned, his underwear soaked in sweat. His trousers were large and baggy, his feet encased in dirty white socks. An oscillating fan on a dresser was turned so that its breeze would pass over Daugherty, but obviously it was not enough to cool his formidable body.

"Who are you?" Daugherty demanded querulously. "What right you got to come bargin' in here thisaway?"

Waddy said, "We're the law, and we've come to arrest you."

"To arrest me? You got nothin' on me." Daugherty brought up a huge, flabby arm and wiped a sleeve across his sweat-beaded forehead. "I been right here all the time. I don't know nothin' about your sheriff gettin' hisself killed. It was somebody else done that."

"Who said anything about the sheriff?" Slim asked.

"I heard it. One of my boys come in with the word."

Slim said, "He was wrong, then, because the sheriff's not dead. But there's three of your men layin' out yonder, and *they're* dead."

Daugherty's jowls quivered. "My boys? Dead? Whichaones?"

"There was one called Irish, and one called Skinny. And there

381

was the one you hollered for just now, Turk. He won't be an-
swerin' you anymore."

Choctaw put in triumphantly, "He wound up in a slushpit.
Just like Ox."

Daugherty trembled. Slim half expected him to collapse like a
big canvas bag filled with water. Daugherty sank deeper into a
sagging davenport. He rubbed a hand over his rubbery face.
"My boys. I can't believe Buckalew killed all three of them."

Slim told him, "Irish and Skinny killed each other. A woman
called Lydia shot Turk Radke."

Daugherty shook his head, not wanting to believe. He looked
around desperately. "Where's the rest of my boys? You-all done
somethin' to my boys?"

Waddy had gained confidence, seeing that Daugherty was
helpless without his men around him to carry out his orders.
"They're on their way to Odessa for a long ride on the train.
You're the only one left." He lifted a set of handcuffs from his
belt. "And now, Mr. Daugherty, you're under arrest. Stick out
your hands."

Daugherty's face reddened. "You can't hold me. I've got lawyers. You can't put me in no cracker-box jail."

Waddy said, "I been thinkin' about that. I been wonderin'
what Dave would do. You ain't goin' to jail, Mr. Daugherty.
You're goin' on the chain!"

Waddy fumbled with the cuffs, trying to fit them over
Daugherty's huge wrists. Hap chuckled, watching the effort.
Slim failed to see the humor.

An excited voice called from the hallway. "Boss! Boss! We got
to get out of here!"

The man called Frenchy burst through the open doorway. His
appearance caught Waddy by such surprise that he did not even
try for his pistol. Seeing what was happening, the wide-eyed
Frenchy jerked an automatic from his pocket. "All of you raise
your hands. Be quick!" His hand shook a little.

Dry-mouthed, Slim realized it would not take much to cause
Frenchy to pull the trigger. He lifted his hands to shoulder level,
dreading recognition.

Daugherty pushed himself up from the davenport and shoved
Waddy aside. His face showed an immense relief. "Good ol'
Frenchy. I thought they'd shipped you out with the others."

382

"I seen them comin', and I hid. I got your car outside with the motor runnin', Boss. You better grab your shoes."

Daugherty bent over, grunting from the effort. He picked up a pair of big shoes that lay where he had kicked them off, one of them topside down. He did not take time to put them on.

As Slim had feared, he found Frenchy's attention fastened upon him. "You're the pearl diver that like to've broken my hand. Come on, you're goin' with us to make sure the rest of this bunch don't give us any trouble." When Slim hesitated, Frenchy beckoned with the muzzle of the pistol. "I said come on!"

Slim glanced at his friends but knew there was nothing they could do to help him. Tingling with apprehension, he went out the door behind Daugherty, wondering what they would do when they were through with him.

Frenchy brought up the rear, shouting to the others, "You-all stay back now, you hear me?" To Slim he said, "Boss has trouble with stairs. You take his arm and help him down."

Slim grasped Daugherty's left arm. It was sticky with sweat. Frenchy moved to the other side and took the big man's right arm, holding the pistol in his free hand. Daugherty felt his way down the steps slowly and carefully, stumbling once, almost dragging Slim off his feet. Slim kept his eyes on Frenchy and that pistol, watching for any chance.

Near the bottom of the stairs, Frenchy looked forward. "There's a rug down there, Boss. Careful you don't trip on it."

Slim gave Daugherty a hard shove toward Frenchy. The big man gasped in surprise and tried to catch his balance. Slim had a glimpse of Frenchy's startled eyes as Daugherty's great bulk hurtled toward him. The two men crashed against the railing and splintered it like two bulls smashing through a corral fence. Slim heard the breath gust out of Frenchy as Daugherty fell on top of him. Frenchy groaned. All Slim could see as he knelt to retrieve the fallen pistol was Frenchy's right hand reaching out from beneath Daugherty's body. The fingers appeared to be broken.

Slim heard Hap's bemused voice from the stairway behind him. "You know, I had a horse fall on me just like that one time."

Dave Buckalew had been dozing, half in and half out of sleep. A shadowy form moving between him and the window's morning sunlight finally brought him awake. He forced his eyes open and focused them on Doc Tolliver. "What time is it, Doc?"

"What difference does it make? You're staying right here."

Dave had come out from under the ether last night and realized he was in one of Doc's white-painted hospital rooms. Most of it remained a blur to him. His last fully clear recollection was of being in Henry Stringfellow's car, with Lydia holding him. He had a dim memory of Waddy Fuller telling him something about rounding up Daugherty's men. It had not made much sense to his ether-dulled mind at the time, and it made even less now.

"Has Waddy been around this mornin'?"

"Him and several more. A few of them are still out there. I told them you wouldn't be fit for company, but they've stayed anyway."

"Send them in, would you, Doc? I've got to know what's happened."

"Are you sure you wouldn't rather rest awhile longer?"

Dave managed to put a little of a sheriff's authority into his voice. "Send them in."

He counted them as they came through the door: Slim McIntyre and the girl Tracy from the Dutchman's. Uncle Henry Stringfellow. Knox Anderson. Waddy Fuller. He heard a thumping sound in the hallway. Victor Underwood entered on crutches, his leg in a cast. Elise Underwood had her slender arm around him.

Slim spoke first. "It's good to see you awake, Mr. Buckalew. For a while there, we didn't know . . ."

Dave kept watching the door. He felt keen disappointment. There should be another. "Waddy, you tried to tell me somethin' last night about Big Boy Daugherty's bunch, but I couldn't hold onto it."

Waddy replied eagerly, "They're all gone."

Henry Stringfellow said, "It was the community, Dave. I told you folks'd sooner or later get enough of Daugherty's mob. Caprock chewed them up and spit them out."

Waddy motioned toward Knox Anderson. "Mr. Anderson and some of his hands, they shipped Daugherty's men out of Odessa last night. I told them they'd better not ever come back. Put the fear of God into them, I did."

"Daugherty too?"

Waddy said, "He's on the chain. Looks like a big ol' bullfrog, squattin' out there on the courthouse square. A Texas Ranger name of Grissom phoned the office this mornin', wonderin' if you're gettin' tired of Daugherty and his outfit. Said he thought it was about time to come down and make a raid before they owned everything in town. Seemed a little put out when I told him we'd beaten him to it. He said they'd finally gotten enough evidence to make a case against Daugherty and offered to come take him off our hands. I said sure, it'd be good riddance."

Dave nodded weakly. "It would be." He turned to the Underwoods. "Things are a little muddy in my mind, but it seems to me you-all brought in your well, didn't you?"

Victor Underwood drew his wife to him. "Elise did, she and a good crew."

Knox Anderson said, "When you feel up to talking business, Dave, I'd like to discuss a lease on your ranch. It's not far from Victor's well, so the chances for oil ought to be good."

Dave was not sure he wanted the place messed up with oilwells, but on the other hand they might pay him enough to buy more land, maybe the Clive ranch. "Since the Underwoods found the oil, I ought to give them first refusal."

Victor Underwood said, "We've already talked about it. We've thought we could make it a joint venture."

"Maybe. Right now my head's not straight enough to be talkin' business." He looked at Slim. "You've had a good taste of the oilfield now. Are you about ready to go back to punchin' cows?"

Slim said, "Not yet. I think I'll give this oil business a little more time."

A little more time, and then more again. The world had lost another cowboy, Dave figured. He looked at Tracy. "How's Autie? Feelin' pretty good?"

Tracy's face fell. "Too good, I'm afraid. He came in to town last night. Drank an awful lot. Choctaw and Trinidad have taken him back out to the well, but I don't know if he'll stay. I guess we expected too much."

Slim put his arm around Tracy's shoulder. "We'll keep watchin' out over him."

That probably wouldn't be enough, Dave thought. Autie had too many devils riding on his back.

Slim said, "I'd better be takin' Tracy back to the café. The dinner crowd'll be startin' in pretty soon."

Dave said hopefully, "Maybe she won't have to work there a lot longer."

Slim gave Tracy's shoulder a squeeze. "That's the way I've got it figured. So long, Mr. Buckalew. We'll be lookin' in on you again." Dave watched them warmly as they went out the door arm in arm. There might not be much chance for Autie, but Tracy and Slim were a new generation, and every new generation brought a renewal of hope.

Everyone seemed to have run out of anything to say. Dave waited for someone to volunteer what he wanted to know. Finally he asked, "Anybody seen Lydia?"

No one answered for a minute. Elise and Victor Underwood looked at one another. Henry Stringfellow stared at his pipe. Finally he said, "She's gone. She went to Odessa and caught the train."

Dave lay back on his pillow and closed his eyes. He wished he could sink once again into the mercy of sleep. The pain from the wound was small against the one in his soul.

Elise came to Dave's bedside. "I talked with her a lot yesterday while we were waitin' to see if you'd live or die. She said she isn't good enough for you, said if she stayed everybody would talk. She didn't want to shame you."

Dave's throat was tight. "I wish she'd spoken to me first. I lost a good woman once, worryin' about what people would say. I'd've held onto Lydia and let them gossip all they wanted to. I wouldn't give a damn anymore."

"She said she was goin' home to East Texas."

"But I don't know where her home is."

Elise squeezed his hand. "I do. I'll tell you if you decide to go."

The doctor came in. He felt Dave's pulse, then his forehead. "A little company is good for him, but rest is better. You-all can come back another time."

When they had gone, Dave asked, "Doc, how long do you reckon it'll be before I'm out of here?"

"I can probably send you back to your own room in two or three days, but you won't be working much for a while."

In his mind, Dave saw a pair of hazel eyes. "I wasn't thinkin' about workin', Doc. I was wonderin' how long it'll be before I'm up to makin' a trip on the train."

Author's Note

MUCH OF THE SETTING for this novel is drawn from my own memory. I grew up on the McElroy Ranch east of Crane, Texas, in the middle of the Permian Basin and on the edge of a considerable oilfield. Crane had not existed until the first oil discovery there in 1925, and it was much of a boomtown when we moved to the ranch in 1929. Like most other burgeoning oilpatch communities of its kind, it was still made up largely of tents and shotgun houses, hastily thrown together with no view toward permanence. Most of its business buildings were also of cheap and tentative construction, for no one knew how long the oil and the town might last.

Early Crane had its share of casual violence but was spared

much of the organized viciousness that beset some other boom-towns, the type that invades the Caprock of this story. Some towns managed to shake it off. Others endured it until the boom was over and the mobsters left in search of better opportunity.

Work was hard in the new and developing oilfields, most of the population highly transient. As a schoolboy I found myself constantly having to make new friends because so many of my classmates kept moving away, their fathers transferring to other towns, other fields.

Though parents tried to shield us youngsters from the seam-ier aspects of life, we were aware of the beerjoints and honky-tonks, and we knew that over in one corner of town was a "line" little different from the one that had existed in booming mining and cowtowns of earlier generations. In stark contrast was a strong God-fearing element who saw to it that the honkytonks did not outnumber the churches and that the singing on Sunday morning was as loud as it had been on Saturday night.

Oilfield towns such as Crane offered about as near a classless society as could be found anywhere. The population was made up of working people, few much better off than the rest. In some cases, where a town had existed before the boom, the "old settlers" had difficulty accommodating to the boomers. But in general most of the first generation of Texas-Oklahoma oilfield workers came from a rural upbringing and had much in common with the original residents. Whether they had oil on their shoes or cow manure on their boots, most could find a middle meeting ground.

My father's family were ranch people, while my mother's were tied to the oilfields, giving me a unique view of two contrasting worlds.

It was an exciting time and place for a boy. I would not will-ingly trade that experience and those memories with anybody.

For readers who would like to know more about life and work in the oilfields, past and present, I would recommend a visit to the Permian Basin Petroleum Museum in Midland, Texas, and to the East Texas Oil Museum in Kilgore, Texas, both excellent. The Panhandle-Plains Museum in Canyon, Texas, also has a large section devoted to oil and gas exploration on the high plains.

In addition, a number of fine books present various aspects of the industry in layman's language. Following are just a few:

Boatright, Mody. *Folklore of the Oil Industry.* Dallas, Texas: Southern Methodist University Press, 1963.

————, and Owens, William A. *Tales from the Derrick Floor.* New York: Doubleday, 1970.

Clark, James A., and Halbouty, Michel T. *The Last Boom.* New York: Random House, 1972.

Eason, Al. *Boomtown: Kilgore, Texas.* Kilgore, Texas: Kilgore Chamber of Commerce, undated.

Knowles, Ruth Sheldon. *The Greatest Gamblers.* Norman, Oklahoma: University of Oklahoma Press, 1978 revision.

Lambert, Paul F., and Franks, Kenny A. *Voices from the Oil Fields.* Norman, Oklahoma: University of Oklahoma Press, 1984.

Lynch, Gerald. *Roughnecks, Drillers, and Tool Pushers.* Austin, Texas: University of Texas Press, 1987.

Myers, Samuel D. *The Permian Basin, Era of Discovery.* El Paso, Texas: Permian Press, 1973.

————. *The Permian Basin, Era of Advancement.* El Paso, Texas: Permian Press, 1977.

Olien and Olien. *Life in the Oil Fields.* Austin, Texas: Texas Monthly Press, 1986.

————. *Oil Booms, Social Change in Five Texas Towns.* Lincoln, Nebraska: University of Nebraska Press, 1982.

————. *Wildcatters, Texas Independent Oilmen.* Austin, Texas: Texas Monthly Press, 1984.

Rundell, Walter Jr. *Early Texas Oil, a Photographic History, 1866–1936.* College Station, Texas: Texas A&M University Press, 1977.

————. *Oil in West Texas and New Mexico, a Pictorial History of the Permian Basin.* College Station, Texas: Texas A&M University Press, 1982.

Stowe, Estha Briscoe: *Oil Field Child.* Fort Worth, Texas: Texas Christian University Press, 1989.

There are many more, but these offer a starting place.